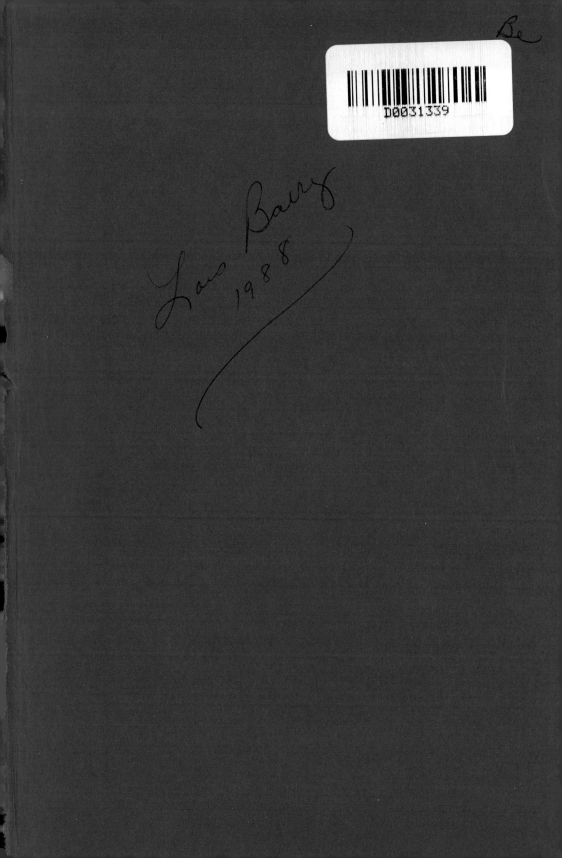

ONCE A GENTLEMAN

ONCE A GENTLEMAN

DONALD JAMES

CROWN PUBLISHERS, INC.
NEW YORK

Copyright © 1987 by Donald James
All rights reserved. No part of this book may be reproduced
or transmitted in any form or by any means,
electronic or mechanical, including photocopying, recording,
or by any information storage and retrieval system,
without permission in writing from the publisher.
Published by Crown Publishers, Inc.,
225 Park Avenue South, New York, New York 10003
and represented in Canada
by the Canadian MANDA Group
CROWN is a trademark of Crown Publishers, Inc.
Manufactured in the United States of America

Book design by Dana Sloan

Library of Congress Cataloging-in-Publication Data
James, Donald, 1931-
Once a gentleman.

I. Title.
PR6060.A45305   1987   823'.914   86-19962
ISBN 0-517-56405-X
10 9 8 7 6 5 4 3 2 1
First Edition

Non cuius homini contingit adire Corinthum.

It is not given to every man to see Corinth.

HORACE

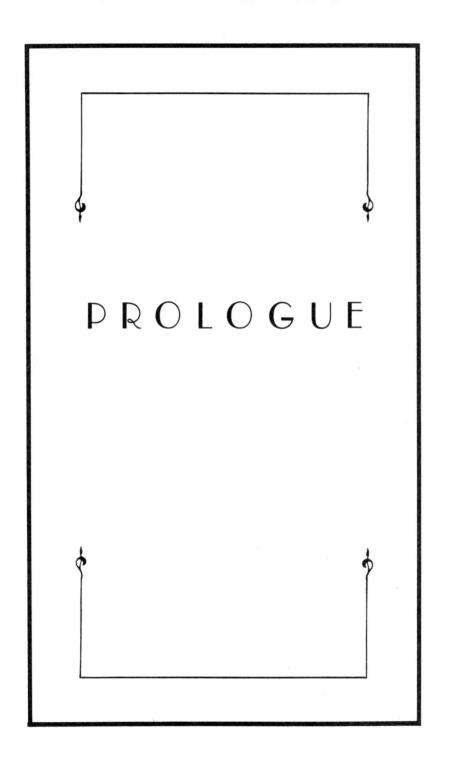

PROLOGUE

Cambridge, 1914. The woman in the white silk dress, her face shaded by the wide brim of her hat, walked slowly in long strides from the hip, conscious of herself and of the glances of black-gowned undergraduates as they passed on the narrow stone bridge that led from King's College to the towpath on the far side of the river. Her breathing was as even as her step. She was tall, slender, and not yet thirty years of age. Her features, regular and formidably set, perfectly achieved an imposing distance that a woman of quality must seek to put between herself and the world.

She acknowledged with only the faintest inclination of her head the raised straw hats of the young men who moved a pace aside to allow her unimpeded passage. Across the years, the Middle European accents of Miss Kantrapp, directress of her Swiss finishing school, came back to her: "Step out, Lady Margaret, step out! Ladies don't *mince*, shopgirls mince. Ladies step out from the hips. Shoulders back, derrière tucked in, eyes grave and distant, acknowledgment of a gentleman's greeting languid almost to the point of indifference. From the hip like so, unhurried, stately, striding, striding. . . ." The English and American girls used to call her Miss Mantrap. Even in 1903 they knew what it was she was teaching.

Before her, Lady Margaret Ryder saw the Reverend Arthur Lampson, the dean of her husband's college. The clergyman stopped and raised his hat. "A perfectly splendid day," he said.

She agreed.

"Are we to see you Lady Margaret, at the garden party this year?"

"I sent my acceptance this morning," she said. "I am particularly looking forward to meeting Mrs. Lampson."

"And she you," he affirmed, nodding vigorously. "I do hope you will become good friends. She's young and needs guidance, I feel, in the sometimes excessively political groves of Cambridge academe. Who is better qualified to give her guidance than the wife of, may one hope, the next provost of our college?"

"My husband is not provost yet, Mr. Lampson."

"We are all perfectly confident that he will be, Lady Margaret. I have sounded the feeling of the college. There is no doubt in my mind that it favors Sir Henry."

"We shall see."

"Indeed, indeed. Meanwhile, I look forward to your meeting with my wife. I shall not delay you further, Lady Margaret. Such a fine day for a promenade, such a fine day. . . ."

Lady Margaret Ryder turned down onto the towpath and stopped opposite the college founded four hundred years earlier by two queens of England. Beside the bridge the willow fronds trailed the water. Giving her parasol a half-turn, she let her eyes wander toward the empty punt tethered to the bank, then across to the ancient brickwork of Queens' College and the line of mullioned windows overlooking the river. She could, of course, turn back now.

And if she did, the summer would be quiet and uneventful and very dull. Yet if she continued on down the towpath, turning across the Mathematical Bridge and into the river court of Queens' College, the summer ahead might well prove dangerous, unpredictable, and very exciting.

She regretted that in her eight years of marriage she had only had one real affair. It invested with all too much importance that extraordinary spring in St. Petersburg with her cousin William. She had loved him for only a few brief weeks along the banks of the Neva. But afterwards, upon her return to England, she had made of him a confidant. She could write to him with the utter certainty that, having read the letter in his study in the great English merchant's house in the very center of the Tsar's capital city, he would open the enameled stove and watch while the pages of her dangerous self-revelations were consumed.

But perhaps it was just that earnest, steadfast quality that had made her fall out of love with him even before she had left St. Petersburg to return to her equally earnest, steadfast husband.

Henry Ryder had suspected nothing. While his mind probed the furthest reaches of philosophical improbability as Professor of Natural Sciences at the University of Cambridge, he was unable to conceive of his wife's naked body striding the carpet before another man, her voice imitating the accents of Miss Mantrap: "Ach, don't *mince*, Lady Margaret. *Shopgirls* mince. The high-born lady uses her hips, like so, or so . . . and the shoulders like so. . . ."

She'd shocked poor cousin William. But captivated him as well, and he had bought her splendid jewelry and begged her to stay with him in St. Petersburg and divorce Henry. But in the end she had had to tell him that all her caprice and laughter and reckless insatiability were not to be reserved for him alone. Probably not for any one man alone.

He had sat opposite her in his study hung with tribal Shiraz carpets, a young merchant prince in an adopted land. "You're telling me, Margaret, that you can love more than one man at a time? I don't understand," he said.

Turning from the fireplace, she had slowly walked the long room, listening to the sound of her heels on the polished oak floor. "I'm not talking about love, William."

"Not love?"

"Not love, William. I am talking about desire."

She had had to suppress her laughter as his pince-nez fell from his nose and his eyebrows shot up like those of a music-hall comedian.

"I could not marry you, William," she had said firmly, "because I could not inflict pain upon you. The truth of the matter is that I desire other men."

He was speechless. Not with anger, or even, at that moment, with unhappiness, but simply speechless.

"I'm afraid," Margaret had continued, "that I would welcome the opportunity to give my body to any young man of sufficient attraction I pass in the street. I am quite incorrigible and I cannot imagine that I shall continue my life in anything but the same vein." She stopped pacing, turning toward him. "My dear William," she said, "I had to tell you."

For a few moments he had sat polishing his pince-nez, watching a sparrow caught in the window alcove between the thick, beveled outer glass and the inner window set a full yard back against the northern winter. Then, getting up, he had released the bird and turned back toward her. "The sparrow is released," he said. "Perhaps it will want to come back, from time to time, as a friend."

There had been other men, of course—furtive, scrambled incidents with tradesmen she had allowed to touch her. Once with a young American in a railway carriage between London and Cambridge. Once with a groom in a friend's stables, who had called her "madam" as he fumbled under her skirts.

She had learned, gradually, to write to William, describing each adventure in more detail than the last, perhaps now after four years giving him in the reading as much illicit pleasure as she found in the recounting.

But since those days in Russia she had never coldbloodedly considered a full affair. She had always too much feared the damage to her husband's position if she were to acquire a fast reputation. He was midway in a brilliant career and had every hope of succeeding to the post of provost of King's College within the year, a position whose responsibilities extended well beyond the world of learning. A wife who dabbled in young undergraduates would be an insurmountable barrier to his aspirations. And yet *this* young man offered a furious attraction to her. He possessed those tall, Germanic good looks that she particularly warmed to. He had a certain shy *gravitas* that made her believe she could trust him. A brief, frantic affair with a young man almost ten years her junior could be the summer's offering. If she walked the towpath, crossed the Mathematical Bridge, and entered the river court of Queens'. Now.

In his first-floor rooms overlooking the half-timbered Tudor courtyard that linked the river to Queens' College Great Gate, a young man reread the letter he had just written:

My dear Cousin,
  You ask me if I envy you, a graduate officer of the Imperial Guard? Of course I envy you, Wolfgang. But then, within a year or so I shall be a Bachelor of Arts of the University of Cambridge, and will you envy me? Probably not, since I'm sure half the family in Berlin is convinced that I spend my time here

playing the English gentleman, drinking excellent champagne and picknicking by the river with beautiful girls. The truth is, I don't do as much of the latter as I would wish. Cambridge is, I regret to report, a *mostly* monastic society.

But you ask me more serious questions too, Wolfgang, about the nature of the English and their determination to confront the German Empire in a European war. I have to tell you in all honesty that I see little or none of this. Of course there is silly undergraduate talk of war. And there are offensive jokes against the Kaiser. But these same young men make jokes against their *own* royal family. There are constant jokes about the gluttony and sexual proclivities of the late King Edward, for instance. We must, I think, remember in speaking of the English that we are dealing with a superficially unserious people. And what lies behind this unseriousness? Perhaps nothing, or very little. Perhaps in this sense the German opinions you quote are correct. But if we miscalculate we will commit a massive, irrevocable blunder.

Dear Wolfgang, do not imagine that I have "gone native." I am still as much a German as I was when I arrived here a year ago. It's true I wear English suits, English boots, and an English hat. But my heart beats to the German drum. It always will.

This letter is to offer my heartfelt congratulations on your commission. It will be an honor for me to follow in your footsteps at Potsdam next year.

Your cousin,
Claus

Claus von Hardenberg sealed the envelope and placed it prominently on a side table to remind him to post it that afternoon. Then, crossing to the latticed window, he looked down into the empty courtyard, frowning.

"Expecting someone?" a voice, slightly layered with an American accent, said.

Hardenberg turned guiltily. "For God's sake, Buzz," he said to the young man lounging by the door. "I told you I'm working this afternoon."

George Amadeus Winslow laughed. "On such a day as this? Listen, we have two plump capons, a Bradenham ham, and a half-dozen bottles of Moët '83. Come on, you bloody Hun, a picnic *sur l'herbe* with champagne and a whole bevy of beautiful girls. Can you resist?"

"Yes," Claus said shortly. "Get out, Buzz."

Winslow nodded amiably. The sunlight caught his golden hair as he leaned back against the doorjamb, watching the agitated movement of his friend about the room. He was the same age as Claus, big and broad-shouldered, but his jawline still suggested the soft fullness of boyhood. "Very well." He glanced around the room. "You've got work to do." He gave Claus a friendly leer. "Although I see no sign of it. No classical text piled on the table, no pert Propertius or tactless Tacitus. Only the decanter carefully to hand, and two sherry glasses polished for the occasion."

"Push off, Buzz."

"This very moment." He slipped back through the door, and his voice floated from the corridor. "Be right back."

Claus reached the window. His mouth was dry but he could feel trickles of sweat on his forehead. He was suddenly certain that she would not come. He stood for a moment between disappointment and relief.

The footsteps outside signaled Winslow's return. He was buttoning his fly. "Sorry, old chap," he said. *"Appel du destin.* What were we saying?"

"I was asking you to push off," Claus said tensely.

"I'm going." Winslow half-turned toward the door. "You know I've always envied you these rooms," he said. "Tucked away discreetly on their own staircase. Ideal for assignation. Best rooms in college."

Claus looked quickly down into the empty courtyard below. "So you've often said. Now be a good chap and leave me alone."

"You know what happened to the last man who had these rooms, Claus?" Winslow pointed upward. "Hanged himself from that very beam with his mistress's knickers. Be warned."

Claus laughed. "Get out of here, you oaf. If you're lucky I'll tell you about it later."

Hands deep in the pockets of his flannel trousers, Winslow strolled out of the room. As he closed the door behind him, Claus could hear the low, whistled notes of "Deutschland Über Alles" on the landing beyond.

Claus turned back to the window. Below him, Winslow

strolled across the court and disappeared through the brick archway. A clock in some belltower or steeple began to strike midday. In the deep shadows between the timber columns of the cloistered walk, Claus caught the flash of a white dress. For a moment he stood rigid. She moved slowly along the cloister, as if to follow Winslow through the arch, and then, at the last moment, emerging into the sunlight, she turned quickly across the court toward the staircase below.

He was trembling now. One last quick look around the room, and he could already hear her steps on the oak stairway.

The heat prickled under the soft collar of his shirt. He snatched a handkerchief from his pocket and patted at his forehead. He was aware that he was acting like any boy at his first assignation, and even while he acted just that way, he managed to smile ruefully at himself. The footsteps continued up and paused . . . and continued again. He had never known a woman. The thought that he might, that in all probability he would, in the next hour or two, was intolerably exciting. Or was he simply deluding himself? Certainly at the luncheon where they had met she had been markedly friendly, but perhaps no more than a mature English lady might be with total propriety to a young German undergraduate. Yet there had been one exchange. She had asked him whether he had considered marrying an English girl, and he had laughingly answered that he was in no position to think of marriage yet. And she had fixed him with her warm hazel eyes and said quite right—and with a pause—but then she understood these modern, long-delayed marriages often imposed intolerable—another pause— strains upon a healthy young man. Claus von Hardenberg was inexperienced, but he was no fool. He knew that that remark from beneath a level gaze exceeded wildly the bounds of propriety. And her acceptance of his invitation to call on him in his rooms had surely borne out his interpretation.

At her knock he pulled open the door so quickly that she recoiled with a quick smile of surprise.

"Do come in." He stepped back and held the door wide.

The brim of her straw hat brushed his cheek as she moved past him. "How lucky you are to have rooms here," she said as she looked around the low-beamed chamber. "I think it's quite the prettiest court in Queens'."

[9]

He closed the door. "Yes, I consider myself very lucky."

"But then you're a Scholar, aren't you?"

"An Exhibitioner," he said.

"Even so, that must put you high on the list for the best rooms."

He shrugged in uneasy agreement. "May I offer you a glass of sherry?" She had moved to the window and was looking down.

"I'd love one," she said.

He poured sherry with hands that were still unsteady. "It was very good of you to come," he said, his back still toward her.

She sat on the sofa and stared thoughtfully at the enormous stone fireplace with the carved college coat of arms and the date, 1573, inscribed above it. "It wasn't good of me at all," she said as she took the sherry glass from him. "It was surely either indiscreet or impetuous or even very stupid. Isn't that the way the world would see a don's wife who visited an undergraduate alone in his rooms?"

"I don't know."

"You do, Claus." She indicated the place beside her on the sofa.

"I mean this is the first time I've received a visit in my rooms," he said.

"Really?" She smiled. "But I thought all undergraduates received visits from the dancing ladies at the New Theatre."

"Some do," he said, flushing.

"But not you?"

He hesitated. "Once. My friend Winslow invited four or five of them."

"Is that young George Winslow? Buzz, he used to be called. Richard Winslow's younger brother. I thought I saw him downstairs in the court."

"You know the Winslows, then?"

"I used to know their father, old Lord Winslow, before he died. He was incapable of resisting a fast woman or a good-looking horse. I'm afraid he wasn't much of a judge of either."

"Did you ever meet Lord Winslow's brother, Thomas?"

She laughed. "Why do you ask?"

"Buzz speaks of him a lot," Claus said. "He's dead now, of course, but I believe Buzz admired him rather."

"I'm not surprised," Margaret said. "Any young man would. Thomas Winslow, Buzz's uncle, was a frightful man-about-town. Said at one time to be the handsomest officer in the Household Cavalry. He asked me to be his mistress."

Claus's eyes widened.

"My dear Claus"—she patted his arm—"Thomas Winslow asked every young woman to be his mistress."

Claus was silent.

"You are wondering, clearly, whether I assented."

Not a muscle moved in his face.

"Nevertheless, you are wondering." She smiled. "The answer is no. The answer is to my infinite regret, no. I was terribly young, just married and deeply disillusioned. But Thomas was already forty years old. He was going gray, Claus. I have always admired rather younger men, you see. But you were telling me about the visit from the ladies of the New Theatre."

"I feel it is not a fit subject for conversation, Lady Margaret," he said hurriedly.

"Really?"

"Yes."

"Is that because they take their clothes off in public?"

"Quite."

"But they wouldn't, indeed logically they couldn't, without an audience."

"That is true."

"Have you been part of the audience, Claus?"

"I must confess I have."

She laughed. "I must try not to tease you," she said. "Now tell me about the visit of the dancing ladies."

"There's not really very much to tell. It was an afternoon visit."

"Yes?"

"A champagne tea."

"A champagne tea?" She frowned. "Really?"

"Winslow refuses to drink anything else." Claus forced a smile. "He claims water's bad for his liver. And tea is a lightly disguised Indian poison."

"And what happened?" she asked, sipping her sherry. "That afternoon?"

"One had a party," he said hesitantly.

"One had a party?" she echoed. "Did you not select your own little cocotte and set her up in convenient lodgings in Laundress Lane?"

"Good Lord, no!"

"Relax, Claus." She reached out a hand and touched his knee. "Tell me, when you leave Cambridge, what will you do then?"

"I go back to Germany. To the army, to take up my commission. In the Potsdam Guard."

"Ah, so you're to be one of those magnificent German generals, enormous of girth, bewhiskered and bemonocled?"

He shook his head. "No, Lady Margaret. I've already decided that my career shall be in military diplomacy."

"You hope to be posted to an embassy as military attaché?"

"As third assistant, to begin with."

"And where would you hope to be? London? Paris?"

"Paris is the plum," he said. "The French army is the biggest and most modern in the world. With the exception of the German army. But in Paris there would still be much to be learned."

"It's said there is a great deal to be learned by a young man in Paris."

"I mean professionally, Lady Margaret."

"Do you mean that a military attaché is little more than a gentleman spy?" She opened her eyes wide. "Surely not."

"No, Lady Margaret. And I believe you're making fun of me. But then, making fun of the Germans is a very popular English pastime, is it not?"

"I've offended you."

"Of course not," he said hurriedly.

She leaned forward, and taking the glass from his hand, she placed it beside hers on the gateleg table. "I didn't risk my reputation in Cambridge to make fun of you, Claus."

"No ..." he said uncertainly.

"I risked it because you are a beautiful young man whom I believe I can trust."

"Trust?"

"Not to boast to your friends about your conquest of the wife of the Lord Provost-elect."

"Conquest?" A pulse hammered in his head.

"No less," she smiled.

"It's you," he said hurriedly, "who have made the conquest."

She took his head in both hands and drew his lips to hers. Gently she probed with her tongue until his mouth opened and she felt him reach out to grasp her around the waist. The tension in his body she found infinitely exciting. But the door behind them was unlocked. And if she had been seen coming here, it was a desperate risk to stay for more than the time it might take to deliver an invitation, or to inquire after the health of a mutual friend.

She drew her head back slowly and reached up to stroke his cheek. "I must go now, Claus. That's all I came to say."

She rose from the sofa and adjusted her hat as he looked at her in bewilderment.

"You're going now? Already?" He scrambled to his feet. "Will you please stay?" he said.

She shook her head. "No. There will be other opportunities. Safer ones."

"But I leave Cambridge soon after the end of term. I am to return to Germany for the summer."

"It will certainly be possible to arrange a meeting before then." She took up her parasol. "Patience, Claus, you'll hear from me soon. If you want to, that is."

"Of course I want to."

He leaned forward and took her around the waist. He could feel her body through the thin material of the white dress. His eyes burned and his throat ached as if he were about to burst into tears. He had no more than a vague sense of the irresistible madness that possessed him as he pulled her toward him. He heard her gasp and heard her voice raised in anger or pleading, but his hands were already on her breasts and she was falling backward onto the sofa.

He crashed down upon her, forcing his knee into the fold of her dress between her legs. He was breathing like a demon, hotly against her neck. Cologne clouded his senses. Her hat had fallen and was rolling across the carpet. Then suddenly his body stiffened.

He raised himself, at first still kneeling between her legs, and then to his feet. "Lady Margaret"—he forced his dry mouth to form words—"please, please accept my apologies."

She stood up and, without speaking, turned to the looking glass and arranged her hair and the bodice of her dress. "Please hand me my hat," she said into the mirror, where his reflection lurked behind her.

He gave her her hat, and she took some moments to put it on. "Of course you realize the door was unlocked all the time," she said.

"I was not thinking. . . .I do beg you to forgive me."

She closed her eyes briefly and nodded toward the door. He stepped forward and opened it and she swept past him, leaving a trace of cologne as she turned at the end of the corridor. Descending the narrow staircase, she was relieved to see there was no one in the sunlit court.

Buzz Winslow, gown flowing behind him, hands deep in pockets, paced morosely beside Claus as they rounded the cloister and passed into the great court.

"That fool, Jack Soames," Winslow muttered. The bell was still tolling as they joined the press of undergraduates outside the dining hall.

"What about Soames?"

"Induced me to spend a precious afternoon with a couple of girls he'd met. Enticingly common, he claimed. Shopgirls, he even hinted at. Ready for the Beast if we played our cards right."

"And what were they?"

"A pair of prissy vicars' daughters, damn his eyes. Never taken the Beast in their lives. Their only interest in this life was to debate the literal truth of the New Testament. One even brought her Bible along with her for handy reference."

"So you drank champagne and listened."

"For as long as I could. Between close textual exegesis I inserted a suggestion that we take a turn in the punt. . . ."

"'The covered creek free from prying eyes . . . '?"

"Refused. I then suggested a game of hide-and-seek. . . ."

"'The school woodshed to which you have the keys . . . '?"

Winslow nodded gloomily. "Equally refused. So the furies munched their way through the Acts of the Apostles and the best part of a whole game pie and contrived to reveal not so much as a fat ankle between the pair of them. Still, I have a tryst on Tuesday with a liberated shopgirl from the butcher's."

"Liberated?"

"We had a long chat, my dear fellow, over the purchase of a pound of sausages. She put herself forward very bravely. Mind you, she was wielding a huge butcher's cleaver at the time. Still, I've high hopes that this one will have the courage of my convictions."

"These shopgirls," Claus said doubtfully, "are they always like that?"

"'Course they are, old chap. They love the Beast. Can't get enough of it. Stands to reason. They're members of the working classes."

"What does being members of the working classes have to do with it?"

"Don't be naïve, my dear fellow. The working classes of England are the salt of the earth. They were created, more or less in God's image, to serve and pleasure their betters. Keystone of the Protestant religion." He nodded to himself. "Jolly decent of you to invite me to dine in hall, Claus. Hope it's better than last time."

The bell stopped and the undergraduates flowed into the dining hall and stood at the long oak refectory tables, awaiting the arrival of Masters and Fellows at the high table. In the shuffling silence, Claus remembered the letter in his pocket. It had arrived that morning in an expensive, handmade envelope carrying the Gorringe family crest. Its contents could be guessed with more or less complete accuracy. It would comprise first a complaint that he had not visited the Gorringe family home since March or December or whenever. And it would follow up with an invitation, almost a summons, to a weekend house party.

The Gorringes were the closest remaining friends of his Uncle Jurgen, who had served as military attaché in London back in Victoria's time. He would have to reply with polite expressions of regret, so the letter would have to be read. And not only read but answered. The Gorringe estate was in Suffolk not thirty miles from Cambridge and excuses would not be easy.

Tearing open the envelope, he saw to his surprise that it contained a letter rather than a printed invitation card. It came from Lady Cynthia Gorringe and read:

My dear Claus,
    It seems nothing short of tragic that you have been in univer-

sity residence for three whole terms and yet we have not induced you to come to Kentworth Hall for other than the christening of Bertie's firstborn and the sad funeral of my dear mama. . . .

Claus winced and noticed that the shuffling of the hungry undergraduates had stopped. The door to the Senior Common Room had opened and the Fellows of the college were processing toward their places. He clasped his right wrist with his left hand and stared at his shoes. *"Benedice benedicat,"* a voice intoned, and one hundred and fifty undergraduates scraped back their benches and sat at table.

Winslow was talking to someone on his left. *Dear mama's funeral.* Yes, Claus remembered that. A weekend of somber horror: tall, black-hatted coachmen, and black-and-silver caparison for the horses of the cortege. He shuddered and returned to the letter.

. . . Before you go back to Germany, which surely must be soon, you must—I really mean *must*—come to stay. Two weekends are available, the first this coming weekend. The other is the last weekend in July. For many reasons I suspect that will be the one you will choose.

Write to me by return post. I am quite certain your dear uncle would be most upset to hear that you were too occupied to come to see us.

For the rest of the guests, I can promise some most pleasing personalities. Lady Diana Winslow is a charming young thing of not much less than your own age and will be accompanying her mother, Lady Winslow. The Desboroughs, of course, and their friends Mr. Carstairs and Miss Wright. In addition there are four or five others who have not yet confirmed acceptance, one at least with whom you are acquainted, Lady Margaret Ryder, who asked particularly to be remembered to you when I met her last week. . . .

"What is it?" Winslow was half-turned, looking at him strangely. "Not bad news?"

"No." Claus stuffed the letter back into his pocket. "Not bad news at all. It seems I'm to meet your sister at the Gorringes at the end of the month."

"Oh, God." Winslow bent his head and began to spoon onion soup noisily from his plate.

"What's wrong with my meeting your sister?"

Winslow lifted his head from his plate and, pulling out his handkerchief, dabbed at his mouth. "Foul soup," he said. "Nothing wrong with your meeting Diana, old chap. Everything wrong with *her* meeting *you*. She's fourteen years old. Fifteen, perhaps, now. She'll fall desperately in love with you and plague me for invitations up here every weekend of next term."

"You think your little sister's an incurable romantic, do you, Buzz?"

"God knows what she is, old boy," Winslow said gloomily. "All I'm worried about is how the devil I'm to satisfy the demands of the Beast with my sister hanging around me every weekend."

"Excuse me, gentlemen." The college steward was standing behind them. "Count von Hardenberg, a message from the Master, sir. He would like to see you in his rooms immediately after Hall."

Claus frowned. "Did he say what for?"

"No, sir. He did stress that it was urgent."

As soon as dinner ended, Claus left Winslow, promising to meet him later in the Common Room for coffee, and made his way to Sir Hubert Thompson's rooms.

It was months since he had first met Sir Hubert. In the first week or so of the winter term it was the practice of the Master to invite new undergraduates for a glass of sherry and a disquisition upon the opportunities and pitfalls that lay ahead. Sir Hubert had covered the opportunities incisively enough. It was when he came to consider the possible dangers a young undergraduate might be exposed to that he seemed less comfortable. Pulling at his gray mustaches, Sir Hubert had swirled his sherry in the glass. "Infection," he growled.

Claus had looked at him in astonishment. "Sir?"

Sir Hubert sucked sherry from the glass and drew it noisily through his teeth. "The inevitable, *inevitable* result."

"Result of what, sir?" Claus asked hesitantly.

"Tell you a story." Sir Hubert scowled at him from under his thick gray eyebrows. "Two young men. First-class minds. This college, '08. Perhaps '09. Both first-class minds. One of them got married. Two children. Fine boys. The other took to yellow French novels. This chap Maupassant. Another one, Zola. Inevitable result."

"Sir?"

"Infection." Sir Hubert shook his head sadly. "First-class mind."

He extended a huge hand to Claus. "Keep a straight bat, my boy. Only way. Understand me. Only way."

With his tree trunk of an arm around Claus's shoulders, he had conducted him fondly to the door.

Since that first baffling meeting, Claus had slowly improved his understanding of the bachelor mathematician who was Master of the college. Watching him now as he poured port for them both, he saw the old man's mouth compressed with anxiety and realized that something different from the unmentionable concerns of the "infection" speech was occupying him.

"I came as soon as I could, sir," Claus said, taking a glass of port. "The college butler said you wished to see me urgently."

"Sit down, Hardenberg," Sir Hubert said, standing before the empty fireplace. "I believe I'm doing the right thing. Though one has no real guide in these matters. The principle I must accept is my responsibility as Master to the undergraduates of the college." He paused. "What are your plans for this summer, my boy?"

"I've just come back from the Dean's reading party in Wales. I was planning to stay up for a few more weeks and then return to Berlin in the middle of August."

"I see." Sir Hubert shifted his great bulk from one foot to the other. "You are aware that today Austria delivered an ultimatum to Serbia."

"I read about it in the evening newspaper, sir."

"You are also aware, of course, that your country is closely allied with Austria."

"Yes."

"If I were you, my boy, I'd pack my bags and go home for the vacation. By the time term begins, it could all have blown over, of course. No doubt the diplomatists on both sides are all hard at work."

"Do *you* think there will be a war, sir?"

"I'm a mathematician. Frankly, numbers have always been easier for me to understand than people. But add Austria and Germany against Serbia, Russia, and France, and any fool can see Europe is heading for troubled waters."

"If there is a war, will England come in?"

"Yes," Sir Hubert said quietly. "I believe the answer is yes. Which is why, as Master of this college, I am suggesting that you most carefully consider your position in the next few days. Now drink up your port, my boy. You understand me. Nothing official, I'm not suggesting you resign from the college or anything like that. Just think about a visit home to Germany." He stretched out a huge hand. "And I hope to see you back here next term."

Claus came clattering down the staircase from Sir Hubert's room and stood gulping air in the moonlit courtyard below. He knew that there could not possibly be a war. Certainly he knew there could not possibly be a war until he had experienced the full forgiveness of Lady Margaret Ryder.

INNOCENT
PARTIES

ONE

Events have shown that I am not a gentleman. Least of all an English gentleman. Yet I still believe that if America's gift to the world has been equality and that of France individuality, and that of Germany discipline, England's gift has been the idea of the gentleman. Each national offering has, of course, been flawed by almost all that history can recount, but without such elusive ideals the world would be poorer. And of them all the most elusive is that of the *gentleman*.

My name is Claus Thomas von Hardenberg. I came to England in the autumn of 1913 in rather unusual circumstances. I was brought up on a very modest family estate in Prussia, sharing a tutor with my many cousins and receiving lessons in English from my mother, who spoke the language fluently.

The years seem to have gone a long way toward eradicating detailed memories of my early childhood. There were, I believe, upwards of a dozen young Hardenberg children growing up on the estate. Sometimes, as I look back, it seems to me that we lived in a world of perpetual summer, although I can still just recall memories of boar hunts in the snowy forest that made up much of the estate. The *Schloss* itself was really more a large, tumbledown, fortified farmhouse than a castle. But it had a drawbridge and a moat and it was the practice of the villagers to bob a curtsey or tip their hats to us children by the time we reached the age of eleven or twelve.

We knew, of course, that we were poor and that parcels of land were always being sold to pay for a dowry for one of the older girls or military school for the boys. But I think that, at least as very young children, we associated poverty with nobility and believed that only traders and the local corn chandler could be rich.

The adults in our lives were mostly women. As far as I can remember, every single male was in the army or in the public administration in Berlin. Perhaps there was a grandfather of one of my cousins who lived in a tiny apartment overlooking the stable courtyard, but that too is a dim memory. For the most part, men passed infrequently through our lives. This is undoubtedly the reason my childhood was reasonably advanced before I became curious for details about my dead father. I remember the occasion well enough. One of my older cousins, Wolfgang, had constructed a large cut-out family tree. On every drooping branch of the cardboard conifer he had recorded members of the Hardenberg family in his own eccentric groupings. Since we have some claim to go back to the Teutonic knights of the eastern marches, Wolfgang's genealogical line was both overcrowded and confusing. But what was clear to me was a strange and simple fact that had never occurred to me before. Growing up among all these Hardenbergs, I had never questioned the fact that my name too was Hardenberg. My mother, born a Hardenberg, was *still* a Hardenberg.

Illegitimacy was no more to me then than an intriguing mystery. My mother, to her credit, faced the problem squarely. We were sitting in a bare schoolroom that looked out over the moat and away across the flat pine forests to the unending east. If you walked and walked and walked all day and all night, Wolfgang claimed, you would arrive in Moscow. There the Tsar, who would be awfully pleased to see you, would give you a sable fur, a sleigh, and two Russian ponies to carry you jingling merrily back home.

I was probably thinking as much about the sable fur and the crackle of the sleigh across the snow as anything else when my mother beckoned me to leave my desk and come and stand next to her chair.

I crossed the room, glancing out of the diamond panes of the leaded windows across the snow-tipped trees to Muscovy. My mother, rather severe in a dark brown dress, her fair hair drawn back into a bun, was probably not more than thirty at that time. I was perhaps ten or eleven.

"You wanted to ask me something, Claus," she said. "Something about your father."

I don't think I felt any embarrassment. I told her about Wolfgang's cut-out family tree and the minor mystery it had revealed.

For a moment or two she was silent. "When I was very young," she said, "I went to England as a governess to the young boy of an English noble family. He was about your age, and I was to teach him German. The family lived in an enormous house with dozens and dozens of servants, and each weekend there would be house parties, and sometimes even the Prince of Wales, the English king as he is now, would come and bring friends for the shooting."

"Did you like England, Mama?"

"Oh yes. For that reason I have always insisted on your English lessons even when some of your aunts were less demanding of your cousins. But let me go on. While I was in England I met the man who was to become your father."

"An Englishman?" I remember still that first thrill of excitement.

"Yes, an Englishman."

"Was he an English lord?"

"He was the brother of an English lord."

"What was his name?"

"Thomas Winslow."

"Thomas Winslow. Thomas Winslow." I repeated the name a few times and decided that I liked it.

"Your father died shortly before you were born. When I returned to Germany with you as a small child, there seemed no reason to give you an English name when you were to be a German child. In any case, I was very proud of our Hardenberg name. So I decided to keep it. For both of us."

For a year or two the explanation more or less sufficed. At some point I realized that I was illegitimate, but in the closed Hardenberg circle I can't remember that the fact caused me any distress. Obviously, though, I was aware of the need for some delicacy because I did not again talk to my mother at any length about my English parent until one day just after my sixteenth birthday. And it was she, not I, who brought up the matter.

"I have made arrangements for you to go to Berlin, Claus," she said in an abrupt, agitated manner that was unusual for her. "There is a visitor there from England who wishes to see you."

We were walking across the stable courtyard. I stopped at the great carved wooden staircase that led up to the family apartments. I could form no question to ask, and I could see from her face that it was better to ask none.

When after a moment she recovered her composure, she smiled as if nothing had passed between us. "Do you remember I told you that I had been a governess in England to a young boy of ten or eleven?"

"Yes."

"His name is Richard Winslow. Lord Winslow, now that his father has died. I suppose he must be about twenty-five years old by now. In any event, he is in Berlin. He would like to see you."

"You'll be coming too?"

"No, Claus. I'm far too busy with sickness in the village and Frau Kramer expecting her baby at any moment." She put her hand on my arm. "I want you to go alone, Claus. You can stay at the Potsdam Guards Barracks with Uncle Jurgen, and you can see all the wonders of the new Berlin that His Majesty is building."

I was not convinced by the excuse of sickness in the village, or of the need for her presence at the Kramer birth, but I was unwilling to probe further. I did, however, ask one more question. "This young English lord," I said, "is he my cousin?"

She hesitated. "Yes," she said. "Richard is your cousin."

I met Richard Winslow for the first time two days later in the Adlon Hotel in Berlin. Strangely, he was much as I expected, a tall, slender, brown-haired man, very easy and self-possessed. He offered me tea in the lobby and complimented me on my English and plied me with questions about my mother, to whom he seemed greatly attached. He was in Berlin, he explained, on the business of the British Foreign Office, and had a day or so free before discussions at the Wilhelmstrasse were to begin. He would very much like, he said, to spend the time with me. Since we were cousins, it was time that we got to know each other.

At sixteen, I was immensely flattered, and for the next two days we ate lunch and dinner together and visited the theater and walked around the wide alleys where the new Berlin was rising in great blocks of pale gray stone. On the last night we had dinner with my Uncle Jurgen at the Guards mess, a splendid uniformed affair with only Richard and myself in civilian evening dress. Regimental silver and glass glowed in the candlelight. It was the career I had decided on for myself, and I felt, despite the fact that we were both my uncle's guests, that I shared in some way as a host to this splendid evening.

Afterwards we went back to the Adlon, where Richard had taken rooms for me. Sitting in the lobby with brandy and cigars, I felt my provincial childhood in Prussia slipping away forever.

"You've never been to England, Claus," Richard said, lighting his cigar. "Do you imagine you'd like it?"

"I couldn't fail to." My enthusiasm was genuine enough to quell the slight queasiness from my first cigar.

"I'm glad we've come to know each other," Richard said. "After these two days, I feel I know you well. You see"—he leaned forward—"I am now the head of the family. The English side of the family, if you like."

I looked at him through the hanging blue cigar smoke. I had never thought of myself as having an "English side of the family."

"I've already talked at some length and very frankly with your Uncle Jurgen, and I think I understand the circumstances of the Hardenbergs. I owe it to you to speak equally frankly. The Winslow estate, at the time of my father's death, was mostly heavily mortgaged. It has taken three years of sales and considerable retrenchments to pull things round."

He saw that I was baffled, and laughed. "I'll come to the point, Claus. I have put aside a certain amount of money that I believe is owed to your mother and yourself. Your mother has refused either a capital sum or an allowance, and I understand why. I have, however, persuaded her to allow me to make some provision for you."

"Some provision?"

"Yes. The males in the family have always completed their education at Cambridge. My proposal is that the estate pay for your education and, of course, general support for three years at Queens' College, Cambridge."

"You want me to go to England?" My mind was turning uncertainly between excitement and alarm at the proposal. I had hardly traveled outside Prussia, and the prospect of living the life of an English gentleman for three years terrified me as much as it appealed to my ego. It was then that I remembered my ambition to enter the Imperial Guard.

"It's not I who want you to go to England, Claus," Richard was saying. "I think your father would have wanted it, but perhaps that's not the most important consideration. I believe your mother would wish it."

"Would that mean," I asked carefully, "that I could not enter the Guard?"

"Far from it," he said. "Three or even two years at the University will provide an effective stepping stone to Potsdam. Your uncle Jurgen confirmed this. Do you want time to think about it?"

I shook my head. I had an image of the life at Oxford and Cambridge from my mother. More than that, I was already swelling with pride at the thought of what Wolfgang and the others would say when I told them.

"I think it's a great honor," I said in my sixteen-year-old attempt to rise to the occasion. "I will do my best to acquit myself well."

Again, Richard Winslow laughed. "Go there and enjoy it, Claus," he said. "Make lots of friends and do what you can to make sure our two countries never blunder into war."

I arrived in Cambridge late for the beginning of the winter term of 1913, the Kiel ferry, a brass-and-mahogany bucket called the *Cuxhaven*, having been forced by bad weather to stand off Harwich for two days and nights. It had been intended that I should go to London and stay that first night in England at the Winslow town house in Ebury Square, where I was to meet the family—that is, Lady Winslow, who had survived her husband; young George Amadeus, or Buzz as he was known to the family, Richard's younger brother who was going up to Cambridge that term; and Diana, an even younger sister, barely more than a child. But when I telephoned Richard Winslow from the wind-battered harbormaster's office at Harwich, he suggested I go straight to Cambridge, where his younger brother, Buzz, would already be in residence. I thus missed this first opportunity to meet the two female members of the Winslow family.

My first days in Cambridge I found quite overwhelming. I had imagined that the University would be four or five imposing buildings, each one devoted to History or Philosophy or Medicine or Law. What I never suspected was that every one of the ten thousand undergraduates would be housed in apartments in medieval college buildings that utterly dominated the center of the town. Nor did I suspect that we would be served meals in a medieval hall or, twice a day if I chose, on great silver platters in my rooms. At the same time, port and cigars were freely available from the buttery merely on the signing of a chit, and younger dons were addressed with a freedom and lack of reverence that at first unnerved me.

In addition to all this, Richard Winslow had deposited five hundred pounds to an account in my name at Martin's Bank in Trinity Street, and on that first misty autumn afternoon, having invested an English shilling in a large cream almond cake from Fitzbillies, I walked down Silver Street with the words of old Herr Kammerman singing in my head, or rather the rhythms of Horace quoted to me by Herr Kammerman: *Non cuius homini contingit adire Corinthum.* "It is not given to every man to see Corinth."

Nor is it given to every young provincial German to know George Amadeus Winslow.

On that day of my arrival at Cambridge I had walked along the river behind my own college and found myself at dusk staring breathless at an assemblage of buildings on broad lawns, and a vast, soaring Gothic chapel that I discovered, on inquiring of a passing undergraduate, to be King's College. Crossing the stone bridge over the narrow River Cam I walked through the massive court, the lights from the windows of undergraduate rooms sparkling in the October mist. At the porter's lodge I left my card for the Honorable George Amadeus Winslow with a note saying I would give myself the pleasure of calling upon him tomorrow afternoon. I was, I suppose, a very formal young man in those days. But formality, I soon discovered, was not something to be maintained easily in the presence of Buzz.

I entered his rooms that next afternoon to find a chaos of empty champagne bottles, clothes strewn across armchairs, a broken-legged table, half-collapsed. A tall young man with a round, youthful face and smooth, improbably blond hair stood coatless in the middle of the room. "Claus von Hardenberg," I introduced myself, clicking my heels.

We shook hands. "Devil of a party last night," he said. "My servant's refused to clear up the place until I'm out of it. Can't blame him and can't bribe him. So just have to make the best of it, old fellow."

"Would you like me to help you clear it up?"

"Good God, no." He waved his arms to encompass the impossibility of the undertaking. "Sorry I missed you in London. You've met Richard, of course."

"In Berlin, last year."

"Marvelous fellow," Winslow said. "Terribly worthy. Thank God he's got charge of the declining family fortunes. We're on the edge of penury as it is, old boy."

I looked down at the empty champagne bottles stacked in corners and rolling across the carpet.

"Appearances, my dear fellow. Must keep up appearances. Here, there's one bottle unopened." He disappeared into his gyp-room and came out with a bottle of champagne and two dripping glasses. Opening the bottle, he poured for us both. "Great shame about your boat," he said. "My mama and my sister were dying to meet you."

"I am very sorry to have missed them. But there'll be other opportunities. Is your sister tutored in London?"

"When she isn't away at some frightful place in Switzerland. She comes back gurgling French and German like a strangled peahen."

"Richard showed me a photograph of her. On horseback."

"She's something of a daredevil, Claus, to tell you the truth. A very fine horsewoman already, but over bold on the hunting field. Over bold altogether, by God!"

"I look forward to meeting her," I said. "And your mother, Lady Winslow."

"We're all that's left of the closest family—Mama, Diana, Richard, and I." He paused. "And you, of course." He handed me a glass.

I believed I could feel a flush rising on my cheek. Whether it was apparent or not I have no idea. Certainly it was not necessary. The careful nonchalance of his manner in the next few minutes was something I was never to forget. It was to make me grateful to him for many years to come.

He raised his glass. "Welcome, Claus," he said. "This is a meeting that should have taken place many years ago. Would have saved embarrassment all round. Too late now, and no need. Richard's done the right thing—trust Richard."

We touched glasses and drank. "I suppose you never knew your father," he said.

"No."

"Tell you the truth, old boy, he was a bounder. So was mine. Richard's the first decent chap we've had in the family for years," he said. He slapped me on the shoulder. "Present company excepted, as the shopgirls say."

It was the beginning of much more than a friendship. Without Buzz's vast network of Eton and family connections, I might well have settled for a quiet, even studious existence in my comfortable rooms in Queens' College. But with Buzz's more flamboyant circle drawn from undergraduates from King's and Trinity College, there existed no possibility for a quiet life. We went to parties and the races, we played the murderous game of rugby football or rowed on the upper reaches of the Cam. We got outrageously drunk and smoked cigars, but most of all we talked about, thought about, and intermittently pursued girls.

The leader of our group was undeniably Buzz. Sir Harry Towers was a young man, red-faced, overweight, and already squirearchical; Billy Danvers, the Marquess of Belfort's heir, was tall and extraordinarily thin; the Saunders brothers were excessively physical, like a thousand other undergraduates of that time: boxers, footballers, and one a racquets champion, holder of a "blue," as it was called, an honor awarded for playing against Oxford. Charles Vanerl Chrysler was an American, a year or two older than most of us, a big, rawboned youth at this time, quieter than most but still capable of those outbursts of alcoholic excess that we all affected to admire so much. The Honorable Tom Boscowan was a "tough," a powerfully built Anglo-Irishman, his temper always on the shortest possible fuse.

There was much posing. To strike an attitude was the currency of our relationships. We were too shy and too confident at the same time. Above all we feared sentimentality.

Quite early in the term we decided to form ourselves into one of the private dining clubs then, and probably to this day, so fashionable at Oxford and Cambridge. We chose to call ourselves the Corinthians, because, as I understand it, the Corinthian tradition in English private schools of the period suggested a certain muscular attitude to life, a touchiness in respect of what we believed was our honor, a readiness to respond to imagined slights. In addition, I had wheeled out old Herr Kammerman's line from Horace, "It is not given to every man to visit Corinth." And that seemed to us, warmed by the self-satisfaction of our youth, to provide just the touch of exclusivity on which our style of life depended.

Thus we became the Corinthians. We registered the name with the bursar and recorded our function as a dining and debating club. The college steward was instructed to lay down in our names an initial six dozen bottles of port, and Charles Chrysler contributed from his own pocket, or that of his unbelievably wealthy family, forty dozen Krug '98, enough champagne, we calculated, to take us comfortably through the eight club meetings we planned to hold in the coming spring term of 1914.

We met every day together, at least three or four of us, and sometimes the entire dozen members of the club. We went to pubs together, we hired half a dozen punts and traveled the river in convoy. We shouted, jeered, waved, laughed together. We were a tight-knit group, the young men of the tribe, the chieftains' sons. Only Leslie Lazard-Cohn was different. He had been educated exotically in Paris and Madrid. He spoke several European languages (I could vouch for his German) and was reading Natural Sciences with more success than he was prepared to admit to us.

He had attached himself to Buzz early in the first term, and despite a number of swingeing rebuffs from other Corinthians, he had managed to establish himself as, if not a member of the group, at least its court jester. Buzz was his protector.

The truth is, none of us liked Jews very much. They were seen as too ostentatious, too ingratiating. Above all, not quite gentlemen. Lez Lazard knew exactly the nature of the stereotype, knew what was expected of him, and gave us what we asked. Why? He was, of course, desperately anxious to belong, on any terms. But I think it was more than that. I think he himself believed that his exclusion was just, so powerful was the idea of the gentleman. Of course, neither he nor we were aware that the idea had already begun its long descent into decadence.

Charles Chrysler was at the other end of the scale from Lazard-Cohn. He was immediately recognizable as one of us. His manner was North-American-relaxed. He was the only one among us who had a serious knowledge of the wines we pretended to be familiar with; he was a natural sportsman, a rider of courage and confidence; his dress was a careless mix of New York and Savile Row. And he was rich. But then, so was Lez Lazard. So what was the difference? In terms of Aryan looks, Lez was as fair as Charles was dark, his nose straight, his tailor the best that Cambridge and London could offer. But he wore an extravagant diamond ring to amuse us with his Levantine vulgarity, and would delight in telling a story against himself, against his Jewishness. Above all, the difference between Charles and Lez Lazard was that Charles never apologized, never explained. He never felt the necessity.

The day arrived when the subject of Lez Lazard becoming a Corinthian could no longer be delayed. Solemn eighteen-year-olds as we were, we trooped, one by one, into the billiard room of the Pitt Club, which provided such facilities to infinitely less important clubs, such as our own, and used its election box to decide Lazard's fate. The system was simple. A mixed basket of snooker balls stood on the center table, two or three dozen red, white, pink, blue, and green ivory spheres—and, among them, a half-dozen black. In most Oxford and Cambridge club rules, one black ball placed in the box was enough to ban a membership application.

We had considered the whole question pretty seriously. Lez Lazard, it was generally agreed, was a first-rate chap to spend an evening with. He was outrageous on the subject of women, generous, a good drinker, and a man who appreciated a first-class riot. But still, doubts about him had been expressed. Billy Danvers squirmed uncomfortably and said he liked Lez as a man, but felt he had to ask if that was really enough. One really was obliged to think of the future of the club. Within the coded speech of the gentleman, we all knew the concern he was voicing.

We looked naturally toward Buzz, but he rocked back in his seat in the bar of the Anchor and said nothing. It was Charles Chrysler who spoke up for Lez. "The chap's a Jew," he said firmly. "Come out with it if you don't want a Jew as a member. Personally, I think he's a good man who can hold his own."

"Can't we all," Buzz said. "But only as a last resort."

"You know what I'm saying," Charles said. "I don't mind saying I'm voting *for*."

"Good chap," Buzz said. "No more chat, let's get to it. I've arranged with the Pitt Club to service us this afternoon." He got to his feet and led us up Silver Street and along King's Parade.

The Pitt Club, to which all except Lazard himself already belonged, had provided two monitors, and with due ceremony we were conducted, one at a time, into the billiard room to cast our vote. The whole process took less than five minutes. Afterwards the senior monitor emerged carrying a tray, which he ceremoniously showed to each Corinthian in turn. Lez Lazard had been rejected by ten black balls to two colored. A red and a blue nestled among the smooth surfaces of the blacks.

I had voted black, swayed, as most of us clearly were, by Billy Danvers's mumbled reservations. Charles had announced his intention not to blackball Lazard. So who else had gone his own way? We all knew it could only have been Buzz.

Meeting Lez afterwards, I felt deeply apologetic. I did not intend to reveal details of the voting, and he did not expect any. "It was a close-run thing," I said, my hand on his shoulder.

He nodded.

"Really."

He shrugged as if accidentally shrugging my hand away. Then he grinned, his lips slightly twisted. "Another time," he said. "Another place."

From time to time, as a club, we paid visits to Oxford. There we found most in common with the recently formed Cribb Society, named after Tom Cribb, the bare-knuckle boxing champion of the previous century. They too subscribed to Corinthianism, and greatly envied us our name. We met on the first occasion for dinner at the Mitre, where we had reserved the long, oak-beamed upper room. We were two dozen strongly built young men replete with pheasant and claret and Stilton cheese and vintage port. We clasped one another in love or menace. The Corinthians proclaimed Oxford to be a decent enough little place, suitable for those from the lower evolutionary scales. And Cambridge, the Cribb men inquired—was it not a collection of thatched privies somewhere in the fens? By dinner's end we were spoiling for a fight. It was Buzz who proposed to the Cribb president the resolution. We should retire after dinner to Christchurch meadows. There, adequately supplied with champagne carried down by the Mitre Hotel waiters, we should pair off one Corinthian against one Cribb man. Each contest, bare-chested and bare-knuckled, would last until an adversary went down and stayed down for the count of twelve. There was one rule only: blows were not to be struck above the neck.

We fought. My opponent was a square-shouldered, pug-nosed Etonian bruiser named Lumley, who was the son of the duke of somewhere, a solid puncher who almost caved in my ribs with his first tornado attack. I can see the image still: the lights along the towpath sparkling through the almost leafless trees; the pairs of young men stripping to the waist in the misty autumn air, shaking hands, and hurling themselves at each other.

Cries of encouragement came from the lighted windows of a college behind us (was it Merton?) and young men in striped scarves and heavy topcoats came running down the meadows to watch. I went down once, then again. Lumley caught me unintentionally with a wild blow, high on the cheekbone. I went down again. But a Corinthian never gives in. I staggered to my feet and hit him with a rain of blows, and as he reeled back across the meadow beneath the ancient Oxford town wall, I called up all my last reserves of strength and hit him again and again.

It had no effect whatsoever. He charged forward and seemed to ride all over me. A green water level seemed to rise before my eyes as if I had been gently and painlessly submerged in a pool. Buzz was helping me to my feet. "Utter Visigoth, that chap Lumley," he said cheerfully. "Was at Eton. Always will be. You drew the black ace when you got him, old chap. But you got in a few good ones."

Lumley came across with two glasses of champagne. He handed me one, grinning hugely. "I thought you had me there," he said. "Right under the heart. What a puncher! I thought if I didn't go for you hell-for-leather, it would be the end of me. I was nearly finished, old chap, no mistake."

The right side of my face ached from temple to jaw. My ribs were bruised. But I was supremely happy. Everyone had heard what Lumley said.

We were equal, Oxford and Cambridge, at a dozen contests each.

A number of young men had gathered around us, some few notably a year or two older than the rest. It transpired that they were officers of the Brigade of Guards, visiting friends in Merton College. The suggestion was put to Buzz that it might be amusing to fight a Battle Royal. The Cribb Society and the Corinthians should each choose two champions, and the Brigade would put up two more. Buzz and Harry Towers were chosen for Cambridge, and George Westmorland, who was the Cribb president, and Lumley were to fight for Oxford. Two young Guards officers stripped to the waist and came forward.

I had no clear idea how a Battle Royal was fought, and I watched with astonishment as scarves were used to blindfold the contestants. Gloves had been called for and brought from Merton. The spectators formed a rough square about the size of a boxing ring.

On a signal the six contestants, propelled by friends on the edge of the ring, stumbled forward, flailing their arms wildly. Three or four blows seemed to connect at the same time. Heads cracked together. Noses spurted blood. As blindfolded figures came to the edge of the ring, a great concerted roar went up, glassfuls of champagne were thrown over the gladiator, and he was propelled back in the direction of the battle.

Buzz, I quickly recognized, was adept at the sport, if sport it was. He would advance crouching low, one gloved fist held out to seek the enemy, the other ready to deliver a punishing blow. He was a professional among amateurs. When the five others were rolling on the damp grass, he was declared the winner by acclamation.

It had been decided that this, our first term, should end in a monumental thrash, and Buzz, as our president, was responsible for deciding the form that the party should take. On the last day of the term, therefore, I was not surprised to receive instructions on club writing paper to be at the railway station at three that afternoon, wearing evening dress and adequately funded. We were informed that a compartment in the London train had been reserved for our use, and that a supply of the club's favored beverage, what we now called Chrysler '98, had been delivered to the railway station. The Corinthians were off on their first big adventure.

I arrived by hackney at the station to find half a dozen young men in white ties, long black overcoats, and tall silk hats striding about the waiting room, attempting to conceal their ill ease before the other travelers with an arrogance of voice and manner. There was, they told me, no sign of Buzz.

The station clock was already showing five minutes to three when we trooped out onto the platform for the London train. Standing in a worried huddle of silk hats, we listened to the whistle of the approaching train and wondered what our next move should be. Buzz, we realized, had said nothing in his letter about being there himself.

With a final blast on its whistle the train came into sight. Forlorn, we scanned the long platform in both directions. There was still no sign of Buzz. Fellow travelers, overhearing our anxious discussions, smiled to themselves. The train had pulled to a stop and we were still arguing about what to do when a guard approached us. "Good afternoon, gentlemen," he said, touching his peaked cap with the stick of his flag. "Would I be right in believing you are members of the Corinthian Club?"

I still recall the smiles of relief that greeted the guard's approach. We confirmed that we were indeed the Corinthians, and were led by him to a first-class compartment at the rear of the train. Grateful hands thrust half-crown pieces upon him. In the corner seat of the compartment sat Buzz, his feet upon the seat opposite, a glass of Chrysler '98 raised to greet us.

We tumbled in, laughing, all speaking at once.

"Silk hats on the luggage rack, gentlemen," Buzz roared above the din. "Help yourselves to champagne. I hereby call an extraordinary meeting of the club. Billy, as secretary, you'll have to commit the details to memory."

We settled down as the train pulled out toward London, no longer the lost, uneasy youngsters of a few moments ago, our confidence restored by champagne and cigars and first-class compartments and most of all by Buzz. And, I suppose, by the assurance that privilege did after all exist, inviolable, in our world.

I had never yet been to London, having missed the opportunity at the beginning of the term. I had of course heard a great deal about its sprawling size and had read Heine's essay on the commercial heart of the British Empire. But I was totally unprepared for the vast numbers of people scurrying about the railway station, the jostling hackney cabs, both horsedrawn and automobile, the cheerful porters bawling to one another and to their clients as they thrust their way through the crowds. There were sailors everywhere.

From the taxicab on the interminable drive from Liverpool Street station to the Winslow family house in Chelsea, Buzz nonchalantly pointed out the sights. I affected a nodding indifference to Trafalgar Square and Whitehall, Downing Street and the Houses of Parliament. Yet as we entered the great squares of town houses called Belgravia, I found it difficult to conceal how impressed I was by the pillared white buildings, six and seven stories high, each large enough to house a dozen families.

We entered into a hall of rose-colored light. Black and white diamond-shaped floor tiles filled the space before soaring mahogany doors. A full-length portrait of a tall, rather sullen-looking man in coronation robes occupied most of one wall. A butler saluted Buzz with friendly deference and directed a footman to take our coats.

We were greeted in the long drawing room by Lady Winslow. After Buzz had introduced her to those of us she had not previously met, she turned back to me and led me aside. She was a heavily built, formidable lady in her fifties, with gray hair that had been lightly tinted auburn. It would have been normal at that epoch to have addressed me, as one of her son's friends, as Mr. von Hardenberg. She chose instead to call me Claus, but I could detect no friendliness in the use of the name. Nor could I detect any real interest in her questions about my life at

Cambridge. When I told her I was reading History, she nodded. When I added that my German was useful for reading documents in European history, she murmured, "Of course." In particular, she made no effort to ask about my family in Germany. My mother received not a mention.

"I much regret that your daughter, Diana, is away from home at the moment," I said.

She frowned either in puzzlement or a more general disapproval. "Why is that?"

"I very much look forward to an opportunity of meeting her," I said, adding ingratiatingly, or so I thought, "the photographs I've seen promise a very lovely young woman."

"Diana is a child," she snapped. "Worse, she is a child plagued by a special sort of romanticism. I sometimes fear for her stability. Frankly, Mr. Hardenberg, I see no advantage in your meeting Diana at this stage."

I was desperately embarrassed.

"Poor Buzz has already suffered exile for her romantic inclinations," she said. "It would be really too much if she fixed her predatory affections upon you too."

I was rescued by the arrival of Richard Winslow, home from the Foreign Office, and it was noticeable that shortly after he had returned home, his mother left us. I was greatly relieved. It was the first time I had suffered that peculiar bloodless hostility, more than disapproval but less positive than dislike, which some Englishwomen choose to project. And it would in any case be many, many years before I understood Lady Winslow's feelings about me.

When she had gone, the butler served us whiskey and soda, and Richard questioned me in a leisurely yet interested way about my life at Cambridge. The truth was, of course, that I felt I spent a great deal too much time away from my studies, but it appeared that Richard had recently met Sir Hubert, the Master of the college, at the Oxford and Cambridge Club here in London, and Sir Hubert had given him a satisfactory first-term report.

We finished our drinks and Buzz rang the bell for our hats and coats. "Diana will be devastated at having missed you, Claus. She is, I'm afraid, just that age."

Richard Winslow laughed. "It's not every fifteen-year-old girl who suddenly acquires a handsome cousin out of the North German forest. Buzz teased her outrageously when they first heard you were coming to England. Blame it all on him." He turned to Buzz. "Incidentally," he said, "where are you fellows off to now? All dressed up as you are, I think I detect every sign of an impending good thrash."

Buzz said evasively, "You could be right."

"Music hall, supper, and whatever divertissements London town can offer, then back, pale and wan, on the milk train to Cambridge?" Richard crossed to the door.

"That's the sort of thing," Buzz said.

When Richard had left and the coats had been distributed by the footman, we stood, hats in hand, looking expectantly at Buzz.

"There's a taxi rank just around the corner," he said as we left the house.

We walked toward Sloane Square, I beside Buzz.

"I'm afraid, Buzz," I said cautiously, "that I might have offended your mama."

"Not difficult, old chap," he said, puffing at his cigar. "What did you do?"

"I'm not too sure. I was simply talking about Diana."

"Oh God."

"What was wrong with that? I just said how much I was looking forward to meeting her."

"Yes, I can imagine that caused the tight-shoe face. You didn't say how tall and blond and pretty Diana was, I suppose. That's calculated to light the fires of her wrath."

"I may have said something—yes, I think I did."

"Truth is, old chap," Buzz said, "and I can tell you because we're all family, my mama has got something of a down on Diana. She says Diana's head is stuffed with the most unsuitable romantic notions."

"Romantic notions about what?"

"About anything and anybody, old chap. Even about me in Mama's view."

"Is that what she meant about your being exiled to America?"

"God, you know how mothers are," he said. "She thought sister Diana was getting a little too sweet on me. Just an excuse, really. I was pushed off to America because Mama thought if I was going to sow any sixteen-year-old wild oats, I'd best do it three thousand miles away and not in the receptive bellies of her friends' daughters. That's the truth of the matter. Diana didn't really come into it."

In Sloane Square a line of motorcabs stood waiting for fares. Billy Danvers joined us.

Buzz gestured grandly. "Our transport awaits us."

"And where do we direct the cabbie to?" Danvers asked. "The West End?"

"No." Buzz shook his head, smiling. "No, tonight we're going south across the river. To Battersea. Tonight, gentlemen, we are slumming. I've booked us into Mrs. Bashford's."

"Mrs. Bashford's?" We were all equally at sea.

"Ma Bash," Buzz said with a slow, puckish smile, "runs the best house in south London."

With the exception of Buzz, I *think* with the exception of Buzz, none of us had ever been with a woman before. During club dinners we had all more or less confessed our virginity to one another. Now it seemed to me that the demands of Corinthianism required action. But I was mortally afraid. My ignorance of the female body was even more complete than at that time I believed. Worse, I feared disease, that dread shadow of infection that hung over every young man who was not utterly chaste. Every young woman, too—but for them the shadow could pursue them to the marriage bed. And often enough did.

Mrs. Bashford's house in Ethelburga Street, Battersea, did nothing but underline my unease. I had never entered so small a dwelling, the hall of which was no more than a yard wide and in which a dozen large, top-hatted undergraduates jostled and stamped like yearlings in a crowded stall. On the stairway Ma Bash appeared as a small, slender woman in a low-cut yellow gown, with an air of refinement behind a lifetime's habit of command. She took charge immediately, and within minutes we were settled at two tables in a tiny, red-lit parlor, being served champagne, which was undoubtedly hock and seltzer, by gray-faced waitresses who were naked from the waist up.

The supper was roast lamb and summer pudding and a decent enough piece of Stilton with cheap claret and even cheaper port to follow. But we roared and shouted and joked our way through it, and fondled the bare-breasted girls and drank toasts to Buzz as our president and only provider.

Yet I think that hanging over all of us, again perhaps with the exception of Buzz himself, was our worry about the way the evening must end. In the room across the hall, another party, apparently of commercials, had already finished supper, and from my position I could see a man disappear upstairs from time to time with one of the girls. They would be gone for no more than ten or fifteen minutes and return to jeers and shouts from their fellows.

At about ten o'clock the other party left, and a few minutes later Ma Bash led her young ladies into our parlor. They were better-looking girls than the waitresses. They wore dresses of extravagantly low cut and their mouths were rubbed with rouge, and they eyed our group with the same lip-pursing superiority that was Mrs. Bashford's stock-in-trade.

A complete quiet fell on the room. Mrs. Bashford walked forward and leaned over Buzz, her bosom pressing against the side of his neck, her head up as she passed her eyes across the rest of us. "Well, young gentlemen," she said. Her eyes, heavily mascaraed, seemed to me to glitter with something approaching malice. "I've a rule in this establishment." She nodded toward the girls. "Betsy and Sarah and Margie and Hoppie take the virgins. I take the big men-about-town."

I was sitting next to Buzz and Mrs. Bashford's yellow satin dress was spilling across my shoulder. From somewhere within the folds of material her hand moved, circling my neck, the fingers brushing my mouth. I was trembling like a leaf. "This blond one here"—she smiled down at me—"I'll bet my Derby Day shilling he knows where to put it."

The table erupted in laughter, the undergraduates sweating, nervous-eyed, the girls screeching in pretended shock at their mistress's candor. Mrs. Bashford turned her attention to Buzz, who was lounging back in his chair, a cigar clamped between his teeth. "And what about you, young sir?" she said. With one finger she slowly stroked the underside of his cigar. "Well? Yes or no?" She was staring down at him with savage pleasure. "Yes . . . or no?"

With an obvious effort, Buzz pulled the cigar from his

mouth. "Why not?" he said. But she had already turned away. Bending over me, she took my hand. "Come along, blondie," she said. "We'll leave your friends to sort themselves out."

My adolescent fumblings are no real part of this account. Mrs. Bashford took me upstairs to an even tinier room where almost every foot of floor space was taken up by a wide brass bed. She sat down on it, pulling her yellow skirts up high on her thighs.

I stood opposite her, watching the play of the paraffin lamplight across her face.

"You're not worried, are you, dear?" The malice seemed to have drained from her. She was matter-of-fact, bored. "There's a first time for every young man," she said. "For most of them, it's over in the blink of an eyelid."

I rested a hand on the high brass bedpost. The coal fire at my back drove waves of heat through my coat.

"Sit down next to me," she said.

I sat beside her on the bed and she dangled her hand between my legs. "You're not to worry. I run a very clean house, you know," she whispered in my ear. "Any of my girls get caught and they're dismissed immediately. As for me, I'm much too careful."

So, with a kindness I would not have expected of her, she coaxed me through the act. For a few brief minutes I suffered agonies of shame and revulsion, flayed on by a strident lust over which I had, by then, no control. When I rolled off her, she fumbled under the pillow for a packet of Woodbine cigarettes. "You just want to run away now, don't you? You don't think you'll ever want to do it again. But you will," she said. "I promise."

I sat on the side of the bed, pulling on my clothes. Sweat poured down my face and dripped onto the stiff white front of my shirt. As she bustled about behind me, talking of all the young men she'd broken in her time, a feeling of exhilaration spread over me. I stood up, brushing sweat like tears from my eyes.

"That's better," she said. "Have one of these gaspers." She winked. "You don't want to go down quite yet, do you?"

I sat down on the bed and smoked one of her cigarettes and paid her the sovereign she asked. "On Sunday nights," she said, "we don't take parties. Gentlemen come here in ones and twos.

[43]

A few glasses of champagne. All much more relaxed. Think about it." She nudged me. She was right. I was already.

We all gathered at a green-painted cabman's coffee stand on the Chelsea side of Albert Bridge later that night. Under the encouragement of the cabmen, only Buzz wasn't boasting of the delights of the evening at Mrs. Bashford's house. I handed him coffee in a cracked cup.

"What is it, Buzz?" I said. "Wasn't your girl up to the mark?"

"Good enough," he said brusquely.

"Which one was it?"

"Does it matter?" he said. "You couldn't tell one from the other. I hope you didn't let the old bag give you the pox."

Not yet fully aware of it, I was already beginning to assume an apologetic role. Somehow I had begun to sense the need to protect him from the awful demands his pride made upon him.

"I didn't let her get that close," I said.

Charles Chrysler came up and put his arm round Buzz's shoulder. "What a thrash," he said. "First house I've been to. When are we going again, Buzz?"

I flinched as Buzz shrugged Chrysler's arm from his shoulder. "Never. We'll find somewhere else next time."

He slurped coffee from a thick-rimmed cup and looked away from us, past the lamplight around the coffee stand and into the darkness of the river. Years later, when I knew him so much better, I got to know what these cataleptic moments were. Almost anything that touched his obsessive sense of being slighted could induce a long minute in which he would stare fixedly, his teeth catching his lower lip, his head at an unnatural angle. At first I thought it was a pose. I confused it with one of a dozen postures that he could adopt, usually with a reckless, good-humored theatricality. But I discovered that I was wrong. The withdrawal was real, as real as the vulnerability that made it necessary. But what remained a mystery was his emergence from these moments, his armor forged whole again in the fiery seconds he had been away.

He turned back toward us, smiling. "I shall consult my spies," he said. "In any event, I'm convinced we can do better than Ma Bash's house." He hurled his steaming coffee across the damp cobblestones and tossed the empty cup to Chrysler. "Next time," he said, rapping the cobbles with his silver-topped ebony stick and addressing us all, cabmen and Corinthians alike, "next time we shall pluck virtue from ripe, soft-faced girls. We shall penetrate their sweet dreams and the virginal sweetness of their bodies. Only Claus will be peeved."

"Why should I be peeved?"

He lunged forward and dug hard at me with his stick. I gasped angrily at the pain in my ribs. "Never take offense," he said, lifting a hand. "A gentleman never takes offense." And he danced off around a gas lamp, silk hat in one hand, stick under his arm, improvising to the tune of a Marie Lloyd song:

> *"She may be gray, her tits might sag.*
> *She may be the most frightful old, old bag.*
> *But never mind, all love is blind*
> *Especially that . . . old . . . Junker . . . kind. . . ."*

The cabbies, grizzled men in caps and long mufflers, grinned and stamped out the tune. One of them turned to me, wiping coffee from his mustache. "You've got a character there, sir," he said. "No mistake."

We caught the four-thirty milk train from Liverpool Street, tumbling exhausted into our reserved seats and only really registering that Buzz and Tom Boscowan were not with us as we pulled out of the station. Charles Chrysler offered me a cigarette. "Do you know what has happened to Buzz?" he asked carefully.

I yawned. "He's got more energy than I have. I just want to be rolled up in bed. Alone."

"You know Tom Boscowan's with him?"

I nodded, taking a light for my cigarette. "Wherever they are," I said.

"They've gone back to Mrs. Bashford's."

"God, they're insatiable."

Charles shook his head. "They've gone to smash the place up."

Billy Danvers leaned forward, his long giraffe's neck swaying

[45]

his head from side to side. "Harry Towers has gone too," he said. "He's a solid chap. He'll keep them out of trouble."

"The only thing that'll keep Buzz out of trouble tonight will be a pair of arms of the noble law," Charles said. "He's got the devil in him, God knows why."

We arrived at Cambridge before dawn had broken, and made our way to our colleges by hackney. I rang the bell at the gate of Queens' and presented my Exeat to the porter. "Have a good night in town, sir?" he asked, lifting an eyebrow.

"Yes, thank you, Gibbs," I said. "How long before breakfast?"

"They're just laying up in Hall now, sir. I can arrange for something to be sent up to your rooms, sir, if you are"—he licked his lips—"really feeling done in."

"No, thank you, Gibbs." I lifted my stick and strolled off toward the Hall. I rather liked the idea of breakfasting in white tie and tails among my more sober-minded peers.

Five minutes later I was half-slumped over my eggs and bacon when Gibbs appeared stoutly at the entrance to Hall. As he tiptoed toward me I could see that he was trying to compose his face. "If I could just have a private word with you, Count Hardenberg," he said, bending over me and speaking in a loud whisper.

"What is it, Gibbs?"

"In private, sir?" His eyebrows rose and flickered in the direction of the door.

I got up and stumbled after his portly figure. In the anteroom I stopped. "Yes, Gibbs?"

"A message for you, sir. Conveyed by telephone from Battersea Magistrate's Court."

"Battersea?"

"It concerns Mr. George Winslow, sir, of King's College. Of course the gentleman is well known to me. Indeed, he has been very generous in the past on a number of occasions."

"What was the message?"

Gibbs hesitated. "It was to ask you to go immediately to London with fifty pounds, sir."

"Fifty pounds?"

"That was the sum Mr. Winslow and two others were fined, sir, at the morning court. They're at present detained at Battersea police station, sir."

I gave Gibbs five shillings and went up to get changed. Then I drew fifty pounds from Martin's Bank and set out again, wearily, for the train station.

We drank champagne before dinner that night in Charles Chrysler's rooms. The full dozen Corinthians toasted Buzz and dark, lowering Tom Boscowan and round, red-faced Harry Towers.

"How was it?" Buzz roared in answer to somebody's question. "First-class, old chap. We went through the place like a dose of salts. Some of the girls had ancient, old dodderers rolling on top of them. Ma Bash was in her nightie with some cream of flour and asses' milk smeared all over her face. Utter uproar, of course. Screams, shouts, breaking glass. Tom hurled a chamber pot clean through a window and out into the street. Harry chased some old chap in his shirttails out into the front garden. By the time the bobbies arrived, we'd draped half of Ethelburga Street with a colorful collection of Ma Bash's drawers."

The noise in Charles's rooms was deafening, the tobacco smoke so thick I felt I could hardly breathe. Everybody seemed to be talking at once. I had drunk too much champagne to stay awake longer. As I drifted into sleep I could hear the babbling congratulations offered to Buzz and Harry and Tom Boscowan. I was also aware that none of them had mentioned that the police charges had included a complaint that Mrs. Bashford had been punched several times in the face.

T W O

I stood on the guard's platform at the rear of the last carriage as the little train clattered and snorted its way through the summer Suffolk countryside toward the home of Lady Gorringe. Leaning on the mahogany rail, watching the wind carry the smoke from the tip of my cigar, I was forced to admit that I understood something at least of why the young Cambridge poets were so proud of their land. A young man named Rupert Brooke at Buzz's college, King's, was already making something of a name for himself with what seemed, to me at least, to be a too-strident patriotic tone. But letters from Wolfgang revealed no different feeling in Germany. Already, after a year in England, I felt myself somewhere astride two horses.

The train clattered on through a rolling land of ordered fields and thick hedges where every horizon offered a stone church tower or a village of pink-walled cottages strung together along a main street and punctuated by a school, a line of small shops, a coaching inn or two. And often in the distance, on a hill behind the village, the warm red brick of an Elizabethan manor house would advertise the presence of the squirearchy or the country house of one of the land's great families. It was a long time since this countryside had been organized for defense.

By my pocket watch it was just after three o'clock. The guard emerged and stood beside me at the rail. "Sudbury in a couple of minutes, sir. Would you be one of Lady Gorringe's guests at Kentworth?"

I confirmed that I was. I never ceased to be astonished at the British genius for class identification. There were a dozen or more people traveling on this train all more or less as well dressed as I was.

Yet just as I had acquired the subtle trappings of Englishry, the guard had equally trained himself to recognize them, the dark-checked weekend suit, the polished handmade boots, the three pigskin gladstone bags in the luggage van, slightly worn but well saddle-soaped. I was well aware that outwardly I had changed a great deal in a year. And I was not, vain as I was, displeased with the result.

With a brave blast on its whistle, the little train announced its successful ascent of the final incline before Sudbury Station.

"Not to worry about the bags, sir," the guard said. "I'll put 'em out for you. Lady Gorringe will've sent young Tom down from the house. These weekends he's there to meet all the trains."

I thanked him and placed a shilling into his hand, then walked back along the train to my compartment. I was in fact a good deal less composed than the admiring guard imagined. I had seen nothing of Lady Margaret in the two weeks I had been writing the preliminary examinations to Tripos, but the memory of that brief ten minutes in my rooms at Queens' excited a throb of lust every time I thought about it. I wasn't in love, that I knew. I had no urge to write poetry or moon about Cambridge in the hope of seeing her. But by the end of this weekend I supposed my feelings might be quite different.

The train stopped. I took my pale gray homburg from the luggage rack and swung open the door. Along the short platform I could already see the guard handing down my bags to a stocky young man in a brown uniform and black cockaded top hat. I slammed the door after me and crossed toward the exit sign, then stopped and pretended to read the train timetables in order to give the footman time to reach me. It was too hot a day to make anyone run the length of the platform with three heavy bags. My mother had taught me that no servant was beyond a gentleman's consideration.

A family passed behind me on the way out, a solid middle-class Englishman in high collar and brown bowler hat, the local lawyer, perhaps, his wife as solid a female version of his confidence. Was it conceivable that the three little boys in sailor suits skipping before them would, in years to come, be fighting my own small cousins in some great set-piece battle on land or on the high seas?

Puffing, red-faced, Lady Gorringe's footman came down the platform. In his round Suffolk accent he introduced himself. "I'm Tom, sir. You must be Count von Hardenberg."

I nodded, turning from my examination of the timetables.

"If you'll come this way, sir, I've got the carriage just outside."

I fell in beside the powerful, wheezing figure.

"We've a lady wiv' us, sir, going up to the 'all. She come down wiv' a party on the earlier train but she'd to buy things in the village, so she waited on."

"I see." I felt a lift of excitement.

Tom put down the bags at the entrance to the booking hall. "I'll take your ticket, sir."

I gave him the ticket from my waistcoat pocket and walked through the hall and out onto the dusty forecourt of the station. An open carriage stood there, an unpretentious two-hander. A woman, her face obscured by her parasol, sat in the back. I crossed toward it. "Good afternoon, Lady Margaret." I put one foot on the mounting step and the carriage rocked visibly.

"I beg your pardon?" The parasol, transferred from the left to the right shoulder, revealed a smiling face, the most beautiful face I had ever seen. Not just in the regularity of the features or the golden yellow hair scooped under the wide straw hat, but in the full line of the mouth and the blue eyes open in surprise.

"Please accept my apologies," I said as I looked up at her.

"You imagined that I was Lady Margaret Ryder."

I hesitated. "Yes."

"Then no apologies are necessary. It's an immense compliment."

I stood, one foot still on the mounting step. I had never seen a more extravagantly beautiful girl. I withdrew my foot. "Claus von Hardenberg," I said, and found myself clicking my heels as I would have at home.

She laughed. "I *know*," she said. "I plotted it to have a few minutes together by ourselves. I'm Diana Winslow, you *idiot*."

I could see now by the way she spoke, by the emphasis she laid on the words, that she was much younger than I had first imagined. But I still found it impossible to conceive that this young woman was Buzz's fifteen-year-old sister. She wore a long cream dress held by a wide belt of a dark green material.

Her figure was that of a slender, mature young woman. Composed, her face attained the slight haughtiness that was considered fashionably desirable, but a smile had the immediate effect of a burst of sunlight. One might have searched in vain for clues to her character in the set of her eyes or mouth, but the truth was different. Her character, as I later learned, was less reflected in her face than it was a reflection *of* her face. She was a girl to be haunted forever by her own utter loveliness.

"I was determined to meet you before you went back to Germany for the holidays. I've been plotting to meet you for a whole year, and Buzz is such a cad, he absolutely refused to invite me up to Cambridge for even one miserable weekend. He was no doubt too terribly busy chasing shopgirls. Do you chase shopgirls, Claus?"

"No more than your brother does, Lady Diana," I said nervously.

"You're my cousin," she said. "You must call me Diana."

"Very well. Diana." I climbed up and sat next to her. "I'm honored to find I have such a very beautiful cousin," I said.

"Oh, everybody says that." She waved her white-gloved hand dismissively.

"You wouldn't be pleased if you were ugly," I said, smiling.

"Of course I wouldn't. But whenever men want to treat me as a little girl, they always tell me how pretty I am. The fact is, Claus," she said seriously, "I'm growing up. Rather fast, I think. And it's all of a piece. Mama treats me like a child. Richard will never talk to me about the family finances. And Buzz refuses to invite me to meet his friends in Cambridge. Now I want to ask you in all seriousness, Claus, are we to be friends?"

"I'm sure we shall be," I said, uncertain how to react to her determined manner.

"And are you prepared to treat me as a young woman?"

"Yes. Although I'm not sure I know exactly what that entails."

"Perhaps you're not completely grown up yourself yet."

Across the station forecourt, Tom came lumbering toward us with my cases.

"You see," she said earnestly, "it's very easy for young men. They drink their first bottle of champagne, they smoke their first cigar, and they have their first affair, and at that point they announce to themselves and the world that they're grown up."

I found, in my embarrassment, that I was hoping Tom would reach us before she could go on. But as I watched him he stumbled slightly and one of the gladstones slipped to the ground. While he was repositioning the bag under his arm, Diana continued. "For a girl," she said, "it's obviously quite different. Champagne and cigars are out, and one can't respectably embark on an affair until one is a married woman. So you can see how someone in my position is dependent on friends like you."

"I promise I'll do my very best," I said, "to treat you as a young woman."

She smiled her brilliant smile. "And I in turn," she promised, "will do my equal best to reciprocate."

With a muttered apology, Tom loaded the cases and himself clambered into the driving seat. Flicking his whip at the pair of bays, he set the carriage on the road to Kentworth, the iron-rimmed wheels crunching along the gravel roads.

The Tudor manor house that had been the home of the Gorringe family for over three centuries was not untypical of the great houses in this formerly wool-rich area of England. The red brick body of the house was set with stone wings at both ends, capped by lead-roofed towers. Midway between the wings the main entrance, of faded limestone, rose to a squat belltower of considerably greater age than the rest of the house. Indeed, many of the old walls that lined the moat, and the ruined Norman arches that could still be found in the thickest parts of the gardens, indicated that an extensive priory had stood on the site before the days of Dissolution.

The force of Diana's determination to be recognized as the young woman she felt herself to be had diverted the excited apprehension I felt about meeting Margaret Ryder. But as the carriage halted outside Kentworth in a bustle of greetings and directions to servants, my nervousness returned.

Lady Winslow greeted me with smiling hostility, her face tensed in fury at the discovery that Diana had plotted to come down to the station to meet me. Lady Gorringe was the kindly, somewhat distant lady I recalled from my first term at Cambridge, arranging for me to be seen to my room while watching the end of the drive for the first sign of a new carriage or automobile bringing further guests.

The interior of the house was quite extraordinarily gloomy. Diana had been peremptorily dispatched to the gardens, and I found myself climbing great oak staircases alone, behind a green-jacketed serving man. We were to be nearly twenty guests for the weekend, he confided. The house, he added with something approaching a snarl, would be bursting at the seams.

My room was at the end of the corridor, oak-beamed and mahogany-furnished, and when the servant had left me I stood at the latticed window and looked down on the gardens at the rear of the house. A dozen or more guests were strolling in groups of two or three among the flower beds. In the center of the lawn, tables had been set up, and servants were carrying large trays of sandwiches and silver teapots and hot-water jugs from the house.

I turned away from the window at a knock on the door. Margaret Ryder was standing in the doorway, framed by the darkness of the landing beyond. She came forward, smiling, closing the door behind her. "I couldn't sleep last night for worry," she said, "that you might not come."

"How could I possibly have changed my mind?" We stood a foot or two apart in the middle of the room.

"The international situation seems so threatening." She reached out and took both my hands. "But for this weekend at least we can put it from us, can we not?"

She had moved very close to me. Diffidently I placed my arms around her. I must have been standing stiffly, awkwardly, because she reached up and put one hand around my neck. "We have no need to worry here, Claus," she said in a half-whisper. "There are just the two of us on this landing. Your room and mine. And the servants have been told they are wanted only at very special times."

"The servants have been told? By whom?" My alarm was evident.

"By Lady Gorringe, of course."

I broke away from her. "Lady Gorringe knows I came here to see you?"

She shook her head, smiling. "But of course she does. I asked her to arrange it for me. My dear Claus, don't look so shocked.

There'll be at least three love affairs being conducted here this weekend. A hostess assigns rooms with discretion."

"And the guests, will they know?"

"They won't *know* anything. What they guess at or gossip about is their own concern, not ours."

We came together, and I was astonished to find this cool, mature woman now trembling and gasping with lust. Inexperienced though I was, it was not difficult to read the symptoms. As I kissed her she began to range her hands freely over my body. I knew that both of us realized all this was no closer to love than had been my encounter with Mrs. Bashford. But to a young man of eighteen it was incredibly exhilarating to be given the freedom of a woman like Margaret Ryder, to be able, to be invited, to be encouraged to remove her dress, to caress her body, and to delve into her flesh.

She was formidably uninhibited, lewd with her expressions of pleasure as I penetrated her. As I lay beside her after I had spent, I remember thinking how decorous Mrs. Bashford had been by comparison.

Margaret touched my lips with her fingers. "You're thinking what a dreadfully lascivious woman I am."

I denied it, of course, and she laughed carelessly. "We have the whole weekend before us," she said, rising, "but now we must go down and take tea with our fellow guests."

The next hour was among the most uncomfortable of my life. Not only did I know that Lady Gorringe was aware of my purpose in accepting her invitation, but I felt certain that she must now know that that purpose had been consummated. Beyond that I feared the suspicions of the other guests, and above all of the wall-eyed Lady Winslow, whom I incompetently partnered at croquet. "Your mind, Claus," she snapped, "is clearly on other things. Pray concentrate."

After croquet I was introduced to those of my fellow guests whom I had not yet met. They were all very much older than I, the men amiable in a rather bored, distant manner. My German name stirred a tiny eddy of interest. Yesterday's German ultimatum to Russia to discontinue her mobilization had by now run out, but I can't recall that on that sunny summer afternoon in the English countryside, anybody considered that any fateful step had been taken. The news of the Russian reaction had not yet reached us, but it was generally expected that Russia would back down. I think most who gave an opinion that afternoon considered that the crisis would be over by the close of the weekend.

I readily confess that my own concerns that day were not with the international situation. If, among my fellow guests, I found Englishmen condescending to my country and patronizing to my youth, I found Englishwomen very much more difficult. I was of course absorbed by my own guilty secret, which was perhaps not a secret at all. Every simple question about Margaret Ryder I translated into a leering accusation. Inquiries about my acquaintance with other ladies in the house party I imagined to be thinly disguised questions about when and where I had last slept with them. I was the fornicator at the feast.

"You look on edge, Claus," Margaret Ryder whispered as we drifted together away from the tea table.

"I *am* on edge," I said through clenched teeth.

"Why? Because you imagine they all know what we've just been up to?"

"Don't they?"

"Of course not, my dear," she said. "Whatever affair they think might be brewing between us, they wouldn't for a moment think that anything has happened already, this afternoon."

"Why not?" I asked, baffled by her certainty.

"Because," she said, "with a whole weekend of challenge and response before her, no lady would allow herself to be rogered before tea on the first day. It simply wouldn't be done. Not before tea."

"It was," I said primly.

"And very nicely, too." She patted my arm. "General," she called to a man weaving his way across the lawn toward us. "Have you met Count von Hardenberg, a dear, dear friend?"

Only Diana afforded me some relief. She insisted on detaching me from the ancient general, who wished to lecture me on the inherent weaknesses of the German army, and on taking me off into the lower part of the garden to show me the medieval ruins.

"Remember, Diana," her dragon mother said as we passed, "we shall be going up to dress for dinner in ten minutes." She bared her teeth to me in a smile. "I absolutely insist you do not bring her back late."

We took a path half-concealed among azalea bushes at the end of the lawn, and in the cool shade of the copse I felt nothing but relief to be away from the adult guests. Whether or not I included Margaret Ryder among them at that moment, I can no longer recall. Probably I did. My lust was temporarily sated. I was much more comfortable with Diana, who was younger than I but much closer to my own age than my newly acquired mistress or any of the other guests.

"This is my first real house party," she said, taking my arm. "Do you think, Claus, that life is to be a series of horrendous gatherings like this, stretching into old age?"

"Horrendous?"

She nodded vigorously. "I'd sooner be back in the nursery, playing with my dolls' house. Nobody here, except you of course, is in the least interested in me as a person. 'Ah, what a pretty child Diana is,' all the women say before they move on to talk about the servant problem or the price of an afternoon dress at Longani's."

"And the men? What do they say?"

"They don't. They just look. In a certain way. They're like scrawny-necked vultures sitting on the fence, waiting for me to get a year or two older. I may be very young, Claus, but I know what's on their minds."

"I think I detect the influence of Buzz," I said as we wandered beneath a section of ruined arch and she detached her arm to sit on a huge block of stone.

"Buzz is very good to me," she said. "He answers all my questions. About men and women, I mean. Mama still insists that children come to couples mysteriously by what she calls the act of marriage. When I asked her how *you* were born, despite the fact that my uncle and your mother were not married, she became awfully cross and told me that was not an appropriate question for a young lady to ask. Personally, I should have thought it was most appropriate. Anyway, I went to Buzz and he soon cleared up the mystery."

"He did?" I said. I think I was blushing.

"Oh, we're great friends," she said. "Most girls of my age simply don't have the opportunity to discover the details."

"Of course not," I said.

"Buzz tells me that on her wedding night our cousin Mary Darlington wrote in *desperation* to her mother, 'Dear Mama, I fear Henry is *no gentleman!*' At least, Claus," Diana said earnestly, "*I* won't be dashing off pathetic little letters to Mama on my wedding night."

I was hideously embarrassed. "Richard," I said, in an attempt to change the subject, "is he a friend too?"

"Of course, but Richard, I have always felt, was *in loco parentis* even before my father died. Buzz is totally different."

"He's more your age."

"Not simply that. We grew up together. We shared a nursery for years and I, of course, was such a frightful flirt."

She must have seen my expression change. "Goodness, yes," she said. "I was utterly outrageous, the way I flirted with him. Sisters often do, you know."

I said I didn't know.

"It's rather a dreadful family secret, but that's why Buzz was sent to America. He must have told you. Anyway, you know he spent lots of time there; he even *talks* like an American. That's how it happened."

"I see."

"The plan was to cure me of my unnatural obsession with Buzz. Of course, there was nothing unnatural about it at all. I was just learning about men from the only available man in my life."

"I'm sure there were other reasons for sending Buzz to America," I said.

"The other reason was that Buzz had such a frightful crush on *me.*"

"I see."

"You must know these things happen. Byron, for example. He was utterly besotted by his sister Augusta. Buzz told me that."

"I see," I said for what seemed about the fourth time. "What did Buzz think about being sent to America?"

"Oh, you know Buzz, he's frightfully grand about everything. I suspect Richard gave him an awful wigging about it. And he's *not* the young man to take well to a wigging from anybody. Although Richard can be so severe that I suppose

Buzz had no choice. Anyway, it hasn't changed him a great deal. He may pursue shopgirls all over Cambridge, but he still gets frightfully jealous of anyone I seem to like. I told him when he came back from America that I rather liked our cook's son, Georgie Podsner, and he was positively furious."

"I think we should be getting back," I said. "Your mother said ten minutes."

She stood up. "Are you desperately afraid of Mama?" she said, laughing.

We walked back through the old priory arch and onto the pathway between the azaleas.

"I'm not sure your Mother likes me very much," I said carefully. "Is it something I've done that has offended her?"

In a sense I was surprised at myself that I should have asked the question. With anyone else, on the basis of a few hours' acquaintance I would not have dared.

Diana was laughing. "We had a frightful family row last year when Richard said he was going to Berlin and he intended to see you. Of course, nobody would tell me anything much. Except Buzz. But Mama absolutely forbade Richard to write to your mother. And Richard absolutely insisted. The air was *black*. For days Mama threatened to go and live in our house in Essex, and Richard walked about with never a smile on his face, but finally he got his way."

"Do you know how?" I asked casually.

"Apparently Richard told her one day that it was a matter of his own obligations as a gentleman, and that if Mama continued to oppose him he would have to ask her to take up residence apart, because he would not tolerate her opposition in this matter." She laughed with delight. "Richard can be awfully frightening when he's angry, and I think Mama knew she had come up against a brick wall. With Papa, of course, it was different; she always had her way."

We emerged onto the lawn, and Lady Winslow immediately claimed Diana to take her to dress for dinner. I suppose it was about seven o'clock, the sun still high enough to warm the backs of the guests as they drifted toward the house. Margaret Ryder joined me.

"What a very pretty child Diana Winslow has become," she said.

I smiled. "She complains that nobody says anything else about her."

"Is there anything else to say? She's a child and she's rather pretty. She should count herself lucky. Especially since her cousin seems to find her so."

I remember the astonishment I felt at the realization that this mature woman was suffering a thrust of jealousy. And that I had excited it.

"Richard Winslow, Buzz, I find all the Winslows unusually attractive."

She recovered herself and laughed. "You caught me out, Claus," she said. "Even the merest touch of jealousy is disagreeable in a woman. In a man it's romantic; in a woman, shrewish. Isn't that right?"

I had no answer. I was saved by one of the guests I had met earlier, a young Member of Parliament named Charles Dacre, who joined us from the direction of the house. "Hardenberg," he said, "I've a question for you. Excuse me, Lady Margaret, but I think young Hardenberg can be of assistance."

I was relieved and indeed flattered.

"I've just been talking to London on the telephone," Dacre said. "It appears that the Kaiser yesterday gave a *Kriegsgefahr* order yesterday evening. What exactly does that signify?"

I hesitated. I felt suddenly, in this totally English setting, a powerful sense of my German origins. I knew what *Kriegsgefahr* meant; I had heard my uncle Jurgen use the term often enough, and my other army uncles, when the maneuver season came round. But I knew this was no part of a maneuver. "Literally," I said, "it means 'danger of war.' A *Kriegsgefahrordnung* is a preliminary to a general mobilization decree."

Dacre stood silent, sucking in his lips. "Thank you," he said after a moment. "Thank you."

"Does this mean Germany is preparing to mobilize against Russia?" Margaret Ryder said. "Does this mean it's all serious?"

"It's serious," Dacre said shortly.

"And as for Germany mobilizing against Russia," I put in, "remember, Russia ordered a general mobilization two days ago."

"There'll be a conference," Margaret Ryder said briskly. "Austria and Russia will take a little bit of Serbia and honor will be satisfied. I'm going to dress," she said. "I shall leave politics to the gentlemen."

[59]

Lady Winslow was hurrying across the lawn toward us, her face black with anger she made no attempt to disguise. "I've just received a telephone message from my son Richard in London," she was addressing me.

We stood in an awkward group as she took a deep breath. "It appears that Diana has invited two young friends to stay with her for tonight. An invitation she has carelessly forgotten. They are at this moment being entertained by Richard in London. Diana obviously must return to London immediately. My son asks that you escort her."

"Of course," I said. "Of course."

She could barely control her anger. "There's a train from Sudbury at half-past seven. If you pack a bag, Tom will drive you there in a motorcar."

She turned to Margaret Ryder. "I'm sorry, Lady Margaret. My son insists."

So she knew. But after what Diana had told me, I realized it made no difference in her feeling toward me. I hurried away to the house, and began packing the smallest of my bags.

Margaret Ryder came into the room as I was pulling tight the leather strap. "You'll be sure to be back tomorrow?" she asked.

"If there's a train, I'll be back tonight. I'll ask at Sudbury Station."

She came forward and put her arms around my neck, kissing me, open-mouthed. "Do you think it's stupid of a woman my age to be worrying about the prettiness of a child?"

"It's unnecessary."

"Hurry back," she said. "I'm *aching* for you."

I remember I was not pleased. As little as I was enjoying the house party, I was prepared to endure the mixture of embarrassment and tedium for the prospect of sharing a bed with Margaret Ryder. The first time I would have spent a whole night with a woman.

I spoke little to Diana as Tom drove us along the country lanes to Sudbury. A few minutes before half-past seven we pulled up in the station forecourt, and by the time cases were unloaded, the train was pulling in at the London platform.

Alone in a first-class compartment, Diana and I sat opposite each other.

"You're very angry," she said. "I can tell."

"Not half as angry as your two friends waiting in London."

"Is it because I've interrupted your love affair with Lady Ryder?"

I sat back in my seat. Her dragon mother knew, she knew. Everybody knew.

"There is no love affair with Lady Ryder," I said. "What a preposterous idea."

"Buzz said he thought there was."

"Buzz?"

"Well, at least he said he couldn't for the life of him imagine why you were going to spend a weekend at Kentworth. You'd said often enough that you wouldn't go again if you could possibly avoid it. Check up on which room he's in, Buzz said. His guess was that you'd be next to Lady Ryder. And he was right."

"It has no significance," I said sullenly. "On that basis, half the guests at house parties would be having affairs with the other half."

"Perhaps they are. Buzz says he can't see any other purpose in a weekend. And you must admit it can't be for the *intellectual* interest."

"This is an absurd red herring," I said. "The fact is, you have two friends waiting for you in London whom you invited for the weekend."

"But I haven't," she said calmly. "And I didn't."

I pulled my cigar case from my pocket. "You didn't?"

"Will you be asking my permission to smoke?"

"Yes."

"Then I grant it." She laughed.

"You say there are no friends waiting for you in London," I said slowly, the vision of Lady Winslow's thunderous face uppermost in my mind. If I thought anything at this moment, it was that this extraordinary girl was again "plotting," this time to abduct me for a weekend in London, and I was frankly terrified. "Did Richard telephone? Or did you make that up?"

Her face was composed now, her blue eyes too serious for me to believe any longer in a wild schoolgirl prank. "Richard telephoned," she said. "He spoke to me first and then to Mama. You know what he said to Mama."

"Yes. What did he say to you?"

She got up and came to take the seat next to me. "He told me he was to tell Mama a lie and he apologized for the hot water it would get me into. But he said that it was a lie we would have to keep up for always. For his sake."

"I don't understand that."

"Nor do I. But he was treating me like a person. Someone he could confide in when he couldn't confide in Mama."

"So there really are no friends waiting for you."

"No."

"And this is all Richard's doing because he wants you in London for some reason?"

She shook her head slowly. "He wants *you* in London for some reason, Claus. Not me. I'm only the excuse. He wants *you* to be there."

At nearly eleven o'clock that night we stood opposite Richard Winslow in the long drawing room at Ebury Square.

"Whiskey, Claus, before I begin explanations," he said.

"And I will take a glass of champagne," Diana announced.

I saw Richard's head turn quickly. Then he nodded. "Yes indeed," he said with his reserved half-smile. "Why not?"

For a few moments he busied himself pouring drinks. "I'm sure," he said, handing Diana a glass of champagne, "that my mother will see through my subterfuge. That's not important. There are times when to lie is more honorable than to tell the truth."

"I don't understand," I said. "If the subterfuge is to bring me to London, I certainly don't see through it."

He nodded, handing me a whiskey and soda. "I have to be back at the Foreign Office in a few minutes," he said, "so I shall be very brief. You must catch the train from Victoria tonight. You must return to Germany immediately, Claus."

I sat opposite him, blank-faced.

"Germany has declared war on Russia," he said. "More than that, at seven o'clock this evening German troops invaded Luxembourg. This can only mean that Belgium and France are next. England and Germany will be at war in a matter of hours."

I remember his tall, frock-coated figure. I remember Diana's white face. I remember the ticking of the clock in the silent room. But I have no memory of how I answered. I know I felt a rush of anger at the idea of a noose tightening around Germany's neck. I know this anger was obliterated by the thought that it was Germany who had declared war. And this thought was replaced in turn by some confused attempt to justify to myself the action taken by Berlin.

In all probability I said nothing at all, but sat there close to tears, swamped by the impossible idea of England and Germany as mortal enemies.

"Is all this certain?" I managed to ask after a few moments. "Must it happen?"

"I believe it will," Richard said gravely. "We may have a few hours longer, perhaps even a day. But the Rubicon is crossed. I believe Europe is about to commit suicide."

"One thing I don't understand, Richard," Diana said quietly. "Why is it Mama is not to know?"

He hesitated, pulling at his lip. "At a meeting at the Foreign Office an hour ago," he said, "we discussed whether or not to restrict the movement of German citizens out of the country from tonight."

"But we're not at war yet," Diana said.

"The War Office believes that by such a restriction we might usefully prevent several hundred Germans of the officer class being available to fight against us."

"Is that your view?" I asked.

"I made it clear I thought it a despicable preemptive act. British citizens are still free to leave Germany. That was confirmed by telegraph during the meeting."

"Was a decision taken?"

"Not yet. A decision will be made at nine o'clock tomorrow morning."

"And Lady Winslow?"

"I am afraid that if I had told her the truth, she would have refused to pass on the message."

Diana leaned forward in her chair, biting her lip.

"It was not a risk I was prepared to take," Richard said briskly. "You have every right to return to your homeland. Your mother has already been sufficiently wronged by the Winslow family. I will not be part of any further wrong."

I made a clumsy effort to thank him, but he would have none of it.

A few minutes later he left with assurances of his goodwill both to myself and to my mother, which deeply touched me. As I turned away from him I could see the tears welling in Diana's eyes.

"I shall go to the station with you," she said. "Don't say no, because I intend to, whatever you say."

Just before midnight we stood together at the ticket office of Victoria Station. The gas lamps hanging from the iron roof arches threw yellow circles of light down through the rising steam. Newsboys with thin cockney voices proclaimed the rape of Luxembourg. Porters pushed trolley loads of cases toward the continental boat trains to Dover, Folkestone, and Ramsgate.

We walked over a twenty-foot-long chalk inscription, white on the black macadam beneath our feet: HANG THE KAISER— LONG LIVE THE TSAR. Clusters of Union Jacks seemed to be draped from every bookstand and coffee stall. I was awash with misery.

Holding tight to my hand, Diana led me past the ticket collector and onto the Dover platform. "You musn't mind so much, Claus," she said. But tears were trickling down her cheeks too.

I felt desperately young and frightened. It seemed to me, walking hand in hand with Diana, that all the veneer of assurance I had learned from Buzz and Cambridge, from the Corinthians and Mrs. Bashford, had slipped away from me. Would there be English policemen examining my German passport at Dover? Would I be taken aside (just a formality, sir) to where hard-faced men in bowler hats waited in a green-painted room? All that privilege had given me, its obverse had snatched back in a single hour. I felt hunted and alone. Apart from Diana.

The guard's whistle blew. Porters moved down the length of the train, slamming doors.

"You can kiss me if you like," Diana said, "since we're such good friends."

I put down my case and took her in my arms and hugged her to me. Then I kissed those smooth, perfect lips. For the first time.

[64]

THREE

On the train to Dover I wrote to her. I can't remember what I said. But I posted the letter in Calais the next morning, before boarding the train for the Belgian border. For the whole of that Sunday we remained in the sidings as trainloads of young French soldiers were given priority. Next morning, on Monday, August 3, we began to move, slowly, with many lengthy stops. We crossed the border into Belgium late in the afternoon—barely an hour, I discovered, before Germany declared war on France.

The seemingly interminable journey continued all that night. On the German border we waited in the early dawn. For an hour it seemed certain that we would not receive permission to move. Then we rolled forward, the wheels clanking across the points, past the Belgian frontier post and into Germany. On the German side, long columns of troops in cloth-covered spiked helmets and field-gray uniforms patiently lined the roads. Behind them, horsedrawn artillery and yet more infantry stretched back for miles. As we drew past the mobile field kitchens with their smoking chimneys, the great column seemed to shrug itself and move forward. The invasion of Belgium had begun.

Within a month I was swallowed up in the maw of the military machine. I never went to Lichterfelde, I never joined the Brandenbergers. I became instead, after six months of infantry training, a company officer in the 169th Regiment, a humble line formation, an assemblage of men from the vineyards of the Rhine, the slums of Berlin, and the alleys of Munich. In training we became friends, in the front line we became comrades. It was the first time in my life that I had lived with the working classes. While we sat in quiet parts of the line I absorbed their jokes, the stories of their lives, their infinite sentimentality, and I learned to admire their remarkable resilience. For their part, they found it astonishing that I had been to England, had been educated there and even had English friends. Before an attack we would huddle in a forward trench together and they would ask me in whispers, "What will the Tommies be thinking now, Herr Leutnant? Will they be as scared as we are? Will they all be mad drunk on rum before they go over the top?"

I pretended knowledge of the British workingman soldier that I didn't of course have, and I think it reassured my boys to listen to my inventions, which made the Tommies no different from themselves.

By the luck that follows some men in war, the 169th occupied mostly quiet sectors throughout 1915. By the end of the year we were seasoned frontline soldiers, well able to take care of ourselves in normal conditions. To describe our lives as a vision of hell or a new dimension of human savagery would have been, for the most part, far wide of the mark. We played skat, we dug revetments, we drank schnapps when we could, and we smoked cigars that still came in parcels from home. From time to time someone would be wounded. Rarely, a member of the company would be killed.

Yet we had no illusions. We heard of other parts of the line where the French Poilus or the Tommies had hurled waves of men against our machine guns in fruitless attempts to gain a hillock or a shattered wood. Most of all, the war closed down upon us like a thick smoke cloud, obscuring our memories of the past, creating a whole self-contained world in our fifty-yard-long line of trenching, a world where a chaffinch chirping on the barbed wire caused men to gather to watch its innocent freedom of movement.

In the late spring of 1916 we moved in motor lorries south toward the River Somme. I was twenty years old. I had given up praying for the end of the war. It seemed to me, as it seemed to all of us in the front line, that there could be no end. The two sides seemed so evenly matched in numbers and equipment, and the machine guns behind barbed wire so effective against the flesh of men, that there could be no decision. A sort of apathy had overtaken us. Or perhaps a skepticism. We paid no real attention to the war news any longer. An advance here, an attack repelled there, we knew what it meant. A hundred yards to be lost again in the next day's counterattack.

But our arrival on the Somme abruptly shattered our lethargy. At the first officers' order group behind the line at Bapaume, I listened with horror to the details of the *Grosse Vorstoss*, the Big Push, which the British were planning. We were not short of details. Our engineers had tapped into their field telephone links. On the Somme, we were told, the British were looking for nothing short of a major victory. The colonel conducting the order group did not smile. "A major victory against our defenses here is impossible," he said. "They will lose fifty thousand men in the coming battle."

The colonel proved wrong, as the world now knows. British losses on the first *day* amounted to fifty thousand dead, and the battle was to last from July into autumn.

As I was leaving the order group in the old corn market at Bapaume, I heard a voice behind me shouting my name. I looked around to see my cousin Wolfgang, a major now, elbowing his way toward me through the crush of officers.

"I saw the 169th had been transferred down here," he said, pumping my hand. "I've been watching for you for a week."

There was time to find ourselves a corner table in the Estaminet Hugo and order ourselves a cognac. Wolfgang had changed as much, I suppose, as we all had. His face was thin and seemed almost lined, although he was barely twenty-four. I noticed he smoked cigarettes incessantly, held just in front of the mouth between yellowed fingers.

"And when you were last home?" he asked. "How was everybody, your mother, Uncle Jurgen?"

It all seemed so long ago. I answered his questions, but I saw that, like mine, his interest was distanced by the present. After a few brief questions and answers, we turned with relief to what really absorbed our interest, the strength of our own defenses in this part of the line, the accuracy of English artillery, and above all the reality of the Big Push.

Wolfgang had been in the line here for over six months and assured me that our trenches and redoubts were as well prepared as anything he had seen. Since Christmas his own regiment had worked like miners, burrowing into the chalky soil, constructing deep galleries protected by low concrete kennel entrances. If the English had decided on this sector for their Big Push, they were ill-advised, he said.

We ordered a bottle of brandy. Although we had corresponded intermittently, we had not met since the autumn of 1913, when I had left for Cambridge, and he was interested in my view of the English.

"I believe," he said, "that this war will not be won by the nation with the most men or even the most numerous artillery. It will be won, and should be won, by the nation that in the end has more faith, more belief in its culture."

"By culture," I said, "you don't mean its poets, musicians, and painters."

"Of course not. I mean an overall and intrinsic confidence. A belief in the very structure of our national lives."

Perhaps I smiled. I did not wholly disagree with him. But the earnestness of his proposition was so un-English that I, a part product of Englishry, found it hard not to smile.

"You disagree?" Wolfgang said. "You think blood and iron will win this war?"

I shook my head. "No," I said, "mostly I agree. Russia is a spent force, only formidable in her numbers. But Frenchmen believe in France. They have spilled more blood in this war than any nation so far, and you can still hear 'The Marseillaise' across the ramparts at dawn."

"And the English?"

"They are protected," I said carefully, "by a lack of candor. Toward themselves and each other. The cult of the gentleman is unlikely to allow them to lose this war. God knows what value it will have in peace."

"You're not a defeatist, Claus?"

I poured an inordinately large glass of brandy. "All our energies—French, German, British, even Russian—will not be dissipated by this war, Wolfgang. But they'll be redirected. I think you're right to talk about this struggle as a clash of cultures. But the winners will be marked forever. The losers possibly more so. We're all fighting for what we claim to believe in so deeply. I wonder how prepared we are for the distortions that defeat or victory has in mind."

*　　　*　　　*

The shelling was passing comfortably over our heads. I had no way of guessing that this was to be an extraordinary day. No particular feeling of well-being, no company errand that would take me back to a first-class lunch at one of the estaminets in the little villages behind the line, no reason even to think that this would be a mail day, although it was over a week since the Field Post had honored us with a delivery.

Deep in our bunkers, we barely heard the twenty-five-pounders whistling across. And in any case for the last four days they had been firing to balloon observer's orders, registering targets on our second line of defense and on the position of Wolfgang's Guards Division, which was held in reserve behind us. We knew, of course, that it was all preparation for the Big Push—even our soldiers now used the English term—but we were confident that our experience and our trench system would see us through any attack the English could mount against us.

My own company position was a network of dugouts, galleries, and trenches along the south-facing line of Gommecourt Wood, forming the leading edge of a salient that prodded into the British line. From my occasional duties interrogating prisoners brought in by patrols, I knew that the British front line opposite us was held by the 56th (London) Division, short, stocky cockneys mostly, as tenacious as terriers, with languid officers whom we had already faced twice in Flanders last year.

The day, as I said, began no better and no worse than many others in the front line. With the sun on our backs, the company *Feldwebel*, Otto Heiden, and I inspected the thirty yards or so of trench that were our company responsibility. As efficiently as ever he noted in his black book any section of sandbagging that had been blown out of place, or a shattered duckboard slat. Since the arrival of the London Division opposite us, we had displayed a painted sheet above our trenches reading: WEL-COME TO THE 56TH LONDONERS. The object was to proclaim the effectiveness of our intelligence and to boost our own morale. This morning, I remember Sergeant Major Heiden invited me to take a look at the British line from one of the firing steps. An identical sheet was fixed above their lines reading: WILLCOMMEN—169 REGIMENT! Sad, really, when you think about it. But perhaps the little jokes we sometimes played on each other served somehow to remind both sides that there were human beings opposite, though shell splinters and mustard gas took very little notice.

At the end of our rounds, the *Feldwebel* saluted. "If you'd like to join us for breakfast, Herr Oberleutnant," he said, "the post sergeant brought up a nice piece of bacon and a dozen new-laid eggs."

I declined, as he probably knew I must. An officer could not be seen eating bacon and eggs when the men of the company breakfasted on beans and black bread. "Enjoy your breakfast, Sergeant Major," I said. "But make sure the post sergeant distributes the mail before he settles down to his."

I sat on one of the firing steps and removed my helmet. The British front line was no more than two hundred yards away, and from time to time a voice carried on the morning breeze. I had not slept particularly well, and the warmth of the rising sun induced an agreeable drowsiness. I suppose that at that moment my mind was as empty as that of any frontline soldier crouching in the chalky ground in these rolling Somme hills. My nose twitched to the smell of frying bacon wafting from the sergeant's dugout. I lit a cigarette, smoking with my eyes closed.

"Coffee, Herr Leutnant." I looked up to see *Feldwebel* Heiden standing over me, proferring a tin mug. "And a letter for you."

I thanked him and placed the coffee on the duckboards. The letter was from my mother, her familiar untidy hand scrawled across a sludge-green envelope.

I drank some coffee and lit another cigarette. The letter was bulky, perhaps with an enclosure from Uncle Jurgen or one of my cousins now scattered across Germany and the Western Front. I tore open the envelope and saw only a brief note from my mother. Enclosed, she said, was a letter marked in care of an address in Switzerland and forwarded to me at home in Germany. Mystified, I tore open the second envelope. The letter, several pages long, began, "My dearest, dearest Claus. . . ." It was a letter, I knew immediately, from Diana Winslow.

I did not continue reading right away. I sat back with my head against the firing step and let much more than years roll away from me. It seemed to me that I no longer saw the mud-caked boots stretched out in front of me across the duckboards, or the grimy hands clasping the pages of the letter. I had thought very little about Diana or Richard and Buzz and the Corinthians since I came to France. Trench warfare mostly dulls.

But now images of a girl in a white cotton dress sitting on a block of stone beneath a ruined Norman arch filled my mind.

From between the pages of the letter something dropped into my steel helmet. I reached down and picked out a photograph. A most extraordinarily beautiful girl in a nurse's uniform smiled somberly at me. The letter read:

My dearest, dearest Claus,

I am certain that I should not be writing to you, but perhaps by the end of this letter you will see why I have finally come to do what I have wanted to do since the day you left England. In my own way, muddled and sometimes inconsequential as it is, I need to tell you what has been happening to me as the carnage in France continues. You will excuse me if I fail utterly to strike the right note. When one of your Corinthian pals, Billy Danvers, was killed last year at Loos, I wrote to Buzz a silly rambling letter, full of cartoons and tear stains. Buzz was *furious*, but I was so upset, although I barely knew Billy, that I could only tell him it was like whiskey at a wake, or stupid disrespectful jokes that fend off hysteria. When the two Saunders brothers were killed at oh I forget which battle now, I did rather better. But I still upset Buzz with my mad levity.

Yet I think—hope—that I'm seeing things more clearly now. With Richard's encouragement I have trained to become a nursing auxiliary and I work five days and sometimes nights a week at an officers' hospital in a place called the Sloane School at the World's End of Chelsea.

And the World's End it is. They come by motor ambulance direct from hospital trains at *our* Victoria Station. They come without legs and hands and eyes. And I won't tell you they're all so cheerful and brave it breaks your heart. They're not. They weep if they have eyes and they thrash the air in terror if they have arms. And they snarl and sneer and swear. And it breaks your heart.

So what's a silly joke or two in a letter to Buzz or my mother? Though I don't do things like that anymore, I still have the frantic urge to. The whole obscene thing *must* be a joke. Some

[71]

nights on the wards when I'm alone, I even think I hear God laughing.

You understand, Claus, don't you, because we're such good friends.

Now let common sense command my pen. I must not go jabbering on about myself all the time. If this letter ever reaches you, and I think it will, you'll want to know about your Cambridge friends, the Corinthian Dining and Debating Club. First, the club is *still* in existence and furthermore (Buzz's doing) is open to women. I and five or six fellow nursing auxiliaries are honorary members. Meetings are infrequent but uproarious.

Buzz and your American friend, Charles Chrysler, have joined a regiment called the King's Royal Rifle Corps (Richard's regiment, about which more later). Frightfully pukka and apparently known in the eighteenth century as the 62nd Royal American Regiment. This gave Charles his excuse, although, as you know, he'll stick to Buzz until the grave yawns. (Another silly joke. You see what I mean.) Neither Buzz nor Charles has yet been posted to France and indeed this week's good news is that Buzz is to be sent far overseas, probably to India, as a training officer.

Richard is a major in the King's Royal Rifle Corps and was last month awarded the Victoria Cross for action in Flanders. What can one think? When I heard, I sobbed with pride and with horror at my pride. It is unspeakable that our emotions should be twisted and snarled in this way. Richard himself is as cool and reserved as ever. More than that, I think since he came back from France he is somehow distant. He talks very little about the war, although I know it obsesses him. Sometimes I think perhaps he even won the V.C. on purpose, for some special purpose I mean, that he's harboring until the moment's right. Or is this just a girlish excuse for my hero brother?

Other news: The big scandal among the washerwoman gossips of London society is Margaret Ryder. Yes, you remember her! It appears that she had a distant cousin in St. Petersburg, a certain William Collins, merchant, with whom, on a visit to Russia, she had a short but torrid affair. Last year this William died, leaving, incidentally, a very handsome sum to Margaret, but leaving also among his effects letters written by Lady Margaret long after the affair, describing in fine detail her delight in the seduction of grooms and errand boys. These letters found their way into the hands of Lady Margaret's husband, and when used in court even in a bowdlerized version, counsel assured us, they were enough to secure for Sir John Ryder divorce immediate. Lady Margaret, whom I see frequently, now finds herself cut by London society, but apart from that rich and overjoyed. And as she says, if London society won't take her up, the officers of the society regiments are only too willing. Incidentally, she is very sweet about you.

I can write no more into the void. I must hear from you. Write to me whether you are safe in Germany or unsafe in France, whether you are hale or harmed, among the quick or the dead (oops!). Write to me because I still love you desperately. Or because a little fifteen-year-old girl most *certainly* did.

Diana

From the middle of June the shelling got worse, and the night patrolling, at which the British were feared for their skill and savagery, became more and more intensive. Lack of sleep made us increasingly irritable, and the slow accumulation of casualties made us, for perhaps the first time, highly susceptible to superstition. No man would light his cigarette from a match that had already lit two others. Later I heard the British troops also harbored this same fear. Poppies growing from the vertical side of the trench were considered particularly bad luck and were ripped out at the first bloom. Certain men, usually survivors of a shell-burst that had killed others, were thought of as Jonahs, and a hawk hovering above an emplacement was a certain harbinger of death.

The men could be excused their foolishness, they felt the dice so heavily loaded against them. The company officers poured scorn on the very superstitions they themselves observed in private. I never saw an officer proffer a third light, or pass a trench poppy without surreptitiously tearing it out by the roots.

I had written to Diana care of the address in Switzerland the day I received her letter. I told her that for two years I had put England from my mind, that for two years the English to me meant men in mud-spattered khaki who lived, as we did, like animals in the trenches opposite. I told her that her letter had changed everything. It had forced me to delve back again into the past. It had shattered my apathy, and I was deeply fearful of what that might mean to me.

But I told her many other things too. How astoundingly beautiful I thought she had become. How much I too hated the war, or, if that was not entirely true, how shamefully pointless I thought this conflict of Europeans. An expense of spirit in a waste of shame, I had quoted Shakespeare's sonnet on lust. But I think that first letter was muddleheaded and perhaps simply untrue of my attitude to war. Not until the Battle of the Somme began and I was utterly overwhelmed by the ghastliness of what we were doing to each other did Shakespeare's words really mean anything to me.

I will always remember Helmut Feldman's arrival to take the place of a wounded junior officer in the company. He was nineteen and fresh from training school in Hanover, tall, dark-haired, and planning to marry a childhood sweetheart on his first leave. Looking back over the years, I feel that by his very innocence he was marked for death. He believed deeply in Germany's cultural mission to the world, and believed that only the envy of our excellence on the part of France and Great Britain prevented the acceptance of Germanism for what it truly was. The skeptics among the company officers, all of us in one degree or another, took great pleasure in teasing his earnestness and lack of experience.

This grave young man, whose hand was never far from a Bible he carried with him at all times, had no fear of death or injury. God's will, he said, will be done. But he did harbor another fear which he confessed to us with immense seriousness in the officers' dugout one night after he had been with us for about a month. His mother was a widow, he said. She was one of three sisters. His father came from a family of seven, himself and six sisters. And Helmut himself was the only male child in a family of five. The baffling progression of females seemed to spread into the furthest corners of his family. We failed totally to understand the significance with which he invested the fact.

"So. Sisters, aunts, cousins, you're surrounded by women."

"This is precisely the nature of a very delicate problem that I wish to put to you as friends."

We urged him to go ahead. The schnapps bottle was passed around, with Helmut refusing as usual.

"Naturally, I wish to father children."

"Naturally. But you fear you will sire only girls."

"This is true. I greatly desire a son."

A salvo of Tommy shells fell somewhere close. The Primus lamp swung gently. The huge oak beams supporting the dugout roof groaned and settled. Chalk dust tumbled down in the warm light.

"You have no doubt prayed," I said.

"Of course, and will continue," he said.

Our company commander, a middle-aged captain named Forster, shook his head. "In these matters," he said gravely, "God and nature work hand in hand."

We knew Forster as something of a joker and sat back in anticipation.

"Before the war," he said, brushing crumbs of chalk from his mustache, "I was a lawyer in a small country town in the Black Forest. Now the question of producing a fine family of sons was at the very heart of prosperity for these peasant farmers. And it so happens, gentlemen, that I was often consulted by local farmers on some very delicate matters of this very nature." He took the schnapps bottle, paused as a salvo of shells roared like trains above our heads, and tipped it to his lips.

"But I have to confess to you," he went on, "that however much I consulted my colleagues in the medical profession, and indeed in the Church itself, not one of us learned gentlemen could produce a solution with more efficacy than the farmers' own resolution."

"And what was that, Herr Hauptmann?" Feldman asked diffidently.

Forster shrugged as though reluctant to speak. "As I've said, it's a matter of some delicacy."

"I should be grateful . . ." Feldman began.

"Very well," Forster said. "If you insist. These Black Forest farmers, you understand, are big, strapping lads, most of them. A child a year when the wife is young is not uncommon. But if one of them was, as he felt, cursed by a string of daughters, this is what he would do. Forgive me." He turned and winked at the rest of us. "This was the way it was done."

Forster's voice dropped. "The young wife," he said, speaking directly to Feldman, "is taken into the kitchen. There she is

[75]

lifted onto the big scrubbed tables they favor in those parts. And she is invited to kneel on her hands and knees. Sometimes the more considerate young husbands provide cushions to alleviate the hardness of the wood on the bare knees. Next the husband stands on a low chair or stool. And from this position the young husband lifts up her nightgown and mounts."

Feldman was blushing furiously.

"This treatment, I am assured, given twice a day, proves most efficacious in producing a son."

Forster threw himself back on the rough bench he sat on. "There you have it," he said, smiling broadly. "And even if it doesn't do the trick, I am reliably assured that it's well worth trying."

Feldman smiled shyly around at the umbered faces in the dugout. "The Herr Hauptmann is, I believe, teasing me. But when I send him, after the war, a postcard photograph of my five young sons, who will know by what mystery God and nature combined?"

He stood up, slapping his thigh with the flat of his hand, filling the dugout with billowing chalk dust. He looked absurdly young as he put on the heavy steel helmet.

His platoon dugout was at the far end of our company trench. Perhaps two minutes after he had left, we all froze at the crazed shrieking of a shell. The explosion caused the lamp to rock violently, and the blast thumped against the wooden door like a demon intent on entering.

Forster nodded toward me. "Go and see, Claus," he said grimly.

I stepped out into the moonlit trench. One whole firing step had been blown away. Feldman sat in the bottom of the trench, his legs sprawling, smoke rising from his tattered uniform. Ten inches of steel shell casing had hit him like a thunderbolt from Jove. We found it afterwards among the shattered, bloodstained duckboards. The lower part of his stomach had been carried away. I knew, as I gave him morphine, that neither God nor nature would ever give Helmut Feldman the sons he so much wished for.

Was it Diana's letter, or was it the shy, boyish Feldman, or was it simply the steady increase in the shelling in those last June days that wrought the change in me? The shelling, perhaps, was enough to explain it, and the menace that hung over us like a thundercloud. The menace of the coming attack. The Big Push.

We heard rather than saw the buildup taking place. At dusk, as we stood to in our trenches, we would hear the tramp of feet, the distant jingle of bridles, the curses of noncommissioned officers. It was all so immensely familiar. We could almost *see* what was happening there as more and more Tommies were packed into the line.

Then, on June 25, the real bombardment began. Can I ever describe it to anyone who was not there? After the first day I was beginning to believe that the flesh had been shaken from my bones. Down each leg and arm I felt nothing but raw, torn nerves. My head ached constantly with the shattering crack of the explosions and the flinching fear of the shells that overflew. By the second or perhaps the third day we were no longer even attempting to speak to one another. There was little or no water. Fear dried the salivary ducts; my tongue was permanently stuck to the roof of my mouth. The dugout seemed to pitch and toss like a ship at sea as salvo after salvo tore at the ground around us.

There was no sleep. No more than a catnap of a few minutes only, until the roaring, singing, earsplitting sounds began again. It is not possible to remain at that pitch of fear. We were rabbits, not just from the burrows we lived in, but from the frantic, wild-eyed terror that I saw in every face. Yet somehow that extraordinary discipline that German soldiers can drag from the deepest recesses of their minds formed a barrier between us and madness. On the fourth day, in the most intense shelling it is possible to conceive, I looked out through the only company periscope still operating to see the whole of no-man's-land boiling in eruptions of earth like some field of molten lava.

At 7:30 A.M. on the fifth day, a sudden silence fell. I remember crouching in the entrance to a dugout and marveling that there were still birds to sing, marveling even more that they should stay to sing in this evil place.

I don't think I thought for a moment about the reason for the silence. I remember hauling myself up to sit on the dugout step, and looking at my uniform, thick with wet chalk. Then Captain

Forster's voice broke in on my reveries. He was bawling almost incoherently as he ran down the length of trench. I must have understood something because I reacted, shouting to my men to get out of the dugouts and onto the firing steps. I heard my own voice and others mixed with fearful curses and the clattering of boots on duckboards. "The Tommies are coming!"

Our trench line had been almost completely destroyed in the last five days. The neat zigzags were now a series of vast shell holes with a few yards of unbroken trenching between them. The men stood on what firing steps still existed, or threw themselves on the sides of craters. Then, after a minute or two of almost complete silence, when even the birds forbore to sing, we heard the officers' whistles from the trenches opposite, and as I watched, a great line of khaki figures, as far as the eye could see, came scrambling over the mounds of earth, hesitated as they positioned themselves, and began walking forward, their rifles with long fixed bayonets held across their chests.

It was not difficult to pick out the officers in the line, second lieutenants, pistols in hand. I found myself looking across two hundred yards of tortured earth at a young officer carrying a round, dark object under his arm. As I watched, he shoved his pistol into his holster, and taking the round object in both hands, he drop-kicked it toward the German lines.

I felt sick with sadness as the football bounced toward us. From the British lines a great cheer arose, and as they reached the ball a man darted forward to boot it farther in our direction. Then the machine guns of our support company began to chatter.

It was the last playful moment on the Somme. There had indeed been precious few before, although both sides no doubt had had their shy, trusting Helmut Feldmans. But from that moment when the khaki figures began to fall, when they still came on in a blinding storm of bullets, when new battalions scrambled from their trenches among the bursting shellfire of our own counter-batteries, the Battle of the Somme had begun.

That day was July 1, 1916. I survived that day and the next hundred days the battle continued. I have a poor memory of that summer. Captain Forster was dead in the first week. I became company commandant. *Feldwebel* Otto Heiden was clubbed to death in hand-to-hand fighting when the Tommies took our trenches. A few days later we had taken them back, and Kern was dead, and Brucker and Hellmann and Schwarz. And then the toll of dead and replacements and new dead was too much for the memory to handle.

Every day the wounded sat in silent lines, waiting to be evacuated, or lay howling in no-man's-land, where nobody could reach them through the storm of flying steel.

Perhaps it was sometime at the end of the first month that I received another letter from Diana. It contained another photograph, as I had asked. She was sitting on a park bench in a light-colored dress, and was pointing at a duck waddling past. Perhaps at the Serpentine in Hyde Park. It was probably a bad photograph, overexposed, and light billowed across her blond hair. But she was, quite simply, exquisite.

The letter read:

Claus, Claus, Claus,

It was the greatest secret moment of my life! Your letter, I mean, and the news that you are so far unharmed. I had been working late at the World's End, long past the time of the last bus. And the area is not one where taxicabs normally cruise. So I walked back at dead of night along the interminable King's Road, my uniform still covered with blood—looking, I suppose, like a cross between Jack the Ripper and one of his victims, risen.

At Ebury Square I was surprised to find Richard still up, writing letters. We had a cup of hot cocoa together and talked about his plans a little. Then as I started for bed he said casually that there was a letter for me from the Larkman girls in Switzerland.

I scampered up to bed with my prize, still not certain it was a letter from you, but desperately hoping. And it was. And it lies before me on my desk, a trifle mudstained and crumpled. But a letter from you, from the other side of the iron divide.

We've beaten them, Claus. We've devised a cunning system and we've made it work. And neither tinker, tailor, soldier, sailor, censor, or politician has been able to stop us.

But I tremble at the thought that you are on the Somme front. Everybody in England is talking about the Big Push. Probably everybody in Germany too. Will it be like Ypres and Loos? Or worse?

I am so frightened for you all. Among my poor wrecked patients a day or so ago was a German officer, bandaged to anonymity. Oh, you can imagine what I felt! I scurried back and forth for an hour at least until the bandages were removed from his head and I was finally reassured it wasn't you.

You did not say you loved me, but no matter. My plan is to woo you with letter after letter until you can no longer bring yourself to think of any other woman. I care nothing for the French ladies you are no doubt rogering at every opportunity. I'll shock you and delight you and disappoint you with my loving verbosity until you succumb wearily to my incessant blandishments.

You can lie if you like, I don't care. But, oh, tell me you love me and you've never loved another, although you've probably sworn your heart away to any number of fräuleins and mademoiselles and English misses.

You think I am utterly reckless, but I am not. Buzz held a massive party before he left for the mysterious east, and all your old (remaining) friends were there. We toasted the Corinthians wherever they may be, and Buzz spoke, drunk as a pig as he undoubtedly was, very touchingly of you. Then we danced (this was all at our house at Ebury Street) and drank some more and danced on until it began to get light. And to my enormous surprise I received my first proposal of marriage. From lovely Charles Chrysler.

I *think* I was kind and careful, though by nature I am neither, and I declined with many regrets, and not just for his stupendous American fortune. But how was I to tell him that I loved another? And a German officer in muddy field gray, somewhere on the Western Front. Oh God, I hope it's not the Somme.

Now to be serious. I told you about Richard's Victoria Cross. I also told you that I thought he was up to something. Well, he most certainly is. He has meetings here with an officer, a poet, named Siegfried Sassoon, and twice at least, late, late at night with a Cambridge mathematician whom I'm sure you have heard of named Bertrand Russell. What you haven't heard, no doubt, is that Russell is an antiwar activist. He's a strange, sinewy little man with a great shock of brown hair, possibly not too likable

personally, and certainly very convinced of his own considerable abilities. But he has taken a stand. And I believe that
Richard plans to do exactly the same. He intends to take his seat
in the House of Lords. From there I believe he will denounce
the war. What an extraordinarily clever brother I have! How can
anybody accuse a holder of the Victoria Cross of cowardice!

Of course I *am* reckless. I should be writing none of this. But
you must know that not everybody in England raises a patriotic
cheer at the latest casualty lists. I pray that there are people like
Richard and Sassoon and the sinewy Bertrand Russell in Germany. There's a *Punch* cartoon of a skeleton towering over the
battlefields, raising a cup of blood marked "*Civilization*" to his
fleshless mouth. Are there cartoons like that in Germany?

I could write on forever, drooling into the night my half-
thoughts and hopes. Selfishly, I have only one real hope and
that is that you are a hundred miles from the Somme.

None of us will emerge the same from all this. Before the war,
it was a disaster if your housemaid became pregnant by the
footman. My poor antediluvian mother might still think so. But
if we learn anything from this period of death's dominion, we
must learn that to *create* a life cannot be sinful. Bertrand Russell (I
have heard him speak at meetings) would no doubt say I trivial-
ize the issue. But I think not. Leaving a rally at the Wigmore
Hall last week, I accidentally trod on his foot. He scowled at me
in a nasty, *unpacific* manner.

Why should you love me? If God knows, he won't vouchsafe
a clue. I am not ill-favored, sir, nor do I lack the breeding that
every Tommy Atkins struggling forward on the Somme is said
by my mama so conspicuously to lack. But I am an empty vessel
until you fill me with your love. I will clatter about the room,
ringing emptily. I will be scratched and dented and will lose my
value in the market of gleaming virginal pots. Whisper that you
love me and I will pay you back tenfold. I have *masses* of love to
squander. And all on you.

Diana

I was wounded in September. Not seriously. My leg was
broken by a steel helmet blown by a shell-burst that decapitated
my company runner. I was withdrawn first to Alsace and then,
as some complications set in, to a hospital in Berlin.

My uncle Jurgen visited me and we had a cheap, untruthful conversation about the war. Perhaps he believed what he told me. I certainly was lying.

When my mother came I told her more, and I think she understood. But I was still unable to mention the letters from Diana. Perhaps if my leg had not healed so quickly or if my new posting had arrived, I would have got to understand her better. Enough to talk to her about the strange impact England had had on both of our lives.

On one of my mother's visits to the hospital in Berlin, she brought with her a letter from Switzerland. She was, I think, mildly curious about the two sisters who were writing to me from Zurich, but I explained that their brother was a good friend of mine at Cambridge, and that was enough to satisfy a curiosity that was never a highly developed facet of her personality.

I tried during those visits to ask her more about her own time in England, but she wished to answer in no more than gener-alities. She had taught Richard at the home in Ebury Square, and after the end of the London season the whole family had moved to Winslow Court, their house in Essex. It was there she had met Thomas Winslow, Lord Winslow's younger brother. But as I asked about him she became uncomfortable, sitting up stiffly in her chair beside my bed until I felt unable to press her further.

"Was it a great scandal?" I asked her once, as gently as possible.

She smiled then. "Yes, Claus," she said. "It was a great scandal."

"I can imagine Lady Winslow's view," I said. "She was not friendly."

"No, Claus," she said. "Lady Winslow was not friendly."

The letter my mother had brought from Diana was different from the first two. It contained very little news about our friends in London, and much more about the changes she felt were taking place in herself under the nightmare influence of her job at the hospital:

I try to be optimistic. I *think* that is my essential nature. But these days I find myself so beset by melancholia, accidie, the

[82]

black dog, call it what you will. There are mornings when I wake up weeping from a sense of the dreadful waste of it all. And all these terrible, jingoistic popular songs make me *sick*. Especially when Richard tells me how the soldiers at the front change the words into quite filthy but healthy cynicism. Richard has himself changed so much that he is not at all reluctant now to tell me what the Tommies really think and say. Sometimes I wonder if, after all this ends, we shall divide between those who saw the horror and those who stayed at home and pretended it wasn't happening. Through my work at the hospital I hope I can claim to be one of you.

And when it is all over, will I ever revert to being Lady Diana Winslow calling for tea, chiding her dressmaker, or jaunting after a ball to the East End to see the night shifts come on? I will be bitterly ashamed of myself if I do. And yet I'm sure the British class system will continue, perhaps even thrive. And the workers who fought the war (I know gentlemen have fought with just as much blind bravery) will they go back to a land fit for heroes in England or Scotland or Germany or France to live on a few shillings a week?

I wrote to her every few days during the next weeks, and I received letters from her, sometimes two or three at a time. I was not as skilled or uninhibited as she was at releasing my fantasies to another. But it was courtship by letter, and I knew and began slowly to tell her that I was falling in love with her.

I was dependent upon the mad, scrambling effusions of joy that my letters elicited. I began to relax to a point where I could talk about the future. One day in mid-October, when I was walking again with no more than a slight limp, I took a taxicab from the hospital to a village *Gasthaus* reserved for officers just outside Berlin and ordered a bottle of wine and settled down to write to her. I wrote:

Nothing anesthetizes my longing to be with you. Neither morphine nor ether nor the wine and schnapps I sometimes drink in crazy quantities. The war will end, and the conventional wisdom has it that one of our countries will be in the gutter, the other marching the pavement. Any man's—or any woman's—prospects are beyond estimation. So I offer nothing whatsoever beyond the wish to be with you always. I am asking you to marry me, pauper or prince as I may be, native of the Germany of the Kaiser's dreams and of England's fears, or of a Germany more utterly ruined than any modern nation has ever been. Whatever the future, I know I want to spend it with you.

I was discharged from hospital the following week and spent three further weeks' convalescence staying with my mother. Each morning I was up to intercept the mailman. But no letter arrived via Switzerland.

In November a medical board decided that I was no longer fit to return to the infantry, and I was offered and accepted a course at a flying school in Wuppertal. I said good-bye to my mother, and I remember that as I lifted my bag onto the back of the mule cart that was to take me to the station, she looked over my shoulder toward the postman who came bicycling into the yard.

I waited while she took the letters and thumbed quickly through them. She shook her head. "I'm sorry, Claus, nothing from your friends in Switzerland."

In any other circumstances, even in the middle of a world war, I would have enjoyed the flying school, although I attained no more than an average rating, but my four months there were overshadowed by the absence of any word from Diana.

I had written to her, of course. But my fear was that she had perhaps fallen sick and that my letters would come into the wrong hands.

Just before Christmas I wrote again to the Larkman sisters in Switzerland, and within a week I received a reply that left me breathless with pain. They were writing, they said, on behalf of Diana, who asked that I should not communicate with her again.

No more than that. No less. Even now it is all too easy to remember the waves of misery that passed over me. I had no doubt that it was the offer of marriage that had affected her. I reread her letters in a different light now, and I could see, with hindsight, that what I took to be serious declarations, clothed in frivolity, were quite possibly no more than that oddly inappropriate sense of mad humor of which she had accused herself. Could it be so? In the weeks that followed I veered wildly from belief in her to anger and despair. And in the meantime I was posted back to the front.

At that time the air force had just been reorganized in the spectacularly successful fighting system of the "circus." Each circus consisted of a number of squadrons under a recognized ace like Boelcke or Baron von Richthofen or, after Richthofen's death, Hermann Göring. Having proved a competent pilot on the Fokker triplane, but certainly not a particularly gifted flier, I was assigned to one of the less well-known circuses, in the Metz area of the front. It was unfortunate for us that the French squadrons along the Meuse contained pilots of great skill and experience, and our ratio of losses was uncomfortably high. Worse, as the year 1917 progressed, the arrival of the advance guard of the American First Army in the area made available the first American barnstorming pilots, who flew their French machines with more verve than I could ever muster.

The truth probably was that I was now devoted to staying alive. I desired as much as ever a German victory or at least an honorable armistice, but my reasons had subtly changed. My belief was no longer in the rectitude of our cause. I now feared for Germany if the mass hatred of a continent was loosed upon her in defeat.

We flew several missions a week, mainly dawn reconnaissance sorties over Pershing's army positions behind the Argonne Forest. Our orders were to observe and depart quickly, and they enabled me to exercise my discretion without a reprimand for lack of aggression.

The younger fliers, some of them eighteen or nineteen, chafed at the orders. It was their pleasure to allow themselves to be caught by an American squadron, upon which a desperate air battle would ensue. As far as I was concerned, I believe our circus commandant, a cultivated engineer named Messerschmitt—a cousin, I understand, of the now-famous Willy— knew that my heart had gone out of the war. But as an officer who had been through the battles against the British in Flanders and the Somme, I was accorded more leeway than might otherwise have been the case.

Then, on one beautifully misty morning in late August, I brought my aircraft down onto the field and noticed that though I had been assigned a more distant area of the American lines to overfly, only ten of our twelve aircraft had returned. I climbed down anxiously. Two of the planes nearest me had badly tattered fuselages where machine-gun bullets had ripped through the canvas. The excited pilots came running across the field. In their observation area the mist had cleared suddenly, and they had decided to "waggle their asses" at an American squadron just behind the river line. The result had been a running battle in which two of our aircraft had been shot down and two American planes were claimed.

I stomped into the mess. Two German for two American planes seemed to me to sum up this war. With the navigators, that probably meant eight young lives.

The church hall we used as a mess was already roaring with overexcited fliers. Trays of schnapps were being passed from the bar over heads to the far corners of the room. Young pilots, puffing cigars, were describing with flattened hands the banks and rolls that had brought them onto the tail of the enemy. The thickest group was gathered around the bar. Amid the black leather of our own squadron jackets I could see the shoulders of two men in United States khaki. As one of them turned, a stein of lager in his hands, I saw that it was Charles Chrysler.

The American fliers were to be removed to a prison camp that day, and a car and guards were already waiting. But our commandant had insisted that the Americans should first have lunch with us, a not-uncommon practice among aviators in that war.

I seized the opportunity to take Chrysler to a table in the corner of the mess. My pleasure at seeing him was unfeigned, but more important to me was the news he might bring me from London.

Apart from Buzz, I had always liked Chrysler best of the original Corinthians. He was a tall, strong-looking figure in his excellent-quality khaki uniform, his dark hair neatly trimmed, his smile confident, one arm around my shoulder. "By God, it's good to see you alive and well, you bastard," he said.

I sat him down with a large schnapps before him. "Bring me up to date, Charles. I must know what's happening in England."

"Let's get the bad news over first," he said. "The Saunders boys and Billy Danvers got it early on."

I nodded, on the edge of saying that I knew.

"Various wounded," he continued, "not too seriously, except Falconbridge from Trinity, you remember him?"

"I remember."

"Blinded," he said grimly. "And Mark Hetherington lost a leg." He paused. "Closer to home, Buzz is fine, out east somewhere, but Richard Winslow's in the bag."

"Richard's a prisoner?" I couldn't tell him why the information so astonished me.

"In a prison hospital in Germany. Would you be able to find out where?"

"Perhaps," I said uncertainly. "Was he badly injured?"

"That we don't know," Chrysler said. "So far, Lady Winslow has only received the official Red Cross card. Perhaps you could find out."

I promised to do something on my next leave.

"What you don't realize, of course," Chrysler said, eyeing the room with the satisfaction of a victor rather than a prisoner, "is that Richard was awarded the Victoria Cross last year."

"Is it usual," I said carefully, "for a V.C. to continue at the front?"

"Sure. Although Richard did at one time have plans to go into politics. Seems he changed his mind. Let's hope he's not badly hurt."

We drank to that.

"And you, Charles, what sort of a war have you had?"

He shrugged. "It doesn't seem right to say not bad. But that's the truth of it. I joined the British Army in 1915. Richard's regiment had old American connections. I stayed out of serious trouble, learned to fly, and joined the U.S. Army as soon as we came into the war. Now, I guess, I'm out of it for the duration. And as far as that goes, if I'm really honest, I just have one regret."

"What's that? No more chance to down a Hun?"

He smiled. "No." And then suddenly, as if he had changed the subject, "I asked Diana Winslow to marry me last summer. She said no."

"I'm sorry to hear that, Charles. She was only a young girl when I last met her, but astonishingly beautiful even then."

"She looks like an angel now," he said. "Most stunning girl in London. A couple of months ago I tried my luck again."

"And?" My heart was thundering so loudly I thought he would hear.

"This time," he grinned, "she said she would. One good reason I can't wait for this goddamn war to be over and won."

The commandant came to join us, intrigued by the coincidence of our meeting. For lunch he produced champagne, and we toasted Charles Chrysler on the way to his prison camp.

F O U R

On a morning in early September 1917, my life took another of those lurching turns off what seemed up to then
the beaten track. My squadron commandant called me to
his office and, over a cup of good, scarce coffee, asked me if I
would like to go to Africa. He might as well have said to the
moon. For a moment I sat staring at him while he smiled at my
bewilderment.

"The German forces in East Africa," he said, "are fighting an
extraordinary action. Two thousand men with African askaris,
native troops, are playing cat-and-mouse with British forces
under General Smuts, fifty thousand strong. Beyond any other
assistance we can give, they need a reconnaissance aircraft to
keep track of the British columns pursuing them. That aircraft,
if it ever arrives there, will need a pilot."

In the next days I took a map and asked questions of anybody
who pretended knowledge. In 1917 the German colony of
Tanganyika and the British protectorate of Kenya occupied
eight hundred miles of coastline between Portuguese colonial
Mozambique and the Somali lands of the Horn of Africa.
Behind these shores a half-million square miles of scrub and
desert and grassland and jungle and lake and mountain and
valley formed the battlefield for the two empires. Over this vast
area a tiny German force under a remarkable general named von
Lettow-Vorbeck had marched and fought and doubled and
circled and fought again since the outbreak of war in 1914. The
Kaiser had awarded von Lettow our highest decoration, the
Pour le Mérite for his success in holding down the vast enemy
force under General Smuts. Every British and Dominion soldier
pursuing Lettow-Vorbeck across East Africa was one soldier less
on the Western Front. When I passed through the Great

Holenau locks into the Kiel Canal in the U-boat that was to rendezvous with a German blockade runner somewhere off the Canary Islands, I knew no more about the East African conflict, or about East Africa, than that. In my baggage stored below I had a sun helmet lined with red silk, and several uniform bush jackets and pairs of khaki drill trousers. For more formal occasions I had packed my Imperial Air Service mess dress with winged collar and black tie. Nobody had thought to tell me—perhaps nobody knew—that there would be remarkably few opportunities for the wearing of mess dress in East Africa. The value of a good pair of boots I had learned in the trenches, and my pack did at least carry two strong pairs of leather boots, laced to just below knee height, to be worn with flying breeches. My boots, I was to discover, were my only effective provision, material or psychological, for the experiences to come.

When I look back now, over twenty years, at that young man, myself, standing in the conning tower of the U-162 in the blustering, rain-filled wind, as the submarine slid through the Kiel Canal toward the sea, his poignant innocence still affects me deeply. Perhaps, to some, the idea of innocence rings untrue. He had slept with women and killed men. But his view of the world, his *Weltanschauung*, was still that of the year 1914. It was still, in terms of honor and honorable behavior, Corinthian. A long road stretched ahead.

Somewhere off the Canary Islands I was transferred from the U-boat to the comparative luxury and danger of life aboard the *Francken*, a robust tramp steamer built at Bremen more than a quarter of a century earlier. Above the waves, the sea was British. Our captain cheerlessly calculated that we had no more than a twenty-percent chance of landing our precious cargo, which stood crated on the aft deck.

Early in January we rounded the Cape and started north again. I had still not seen land, but I persuaded myself that I felt its presence out there far beyond my view from the port rail.

I was as ignorant of Africa as I could be. But I had accepted the posting from my squadron commandant because it seemed not only to take me far away from the Western Front, but far away, too, from all I felt about Diana. What I never considered, as our tiny blockade runner trailed its shimmering wake through the Indian Ocean, was that Africa would offer me not just a different world but something approaching a different dimension. Of course, I am not the only man whom Africa has struck with its own unique mystery. I use the word in its religious sense because I believe now that only through some awareness of mystery can Africa be touched. It is arrogant to think we Europeans or Americans can understand Africa. But perhaps we can touch its mystery if we reach out far enough.

I am rather pleased, in retrospect, that I have no idea where on the coast of East Africa I first trod. It was night, and the *Francken* rode at anchor in perfect moonlight behind the small row boat that carried me toward the shore.

Before me I saw that the endless stretch of pearl-gray beach was in fact severed by innumerable channels and inlets giving onto hundreds of small, sandy islands, sparsely covered with trees. Whenever the two German seamen rested their oars, the incredible sounds of the African night rose around us, an insect orchestra of beetles and crickets, the croaking of a million frogs, the screeching of God knows what nightbirds, and the yelping of unknown four-legged creatures.

The Fokker reconnaissance plane, amphibiously converted to both wheels and floats, rode, silver-blue, among the islands where it had been towed from the *Francken* earlier and abandoned, as I was about to be, in this strange, sandy marsh that was my introduction to the African continent.

When the German seamen rowed away, I stood on a sandspit of an island twenty by perhaps sixty feet, with one single, almost leafless tree clawing in silhouette toward the moon. The bushes around me were low and dry, and crackled in every faint breeze from seaward. I sat down, and again the sounds of night encompassed me. I had no idea how long I would have to wait. The arrangement was that an officer of von Lettow's *Schutztruppe*, or Defense Force, would make contact as soon after my landfall as possible. What that meant in African terms, in terms of a small force harried day and night by a vastly superior British force, I could not guess. The captain of the *Francken* had ordered that I should be left with a small tent and food and water for a week. No doubt, that reflected his own pessimistic guess at the length of time I should be waiting.

Dawn came at a speed I could hardly comprehend, long

darting shafts of sunlight tinting green the tops of trees, then plunging into the dry bush to reveal strange vermilion flowers. The night sounds stopped. A huge water snake slid between the floats of the Fokker and rested in the shadow. The air changed from sultry cool to warm, and from warm to hot. Herons flapped overhead, and kingfisher-like birds darted for insects across the surfaces of the lagoons. I unpacked my Primus stove and cooked myself some beans for breakfast. Then, in the shade of the brightly flowered bushes, I settled down to read Kleist's *Die Marchiese von O.* Within an hour I was asleep, to awaken only in the late afternoon with a head thumping from the full blast of the sun. That night I was sick and feverish. The sounds of African life around me I found weird and menacing. I dreamed only nightmares and woke with horrible jerking movements that left me suddenly cold and desperately alone. When the swift dawn rose I was already feeling better. I had learned something about Africa.

For a fortnight I lived like Robinson Crusoe, but without the companionship of a Friday. I had built a small encampment of thorn bushes with my tent and fire in the middle. The Fokker rode serenely on the water. But with no idea how close the British were, I dared not take the plane up to look for what I increasingly thought of as the relief column.

I became first short of food, then hungry. A day or so into the second week I rigged up a hook and line on which I caught big flat fish that tasted brackish and sour when I cooked them on a spit. I drank my first bottle of brandy, then my second. The third and last I was determined to retain for a celebration with my rescuers—by the end of the second week this is what they had become for me.

Sometime in the third week I had awakened with the dawn and was preparing to take an early-morning swim when I heard a sound between a bird's screech and an animal's yelp, which just may have been human. It had been so short and sudden and unexpected that I had no chance to identify it. I listened for five minutes or more, but it was not repeated. And then, as I turned back toward the encampment, I heard, this time clearly and beyond doubt, a human voice, high-pitched, calling, first a word or two, then a sentence I could not understand. As it came closer I heard laughter. And the splashing of water.

I sat and laced up my boots. The sounds now came clearly from the end of a narrow channel that disappeared into thick foliage about sixty yards away. I drew my pistol from its holster. The foliage ahead was moving, and suddenly I saw a dark figure sliding into the water. Then from somewhere in the deep sun shadow I heard a voice calling my name.

The man who waded across the lagoon and scrambled up the sand bank to stand at attention before me was an African. He wore crudely sewn leather boots, tattered shorts, and no more than the remnant of a shirt. His hat was a khaki pillbox with a leather chin strap. From the Imperial German eagle embroidered above the brow curved a long and tattered red ostrich feather. He saluted, and I remember his shapeless boots squelching as he stamped his heels together.

He introduced himself as Sergeant Kum. He was, he told me in colorful German, the only survivor of an escort of twenty men who had been bringing the *Unteroffizier* Kern to meet me, but who had been ambushed by a British patrol two nights ago. The *Unteroffizier* had been killed. The rest of the patrol had scattered or been taken prisoner. Sergeant Kum had completed the journey alone.

I got to know Kum in the weeks that followed. He was of the Kikuyu people from the highlands of the British protectorate of Kenya. He was perhaps in his late twenties, but the subject of age, like so many other western identifying data, held no interest for him. He spoke some English and some German, both in a strangely exaggerated manner. His imagery and warmth made me think of him as an Irish African. His view of the British was certainly as ambivalent as that of any Irishman.

He had left his tribal home as a young man after some crime or misdemeanor committed during a *ngoma*, a native dancing and drinking session, and traveled south into the German colony of Tanganyika. It is probable, though impossible to establish, that he had served the British as an askari, a native policeman or military auxiliary. Certainly he conducted himself on the lines of a British sergeant major—resourceful, friendly-rough toward his men, politely skeptical of the abilities of junior officers. The British, he said, were the natural enemy of all Africans, of all African wildlife, and of the very soil and bush of Africa. On the other hand, to the amusement of his German officers, he could frequently be heard castigating his own men, inciting them to "stand up like an Englishman," or, before a battle, to "fight like a Tommy."

I got to know Kum as someone who could live off the land, walk the forests like a leopard, find water where there was none, and tell stories of such improbability that he might well have been performing nightly in some Dublin bar. When, in the eerie lagoon where we first met, I asked him if he had ever flown in an aeroplane before, he had shrugged nonchalantly. "Perhaps," he said. "I can't remember, bwana."

Directed by Sergeant Kum, I flew the Fokker biplane to a *Schutztruppe* encampment north of the great snow-capped mountain of Kilimanjaro at a point near the British rail link between Nairobi and Uganda. It was an unforgettable flight. First there was the irrepressible Sergeant Kum in the observer's seat, whooping with delight, urging me to outfly eagles or to swoop on flocks of cranes, to outpace the zebra herds or the thousands of antelopes that roamed the grasslands. Then there was the country itself. We flew for two hours without seeing a human habitation, although Kum would tell me this was Masai grazing land or the land of any one of a half-dozen tribes. Neither people nor roads, no town or belching factory, no colliery wheel or rising slag heap. To see Africa in this way, before the European had done more than scratch the surface of the land, to see it in its infinite scope and freedom, indelibly marked my imagination. I thought of Europe in the centuries before the Romans; I felt myself at a crossroads in time.

I was a year in Africa, mostly engaged in aerial reconnaissance for commando operations along the Kenya border. My German comrades were two seasoned *Schutztruppe* officers, Major Bitov and Lieutenant Kranz. Sergeant Kum had day-to-day control of a company of askaris numbering about sixty strong with wives no less than that in number, a collection of small children, and not a few babes in arms. I can remember Major Bitov's wry amusement as he watched me survey his tiny force from the rowboat that had brought Kum and myself from the Fokker. The women in their brightest looted clothing, a mixture of gaily colored curtaining and European tea dresses, danced barefoot at my welcome while their men lined up, tattered but military in their bearing.

Over dinner of roast water buck in the encampment—the *bomba*, as I soon learned to call it—Bitov and Kranz explained to me the military situation in East Africa. When war broke out in Europe in 1914, the administrative head of German East Africa, Governor Dr. Heinrich Schnee, had forbidden the German forces to fight. He was not against fighting as such, but he believed it would set the worst possible example for the native Africans to see white men fighting one another and, inevitably, to see one side *lose*. Native rebellion, inspired by the sight of a defeated white army (even though the victors would be white), was in Governor Schnee's estimation the inevitable result. He therefore attempted to open peace negotiations with the stronger British forces across Tanganyika's northern border. Not surprisingly, the British intended to fight. So too did Dr. Schnee's military commander, von Lettow, although his *Schutztruppe* was smaller than the British force. Since those days in 1914, von Lettow had marched his tiny command of some two thousand men back and forth across British, German, and Portuguese East Africa, constantly avoiding General Smuts's British, South African, Indian, and askari forces, which pursued him. In the first three months of 1918 alone, von Lettow's men would march two thousand miles, appearing when the enemy least expected them, raiding towns (and looting them of colorful cloth and food and drink), attacking only when the balance of forces was close to equal. To the British, von Lettow had become a legend. When the Kaiser promoted him to the rank of general, it was the British, under a white flag of truce, who passed on the information to him, as they did when Smuts's signalers intercepted the news that von Lettow had been awarded Germany's highest military decoration.

Apart from von Lettow's main column, three other subsidiary groups were operating throughout East Africa, our own under Major Bitov being the most northerly. My task, with the Fokker biplane, was to reconnoiter and maintain contact with von Lettow's main force.

Despite Major Bitov's warnings, I was shocked by the condition of von Lettow's men when I first located them in the early months of 1918. The entire main force consisted of about two hundred Germans and some sixteen hundred askaris. Even von Lettow's clothing was tattered beyond belief. This German general wore captured boots with the toes cut out to make them fit. His corduroy breeches were torn and bleached gray by the sun. Wracked by malaria, which he contrived to ignore, he was also suffering from a disease of the eyes that reduced his vision to a few yards. Yet somehow his extraordinary personality triumphed over every difficulty. He treated his askaris with a mixture of jocularity and grave respect. Though he could no longer pay them except in occasional loot, they remained totally loyal. It was to be forty years before his African soldiers were paid in full, with interest, by a new German government rising from the ashes of a second world war.

I dined with von Lettow that first time on the border of Rhodesia, which he had now thought to "menace" with his ragtag army. He was desperate to know how the fighting on the Western Front was progressing. I believe I told him things that saddened him. I told him that the British and French were holding as solidly as ever. In addition, the first American army had arrived in France. After four years of war, we Europeans no longer fielded infinite numbers of young, fit recruits. To see the American prisoners, in their early twenties—tall, well-nourished men from another world, confident of victory even though they themselves were captives, was a sight that could not fail to impress us. It was a chilling thought that the New World, the only remaining reservoir of European manpower, was now committed to the cause of the enemy.

If my gloomy disquisition affected von Lettow, it seemed unable to impress Governor Schnee. A tall, mustached man, barely past his fortieth year, Dr. Heinrich Schnee would stand posed like a statue, his eyes narrowed, as he listened. His object was to acquire some of that gravity which von Lettow, sprawling on a lion's skin, so naturally commanded. Poor Schnee, as I thought of him then, carefully calculating the effect of his words, could still not retain the attention of the most junior officer present. He insisted on being addressed as Governor, and most complied, but the respect he craved flowed uniquely in the direction of the small figure of the general.

Four years after the outbreak of war, native rebellion was still uppermost in Dr. Schnee's mind. Perhaps he was no less a personality than the run-of-the-mill colonial bureaucrat, but it seemed to me that war had taught him nothing. He still believed, despite the evidence of the askaris under von Lettow's command, that Africans were necessarily shiftless, disloyal, cowardly, and unclean. He had, undoubtedly, a sense of mission in Africa. But it was not to bring European civilization to the continent. It was to civilize the continent *for Europeans*. It was a distinction I appreciated only hazily at the time. I was to learn much more about it later.

Sergeant Kum, who acted as my navigator, met Dr. Heinrich Schnee on several occasions. He would always address him with Irish-oriental excess as "distinguished Governor" or "most learned doctor and Governor." Schnee never saw the twinkle in Kum's dark eyes. But then he believed that Africans were as humorless as he was himself. "The native," he once told me, "is incapable of humor. That is undoubtedly a concept derived from the civilizing influence of education which they lack entirely. Laughter is of course quite different. It is known to the higher primates and to natives. It is usually the result of some disastrous incident befalling another. It is cruel, barbaric."

I once asked Kum what made him laugh. He thought for a long time, poking with a grass blade between his teeth. "I laugh when I am happy, bwana," he said at length.

"Only then?"

"What other reason is there to laugh?"

I shrugged.

"Why do you ask me questions about laughter, bwana?" he said. "Is it because there is not enough of it in your own life?"

Early in the summer of 1918 we were flying, Kum and myself, low over English farms in the Rift Valley when I heard the sergeant shouting like a lunatic behind me and felt his finger prodding into my back. I had no more than half-turned toward him when I saw what he had seen. Swooping down toward us was a De Havilland pursuit plane. In the vast spaces of East Africa it was incredibly bad luck. I don't suppose the British had more than a dozen aircraft operating between Nairobi and the southern border of Tanganyika, and one had found us.

We were unarmed but for a rifle that Kum carried, and with our floats, our airspeed was well below that of the De Havilland. Behind me Kum, for once, was silent. I watched the

British pursuit plane as its airspeed continued to increase in its dive toward us, and realized with a massive sense of relief that the pilot was inexperienced in aerial fighting. It was a cardinal Western Front rule to dive onto the tail of your quarry. To swoop down on him amidships required an almost impossible calculation of the enemy's airspeed.

Waiting until the De Havilland was no more than eighty yards from us, I gave the Fokker full throttle and pulled hard on the control stick. The Immelmann turn was invented by a far more skillful pilot than myself. Essentially you climb at full power with the stick back, as if going into a loop. At the top of the circle, while hanging by your belt upside down, you hold full power and make a half-roll to bring the aircraft level again. Thus you emerge at the top of the half-loop in level flight and traveling in the opposite direction. I executed the maneuver with less grace by far than the German air ace who had devised it, but it left the De Havilland diving away from us, its machine gun chattering into the empty air.

It was in Kenya the very last week of the long rains, and sparse clouds hung across the hillsides to our right. Sergeant Kum was slapping the side of the aircraft in his delight at our evasion, urging me to go on the attack. But death could come as easily, though not as often, in Kenya as on the Western Front. As the De Havilland turned back toward us I banked the Fokker and made for the safety of the clouds.

For the next half hour we flew in and out the scraps of cloud while the De Havilland, like a buzzard lazing on the warm currents, circled above us. It was a question simply of whose fuel would last longer. As the needle on the gauge in front of me touched the red mark I put the biplane into a final dive toward a huge lake that I had already selected as its possible final resting place.

Kum and I sadly scuttled the aircraft by igniting the last liters of fuel as she rode on the surface of the lake. Above us, the pilot of the De Havilland waggled his wings and flew away down the great valley. I looked at Kum as we reached the bank and dragged ourselves through the thick papyrus grass that invaded the shallows. From a high point we both turned to watch the last moments of the Fokker as the flames roared from the canvas-covered wings and the skeleton, now revealed, rocked down on one sinking float and, with a hissing of charred cloth, disappeared below the surface.

"It is no matter, bwana," Kum said, consoling me. "We will make another one."

It was not the problem that faced us at the moment. Major Bitov's column was over eighty miles away, marching east from Njoro. There was no possibility of catching up with him now.

I put the problem to Sergeant Kum and told him that if he wished to rejoin his own people in whose tribal area we were, he should remove the German insignia from his uniform and invent a tale to cover his absence. I was still uncertain as to the original reason for his defection to the German side, but I had no doubt of his ability to account for his years away.

"I will stay, bwana," he insisted. "I will help you cut the wood to build a new aeroplane."

I explained carefully that a new aircraft could not be built as a boat or even a new bullock cart might be. In Germany, I told him, huge factories produced wheels alone, or propellers or engines. Hundreds of men labored in separate places to make the many pieces that made up an aeroplane.

I could see he was unimpressed. I think he saw my reluctance to overcome these difficulties as a sign of lack of moral fiber. "The English," he announced, again revealing his own ambivalence toward them, "would build a new aeroplane. That is sure."

In the face of his certainty I could make no reply.

"No matter," Sergeant Kum continued. "The baroness memsahib will give us food and shelter. We can rest there and then march into the morning sun to find the column."

"Kum," I said firmly, "we must give up all hope of rejoining Major Bitov. I, at least, will be a prisoner of war. You must do as you choose."

"I will guide you to the baroness," he said.

"Who is this baroness memsahib?" I asked him. "And how is it you came to know her?"

"She is a memsahib but she is not English," he said. "We will be safe with her."

It was all he would say. Some twenty-five miles away lived a baroness who would undoubtedly offer us food and shelter. Why did I decide to walk the twenty-five miles to the baroness's farm? Probably because it was in any case the nearest European house to where we were. And if I was to surrender, it seemed I might as well surrender myself to Kum's mysterious baroness as to any other settler.

We marched all day in brilliant sunshine or through sudden slashing rain squalls. There were many tracks through the grassland, and as the day drew on I could see the marks of motor vehicles on some of them. I calculated we were not much more than fifty miles from Nairobi, but the proximity of British troops in large numbers no longer held any fears for me. I was convinced I should be a prisoner of war within hours.

Shortly after nightfall, when we had been following substantial cart tracks between cultivated hillsides for the last hour, Sergeant Kum led me toward a long, low farmhouse, roofed in thatch and with lights twinkling at the windows. Bidding me wait under a great acacia on the lawn, Kum disappeared into the darkness around the side of the house. Within a few moments the front door opened and a tall woman stood in the rectangle of light. Kum, I could see, was standing behind her.

She stepped out onto the terrace, holding the lantern high in one hand. The other hand held a chain attached to a cheetah's neckband. "Do come in," she called.

I began to walk across the lawn. The cheetah beside her growled and she quieted it. Then, handing the lantern to Kum, she came forward to greet me. She was a tall woman of perhaps thirty, with pale hair drawn back off a long, suntanned face. She was what, in those days, we called handsome rather than beautiful.

As I stepped into the light from the doorway, she stopped and a slow, pleasant smile crossed her face. "You really *are* a German officer," she said looking at my uniform.

"Yes." I stood awkwardly before her. "Captain Claus von Hardenberg." I brought my heels together.

"Come in, Captain," she said. "My name is Catherine Esterhazy." She held out her hand. It was rough-skinned, a working woman's hand, though her manner had already shown her to be something else.

"A German," she repeated as she led me into the house.

"Kum, of course, is such a dreadful fibber that I didn't know what to expect."

We entered a large, long room furnished with some locally made pieces, a grand piano, and Persian rugs on a red-tiled floor.

"I can offer you whiskey and soda," she said. "Please sit down."

"You're very kind," I said. I sat in a deep armchair.

She pulled a cord and a bell rang in some other part of the house. "Kum told you, I imagine, that I am not English?"

"He told me very little, Baroness," I said.

"My husband is—was—Swedish," she said. "We divorced six years ago. Since then I have run the farm by myself. Not, of course, entirely by myself. Until the war I had an English farm manager, who is now with the army."

"But you yourself are not Swedish," I said carefully.

"I carry a Swedish passport," she answered firmly.

"But from your accent I would say you were American."

She smiled. "I was born in Minneapolis."

"Your country is at war. Against mine."

The broad smile faded. "Kum has assured me you are a good man. A gentleman, he says. I know him to be an excellent judge of character. He never exaggerates when he talks of friends. But I have to know what you think about this war, Captain."

For a moment I sat silently before her. I considered all the things I might say about the war, about the tragedy of a whole generation of young Europeans and now Americans being torn limb from limb by flying iron. I thought to say that the emperors and kings and presidents had failed us all. But I said simply, "I think the world will pay for the wrong turn we took in Europe in 1914. I think the world will probably continue to pay for the rest of the century."

The door opened and Kum entered. He carried a silver tray on which stood a decanter, glasses, and a soda syphon. After placing the tray on the sideboard, he bowed and retired without a word. It was as if he had worked at the house forever.

"You know of course that Kum worked for me?"

I waved my hand toward the door. "It's as if he never stopped."

She laughed. "He had no need to. There was a little trouble after a *ngoma* here. The young men fell to boasting about their fathers' cattle. It was over the question of the ability to buy a suitable wife. Drunkenly, in the darkness, Kum released some of his rival's cattle from a compound and one of the cows fell among some rocks and was killed. By the time I had compensated his rival's father, Kum had disappeared. Is it really true, he's been fighting with the German army?"

At her invitation I poured whiskey for us both as I filled in the details of Kum's years of absence.

"And you, Captain. Are you resigned to being a prisoner of war?"

"I've no alternative," I said. "I can't possibly rejoin the *Schutztruppe*. Surrender is the only solution."

She shrugged. "We're very isolated here," she said. "I have few friends who call now. If you wish, you may stay here for a week or two while you consider what you are to do."

I told her I could not do that. Harboring an enemy national would put her at serious and unnecessary risk.

"I would claim," she said calmly, "that you told me you were an English officer invalided from the army. You speak English without accent, as far as I can detect."

Thus I stayed with the Baroness Esterhazy. At first for a week, and then for two. When the rains stopped I began to help her with the farm. Sergeant Kum appeared to have taken up his former existence without problems. On the farm he was in charge of the oxen, the horses, and the ancient French motorcar. It was a prestigious position that gave him power over the other workers. At dawn when I rose I would hear him exhorting his minions. I was content to watch him laugh as we passed on our way to our duties. By his own definition, he was happy.

Catherine Esterhazy was happy too. There were mysteries about her that I thought I would never fathom. She told me much about her life with her handsome, wild young husband, but she never told me all. He had brought her to Kenya as a young bride and she had loved it. But for him, as she described it, Kenya had become a prison. Yet this difference was not enough to explain the divorce. Sometimes she even said that she had loved him enough to leave Africa and follow him back to Europe. I lacked the courage to ask her why she had not done so.

She was a lonely woman, yet strong. She reminded me of women I had read about on the American frontier at the end of the last century. But she was also well-read in European literature. As a Swedish neutral, the war offered her nothing but sadness.

One day after I had been on the farm almost two months, she drove into Nairobi with Kum. When she returned, I pressed her for the latest war news. The German army in France, she said over dinner, had launched a massive and successful attack on the British sector of the front. For some weeks the Germans had advanced until it began to look as though they would reach the Channel coast. Then their drive had faltered. The British had struck back. The French army had begun to move forward. The Americans had gained a significant victory in the Argonne Forest. In Nairobi the armchair generals were beginning to talk as if the war were almost over.

I found I was not saddened by the news. I still wished desperately for an armistice that would leave the German state intact. I no longer clearly knew why. I had no faith in the Kaiser, no faith in Germany's unique civilizing mission in Europe. But I suppose, like most of my class, I feared the disorders of defeat and the vengeance of the victors. From my place on the baroness's farm in the Ngong Hills, I could not know how justified my concerns for Germany were to be.

The summer months drifted on. From Catherine Esterhazy I learned as much about Africa as any European could teach me. She took a view of her African neighbors and workers that was totally affectionate and at the same time firmly unsentimental. Most of all, she respected them.

I remember one night when the coffee harvest had been finally brought in and the corrugated iron-roofed sheds were stacked high with sacks. The lantern light gleamed on dark brown faces as the last bags were hauled in and we stood together, a warm bond of achievement between us. Kum, who had practically become the farm manager by his sheer assertive determination to fill any power vacuum, was organizing the unloading and unharnessing of the last oxen.

"You know that Kum has asked me to teach him to read?"

Catherine said as we stood dusty and sweating ourselves among the sweating workers. "Do you think I should?"

The work songs rose around us. My surprise at her question caused her to move closer to me. "We westerners must decide what we're doing here," she said quietly. "Are we transients? Are we to stay?"

"I thought that was never in doubt in your case," I said.

She turned and walked from the shed. I followed her up the path toward the house.

"They say our object is to bring civilization to Africa," she said as I caught up with her.

"And after four years of war, you doubt that civilization?"

She shook her head. "No," she said. "I have some doubts, of course, but I am incapable of imagining an alternative. Many Africans themselves are beginning to be incapable, like me, of seeing an alternative to our civilization. Am I to teach Kum to read? If we go that course, we must accept its consequences. If we offer our civilization to Africans, we must offer it fully. As you can see," she said wryly, "I've been studying my crystal ball."

We walked on back to the house. "I suppose you've wondered," she said, "why I live so isolated a life here. Or why I did at least until you arrived."

I was silent.

"You must have thought it strange that I never asked any of the young Nairobi officers to the farm."

"No," I said. "I suppose I thought you felt they had other interests. Not African interests. After all, they will be going back to England when the war ends."

We stood together on the terrace, the hall light on her strong, handsome face. "No," she said. "I am as inclined to the company of men as any woman. I'm sure you know that."

"Of course."

"I would like to marry again," she said. "A good man. Someone like you, perhaps." She paused. "For various reasons it won't happen."

"It will," I said. "With someone, it will."

She shook her head.

I put my arms around her and drew her toward me, but she averted her head so that I kissed only the side of her cheek.

*   *   *

During that summer we built a lake. Catherine Esterhazy's farm occupied an area of several hundred acres covering two low slopes within the Ngong Hills themselves. The farmhouse was on a wooded incline next to a source that provided water for the house and for the animals. But one year just after the war began, the source had simply disappeared. Its disappearance had coincided, more or less, with a minor earthquake the area had suffered, and it seemed not unreasonable to guess that the source had been diverted underground. Whatever the cause, the effect was that water now had to be hauled from a stream that rose between the two hills, and the oxen had now to be led on a lengthy journey to be watered after their day's work in the fields.

It was my proposal, of which I became inordinately proud, that we divert the stream to force it to flow in a half-mile loop around the base of the more southerly hill, into a low cup of land in front of the farmhouse, and out again to continue its half-loop back on its original course. I saw the whole maneuver as a sort of Immelmann turn on the ground, and spent many a night with a glass of Catherine's whiskey, working on the drawings for the new project.

Catherine herself was somewhere between amused and impressed. Kum was frankly skeptical. "With enough men," he said, "you could dig up all of Ngong and move it closer to the sunrise."

I asked him why anyone should want to do that.

"It would," he said reflectively, "improve the memsahib's view of the morning sun."

There were times when I remained deeply uncertain of Kum's meaning. When I recounted the story to Catherine, she looked thoughtful, smiled, and found some urgent task she had to do.

The construction of the first dam proved a nightmare. Days were spent up to the waist in the freezing fresh spring as I struggled to build a rock wall against the water's flow. Kum, with his usual generosity of spirit, would leap into the water beside me. The other Africans whom I had hired to carry the rocks down to us wisely considered haulage the extent of their task. It was not difficult, even with my limited knowledge of their language, to know that they thought the bwana had taken leave of his senses.

And of course he had. Because he had not considered that

the second dam, which would redivert the water back on its original course, should have been built first, in the dry, before the diversion was effected!

Yet the day arrived when both dams were completed and the second dam, which had been washed away once, had now been rebuilt and the lake was filling in front of the house and the farm *totos*, the children, were leaping in and out, screaming in delight. There was no doubt that it was an immense success. But it was a great deal more than that. It was the first real practical achievement in my life. It had nothing to do with gentlemanly carousing in Cambridge or wading through the stinking, corpse-littered mud of the Somme. It was a creation of genuine beauty, so much so that I would sit on the house veranda and simply stare at it unbelievingly as the herons and ibis and kingfishers and quail came to use it.

Catherine, catching me in my self-satisfied reverie, would stand, placing a hand on my shoulder, and nudge me with her hip. "All my own work," she would say with a smile. Or perhaps she would nod and say, "I think you've convinced even doubting Kum."

I had. If the lake was important to me, it was even more important to Kum. Predictably, he had in the last months made such speed with his reading and writing that he now picked books and read aloud with remarkable facility. Of course, every passage from Dickens or H. G. Wells or an illustrated history of England raised a thousand questions, and I think it was in relation to the answers Catherine and I tried to provide that the lake made an enormous difference.

Before the lake, Kum, though he had used European firearms and traveled in trains and even an aeroplane, retained an essential skepticism in his dealings with white people. As if, in some way, he had never clearly understood what motivated them to make a gun that could kill a man, or an aircraft that could be forced down by another aircraft. I'm sure it's too much to say that the construction of the lake changed all this. But it contributed something to his altered view of what white people did. Not because he had previously doubted their ability but because he had found their objectives trivial.

Within days he was ordering the watering of the farm animals at the outlet end of the lake, and had settled the inlet point where the houseboys should draw the clean spring water. Eager, I suppose, for praise from Kum for my achievement—I was still of course a very young man—I asked him one day what he thought of the new lake.

He stood with his hands on his hips, in his impeccably clean shorts and safari shirt, looking, apart from his color, as much like an English settler as I in my ragged uniform looked like a native. "If all the tribes came from the north to dig with shovels to move the hill closer to the sunrise," he said, "I would turn them away."

"You approve of the lake?" I persisted.

He nodded. "It is good."

F I V E

uring all this time I worked on the lake, my friendship with
Catherine Esterhazy continued to deepen. Over dinner or
a whiskey and soda after dinner she would talk about her
girlhood or her meeting with Esterhazy. I learned, on those
warm evenings with the French doors open to the African
night, about her Swedish-American family in Minneapolis.
About the day she had graduated from high school and found
that an extra guest had been invited to the celebration, a
young, dark-eyed man, aristocratic Hungarian by origin, now
emigrated to Sweden to work in the great Nobel factories
outside Stockholm. He had been to London and Berlin and,
above all, Paris. At twenty-six years of age he had had stories to
tell of Rodin or the anarchists. He had witnessed the bombing
of the Café Terminus and the public execution of the perpetrator, Henry. Now he traveled through the United States, selling
dynamiting products to quarries and construction companies.
But his great, driving ambition was to farm in the new English
protectorate in East Africa.

She had married him against her parents' wishes. Although they
were first-generation immigrants, they already felt the young Count
Esterhazy to be too "foreign" for their daughter. They preferred by
far one of the young American boys of the family next door.

For her dowry they had provided the money for the passage
and farm in Kenya. They were well off rather than immensely
rich, and farmland in East Africa was cheap. So Esterhazy and
Catherine arrived together, and the reality of the backbreaking
work to create something from even a rich wilderness had
proved too much for the count's spirit.

She had told me the story once or twice before—not in
obsessive repetition, but adding new details on each occasion.

Yet she stopped every time at this point. She never explained why she had not gone with him back to Europe.

It was no real barrier between us. I knew that she was not inviting questions on those last months of her marriage, and I had no wish to press her. If I had loved her it would no doubt have been different. But what I felt for her—physical desire certainly, respect, affection, and friendship—all somehow fell short of love.

We lived outwardly, I suppose, like man and wife. We ate breakfast together and discussed the day's work; we had dinner together and sometimes danced to the old, crackly gramophone. We stood with our arms around each other's waists at a *ngoma* and watched the young *morani*, the warriors, dance before the maidens. But since the night of the coffee harvest we never drew closer, we never kissed.

I had told her about Diana. Once, drunkenly, I showed her one of her letters. I remember she read it once, quickly, then again with painstaking slowness, like a seven-year-old. "Is she really such a girl?" she asked as she handed me back the letter, reluctantly it seemed.

"I only know her through her letters," I said. "She was not much more than a child when we met. And that was on one single day. You think, of course, that I was incurably romantic, or simply adolescent, to imagine that anyone could fall in love by post."

"You mean I don't take seriously what you told me?" she said.

I had drunk too much whiskey, but I could not miss the sharpness of her tone. "No, I don't mean that. Of course I don't mean that."

"Good." She stood up to go to bed. "Good," she repeated, turning away. "Because I am bound to take seriously anyone you have been in love with. Are you still?"

"I don't know," I said.

"That means yes."

I watched her as she turned back toward me. Her pale yellow dress, of prewar fashion, showed her swelling breasts and bare, suntanned shoulders. Did I love Diana Winslow? Did it matter if I did?

The face of the woman before me had softened. "It means yes, doesn't it, Claus?"

I stood up, fighting the desire rising within me. I could so easily have lied. I wanted to. "It means yes, Catherine. I suppose you're right, it means yes."

She nodded, relaxed and comfortable now. "Let's have a nightcap." She turned to the whiskey tray and I realized she was relieved.

It seemed to me, for all that, that there were a hundred occasions on which we might have become lovers. There were evenings when we celebrated some small achievement on the farm, the birth of oxen or the recovery from influenza of one of the *totos* whom Catherine taught in the farm school two mornings a week.

The night of the lions sticks in my memory. I had been asleep an hour or so when I was awakened by a furious rustling on the thatched roof above my bed. My first thought was that it was a leopard from the woods above the northern hill. In the early days of the farm, when the roof was of corrugated iron, it was not unusual, Catherine had told me, for a leopard to leap onto the roof and lie enjoying the heat radiating from the warm galvanized iron below him. This night I rose and took a rifle and went out onto the veranda, but there was no sign of a leopard, and no sounds of alarm came from the oxen compounds, so I returned to bed. I have no clear idea how much later it was that all hell broke loose. Catherine was screaming at me to wake up. Every animal in the yard and compound was braying or trumpeting or clucking or neighing. Kum was shouting for me as I threw open the bedroom windows. "Come quickly, bwana. Bring two rifles."

I ran down the stairs and grabbed the rifles from Catherine. Kum was standing in the yard, thumbs hooked into the waistband of his shorts. "A lion broke into the compound," he said. "Perhaps two."

He unhooked a thumb and took one of the rifles. He opened the breech with the skill of long practice, checked that the rifle was loaded, and drove a round into the chamber. Together we entered the compound. I had seen a fox in a chicken yard, and in Germany I had seen a starving wolfpack break into the kennels, but I had never seen animal devastation like this. The lion kills by leaping on the back of its victim and breaking the neck with its paws wrapped around the throat. But even the boundless power of a six-hundred-pound lioness cannot break an ox's neck. Instead, the teeth are used to gnaw and tear and sever until the muscle and arteries have been destroyed. The result is like an abattoir of drunken and incompetent slaughterers. Blood spurted, poured, and gushed. Oxen, their hindquarters half torn from them, trumpeted the wildest fear I have ever seen. Of sixteen oxen, we had lost eleven. Eight of those eleven we shot ourselves. The rest, the lions got.

I was advised by Kum. He believed there were at least two lions, probably lionesses. Certainly they were not sated. While others were quieting the remaining oxen, we used a mule to drag the huge black body of one of them up the hill toward the woods. In the middle of the track we left it, and withdrew into thick bushes about thirty yards away.

It was a night when the moon was less than full, but gave enough light to see clearly the great humped carcass we had left as bait. I will admit that as the hours passed I began to lose faith in Kum's abilities as a lion hunter. Every sort of animal, recognizable or too small to more than hear, came to sniff and tear and feed on the carcass. Jackals and hyenas circled it and were driven off by a leopard, which licked and hissed and slunk off into the darkness.

And then suddenly the lions appeared. In line they approached down the track, a female, a male, and another female. There was one moment only, as I eased off my safety catch, when a great face turned from the oxen to glare stonily toward the bushes in which we were hidden. But we shot the great beasts down with comparative ease, Kum taking two to my one.

There was jubilation on our return. Tiny children were taken from their beds and Catherine handed out beer to celebrate in the first light of dawn.

Catherine met me on the veranda. The first sun rays were making black-red pools in the surface of the lake. She took my hand and led me down the steps toward the edge of the water. Then, turning, she pointed to the thatched roof. It looked as if a storm of incredible violence had struck it.

"They are great, powerful beasts," she said. "A pride of lions can easily take two or three children before they're driven off."

We returned to the house and ate bacon and eggs and drank champagne. It was not at all difficult to see that she was troubled. I thought at first there might be other lions in the forest, but she shook her head.

"I thought we were celebrating," I said.

For a long time she sat with her head down, twirling the stem of the champagne glass between her fingers. When she lifted her face toward me I could see that she was crying. "No," she said, "we're not celebrating. We're saying good-bye."

Her words hit me with the force of a blow. I sat opposite her at the table, unable to speak. She did nothing, I saw, to wipe away the freely flowing tears. She lifted her champagne and drank.

"Yesterday," she said, putting down her glass, "two policemen came up from Nairobi. You were up on the north hill plantation at the time."

"What did they want?"

She wiped away her tears now, using both hands. "They had heard talk from an Indian trader of a new estate manager here. A white man. They thought it unusual that they had no record, although they assumed you were an ex-soldier, possibly demobilized for health reasons."

"What did you tell them?"

"I told them they were exactly right. You had been wounded in the campaign against von Lettow and released from the army. I invented a name that they said they would check against their records. They were perfectly amiable and suspected nothing. You see, I have a certain reputation in Nairobi. The rather eccentric American-Swedish baroness who's known to cultivate her privacy."

"They'll be back."

"Of course. Whether you wait for them or leave immediately, I shall lose you."

I got up from the table and poured myself some whiskey. I needed something stronger than champagne to face the next turn in the road of life.

"There is one other thing," she said, rising and standing beside me. "The German armies are retreating all along the Western Front. The war is almost over."

We stood looking at each other blankly for what seemed a long, long time.

"You know I love you," she said finally. "You've known that for months. Equally, I know you don't love me. But all the other things I know you feel for me have great weight. I know how much sometimes you've wanted to go to bed with me."

"Very often and very much," I said.

She nodded slowly. "You're leaving now," she said. "I suppose if the war is ending you will be repatriated to Germany."

"I can't imagine the British will be anxious to allow former German officers to stay on in East Africa."

"No." Absently, she took my whiskey from my hand and drank it. "I don't think I could have told you unless you were leaving," she said.

"Told me what, Catherine?"

"Explained. Told you why I never agreed to sleep with you, much as I want to."

I stood before her in awkward silence. I knew she was going to tell me something about her husband. Intuitively I knew too that it would be the reason for their divorce. At least, looking back over the long years I think I did. Perhaps not. Perhaps I was just a young man in a tattered uniform on the brink of captivity, whose country was equally on the brink of horrendous defeat. And she was just a tall, handsome American woman, older than I, desirable and unattainable for reasons of which I had no understanding at all. Time anesthetizes pain while it warms our self-estimation. "As much as you want to," I said. "As much as you want to sleep with me?"

She shrugged helplessly. "Yes. As much as I want to, I won't. Even now, when you're leaving. I dare not."

"Will you tell me why?"

She closed her eyes in misery more than I could stand. I reached toward her but she pushed gently away. "Yes, I must tell you why. I am sick, Claus. My husband left me *sick*."

Of course I knew what she meant.

She nodded. "Syphilis," she said briskly now, like a doctor diagnosing. "Syphilis. Treatable to a degree. Incurable in fact. Syphilis," she said, her voice rising, "eating, gnawing, ratlike *syphilis*."

I took her in my arms and carried her to the sofa. We sat there together for God knows how long. Then, from somewhere beyond the veranda, I heard English voices asking to see the baroness and her new farm manager.

Sergeant Major Lusk of the Royal Military Police was a powerfully built man of middle height. He was, I suppose, about forty, a Londoner I would guess from his accent, quick, tough, and dangerous as an interrogator. I don't mind confessing that I was intimidated as he sat opposite me behind his desk, his red-topped service cap placed just so beside the papers relating to my case, his white military police crossbelt gleaming in the sunlight.

"Now, Captain," he said carefully, "I shall be asking you to sign a statement later. For the present, you admit to being an officer of the German Air Service, a Hauptmann or captain by rank, Claus Thomas von Hardenberg by name. Is that correct?"

"It is."

"Briefly, you claim to have attended the University of Cambridge in England during 1913 and the first part of 1914. This accounts for the quality of your spoken English."

"If it's important, I received English lessons from my mother as far back as I can remember."

"It's important, Captain, for this reason. There are clearly only two possible explanations for your activities at Baroness Esterhazy's farm. One is that you are what you claim to be, a straightforward air officer on the run. No problems there."

"And the alternative, Sergeant Major?"

Lusk adjusted the position of his hat on the desk by a fraction of an inch. "The other possibility, Captain, is that you were using the farm in the Ngong Hills to spy on British military movements from Nairobi."

I was frightened. For Catherine as well as myself. It was not, as I knew, an absurd suggestion. With a radio link to Bitov's column, I *could* have passed some very relevant information.

"What do you say to the alternative, Captain?" Lusk asked quietly. He leaned forward and offered me a cigarette from a packet of Sweet Aftons. I took one and he came around the table to light it for me. Yet these politenesses did nothing to mitigate the fierce aura of efficacy that surrounded him.

"Well, Captain, what *do* you say?"

I inhaled the cigarette. "My answer would be in three parts," I said. "First, you must have a record of the engagement that brought down my Fokker reconnaissance aircraft."

"We have."

"Second, I am wearing the uniform of the Imperial German Air Service."

"Yes," he said doubtfully. "Not much to distinguish it from standard civilian settler's work clothes, though."

"Perhaps not, Sergeant Major, but it *is* a uniform."

"Third point?"

"To prove me a spy, you would have to establish how I passed on any information I might have acquired."

Lusk smiled. "Before the war, sir," he said, "I was a copper, a policeman on the beat in London. In my experience, it was the guilty ones that had the best stories. The innocent usually bluffed and fluffed a bit. You see what I'm saying, sir. I'm wondering if your answers aren't just a bit too pat."

"It's a question you must resolve, Sergeant Major Lusk. I can only assure you again that I have told the truth."

"Part of the truth, Captain."

I was now thoroughly alarmed. Behind the cheerful cockney accent I felt a mind working whose incisiveness could endanger Catherine.

"Which part of the truth do you believe I have omitted?"

"According to the report here—and it completely corroborates your statement—your Fokker biplane was forced to land on Lake Nwedn. You chose to land because the British fighter was faster and more heavily armed."

"That is correct."

"No aerial battle took place?"

"The first pass only."

"But no machine-gun bullets from the De Havilland actually hit your aircraft."

"No. I don't understand what's troubling you, Sergeant Major."

"I think you will, Captain. Tell me, a Fokker reconnaissance plane normally carries an observer-navigator, does it not?"

Of course, it was the only weak point in my story. Lusk had found it immediately.

"What I'm wondering, Captain, is why you never mentioned him. Second, where is he now? He wasn't killed in the dogfight, was he?"

"No," I said. "My observer was a native. He chose to make his own way back to his tribe after we destroyed our plane."

"Which tribe would that be, Captain?"

"I haven't been in Africa long enough to know," I said. "He came from German East Africa, of course. Somewhere south of Mount Kilimanjaro."

Lusk nodded. "He could have," he conceded.

I remained silent.

"Unusually intelligent, was he?"

"An intelligent man, yes."

Lusk stood up, blocking the window. "So you walked nearly thirty miles until you came to the baroness's farm."

"Yes."

"Was it the first farm you came to?"

"Yes."

"There are a number of others on what must have been your route. You weren't attracted by them?"

"I don't really recall seeing any others."

"Very well. You arrived at Baroness Esterhazy's farm and you passed yourself off as a wounded British officer, medically discharged."

"Correct."

"The baroness offered you a job as her farm manager, and you accepted."

"It seemed preferable to a prisoner-of-war camp."

"Quite so, Captain. And you are telling me that you never met the baroness before. In Europe, say, before the war."

"Never."

"You just walked in through the front door, so to speak, and she offered you a job."

I nodded.

Outside, a rather tinny band was playing a hymn on a trumpet and three or four tambourines.

"Salvation Army," Lusk said, almost to himself.

Then, piping above the trumpet and tambourines, a very

young girl's voice rose, chanting, "Salvation Army, all gone barmy!"

Lusk put his head out of the window. "Pamela!" he roared. "You come up here, my girl!"

He turned, abashed, back from the window. "My daughter Pam, I'm afraid, Captain." He sat down slowly. "So, Captain, we were saying you just walked in through the front door of Baroness Esterhazy's house and she offered you a job. No questions asked."

"Of course she asked questions," I said, "but I was able to satisfy her that I was who I said I was."

"An English officer?"

"Sergeant Major," I said, leaning forward, revealing no doubt the level of my anxiety, "I give you my word as a gentleman that I was not spying."

"I don't believe you were, Captain." He stood up, walked to the door, and, opening it, called for my escort. "No, spying doesn't quite fit my book, Captain. But one or two other things still don't, either."

I could hear the boots of the escort stamping along the corridor toward Lusk's office. I hoped they would get here before he could ask any more questions.

"No," he said thoughtfully, his thumbs in his white blancoed belt, "one or two things still don't fit."

The escort stamped to a halt at the door. "Good-bye, Sergeant Major," I said.

He stood stiffly at attention. "Good-bye, Captain," he said. "Or *au revoir*, I would guess." He pronounced the French execrably.

As I was marched through the outer office, we passed a pretty girl about ten years of age. Long brown hair curled about her shoulders. She was playing hopscotch between the desks of the empty office, and I could see by the movement of her lips that at each hop she was chanting under her breath, "Salvation Army, all gone barmy. . . ."

My escort had halted me at the door of the outer office while some piece of paper was being filled in. Lusk's daughter had turned at the far wall and was now listening with widening tawny eyes as the escort commander gave the duty clerk the details: Officer Prisoner of War. German. Captain Claus von Hardenberg.

"Are you really German?" the girl asked, pointing a long finger at me.

"Yes, I'm a German, Pamela," I said.

"Gawd," she said. "Fancy that. A bleedin' German."

"In here, my girl!" Lusk's voice roared from behind me, and Pamela scurried into his office.

As my escort marched me away, I heard Lusk's door closing behind me and Pamela piping, "How come he don't speak like a German, Dad?"

Nairobi was not, in those days, the city of the postwar years. Its rapid expansion to accommodate military needs had left it more a township of the American West, with boardwalks and muddy streets. My prison quarters were in the clapboard Suffolk Hotel. I was fed English soldiers' food, not good but adequate, and I was given access to the military news sheet the British published every other day. My own capture in the Ngong Hills was recorded in a small item. I saw with some satisfaction that my own claims were reported. "The German officer," the *Military Record* stated, "had successfully passed himself off for several months as a discharged British officer." No mention, thank God, of spying.

But I had less cause for satisfaction with the *Military Record's* account of the progress of the war on the Western Front. From Germany's point of view, the news was not good. The retreat of the German armies continued. We were on the edge of defeat.

My second interview with Sergeant Major Thomas Lusk took place in the same office a few days after my capture. I stood up when he entered, and he saluted and invited me to sit down.

"No complaints about your treatment, I hope, Captain."

"None at all."

"Good. I've located a number of captured German uniforms. Officer's khaki drill. You can fit yourself out this afternoon."

"That's most kind of you, Sergeant Major."

He shook his head. He had removed his cap and he now placed it, again, on the right of his desk, its red MP's top and highly polished badge the symbol of his authority.

He sat down. "I went up to the farm to interview the

baroness again yesterday," he said slowly. "I explained the position to her."

"The position?"

"I explained that if she had at any time known or suspected you were a German officer, it was her duty to report the fact."

"Of course she didn't suspect me. Why should she?" I said. "But in any case she is, I believe, a Swedish citizen by marriage."

He grunted. "An American ally by birth."

We sat looking at each other across the desk. As I was beginning to feel uncomfortable under his unwavering gaze, he said suddenly, "I also interviewed the baroness's oxen keeper, Kum. Unusually intelligent fellow."

The phrase was, of course, deliberate. Somehow Lusk had made the connection with the missing observer. Perhaps he was only guessing.

"By his account," Lusk said, "he ran away from the baroness's service sometime early in the war over a misunderstanding about some cattle. He appears to have returned about the same time you turned up, Captain. Was he there when you arrived?"

"I believe so."

Lusk nodded. "He couldn't really explain where he'd spent the last two years."

"How does this concern me, Sergeant Major?"

"You know how, sir," Lusk said briskly. "I've picked up a little German in my time interrogating prisoners. I tried some on Kum. He's quick to cover it, but I fancy he understood me."

I remained silent.

"I'm not expecting you to say anything now, Captain," he continued, "but I believe when Kum ran away in 1916 he joined your *Schutztruppe*. I think he was your observer, sir. And I think when you needed somewhere to hide, Kum took you to the baroness."

He took a new packet of Sweet Aftons from his pocket, handed me a cigarette, and, as he had before, rounded the desk to light it. As I inhaled, he stood above me, looking down. "You won't have heard the news yet, I don't suppose, sir?"

"What news?"

"The fighting's over on the Western Front. Here in Africa too. Germany surrendered yesterday at eleven A.M. The Kaiser has abdicated."

[119]

He turned on his heel and walked toward the door. "Excuse me a moment, Captain," he said. "I've a couple of details to check up on in the outer office."

I felt only relief. The slaughter was finally over. I sat slumped in my chair, smoking the cigarette Lusk had given me. Outside it was raining again. On the farm in the Ngong Hills, the *totos* would be playing in the downpour; Kum would be studying his books with his new voracious appetite for fact; Catherine Esterhazy would be sitting in the rocking chair on the veranda, nursing her sickness and the hope that I could avert her arrest.

In London, Diana would be waiting for the return from prison camp of her fiancé, Charles Chrysler. And suddenly, because I felt that all contact with her had been cut forever, I realized that with the Armistice, I was now free to write to her. Even before Lusk returned, I had begun to compose the first sentence in my head.

Later that night, with the rain drumming on the corrugated iron roof of the Suffolk Hotel, I began writing:

My dear Diana,

I heard today that the great bloodletting is finally over. All those you love who have survived are safe now. But the broken bodies will fill the hospitals for many, many years yet. The great reprimand to all the self-satisfied politicians of the world will not be line after line of neat white nameless crosses, but the one man or two in every village in England, Germany, and France rocking on his crutches to the pub or *Gasthaus* or café. They will not feel proud forever. They should not. Perhaps America, which has escaped everything but the last year of madness, will be able to save our sanity in the coming years. Perhaps I write about the world because I can't bear to write about you.

I'm sure Charles has told you of our brief meeting the day he was taken prisoner. He told me then that you had accepted his proposal. . . .

I took the letter and tore it in half, then in quarters, and on and on until I could tear it no more. Lights shone from a long barracks building opposite, and the maudlin songs of drunken soldiers celebrating victory floated across the road. I was twenty-two years old. I felt intolerably lonely in my country's defeat. I longed to be enclosed in the arms of Catherine Esterhazy as I longed to be comforted by my mother, with Catherine's sickness as the maternal taboo between us.

I tried to sleep in misery, with the sounds of the rain on the roof and the snatches of song. Toward dawn the rain stopped and the soldiers ceased their celebrating. To my relief I discovered that my eyelids were heavy.

The next morning my escort collected me and I was again marched to Lusk's office. After proffering the traditional Sweet Afton, Lusk tapped the papers before him on his desk. "I've completed my report on you, Captain. My orders are that you are to be escorted to Abercorn, where General von Lettow's surrender will formally take place."

He handed me the typewritten document. It was numbered in the left-hand corner of the top page and entitled CAPTAIN CLAUS THOMAS VON HARDENBERG, PRISONER OF WAR. I looked up from the first page, repeating the title: "Prisoner of war."

Lusk nodded. "As you can see, sir, I have concluded in the report that you were not engaged in a spying operation."

"I'm very relieved to hear it, Sergeant Major."

"I have also decided to close down my investigations in two other directions, the Baroness Esterhazy and her African employee, Kum."

I remained silent, even now aware that Thomas Lusk was not a man one took for granted.

"Between you and me, Captain," he said, "I believe that Kum was your observer and led you after that crash to the farm of Baroness Esterhazy. I think it's possible you passed yourself off as British—but most likely that she knew you were German." He paused. "The war's over, I see no point in further investigations. But I want to say one thing, Captain Hardenberg. If you ever feel the need, after a few brandies, to tell the story of the crash and how you really came to meet the baroness, I'll come down on her and Kum like a ton of bricks. Do we understand each other, sir?"

We did. I stood up and shook hands with the Sergeant Major. I believed then that it was the last time I should ever see Thomas Lusk.

*   *   *

I was taken by train to Abercorn, Rhodesia, to be present at von Lettow's surrender. He had announced his decision to the *Schutztruppe* a few days before. Standing before them in the captured British town of Kasama, he had told his askaris in Swahili that the war in Europe was over. "The High Command in Berlin," he said, "has ordered us to stop fighting too. Someday your achievements in the last four and a half years will be recognized. Until then, remember that here in Africa you were undefeated."

Germans and Africans alike were stunned. The men, it was recounted to me, listened with tears in their eyes; the wives and women camp followers, who had marched the same thousands of miles as their menfolk, began to weep and wail.

I was standing at attention with Major Bitov's column in the square at Abercorn as General von Lettow led in the *Schutztruppe* main force. He wore his extraordinary boots with the cut-out toes, tattered khaki drill without any badges of rank, and a sun helmet covered with faded brown corduroy. Behind him his German officers marched at the head of each askari column, and behind them came the chanting wives and camp followers, openly carrying on their heads the goods they had just looted from Kasama. But then, why not? As von Lettow had just reminded them, they were an undefeated army.

The ceremony, with a band playing and much saluting, took place in heavy rain. I found it immeasurably sad—not for the German officers, but for the incredibly loyal askaris and their wives who had fought and marched with von Lettow for so long. As the askaris were disarmed and their women dispossessed of their loot, I watched them marched off in the rain toward their internment camps. They seemed infinitely puzzled as they looked across at von Lettow saluting them for the last time.

I think only Governor Schnee was unmoved by the spectacle in the rain. Now that von Lettow's army was no more, Schnee's civilian status would be reasserted. It was difficult to remember, but nevertheless true, that Schnee was now the official German authority in Tanganyika. It was not to last, of course. Germany's East African colony was soon to go, at a decision at Versailles, the same way as the long column of askaris in the rain.

We German officers were transported to Mombasa as Christmas approached. We were all deeply worried by the confused reports emerging from our defeated Fatherland. Rumors of rebellion in the Imperial German Fleet and revolution and the setting up of Russian-style soviets began to reach us. Perhaps I was the only German officer who did not long to be home.

We were nevertheless allowed by the British military to lead an unusually free life in Mombasa while we awaited the boat that would take us home. General von Lettow and Governor Schnee were allotted a pleasant house, and the rest of us lived two to a room in the same street.

Our sailing date had been announced for Christmas Day, ironically, on board the *Francken*, which had brought me out to Africa. It was some days before that I received a brief note delivered by a British corporal. It read:

Claus, you bounder!
   I couldn't believe my eyes when I saw you among the Huns all lined up at Abercorn. What an incredible performance your von Lettow put up. We're halfway to adopting him as a British national hero!
   Come to lunch Friday. I hear they're shipping you all off back to the Fatherland for Christmas. My God, I've missed you!
                                                                          Buzz

His writing paper was headed "Major Lord Winslow, M.C., 2/4 King's African Rifles." It meant, of course, that if Buzz had succeeded to the title, Richard was dead.

I had never been able to trace the hospital in Germany that Charles Chrysler had told me he was in, and although I suspected Richard had died of wounds, this was the first confirmation I had had. Perhaps as a generation we had become unhealthily inured to the death of our friends and relations. When we met, we talked, Buzz and I, of Richard for a few moments before carefully placing his shade aside. It was the way one did such things in 1918.

Buzz gave me lunch with claret and brandy in the British officers' club in Mombasa. Nobody seemed to find it in the least odd to see a German officer sitting among all these red-tabbed British colonels. After a few moments I forgot it myself. Buzz and I might simply have been taking lunch at the Pitt Club in Cambridge.

In the first few minutes there was no mention of Diana between us, and it seemed to me unlikely that Buzz had known about the letters we exchanged. I therefore told him only about my meeting with Charles Chrysler at the German fliers' mess near the Argonne Forest, and of hearing of their engagement.

"Splendid chap, Charles," Buzz said enthusiastically, "and as rich as Croesus, of course. But mark my words, Claus, what my sister needs is a frequent good rogering. I only hope the Chrysler Beast is up to it."

We were well into our second bottle of claret. "One of our Nairobi security chaps told me you managed the last few months as the sole guest of a beautiful American lady farmer."

I nodded. "Catherine Esterhazy, do you know her?"

"Loved her at a distance ever since I've been in East Africa," he said.

I suppose I looked startled.

He smiled his brilliant smile, painfully like Diana's. "Loved far too many of them at far too great a distance, old boy. Can't really complain, though, by George. Here, the knicker elastic snaps at the merest hint of interest. I'm working my way through consorts of the administration. They blame it on the African air, bless them. Say they weren't at all like this at home."

We stayed long over our brandy and cigars. I found myself suddenly, desperately unhappy. "Diana's wedding," I said, "when is it to be?"

"Not until Charles is out of the pen, obviously. No, the date's not fixed," he said. "But I've already chosen the place."

"You have?"

"In loco parentis."

"England? Or America?"

"Neither, old chap. Venice is my preference. The Chrysler family have just bought the Palazzo Bellini in Venice. On the Grand Canal, not a stone's throw from where Lord Byron wrote Don Juan. 'I learned the art of soldiering and of gunnery/And how to storm a fortress or a nunnery,' " he declaimed as he walked toward the door. "Venice has so much to offer," he said, his arm around my shoulders. "My God, Claus, I'm desperate for my first nun."

Buzz could, I suppose, be dragooned into seriousness for a few moments at a time, but he was uncomfortable with it. His only reference to Cambridge friends killed or injured in France was to "silly Billy Danvers, who galloped like a seventeen-hand hunter straight at a German machine gun."

He himself had had, as the British say, a good war. He had reached the rank of captain in the Greenjackets and had served at the Battle of Loos with the First Battalion, King's Royal Rifle Corps, where he had been awarded the Military Cross. This is, for the British, a decoration of far less distinction than the Victoria Cross, but it is a respectable medal. A Greenjacket captain, an acting major at twenty-two, a holder of the Military Cross and alive to tell the tale, this counted as having a good war.

In East Africa he had spent most of his time in Kenya as an intelligence officer, curiously enough having been responsible for, among other things, tracking down a certain Fokker reconnaissance biplane that buzzed and coughed up and down the Uganda railway line in the early months of 1918.

A good war. Had I had a good war? It was near impossible to compare our situations. I too was a captain and had fought on the Somme, survived it, and been awarded a respectable medal. But I was a child of the defeated nation. At home there were rumors of rebellion; in England the talk was of magnificent weddings at the Palazzo Bellini in Venice.

We were almost at the door when a voice broke across the murmur of diners.

"What's a Hun doing here? What's a bloody Hun doing here?"

I looked around. A young major wearing the badges of the Army Service Corps stood at my shoulder. "And who's the cad, I'd like to know, who would invite him?"

"I, sir, am your cad. Major Lord George Winslow of the King's Royal Rifle Corps." He drew a card from his tunic pocket. "This officer"—he indicated me—"is a friend of long standing, a cousin as well as an honorable former enemy. He will call on you in your barrack tomorrow, where you or your appointed second will choose the time and place for the customary *amende honorable.*"

The Service Corps officer's mouth was sagging. Throughout

the British Army, the Rifle Regiments had a daunting reputation for their skill at arms. "I had no intention of offering you an insult, Major," the man stuttered. "None at all."

"Nevertheless," Buzz said, "we shall meet at the time and place appointed by our seconds."

"Lord Winslow," the major said, "I am offering you an apology."

"I don't know how the . . . *gentlemen* of the Army Service Corps look on these matters," Buzz brushed the offer aside, "but in a Rifle Regiment, good form demands satisfaction. We are fated, Major, to meet at twenty paces, in the cold dawn light. It is," he added loftily, "an *appel du destin*. Nothing less."

We marched to the door and, once in the corridor, reeled away laughing. "You *are* a cad," I said. "The poor chap was shaking in his boots."

"*Appel du destin*, no less!" Buzz spluttered helplessly. And tearing at his fly, he pushed open the door to the lavatories.

Before the *Francken* carried me back to Europe I wrote to Kum, certainly the first letter he had received in his life. I told him that I had been able to arrange for his name to be removed from the records of the *Schutztruppe* and that he would therefore be perfectly safe to invent any story for his two-year disappearance from Kenya that he chose.

I wrote, too, to Catherine Esterhazy. I tried to thank her for all she had taught me about Africa. It was only when I returned again years later that I realized how much she had had to impart.

I attempted also—with great clumsiness, no doubt—to say how sorry I was that we were unable to come together:

I seem to feel some unspoken question coming from you, from the direction of the Ngong Hills: shall I ever return to Africa? I think to that question you have provided the answer already. Each day's work on the farm, each hunting party, each coffee picking, every smell and taste of Africa I was privileged to have received through you. It is almost exactly a year since I arrived in Africa, and I am sure that I shall be back.

S I X

I returned to a Germany in chaos. As I came down the *Francken's* ramp at three o'clock on a freezing morning in Bremen Harbor, I was dressed in khaki drill, with a badly torn officer's greatcoat to keep out the bitter European cold. I had no money, or not more than a handful of marks. But I looked forward to the prospect of pay, and travel warrants and accommodation.

We *Schutztruppe* officers from distant Africa struggled to understand what was happening to us. We did not see ourselves as we were, part of a defeated army. On the dockside there was no military reception office to direct us. Outside the main dock gates, young workmen stood on street corners, hands in pockets, their leather caps pulled low on their brows, rifles slung on their shoulders, butt ends up.

The wind off the sea cut into us and drove squalls of snow along the mean streets of the dock area. A group of *Schutztruppe* officers approached one of the armed workers for directions and were driven off at gunpoint like hungry wolves. Seeking a café, some of us went to the marketplace. The statue of Roland was draped in red cloth; a red flag hung from the town hall balcony; posters everywhere proclaimed that the city of Bremen was under the government of the Soviets. Innocents that we were, we had no idea what that meant.

There were no cafés open in the square, but a few lights were burning in the town hall. I decided, with my old commander, Bitov, to try to find out what was happening.

We pushed open the main door to shouts and curses from within as blasts of snow-laden air pursued us. The floor of the main hall was covered with figures, most sleeping, wrapped in old blankets or newspapers, some sitting in small groups, talking quietly. Whole families sat or sprawled on the great staircase. Small children cried in their sleep.

An old man sitting on an upright chair against the wall, his legs wrapped in newspaper, seemed the only one to show any interest in us now that the door was again closed against the wind. We crossed to him.

"Good morning, *mein Herr,*" I began. "Perhaps you will be kind enough to help us."

He smiled, as if the formality of my request amused him.

"We are two officers from General von Lettow's *Schutztruppe.* With others we disembarked from Africa this morning. We are looking for the military reception center for returning officers."

"Officers," the man said. "You don't look like officers."

Bitov was wearing an old British Army greatcoat. My own German topcoat was without insignia, torn and oilstained. "Nevertheless," Bitov said, "that's what we are."

"Then I should keep quiet about it if I were you. Officers are not popular with the new government of Bremen."

"Government of Bremen!" Bitov said testily. He gestured irritably. "What's going on here? Who are all these people?"

The old man got to his feet, the newspaper falling away from him. "Listen to me, young gentlemen," he said in hardly more than a whisper. "These people have fled from the south of the city. Last night we had news that an army brigade under General Gellsner is marching on Bremen."

"On whose orders?" I must have looked as puzzled as I felt.

The old man shook his head, smiling bitterly. "Germany's not what it was when you left," he said. "There have been revolutions against the new republic in Berlin, Hamburg, Munich, and many smaller towns, like our own. Within hours, every man must choose which side he's on."

"How in God's name can we choose which side we're on," Bitov exploded, "when we know nothing about it?"

A few men from nearby groups had begun to look toward us.

"If you can't choose," the old man said, "find somewhere to hide. By daylight the streets of Bremen will be running with blood."

The old man was right. Just after dawn the first light artillery shells began to explode in the Brill, a square in the west center of the town. Barricades of tramcars and furniture had been erected haphazardly across the streets and were manned by armed workers of this or that Redcommando. When the real fighting began, Bitov and I found ourselves outside Hillmann's Hotel. Machine-gun bullets tore through the wooden tables of the hopeless barricades. Young workers of sixteen and seventeen years old struggled to fire rifles that had, until then, been no more than a revolutionary ornament.

The street fighting was as savage as anything I had seen on the Western Front. It was certainly true that the regular army units, stunned by Germany's surrender and believing it entirely the result of what would later be called "the stab in the back," attacked the Redcommandos with a frustrated fury. In Kaiserstrasse, between the river and the railway station, Bitov and I bandaged wounded women with strips of rag, carried old men to the relative safety of their cellars, and led a column of schoolchildren across factory roofs to a quieter area beyond the fighting.

By noon I had lost contact with my old commander. Perhaps he, as I later learned most *Schutztruppe* officers had done, had joined forces with the regular troops. For me the afternoon passed in a flurry of wet snow and grime and blood. A few images I retain. I remember a hunchbacked worker haranguing his command of twenty frozen adolescent boys: "We stripped the Kaiser of his boots. But the revolution is not complete until we hang every Bremen bourgeois from the lampposts." And *that* while they were under attack from a brigade of veteran frontline soldiers with artillery, mortars, and heavy machine guns!

Another image, of a woman running with a small child, sliding wildly across the snow as bullets pockmarked the doorway she was trying to reach for shelter. I dragged her under cover, trying to calm her enough to get her legs out of the line of fire. But she had recognized my voice, my manner of speaking, and we crouched in the doorway together while she screamed hatred of my origins and class.

When the fighting was over, bodies littered the streets. Along the pavements, great black bloodstains spread through the churned snow. I was recognized by the victorious army units as someone who could not possibly have been on the workers' side of the barricades. The voice again, the manner. But it saved me from prison—or a bullet in the neck.

Had I known more about the issues on that day, who can say which side of the barricades I would have chosen to be on? At that time I saw only a savage courage on both sides, and a Germany I had never guessed existed.

In the next week I made my way to Hamburg, where I attached myself to a unit of army engineers recently returned from the Western Front. I saw there the horrifying results of the wartime British naval blockade: families beyond starvation, wearing rags to keep out the winter cold, cardboard shoe soles against the wet slush in the streets. There was almost no fuel, and streetlights were a rarity. Most nights the sound of gunfire would erupt somewhere in the city, and the houses of the better-off would blaze suddenly from the arsonists' work.

In these desperately unhappy weeks I heard from a cousin that my mother had died of influenza at the beginning of 1918 and that our properties in the east were now part of a Polish settlement.

Nationalist and socialist-communist arguments raged throughout the city. My fellow officers were nationalist to a man. Their belief was that the Soviets, financed by the new Russian Revolution, had contrived "the stab in the back" that had defeated Germany's undefeated army. For myself, I found it difficult to understand what had happened, and even more difficult to decide what should now happen. I attended meetings of wildly disparate groups. One night in the Grenzfass, a beer hall in the St. Pauli district, I heard Hermann Knuffgen speak. "The rich must die," he proclaimed, "so that the poor may live." I thought immediately of the hunchback on the Bremen barricades. This very morning, Knuffgen recounted, his Redcommando had successfully raided a basement arsenal of the Burgerwehr, a counterrevolutionary organization of armed citizens. "A dozen bourgeois of all ages," he told us proudly, "were left dead and dying."

As I left the Grenzfass I was aware of a girl of about my age walking beside me. She was dark-haired, of middle height, and neatly but poorly dressed. As the crowd leaving the beer hall flowed among the tables and benches, I noticed again and again that she would recover her position at my side.

At the doors she lifted her face into the cold night air. "You're far too obvious to be a counterrevolutionary agent," she said. "What *are* you doing here?"

I shrugged. "I came to listen. Is there any law against that?"

She looked me up and down with a completely candid appraisal. "Would you like to spend the night with me tonight, comrade?" she asked.

"I have no money," I said. "At least very little."

"I'm not a prostitute," she said easily. "I believe a woman should approach a man openly. I find drawing-room pirouetting bourgeois and humiliating."

"May I ask your name?" I said.

"Lorelei."

"Is that your real name?"

"No."

I nodded. "My name is Claus," I said. "My real name."

"Excellent." She smiled. "But have you decided, Claus? Do you wish to spend the night with me?"

"I do," I told her.

As that spring of 1919 turned toward summer, I lived, it seemed to me, in two political worlds. My army duties were concerned with rehabilitation work for injured officers, and I saw among them some of the extremes of dread that most of them felt at the prospect of a Red revolution. Once a week, however, I would change into civilian clothes and make my way to Lorelei's room. For her, revolution was the Red Dawn. Before that day it was pointless to talk, argue, justify. It was all so clear, so clean, so honest, and so totally ruthless. But I enjoyed making love to her, and slowly, somewhat bizarrely, we became friends.

For Germany, the days of torture continued. With part of our lands occupied by British and French troops, with a vengeful debt of reparations to be paid, we seemed to stagger from crisis to crisis. In the cities, the children of the poor starved. Limbless men tried to support wives whose only real access to bread was through prostitution. As I traveled the country, I saw in town after town the extent to which the state's law and order had broken down. Instead, the Freikorps, groups of nationalist ex-soldiers, would oppose themselves to the Redcommandos who were present in every port and industrial city. Sometime about now I heard in Bavaria, for the very first time, the name of Adolf Hitler.

I was discharged from the army in the autumn of 1919. The Allies had decreed, not surprisingly, that the Kaiser's former army, several million strong, should be reduced to the 100,000 officers and men of the new Reichswehr. There was no place in it for a conscript officer like myself, whose only real training, as a pilot, was of no use in a force that had been forbidden aircraft. To the misery of my country, which I felt intensely, was now added my own isolation and penury.

That winter it was Lorelei's minute Communist Party salary that kept me from starvation. I now learned what it was to be homeless. As the cold weather came on, I had been forced to abandon my rooms with the widow Hertzman, and those nights I did not stay with Lorelei were spent walking the St. Pauli red-light district or sleeping in one of the great open warehouse sheds down on the waterfront.

My companions were former sailors deprived of work when the Allies took over Germany's merchant shipping, ex-soldiers, many still suffering from appalling injuries, and groups of young people who now seemed to run wild in the city. I grew a beard because to shave daily was no longer possible; my clothes became shabby from sleeping rough; my few remaining possessions were quickly stolen. My days as an arrogant young pseudo-Englishman in prewar Cambridge seemed quite unreal. Africa was separated from the harsh realities of the present by distance, weather, hunger, and perhaps some conscious effort to put those months on Catherine Esterhazy's farm far from my mind.

Five or six times during the early winter, I earned a few marks translating letters for a Jewish company that still retained some contacts with the United States. But any regular work was impossible to obtain. Poverty, I soon discovered, had few consolations. But there were some. Stripped of all possessions but the clothes I wore and the few bits and pieces I carried in my pockets, I sometimes achieved a sort of lightheartedness. If I had eaten that day or was sitting warm around a dockyard fire, I would find myself engulfed by a strange contentment that

I could arouse to something approaching excitement when I contemplated my utter lack of responsibility to anyone. I was, I suppose, vaguely aware that a moral change was taking place in me. I stole bread once or twice from a baker's cart and begged a few pfennigs with fierce ingratitude to my benefactors.

One night as I was sitting with Lorelei over a bowl of soup, she told me that I must not come to see her anymore.

"The party," she said simply, "disapproves of our relationship. It has instructed me to find another lover. A Communist."

I suppose I sneered to hide the fear I felt at being cast out from the comforts of her bed and the little food she was able to provide. "And if the party decrees that you find another lover, you obey."

"Yes."

"Will the party choose him for you?"

She shook her dark head. "Don't pretend you don't understand, Claus," she said. "The party means more to me than any man. Without it, my life would be as empty as yours is. I can't sit all day on the waterfront and dream of Africa or England. I don't want to. I want to believe in a future."

"I'm sorry," I said. "I know what the party means to you. I even think it may be right in telling you to get rid of me."

"You're a bourgeois," she said gently. "Worse, an aristocrat. If you'd been a worker"—she shrugged—"perhaps you would even have joined the party."

"Perhaps. But I think not. It's not that I can't feel the attraction of the dream. It's the violence and the hatred that fuels it that I could never accept."

"The hatred is necessary," she said. "There'll be no revolution without it."

I stood up. "Do you want me to go now?"

I suppose I expected her to say no, to ask me to stay one more night, but she nodded indifferently. Within moments I was walking the freezing streets of Hamburg with not even an occasional refuge available to me.

I now lived a strange life. I would do anything for money. Almost anything. I worked for two weeks as a street sweeper, until the snow thawed and I was laid off. With two desperadoes from the dosshouse on the waterfront I broke into a Swedish shipping office and collected sixty marks as my share of the haul. For a month I lived in a comfortable hotel room provided by a more-than-mature Hamburg matron, until she feared her husband suspected her twice-weekly afternoon visits.

Somehow I lived. The challenge carried its own excitement. In the raw months of January and February I enlisted with a nationalist commando for the price of a meal a day, and spent the evenings breaking up Communist or Social Democrat meetings. At my lowest ebb I waylaid my Hamburg matron in a haberdasher's shop and told her I needed a hundred marks. I remember the contempt on her face as she pulled me behind shelves of calicoes. "And if I tell you I won't give it to you, what then?"

I shrugged.

"You'll tell my husband."

"I didn't say that."

"It's what you mean. It's blackmail," she hissed at me.

Suddenly I felt infinitely weary. "I haven't eaten for two days," I said. "You've come out of the war well. I haven't. I'm not complaining, but I *am* asking for money. That's all."

Her fat jowls shuddered angrily. "I lost two sons in the war," she said. "And my husband became rich. Do you think I wouldn't exchange all this if I could bring my boys back?"

I felt shifty, dirty, humiliated. I turned to go.

"Claus." She pulled at my arm. "I didn't mean it about the blackmail," she said. "I know you're a gentleman."

"A gentleman . . ."

She opened her purse and snatched out three hundred marks. "Take it." She closed my hand over the notes. "Book a room at the Hotel Silberheim for Wednesday." Her eyes glittered. "Just once more. I'll make sure you don't regret it."

One day I wandered into the British Seamen's Mission on the waterfront. It was run by the English Salvation Army and known to be good, *in extremis*, for tea and a slice of bread and jam. But, of course, we would have to sing a hymn or two for our supper. I didn't really object. The round-faced girl in the black and red Victorian uniform smilingly accepted my lie about a lost seaman's ticket and motioned me to a table where mugs of tea and plates of bread and jam were being set. We sang our hymns, standing with our hands clasped piously as if protecting our genitals. The first hymn was "Onward, Christian

Soldiers." I knew the words from Sunday-morning services in little stone churches in England. Well, the sadness was that the Christian soldiers had indeed marched. On August 4, 1914, and against each other.

There were two or three other hymns, rousing melodies from the *Ancient and Modern,* and then one I thought Lorelei would particularly have enjoyed. It was called "All Things Bright and Beautiful," and its first verse assured us without a shadow of doubt that we were high in God's regard. The second verse—I think it was the second—described what was clearly the hymn writer's ideal of society: "the rich man in his castle, the poor man at his gate." God made us, we were told, high or lowly, and he not only underwrote the status quo, but he had actually devised the whole rotten system—He had ordered our estate. Afterwards the round-faced girl, who introduced herself as Lieutenant Jenkins, asked me if I had enjoyed the singing, and I confessed that I had. "You seem an appreciative sort of man," she told me. "Perhaps you would like to stay awhile out of the cold. We keep a few newspapers and periodicals for the more serious type of seaman. You'd be surprised how many there are," she added.

I thanked her and said I would like to accept her offer.

"It must be a very hard life at sea," she said, innocently patronizing, "for a man like you."

"It's a harder life on land," I said, and then guiltily tried to soften the remark with a smile. "Salvation Army, all gone barmy," young Pamela Lusk had sung outside her father's office window. But there are many millions of men in the state I was in that day who have been deeply grateful to them. I certainly was.

I took the pile of newspapers and periodicals and was allowed to sit in a small room with a glowing iron stove. Warm, and full of bread and jam, a cigarette and a glass of schnapps would have completed my pleasure, but the Salvation Army approved of neither. I turned to my reading matter.

The journals were all, of course, in English, and many of them were of an age that suggested they had been remaindered from a dentist's waiting room. They were also an extraordinarily varied collection. There were, for instance, the September 1916 issue of the *Proceedings of the Institute of Mechanical Engineers,* and a copy of the *Lancet* devoted entirely to current developments in the techniques of emergency amputation. It wasn't difficult to guess where all that recent information had come from. There were two copies of the *Tatler* not more than six months or so old. It has to be explained that the *Tatler* was, and still is, a unique journal in that it is devoted almost exclusively to reporting British society. I was reading for some reference to Diana, and I did indeed find a photograph of her at Henley, looking relaxed and beautiful. Charles Chrysler stood beside her, the proud fiancé, as well he should have been. In the group I identified Harry Towers, laughing as good-naturedly as ever. Tommy Wandle, also a Corinthian, was there, and a powerfully built, dark-faced young man I remembered as the Honorable Tom Boscowan, Lord Evered's son. The marriage of Lady Diana Winslow to Mr. Charles Chrysler, the caption noted, having been delayed by the recent death of her mother, Lady Jessica Winslow, would now take place in the spring, possibly in Venice.

There was a second photograph, in a later copy of the magazine. In it, Buzz was at her side in homburg hat and fur-collared coat, escorting her up the gangplank of a liner bound for New York. There she was to meet her future parents-in-law, Mr. and Mrs. Vanerl Chrysler of Connecticut. Lord George Winslow, the caption further told us, who would be accompanying his sister to New York, had had his name linked in the last year with those of a number of the daughters of the most distinguished families in the land.

Buzz, I thought with affection, had clearly already acquired for himself a somewhat raffish reputation. It wasn't difficult to read the editor's intention: Lord George Amadeus Winslow was one of the fast set, to be seen as a serious prospect by the matchmakers of London society only when he had finished sowing his wild oats. In Buzz's case, I could have told them, that would not be for some time.

I placed the two pictures of Diana side by side. Could I really feel all about this girl that I seemed to feel? I had, after all, only met her once, six years ago, when she was still barely fifteen years old. I had received a few letters from her and a photograph or two. How could it possibly be love I felt for her? Or again, why should it not be? What difference did it make if she represented to me that part of my earlier life that was drawn toward England and aristocracy and a life of Corinthian opulence? Was it surprising that in my present condition, a mendacious supplicant for bread and jam on the Hamburg waterfront, I should be drawn to all these things?

I studied her face in the photographs. It had been a long time since I felt that ache that made me glimpse a strange girl and see Diana, quite impossibly, in the street of a small French town behind the front line or, perhaps marginally more probable, in the lounge of the Stanley Hotel in Nairobi, later in the war.

Young as I was, I was aware of the danger. Utterly remote from reality, she was the stuff that dangerous dreams are made of. I did not wish to be haunted by images of Diana for the rest of my life, but at this moment I had few defenses left. When the round-faced Salvation Army lieutenant put her hand on my shoulder and said she was sorry but I would have to go now, I nodded dumbly.

"Ah, you poor man," she said. "You poor man."

One spring day I collapsed in the street. I woke up a week later in an officers' hospital, having survived, I was told, a crisis of pneumonia that brought me close to death. By a minor miracle, a comrade from my old regiment had recognized me as I lay on the pavement.

Sick, fevered dreams have a power beyond our nightly offerings. Before my collapse on the Hamburg Zentralplatz, I believe that I had not dreamed of Diana for the last four months. But during those first tortured nights in hospital she had returned so strongly to me that when I awoke, at last fully conscious, I could think only of her.

In a worn wallet I had kept her photographs and three of her letters. In the well-fed warmth and comfort of the hospital, I resolved one day to find out why suddenly there had been no more letters—why suddenly she had agreed to marry Charles Chrysler.

SEVEN

When I left the hospital I received a letter from Buzz, forwarded from Army Command in Berlin. It carried United States postage stamps.

Dear Old Thing.

Why haven't you written? Why are you silent? Where are you living? What are you doing? Who are you rogering? England's in the grip of the Socialist International. Port, claret, and especially champagne prices (thanks to your countrymen's late activities in that area) have gone through the roof. Never mind. I am spending the most delightful holiday with Diana and Charles. We've traveled all New England and America and have now gone west. California, of course, has never seen a female so delectable. Charlie Chaplin, funny little man that he is, tried to press her into making a film with him! Of course she refused. But one must admire the little chap's nerve. All, all send their love. Harry Towers, Tommy Wandle, Bruiser Boscowan, and Charles of course. Diana sends you an indecently long kiss, and Margaret Ryder's thoughts on the subject are much too impossibly lewd to commit to the United States mail.

America I adore. Charles's family own the best stable of polo ponies in New England, and undoubtedly the finest set of houses from Kentucky to Vermont. I myself am desperately looking for an heiress who is not too obviously Jewish or Sicilian, who is under forty and tolerably slim, who is inordinately tolerant of a husband's peccadilloes, who doesn't actually squint and is generous to a fault. Not surprisingly, they're not all that thick on the ground.

I crave a word from you. All reports from Germany are of

most frightful conditions for the returning troops, officers and men. Put my mind at rest, there's a good chap.

Buzz

I wrote a careful letter in reply. I described conditions in the northern ports as I had seen them. I took care not to suggest that I had *experienced* them. I told him that our estates in the east had been swallowed up by Poland and that I had been discharged from the army and was now looking for employment. It was a flat, factual, but essentially dishonest letter. His reply was a bombshell:

Oh, you fucking idiot. Reading between the lines of your letter, I wept. Friendship's worth more than your Hunnish pride. Be in Venice, the Palazzo Bellini, April 2, for Diana's wedding. Don't fail us. Love and kisses,

Buzz

With the letter was a money draft for a thousand guineas!

I arrived in Venice at the end of March, and took a room at the Hotel San Moise overlooking one of the smaller waterways. For the first hour I watched from my window the unloading of an enormous gondola piled with vegetables on the stone quayside opposite. I felt like a gentleman again. I smile at my use of the term, but I was wearing a good suit, I carried leather luggage, I had tipped the concierge. That warming respect, granted not to the man but simply to the trappings of the man, was again extended to me by porters and waiters, by men and women alike.

But I knew myself to be a hollow shell, a sham. To begin with, I was speaking only English. At the hotel I was taken to be English or American, and I made no effort to correct the impression. Beyond all doubt, I would never be a gentleman again. To be such required a certain naiveté about the world, a certain mind-set, a belief that in no circumstances would you act in an ungentlemanly manner. Of course, the rules were infinitely elastic. They tended, for instance, to exclude trifles like adultery and homosexual philandering. It was much more important to pay one's debts, to honor friendships, to play the game. Important, too, to play the game with a certain lofty style. This, it seemed to me as I watched from my hotel window, was all I had left. The substance had been destroyed in a few short months of poverty; the form I retained for the world to see.

I took a boat to the Palazzo Bellini the evening before the wedding. The sun had set, leaving a great dome of pale light in the darkened sky. The boatman pointed across the water. "The Palazzo Bellini, signor," he said.

Lights shone through windows framed in carved stone. As the gondolier trailed his pole I could hear the sound of dance music coming from the rooms beyond a stone balcony that stretched the length of the peeling, red-plastered wall. We drifted across the broad canal. The domes of Santa Maria della Salute rose above the jumbled slopes of the palace roofs. With a few deft movements the boatman brought us under the water arches and into the vaulted, gaslit canal entrance of the palace. As we bumped gently against the jetty, the man reached up and hauled on a dangling bell-chain.

I paid off the boatman. Water lapped a stone stairway, green with algae. I stepped out of the boat and climbed to the level of a broad wooden door. A butler appeared in fusty green livery. I gave my name and he conducted me up long flights of tiled stairs, along painted galleries, and through domed chambers. Everything around me muttered of decay. Great gilded picture frames hung askew, rivulets of condensation wrought patterns in the ocher-pink distemper of the walls. Stone balustrades sagged, and plaster ceilings gaped to reveal patchworks of lathing. But from somewhere close the sound of music and a hundred speaking voices swelled through the emptiness.

Then a wholly familiar voice echoed from a gallery somewhere above my head. "Look around you, dear boy, look around you. *Si monumentum requiris.* . . . You see a whole civilization crumbling to dust."

I looked up. Buzz hung his head and shoulders over a none-too-safe stone balustrade. "Claus, my dear boy!" he bawled. Then his face disappeared and I heard him clattering down the tiled staircase.

He appeared again on the landing above me. Wearing a cravat and a kilt, he looked perfectly in place in these extraordinary surroundings. He had put on a little weight, and his rich blond hair sparkled in the light of a flambeau. *"Je flippe, je danse,"* he sang. *"Je suis très électrique.* Yum, yum." Leaping down the remaining stairs, he threw himself at me.

"You've made the party," he said, hugging me. "Diana will be joyous. Charles, Harry Towers, Margaret Ryder, Tommy Wandle, they're all desperate to see you again. Let me look at you, old chap. God's teeth, you're thin! A German forest wolf! Still, we'll fatten you up with champagne and good cigars. Listen," he said in that familiar, elegant mix of English and American accents, "I'm babbling on like a court jester. But I have to hide my pleasure somehow. A fool I ever will be in the eyes of the serious world! Have you joined the serious world yet, Claus?"

"One thing at a time," I protested. He was leading me toward the dance music coming from behind high carved doors. I stopped him. "Buzz, I have to talk to you," I said urgently. "The thousand guineas saved my life. But it was madly generous."

"It was yours, old chap." He waved his hand dismissively. "If there had been no war and you had stayed two more years at Cambridge, five hundred a year is what Richard had decreed. Nothing to do with me, old chap."

"But there *was* a war," I said. "And I didn't stay at Cambridge."

"Not another word about it. A gentleman never discusses money." He threw open the doors to a vast salon. Log fires burned at either end. Perhaps a hundred people in evening dress were dancing, chatting in groups, drinking by the fire. Cigarette smoke rose toward great chandeliers. A Negro band played on a raised dais where once Venetian noblemen had received news of ships lost and others safely returned. Ribbons thrown from the gallery were strewn across the shoulders of the dancers or trailed from the girls' hair. A dozen perfumes and a hundred colors, of painted woodwork, of tapestries and girls' dresses, overwhelmed my senses.

Then Diana came toward me. She did not look joyous. Under her pale blond eyebrows her eyes were as blue as her gleaming satin dress. She was more than I had imagined for her, taller, more slender, and, by every conceivable standard by which we judge women, golden. But her face was somber, her sculpted lips untouched by a smile.

Buzz had noticed nothing. He was calling across the heads of the dancers to tell old friends I had arrived.

She took my hand. "Darling Claus," she said softly.

I held her hand for as long as I dared.

"Have you really suffered so much?" I knew she expected no answer. Not here. Perhaps never. She would be married in the morning.

I heard Harry Towers shouting to me from the far corner of the room.

"I must know what happened. I must have an answer," I said quickly. "I need that at least."

She looked shaken now, nervous. "Yes," she said. "You shall have an answer. Just tell me one thing," she said. "Will you always love me? Always?"

"God knows." I felt close to fainting. "God knows," I said.

Harry Towers grabbed my hand. Margaret Ryder flung her arms around my neck. Charles was there, grinning hugely, punching me delightedly in the chest. The party swirled around me. I drank glass after glass of champagne. I talked incessantly. I danced with unknown girls.

The evening became a nightmare. Like the fevered dreams I had just passed through, I remembered scraps of talk only. Harry Towers, red-faced, rocking on his heels: "England's changed out of all recognition, old boy," he told me. "The sparkle's gone out of the champagne. People give you those dark looks as much as to say, 'What right do *you* have to come back unharmed when old so-and-so died?' Always jabbering on about the finest flower of England being left in France. Don't realize it's an insult to the rest of us. What are we, old boy, the survivors? Bloody dockweed? Bloody ragwort? Not the finest flower, old chap, that's for certain. Same in Germany, probably. I tell you, I'm getting out."

"Out?"

"Out of England. Abroad. The colonies. Buzz says Africa's the place for us. A new life. All that."

I remember Margaret Ryder, "Bunty," as most people seemed to call her now, elegant and more outspoken than ever. "Damn the war," she said. "Damn the war. Do you ever think of what a delightful liaison we might have had without it? You were such a lovely boy then. You're not a boy any longer, are you, Claus?

More like, what did Buzz call you, a forest wolf? A cautious, watchful, German forest wolf. Well, maybe you've had your fill of Europe too. You must come out to Africa to see me," she said. "I was left a property out there by my sweet William, my Anglo-Russian cousin."

"Everybody's planning to leave England, you know," voices reiterated all evening. "Buzz says Kenya's a wonderland."

"Yes, a wonderland."

"We're all going, you know. We've all had enough. We're all quite determined."

Buzz, of course, was the prime mover. He saw postwar London as gray and grim. Most important, the Winslow debts would never allow him a decent life in England, he said. He was transplanting the Corinthians, lock, stock, and barrel to Africa. In East Africa life was dirt cheap, champagne a few shillings a bottle, servants a few shillings a month. "I shall call the new world into existence," he proclaimed, "to redress the imbalance of the old."

Did I think they were serious? Charles Chrysler thought it was all daydreams. He had other plans. After the honeymoon was over, he intended to stay in Europe to establish an air passenger line. He had already purchased two ex-RAF Vimy bombers and was having them converted in Paris. "Think of it, Claus," he said. "London to Paris in two hours."

"Will you and Diana live in London?"

"I've taken a house in Mayfair," he said. "You know you're welcome to come and stay at any time."

I enjoyed seeing Tommy Wandle again. Friendly, jovial, he pulled me aside and we sat in a fluted stone alcove on a marble window seat and talked about the war. He had served with Buzz in 1915 in Belgium and he had many stories to recount. He was not—Buzz, that is—entirely amenable to military discipline, Tommy told me, and in the opinion of most Greenjacket officers his military career could as easily have ended in a dishonorable discharge for insubordination as in a medal. Twice his colonel had taken him before the brigadier for refusing to conduct a tactical withdrawal. He was, Tommy said, and I could certainly believe it, a most ferocious trench soldier. Before a battle he would listen to Mozart on the big, red-trumpeted gramophone he kept in his dugout, or would slosh through the mud of the company trenches reading Virgil aloud. His fellow officers called him Mad Amadeus.

"Once we'd gone over the top," Tommy said, "he was really quite mad. He carried a pistol in one hand and a spiked club in his right, and he'd lead his men into the German frontline trench, howling like a banshee." Tommy stopped for a moment and grinned sheepishly. "Good thing you two didn't come face to face."

Amid noise and drink and talk and music the evening rolled on, a carnival with its own momentum. I met more people who talked of Africa: Tom Boscowan, now grown into a cold-eyed lecher with brushed-back hair and a hard, aggressive face; a new friend of Buzz's named Boy Carstairs, a tense, pale-faced young man, the only one during the whole evening who made a point of reminding me I was German.

"Buzz tells me you were one of the original Corinthians," he said with a sardonic smile that challenged me to confirm such an apparent improbability.

"I was one of the charter members."

"Are you full-blooded German?" he asked, as if he were talking to an Indian brave.

"I'm half English," I said, "by blood."

"But German by inclination."

"I grew up in Germany," I said carefully. "My mother lived there."

"You chose the wrong side, old chap." He pretended to laugh. "Were you in the war?" It was an outside guess, an instinct, a hope.

"Chest trouble," he said, pale and angry.

"Lucky man." I turned away.

Buzz, just behind me, was smiling. "Good for you, old fellow," he said. "But don't let Carstairs worry you. He's a good sort when you get to know him. Frightful pouncer. The girls like his tubercular good looks."

He steered me through the madly dancing crowd toward two pretty dark-blond girls surrounded by a knot of young men. The Mowbray sisters, he explained, were both married to immensely dull husbands at home in London. "If the Beast is troubling you for attention," he said, in their presence, "the Mowbray girls can be terribly understanding."

They giggled and fluttered and said how dreadful Buzz was.

But they were both totally under his spell. They too, in the course of the evening, talked of Africa.

Before midnight I took Buzz aside and told him I was leaving.

He cocked his head on one side and gave me his look of theatrical puzzlement.

"I'm still not fit, Buzz," I said. "I need to get back and rest."

"But you're staying here. I'll send a man around to the hotel for your luggage."

"No, Buzz." I shook my head. "It will be quieter at the hotel."

He raised his eyebrows in a way I had once caught him practicing before a mirror. "And tomorrow?" he asked. "Will you be fit enough for the wedding?"

I was silent. "I shall have to see," I said at length. "If not, you'll understand. Both of you. Diana too."

He put his arm around my shoulder. "I know about the letters, old chap," he said. "I know you and Diana were corresponding during the war."

"What else do you know?" In my convalescent weakness I felt close to tears. "What else do you know that I don't?"

"Diana must talk to you," he said. "Now."

"I'm leaving, Buzz," I told him. "I shouldn't have come. It was the money that brought me here. I came to thank *you*, not to make demands on Diana."

He indicated the doors to the salon. "Wait for her outside. I'll get her now."

I left the room and stood for a moment in the flickering shadows of the landing. I could not remember which flight of steps I had ascended with the butler. I took one and passed through a narrow door onto a stone gallery overlooking the open central courtyard of the palace. The air was cold now, and scraps of mist hung about the arched cloisters below. Diana's footsteps sounded behind me.

"Claus," she called.

I could not walk away. I turned back and saw her at the doorway. She came forward, bare-shouldered in the chill of the night. She walked slowly. Raised in her hand before her mouth was a long amber holder in which a cigarette glowed. She stopped in front of me.

"Buzz said you were leaving."

"Yes."

"Before we had talked?"

I nodded.

"Do you no longer wish to know?"

"If you'll tell me, I wish to know."

"I'm cold," she said. "Let's walk."

I moved to take off my coat to give to her, but she shook her head. "It's not a long story."

Guests ran past us along the gallery, trailing streamers or carrying foaming bottles of champagne. From a stone bench she reached down and picked up an abandoned shawl. The jazz music from the great salon on the gallery above us blasted across the rooftops toward the domes of Santa Maria della Salute.

"After I had received three letters from you," she said slowly, "in that summer of 1916, I was already needing words from you as I needed food and sleep. Your letters were the only thing that kept me sane. I mean that. It was only with the help of those letters that I was able to fight the horrid hopelessness of that summer."

Screams of feigned alarm came from the tier of stone galleries above us. Figures flitted past the flaring gaslights in the courtyard below.

"Then one evening," she said, "I returned home from the World's End Hospital. I was tired, miserable, and afraid, always afraid, that you were there on the Somme. . . . "

Her heels clicked on the stone flags, punctuating her words. "Richard opened the door to me himself. He told me there were two men waiting for me in the morning room. He said that they were police officers from Scotland Yard. I suppose I knew. Richard stood beside me as the two police inspectors showed me a copy of a letter—one of mine to you." She stopped. "You cannot imagine the humiliation," she breathed the word, "of your own adolescent outpourings transcribed by a clerkly hand. They read me selected sentences, Claus. They asked me what I meant by this or that. Then they took me—Richard was not allowed to be with me this time—they took me to Gerard's Row police station. That night I appeared before a magistrate and I was remanded to Holloway Prison under the Defense of the Realm Act. I spent two nights in Holloway's Women's Prison, Claus. . . . "

I held her tight to me.

"I was questioned. Richard did God knows what behind the scenes. On the third day I was taken before the magistrate again and discharged. Under police supervision I wrote to Switzerland to say that there must be no more letters from you."

I still remembered, with total clarity, the weeks of waiting for those letters.

"Richard said nothing at all. Although of course we both knew that if the story of the letters ever got out, I had destroyed any hope of his speaking out against the war."

"He intended to do that?"

"Yes," she said. "As a peer of the realm and a holder of the V.C., he saw it as his duty to speak for the soldiers in France, to speak out, he had said to me, against the awful bloodlust of our generals." She smiled bleakly. "A V.C. could hardly be denounced as a coward."

"No."

"In September I began to pick up a few rumors. Margaret Ryder asked me one day—drunk she certainly was—if I'd heard anything from dear Claus lately. There were one or two worrying whispers. Then in November I discovered Richard was to go back to France. Of course he had volunteered."

"You think he too had heard the rumors?"

"And of course knew them to be true."

"What did you do?"

"I begged him not to go. I begged him . . . I promised him I should put a cap on all rumors. I told him I would marry Charles Chrysler. And I provoked another proposal of marriage that same night. Which I accepted."

"Richard went to France nevertheless."

"Yes. Mama, of course, never forgave me."

A handbell was ringing somewhere inside the palace. "Time for bed," a male voice intoned. "Choose your beds now, please." This was greeted with shouts and laughter. "Time for bed. Wedding bells tomorrow early. Time for bed. . . ."

"Wedding bells tomorrow?" I said.

She nodded. Her mouth moved. I saw her teeth glisten in the lamplight.

I could stand it no more. "Charles must be told," I said.

She stopped walking and turned toward me. There was no

alarm, no fear on her face. "It will make no difference," she said evenly.

"For God's sake, it will make all the difference in the world."

"I will marry Charles tomorrow," she said with icy determination.

As I watched her face, a sudden strange thought struck me. "The war's over," I said desperately. "The Peace Treaty is signed. You don't have to marry Charles anymore."

She stood silently before me.

With growing dismay I realized she had not told me the full truth. Perhaps she understood what I was thinking. She had closed her eyes. She stood for a moment, rocking blindly. "I will marry Charles tomorrow," she repeated.

I think perhaps her eyes were still closed as I walked away. I reached a staircase and blundered down into the courtyard. And yet I turned to look back. From a dark corner of the cloister I could see a man moving rapidly toward her. I could hear his voice clearly, his American-accented voice.

"Did you tell him?" Buzz asked urgently.

"Yes."

"Everything?"

She did not reply.

"Everything?"

"I couldn't. I'm marrying Charles. Isn't that enough?" Diana's voice cut through the misty air.

"Claus," Buzz shouted from the gallery. "Come back, Claus."

I turned and walked slowly through the cloister and into the courtyard.

I saw Buzz take her arm and push her forward. Then he turned away, leaving her alone.

I climbed the steps to meet her. She looked dark-eyed, exhausted. I followed her into a small room where a fire blazed in the grate. She stood looking down, her hands stretched toward the flame.

"I know you know very little about your father," she said, still staring into the fire.

I stood behind her. "My mother told me a little. Perhaps understandably it was never very much."

"The night I returned from Holloway Prison," she said flatly, "my mother called me up to her room. She was smoking a cigarette, openly for once. I stood before her, still smelling of prison, while she demanded an explanation. I told her that we were in love with each other and that we intended to marry when the war was over. My explanation provoked a storm of abuse. A most violent and ugly resentment."

"Resentment?"

"Because, unknowingly, what I had told her about us was to force from her a confession of her own."

I was gripped by a fear that carried with it a dreadful finality.

"You know my mother took little trouble to disguise the dislike she felt for you," Diana said. "In reality, it was of course your mother she disliked so much. She was violently jealous of her."

"I don't understand," I said. "Why should your mother have been jealous of mine?"

"You fool," she said gently, "because they were both in love with the same man."

"Your mother was in love with Thomas Winslow?" I said slowly. The fear was growing. "Your mother was in love with her own brother-in-law?"

"Thomas Winslow," she said, turning to face me, "was an attractive rogue. By his liaison with your mother, he produced you." She lifted her head until our eyes met. "By his later liaison with his brother's wife, *my* mother, he sired *me*."

I seemed to be fighting for breath. I took a chair and leaned over it. Diana and I were half-brother and sister. I could have howled with pain. "You weren't going to tell me. You weren't going to tell me," I found myself repeating.

From somewhere behind me I heard her voice. "You know why, Claus," she said. "I'm sure you know why. I couldn't bear the finality of telling you."

She came to me. She had had so much longer than I to live with the knowledge. "It couldn't possibly make any difference to what I feel about you," she said. "But apart from that it makes every difference in the world."

She kissed me recklessly. We clung together while Charles's voice echoed through the galleries: "Diana, Diana, everybody's saying good night. . . . Where is the girl? Diana?"

I knew she could feel the swelling against her thin satin dress. She reached down and touched me. Then she broke away and, without looking back, walked toward the door.

[149]

SOME
OTHER
LANDSCAPE

E I G H T

On November 14, 1931, watched by herds of silent gazelles, a long procession made its way across the open plain toward a rocky knoll rising above the lake at Soysambu. Behind a simple wooden bier drawn by four oxen straggled a column of people several hundred yards long.

In the still, astonishing air of an African morning the migration across the plain was captured with the historic precision of a sepia photograph. Then a breeze lifted from the west and the column was seen to be moving, the dust real dust, rising and drifting slowly back across the brown scar of the line of march. Old-time Kenya settlers in torn and stained bush jackets shuffled through the rippling waves of veld grass beside white-suited officials from the Nairobi government. Uniformed police and army officers walked beside bearded Dutchmen and clergymen in surplices and sun helmets. At a distance, tall Masai *morani* stalked the procession in hide cloaks, their long spears held as staffs. Catherine Esterhazy walked among new settlers she had never before met; ranchers or coffee growers formed their own groups; Nairobi administrators met District Officers they had not seen for months; the twenty or thirty people who formed the group around the young Lord Winslow were notably the best-dressed among the civilian mourners present.

Above, a bank of heavy white cloud rolled silently down from the Mau mountain. On the single outcrop of jumbled rocks that rose from the grass plain, the blossoms of wild aloes flared red. It was here on this knoll, without headstone or mark, that Henry, sixth Lord Delamere, had decreed that he should be buried.

The Nairobi *Banner-Post* had devoted a whole edition to his death. Under a half-page headline, DELAMERE IS DEAD, it recorded:

> Our leader has passed on. It is no disrespect to the Governor of Kenya Colony to say that Lord Delamere was more our leader than any appointee of the government in London could ever be. He was one of us, almost the first to break the earth in a new land. He spent his fortunes on farming experiments for our benefit and his vast energies on political activity designed to ensure that white civilization should remain paramount in Kenya.
>
> In the turbulent days to come there will be no Lord Delamere to lead us. There will be no Lord Delamere to speak for us against that growing number of people in London who believe, in their ignorance, that a society of mixed equal races is possible in Kenya.
>
> But Lord Delamere has indicated the path we should follow. A free and independent Kenya must be our aim, nothing short of a Dominion of Kenya, as South Africa, Australia, Canada and New Zealand are Dominions. But who will lead us along this path? Who will, or can, replace Lord Delamere? Who will raise Lord Delamere's motto on a new African flag: For King and Kenya?

At Soysambu the coffin was lowered, the grave filled, the great stones piled on top to ward off the scavengers of the night. The mourners, streaming back across the plain to where they had left their cars or oxcarts, said little to one another. Old-timers nursed memories of the eccentric Delamere, hair down to his shoulders, leading a drunken party to shoot out the new Nairobi streetlights, or other memories of his great champagne parties for six hundred guests at the old Nairobi Club.

Reassembled at their cars, Lord Winslow's friends drank iced drinks in the shade of large parasols held by African boys. Tom Boscowan, the newly arrived Brick Taylor-Hammond, Sir Harry Towers, and Boy Carstairs all stood in one group around the Mowbray girls, Paula Upton-Mallet and Nancy Hofmanthal.

Others leaned on the hoods of the American cars that the group favored, and drank champagne and laughed at the envious looks of settlers who had not thought to bring their own refreshment.

They were mostly in their late twenties and early thirties, married or partly married, the products of Eton and Winchester, Oxford and Cambridge and the country houses, large and small, of England. There were Americans too, the Ryskamp brothers, friends of Edward, Prince of Wales, and the beautiful, sad-faced Gloria Tate-Adams, who had followed Buzz Winslow to Africa and now resorted to the silver morphine syringe to retain an air of fashionable insouciance in the face of his coming marriage to Lady Margaret Ryder. And others: a Russian princess who lived as Gloria's companion, a Belgian who had made his fortune in the Congo before the age of thirty and had moved to Kenya to enjoy it. Some had even bought farmland and had installed a manager to work it. But they were all still recognizably of Buzz Winslow's set, Corinthians born or liberally adopted.

Buzz Winslow and Margaret Ryder sat on rugs beneath colorful golf umbrellas with Diana and Charles Chrysler.

"Some people," Diana said, "may think a champagne picnic at a funeral less than good form, Buzz. Or do you do it on purpose?"

"Diana, my darling," Buzz said. "I do nothing on purpose. I follow my quite ghastly inclinations. No man can be responsible for his own proclivities—though he may be condemned for them."

"In any case," Margaret Ryder said, "here in Kenya we live in a different world. Where else would one attend a funeral wearing a dress more appropriate for Ascot?"

Charles Chrysler raised his glass to Margaret. "To the next Lady Winslow," he said.

Automatically, Diana lifted her glass to her lips, but Margaret reached forward and laid her finger on her wrist, preventing her. "Diana must not drink," she said with alcoholic imperiousness. "She doesn't approve of the marriage—I can feel it in my bones."

"Rubbish," Buzz laughed.

"Bunty, darling," Diana said, removing Margaret's fingers from her wrist, "I've come a good many thousand miles to show my disapproval, if that's what you think."

[155]

"I *know* you disapprove," Margaret said. "You think I'm too old or too promiscuous or something."

"Please, Bunty," Diana said carefully. "We've been friends since the war. You know how close we've been."

Margaret finished her champagne and held her glass out for more. "You're wrong, Diana," she said. "I *am* good enough for him. I'm exactly the wife he needs."

"Bunty, Bunty." Diana leaned forward and put her arm around her shoulder. "I swear I never said different."

Buzz clapped his hands. "Subject's closed," he said. "Next one to mention it gets a good thrashing."

Margaret responded to Diana's hug. "I do love him most dreadfully, you know," she half-whispered to Diana. "Even if it is in my own peculiar way."

"What do you think about this fellow Adolf Hitler, Buzz?" Charles asked, changing the subject abruptly.

"Not a lot, old chap, to tell you the truth," Buzz said. "One of the great advantages of the African climate, you know, is that it's not conducive to thought. Sport, yes; drink, of course; rogering girls, most certainly. But not thought, my dear fellow." He shook his head. "Definitely not thought."

"He'll take Germany, you know." Charles nodded soberly. "He'll take Germany this election or the next, I'm convinced of it."

"I thought he wasn't too keen on elections," Margaret observed mildly. "I thought he went in for giving political opponents a good beating."

Charles shrugged. "He's known by some Germans as 'Adolf légalité.' Some of his followers think he's too pussyfooting to grab power. Too keen on the law of the land, too keen on elections, they say."

Diana turned her gaze on Charles. "You think it not true?"

"I'm simply trying to make up my mind," Charles said.

"After the last election in Germany," Diana said, "I'm told Hitler personally rebuked the more strongarm elements in his party. He pointed out the party's success with the voters so far. 'God send me elections,' he's reported to have said."

"No, no, old girl." Buzz shook his head. "You've got it wrong there. What Hitler was actually doing was quoting Flaubert. 'God send me *erections*,' is what Our Leader really said. Chap had trouble in that department." Buzz nodded gravely. "Well-known fact."

Now just passing her thirtieth year, Diana Chrysler's physical presence had matured to the point no newspaper photographer or hostess could resist. In New York and Washington she had become sought after as a necessary bait for other guests at fashionable parties. An invitation accepted by Diana Chrysler was sufficient to guarantee the most prestigious guest list. When in London, her photograph was seen weekly in the pages of the *Tatler*, and her friendship with the Prince of Wales guaranteed she was never out of the limelight of the popular press. Yet she herself knew she had done nothing to deserve this attention. She had never been falsely modest about the looks she had inherited. Nor was she unaware that to be known as Lady Diana Chrysler was preferable to plain "Mrs. Chrysler." But despite the storm of public attention that had gathered in her mid-twenties and finally broken around her head, she retained some distance from the blandishments of celebrity.

Perhaps for this reason, the need to do something to justify her fame, she had persuaded Charles to teach her to fly. And once she had discovered she was an adequate pilot of an aeroplane, perhaps it was because of this desire to chase and justify the celebrity she had been already accorded that she began a series of first-time solos across South America and Africa. She was well aware that she lacked the courage or the desperation to fly solo across the great gray Atlantic. She had met Beryl Markham in Nairobi and believed her when she had said she would be the first woman to solo fly the Atlantic. She herself had done much less, taken contained, calculated risks and posed afterwards in flying boots and well-cut breeches, brushing back her golden hair as she removed her flying helmet in Rome or Istanbul or Khartoum or Stanleyville. She was in the minor league of fliers, but she had achieved something at least in pursuit of her own celebrity.

Her life with Charles, she knew, was built on this quicksand. In the years after the war he had used his vast inheritance to build air passenger services across the United States. It had not stopped him from being known as Lady Diana Chrysler's husband, just as George Putnam was known as Amelia Earhart's husband. Diana believed Charles both resented and enjoyed their relative roles. They saw remarkably little of each other in any one year: a fortnight in Antibes, Ascot for the Derby, perhaps a week's skiing at St. Moritz. Then a day or two in Chicago or New York or California, in all perhaps eight out of ten weeks in the year—not enough, the newspapers hinted, to remain truly married.

"Jesus wept," Buzz said in a cockney accent. "Old mother Partridge wants an intro to my famous sister."

A big middle-aged woman, her face brick-red from many years of African sun, had detached herself from the group she was walking with.

Buzz got to his feet and removed his soft-brimmed straw hat as she approached. "Elenor," he said cooly, "how very pleasant to see you. May I present my sister, Diana, and her husband, Charles Chrysler. My fiancée, Lady Margaret Ryder, you already know."

He turned to Charles, who was scrambling to his feet. "Mrs. Partridge farms vast acreages at Nanyuki and at Elmenteita and at Thika and at—"

"I have a number of farms," Mrs. Partridge said, shaking hands with Charles. "Lord Winslow exaggerates, as ever, their extent."

"Sheer modesty on Elenor's part," Buzz said, shaking his head vigorously. "If she doesn't own Kenya outright, there are a lot of people in the colony who think she does. Reasonable mistake, I assure you."

"I came over to meet Lady Diana and her husband," Mrs. Partridge said, turning toward Diana. "Even in Kenya we've heard a great deal about your flying exploits."

"You mustn't make me out to be an Amelia Earhart or a Beryl Markham," Diana said, smiling.

"Nevertheless, to fly across the Sahara in a small one-seater aeroplane is an *exploit*."

"But not heroic," Diana said. "A purely commercial exploit to publicize my husband's air passenger lines."

"Even so, the newspapers considered it to be not without risk for a pretty young woman like yourself. Should you have been obliged to make a false landing, I mean, in the Sahara." She lifted her eyebrows.

"Ah, but she was well equipped," Buzz said. "Charles insisted she carry with her the very latest in chastity belts from Saks Fifth Avenue!"

Mrs. Partridge's face tightened. "Quite so," she said. "I must rejoin my party." She gestured over her shoulder. "Good-bye, Lady Diana, Mr. Chrysler. Will you be in Kenya long?"

"For a week or two at the most. We're here for the wedding, of course," Charles said.

"Yes . . ." Elenor Partridge allowed her glance to fall briefly on Margaret Ryder. "So very pleased to have met you. Rather surprised that you came today, Lord Winslow."

"Wouldn't have missed it," Buzz said, conducting her between the parked cars. "Wouldn't have missed the main event."

"The main event?"

"Delamere meets his Maker. Still not sure who my money's on, I must say."

They shook hands. Buzz watched her walk back to her waiting friends, then he turned, laughing, toward the circle of parasols and golf umbrellas. "They love to hate us," he said as he threw himself down onto the rugs and tipped his straw hat over his eyes, "but there's not one of the old-timers who can resist the notoriety. Except that one, perhaps."

Catherine Esterhazy, striking in a long skirt, a white bush shirt, and a broad-brimmed sun hat, walked back to her car with a settler who farmed on the slopes above Lake Naivasha.

"Who's that?" Diana looked in the direction Buzz was pointing.

"She's the woman who owns the farm at Ngong where Claus lived in the last months of the war. Catherine Esterhazy."

Charles looked at her with interest. "Really? Claus landed on his feet, didn't he?"

"Do you think she knew Claus was German?" Diana asked slowly.

"Certain of it," Buzz said.

"And yet she still allowed him to stay."

"Of course," Buzz laughed. "He was rogering her like mad in return."

Diana turned back to Buzz. "Did Claus tell you that?"

"Tell me what, darling girl?" Buzz rolled on his back and grabbed the neck of a bottle of champagne in the ice bucket.

Charles was still watching Catherine.

"Did Claus tell you he was rogering Catherine Esterhazy all the time he was staying with her?"

"Can't imagine where else I heard it." Buzz poured champagne, spilling it across the rug.

"Either Claus told you or he didn't," Diana said sharply.

Charles turned from his examination of Catherine. His eyes rested a moment on his wife, then he got up and strolled over to where Brick Taylor-Hammond and the Mowbray sisters were laughing together.

"You don't think you were showing just a touch too much interest in dear old Claus's love life?" Buzz said. "Charles might just have considered it a mite unwifely, I would have thought."

"Stop playing with me, Buzz," Diana said, her face tense. "Yes or no. Did Claus tell you he was having an affair with that woman?"

Buzz whistled silently. "No," he said after a moment. "No. Claus said nothing. It was my own fevered imagination. Quite frankly, I've been dying to give her something to remember me by ever since I arrived in Kenya." He angled his head and smiled at his sister.

She laughed suddenly and reached out, pouring the last few drops of champagne in her glass over his forehead. "You are the most frightful bounder, brother mine," she said.

Like Catherine Esterhazy, Gerald Longman had broken new land, living in tents or thatched sheds for the first year, making mistakes with soil and climate, only slowly dragging himself out of debt with the Nairobi banks. Last year he had married the daughter of Inspector Tom Lusk. It was rumored in Nairobi that Lusk had been less than enthusiastic, although to many parents in the lower rungs of the Nairobi administration, Gerald Longman would have been considered an excellent catch for an unmarried daughter. Though still in his mid-thirties, his farming at Naivasha was regarded as a model for others to follow, and already many settlers deferred to his carefully considered opinions. To Tom Lusk, however, he was too old and too pompous for the tall, sprightly young woman his daughter had grown into.

"How are things at the farm, Catherine?" Longman's lean,

tanned face turned briefly toward her. He was a tall, thin-shouldered man, hardened from years of labor on his farm. "With coffee prices as they are," he added in explanation.

"What have you heard, Gerald?" Catherine Esterhazy said, smiling at him. "What are they saying in Nairobi, Pam?" she added as Pamela Longman waved good-bye to her father and came toward them.

"What are they saying about what, Baroness?"

"About my crop this year." She smiled. "Don't pretend you don't know. Your father knows everything."

Pamela Longman's large eyes widened. "Empty talk," she said.

"We've heard that you're not going to make much more than fifty tons this year," Longman said brusquely.

Catherine nodded. "That's common knowledge. But you've also heard something else, Gerald. I don't forget we share the same bank manager."

Longman shrugged his shoulders. The thin line of the collar-bone showed beneath his shirt. "Frankly, we heard this could be your last year."

"I've put in a little money from my family," Catherine said. "If next year's crop does no better, I shall have to sell. But for the moment I'm all right."

They stopped beside Catherine's car.

Longman took out his pipe and began to fill it from a waterproof pouch. "We can't afford to lose people like you, Catherine. Too many newcomers have arrived here these last few years."

Catherine Esterhazy watched the process of pipe-filling in silence. From an intuition rooted in her isolated life, she knew he was making more than a passing remark. Pamela Longman, too, watched her husband in silence.

"The country's changing," Longman said. "Bound to, of course, in some ways. Big Nairobi property companies starting up, that sort of thing."

"It's not a frontier any longer," Catherine agreed.

"It's the new types coming in that I'm worried about," Longman said, suddenly angry. "Aristocratic parasites. Not ranchers, not farmers. Parasites."

Catherine saw that the hand holding the now-filled pipe was shaking.

"Lord this and Sir Harry that. No intention of farming. Remittance men. And women."

"Every new country has some of them," Catherine said.

Sweat glistened in the lines of Gerald Longman's leather-brown forehead. "I was riding above Naivasha last week," he said, "when I came on a beaten circle of grass and a pair of whadyah birds performing a mating dance."

"Very rare," Catherine said. "I've only seen that once or twice since I've lived here."

"Exactly," Gerald Longman said angrily. "That's exactly what I explained to Lady Margaret and her friend Mrs. Hofmanthal as they came riding by. I was trying to be friendly, you see. We're neighbors, after all. I told them not many people had seen the whadyah dance."

"What did they say?"

"You shouldn't let them get you so worked up, Gerald," Pamela said.

Longman fumed at the memory. "They sat there watching from the saddle, these two grand ladies. 'How frightfully, frightfully suburban!' Mrs. Hofmanthal said. 'If he wants to roger her that much, why doesn't he just jump on top and get on with the job?'"

Catherine, watching his angry face, said nothing.

"That's how much interest they've got in this country," he said, snapping his fingers. "Twice times nothing."

The dust from the returning funeral column rose around them, peppery hot in their nostrils. Catherine spoke from some sense of loyalty to people who had once been friends of Claus. "I'm not sure they do a lot of harm," she said.

"I am," Longman said fiercely. "Our future depends on what the people back home in England think of us. If they see us as sex-mad, champagne-swilling time-wasters, how will the London government take us seriously? Lord Delamere claimed the right of the white race to govern Kenya. How could anybody in London take him seriously when they hear of Happy Valley goings-on?"

"Lord Winslow and his friends are a few dozen people at the most."

"Perhaps." He lit his pipe with a series of sharp inhalations. "But you never hear the end of them. Stories about them in the club, stories in the *Banner-Post*. Their influence goes beyond numbers. They come from titled families at home, and some of the settlers here are overimpressed by a title. Some of the wives even more so."

Pamela Longman nudged her husband.

"Oh, I'm not talking about Catherine's title, she knows that," Longman said. "Catherine's a farmer, she couldn't be more different."

Catherine Esterhazy smiled. "I must start back," she said. "Perhaps you worry too much about our image in London. It doesn't seem to me London cares much for us either way, settler or lounge-lizard."

They said their good-byes. For a moment Catherine sat in her open Austin, grimacing at the heat from the cracked black leather seats, and watched the Longmans thread their way through the thorn bush to their own car. Gerald Longman, she guessed, had aspirations to take over Lord Delamere's role as leader of the country's ten thousand whites. Who, she wondered, would speak for the country's two million Africans?

On the night before his marriage to Lady Margaret Ryder, Buzz Winslow arranged a stag party in the Norfolk, Nairobi's principal hotel. Women had been strictly banned from the private dining room that Charles Chrysler had reserved, and another party had been arranged at the Muthaiga Country Club by Diana for what Margaret Ryder called her "last night of demi-mondanity."

The two parties began at about eight o'clock, with lobsters at the Norfolk and foie gras at the Muthaiga. The guests at both celebrations had already consumed large numbers of Trinities or White Ladies, the favored cocktails of the new decade. At the Muthaiga, Anthea Mowbray chose the moment before the rack of lamb to propose a toast. "First speech of the evening," she said, "before we all get too fuddled to speak anything but our minds." She beamed at the ten women around the table, her waved dark blond hair sitting as perfectly as a wig on a hairdresser's plaster model.

Silence fell slowly around the table, aided by appeals from Nancy Hofmanthal.

"Darlings," Anthea Mowbray said, "we're here to help launch our old friend Margaret Ryder on her second marital voyage. I knew nothing about her first husband and so can offer no comment on the past. But I do know quite a little, *quite* a little, about her husband-to-be . . ."

"Who's boasting now?" Gloria Tate-Adams was already slurring her speech.

". . . and he's one of the most ripping men any of us have had the privilege of knowing," Anthea Mowbray continued. "Am I right?"

A chorus of "Hear, hear!" went around the table.

"Let's be serious," Anthea Mowbray insisted. "Of course we're all terribly jealous of Margaret. And I frankly could scratch her eyes out for carrying off such a beautiful prize. But there it is. That's life. Raise your glasses. Very best of luck, Bunty."

"To Margaret," they saluted, raising their glasses.

Diana watched Margaret Ryder rise unsteadily to her feet. Diana found no pleasure in this evening. As more alcohol was consumed, the jokes became more and more overt. Perhaps it was inevitable in the small, close-knit society in which these women lived. She was aware that Buzz had slept with almost all of them at one time or another. And they in turn had slept with some or most of the men now dining at the Norfolk. The record of love affairs, jealousies, one-nighters, and threatened suicides was too complex for anyone to keep any longer. There had been highlights, of course. Alice de Janzie, an etherially beautiful American girl, having abandoned her children in England, shot and wounded her lover, the odious Raymond de Trafford, in Paris. Because the incident, of which she was found guilty but immediately released, had taken place in a stationary train about to depart for England, Buzz had now dubbed her "the fastest gun in the Gare du Nord." Alice, in turn, had come back to Kenya, and fallen in love with Buzz.

There were of course other stories, sadder and less dramatic. Annabel Hartley had committed suicide; Barbara Westminster had been sued by her husband in London to resume parental care of her children—or give them to his sole wardship.

Margaret Ryder was already drunk. She thanked Anthea Mowbray for her speech, refilled her champagne glass, and thanked everybody in turn for being there. Diana, she said, she was particularly touched to see there. Lots of people, she said, were wondering what this marriage was about. "Frankly, Lord George Amadeus Winslow, Buzz to us all, has the reputation of being a frightful pouncer. I'm sure Diana won't mind my saying that there are very few women among our set who haven't been pounced on by Buzz. Facts have to be faced. But then," she went on, "it's no secret to anyone here that my own past is less than virgin white. I like men. Buzz likes women. And I don't think for a moment either of us will change."

At the Norfolk Hotel the private dining room rang to the shouts and songs of the men's party. Toward midnight, Diana passed through the lobby on her way to the suite where she and Charles were staying. She could hear the roaring and cheering from the private dining room. It had been cleared of furniture after the party, the desk clerk told her nervously, and a game of touch rugby had been organized. Bandages and cold compresses had already been called for twice.

Diana paused, listening to the weight of bodies crashing against the dining room doors. She winced slightly and turned away.

"The young stags at play," Buzz's voice said from the darkness of the terrace. He stepped forward under the light. His face was flushed and his blond hair plastered across his forehead. He was holding a drink in his hand. "You look so wonderfully disapproving."

"I wasn't disapproving," Diana said, "of anything except the noise. I was wondering how I was possibly going to sleep with that din below me."

"Still," Buzz said, "there are times you rather remind me of Richard. Do you remember how he used to stand, in his tailcoat, hands clasped behind him, mouth just slightly stern. Astonishing, really, what he could put across by a simple compression of the lips. When I was at Eton I was frankly terrified of him. But I was also tremendously proud when he escorted Mama down to Founders' Day. I loved to see the way these old chaps, the other boys' papas, always deferred to him. Astonishing, really."

She remained silent, watching him sway slightly, uncertain of his mood.

"You've got that same thing, little sister. That *je ne sais quoi.*"

"I wish I had," she said.

He raised his hand. "You most certainly have." He paused. "But then you're someone in your own right. You're the famous aviatrix that Mrs. Partridge and all her clucking friends stop to get a glimpse of."

"I must get to bed," she said, "if I'm to look my best tomorrow for Mrs. Partridge and all her clucking friends."

He stopped her with a hand on her arm. "I'll get you a drink," he said. "It's too early to go to bed."

"I think I've had enough." She took a cigarette case from her purse and offered him one. "One cigarette before I go up."

"How did the ladies' night go?" he asked, lighting their cigarettes. "Or am I not supposed to know?"

"I think it went rather well." She crossed the terrace and sat on a wooden bench facing him. "We escorted Bunty up to her room. I think she'll be all right in the morning."

Buzz stood in front of her, one foot on the bench. "What do you think, Diana?"

"What about?" she said cautiously.

Cheers and applause rose from the dining room behind them.

"About your brother's marriage," Buzz said. He took a mouthful of his drink. "You're surprised?"

"A little."

"You disapprove?"

"Not at all. I've always liked Margaret, you know that."

"Liked her *despite* her rather racy reputation?"

"If you like, yes."

He nodded. "I'm drunk, of course."

She smiled. "I'm sure Charles and the rest would think it a failure on their part if you were anything but."

"I'm drunk enough to tell you why I'm getting married."

She stood up. "Buzz, you'll regret this in the morning if you go on. I can feel it in my bones. Now let's go in and have a drink in the lounge and I'll take myself off to bed."

"I'm marrying for money," he said.

They walked along the terrace and stopped at the stone

[166]

balustrade. The sounds from the dining room were more distant.

"I'm ruining my life, Diana," he said. "Too much drink, too many parties, too many women."

"Marriage could change all that. If you wanted it to."

"I'm utterly, utterly broke," he said. "Credit's at an end."

"You could ask Charles to help you out."

He shook his head sharply.

"Why not?"

"You don't understand, little sister. It wouldn't be a matter of helping me out. It'd be keeping me. For good. I haven't a quid, buck, sou, or shilling to my name."

She turned, facing him. "Then for God's sake *do* something! All right, you ask me if I disapprove of your marrying Margaret. Of course I do! She's too old and she's got the sort of reputation only a man can afford to have. You're throwing yourself away on her. Your whole life before you, and you throw it all out of the window for a few thousand pounds."

"My whole life? You talk as if there were something really there for me in the cards. What is it you see that I don't?"

"Are you telling me you didn't see what was happening at that damn silly funeral yesterday? Are you telling me you didn't see the settlers of this colony running round like so many thousand headless chickens? They're looking for a leader, Buzz, who can take on London for them. Someone of rank they look up to. Someone like you!"

He shrugged, spilling champagne.

"And meanwhile," she said with quiet ferocity, "you huff and you puff and you marry Bunty Ryder instead."

"Perhaps you should have come to Africa sooner," he said.

She stood in the middle of the terrace, her face in shadow. "It's not too late," she said.

He recoiled, only partly theatrically. "Chuck Bunty?" he said. "The night before the wedding?"

"It's for the best."

"Little sister . . . what are you saying?"

She came forward into the light of the terrace. "I won't have it," she said.

He looked at her, frowning.

"Marrying for money is one thing, Buzz." She drew rapidly on her cigarette. "But to seem to be serious about it just won't do. You'll make the most frightful fool of yourself at home in England."

"Save me from myself," he said unsmilingly.

His mood suffered one of those lightning changes she knew so well. He was jubilant. He tossed his glass into the bushes. "God, you're beautiful," he said.

"Don't be stupid." She tried to move away from his encircling arms.

"You remember what a frightful flirt you were when you were young?" His arm tightened, pulling her closer. "I still have dreams sometimes, sweet dreams."

She twisted herself free. "Time for bed, Buzz," she said. "High time."

"Yes." Smiling, he thrust his hands deep into the pockets of his dinner jacket and followed her along the terrace. At the hotel entrance he leaned forward and kissed her lightly on the cheek. "Do you ever think, as I do, that life's a most frightful farce?"

"Yes," she said quietly.

"I've sometimes thought of ending it all, you know. Just sometimes."

"I never know when you're serious," she said.

He patted her cheek. "Nor do I." He turned and started into the hotel. "Good night, little sister," he sang over his shoulder. "Sweet dreams."

NINE

As dawn broke on the morning following her brother's wedding day, Diana sat in her hotel room at the Norfolk, finishing a long entry in her journal. From the street outside still came singing, shouts, and whoops, and from time to time even the crack of revolver shots.

She had removed the oyster silk dress she had worn for the wedding and put on a light peach-colored dressing gown. A tall coffeepot gleamed in the light of the table lamp. Within its bright circle her hand drove the pen across the page, then stopped. She was exhausted, drained now even of any desire to comment on the day's events, on the wedding of her brother Buzz to Margaret Bunty Ryder, her onetime friend.

Closing the leather volume, she locked it with the tiny silver key that hung around her neck as footsteps came unsteadily up the wooden stairs. For a moment or two she stood as her husband fumbled at the door handle; then, smiling, she crossed the room and opened it for him.

"Turning it the wrong way for some unaccountable reason," he said.

"Are you very drunk?" she asked as she packed away her journal.

"Very," Charles said. Reaching for the decanter, he poured himself a large whiskey. "Well," he said, holding the glass poised to drink, "perhaps you'll tell me what in God's name was going on yesterday."

"My brother's wedding to Margaret Ryder is what was going on," Diana said coldly.

"Jesus!" He drank half the whiskey in one gulp. "You realize she intends to cut you dead."

Diana lifted her eyebrows.

"You realize that we won't now be going back to stay at their house in Lake Naivasha because Margaret refuses point-blank to have you there."

"I see."

"Well, if you see, Diana, will you kindly explain enough to make me see too? Because at the moment I'm utterly in the dark."

"Margaret is convinced I conspired with Buzz to reduce her wedding to a farce."

"Did you?"

She hesitated. "I think I can say no. If I'm honest I'll admit that I'm not sorry the farcical element in the ceremony signaled a marriage of convenience. That's what it is, after all."

"Some of the fellows are saying that there's more to Margaret's anger than that. She's furious that you spent the whole reception at Buzz's side."

"She felt left out?"

"Of her own wedding." He paused. "What a mess." He moved his hand toward the decanter again.

"You've had enough for one day," she said. "Why don't you get to bed?"

He let his hand drop away from the decanter. "Yes," he said, "enough for one day." He struggled out of his coat, watching her as she took her peach silk nightdress from the bed.

"There's coffee in the pot," she said.

Charles sat heavily on the arm of a chair and plucked at his black tie. "Do you think much about Claus?" he asked suddenly.

She turned slowly toward him. "From time to time."

"You never hear from him when you're at one of your air sport meetings in Germany?"

"No, I haven't heard or seen anything of him for over eight years now."

Charles took a cigarette from his case and lit it. His bowtie hung around his neck; his collar had sprung from the stud at one side. "Never tried to get in touch with him."

"No."

"You spend so much time in Germany now, I would have thought you might have looked him up."

She stood next to the bathroom, her nightdress over her arm.

"I barely knew him," she said. "I met him once, just before the war, at Lady Gorringe's. I was a child at the time."

"He came to our wedding, of course."

"Yes," she said.

"So you met him just twice."

"Yes."

"Strange."

"I see nothing strange about that."

"Strange," Charles said, "because his presence still seems to hang over us. If you had once been lovers, I can't see that it could have been more potent."

"I certainly can't see that it's Claus's presence that divides us." She came into the center of the room, challenging him.

"Divides us? Yes," he mused. "Something certainly does. Perhaps always has." He finished his cigarette. "I must get ready for bed."

He walked forward and kissed her lightly on the forehead. "I believe," he said slowly, "that at some point, for some reason, you will want to leave me. I'm quite ready for it. I don't welcome it, but remember, I *am* quite ready for it."

"Are you not happy?" she asked.

"You know I'm not."

She paused, then nodded slowly. "It's true, of course. I know you're not. But I do not think it is in my power to do anything about it."

"In your power?" He smiled wryly. "Perhaps not."

She stood stiffly, half turned from him. "Why do you say that? In that manner?"

He shrugged abruptly. "Because I don't *know* if it's in your power," he said. "You're a healthy, beautiful, and talented young woman, but you live like a cripple."

She turned on him in astonishment.

"Yes," he said, "a cripple. One who needs desperately every single crutch to hand. Like a cripple grasping his crutch, I see you grasp at the emotions of the men around you: the German politicians, the aviators, the London playboys, Buzz even. Christ!" He stood up. "Why aren't drinking, dancing, and fucking good enough for you? They're good enough for all the other wives we know!"

*　　*　　*

Later that day, Charles Chrysler wrote to his cousin in New York:

My dear Jake,

My brother-in-law Buzz Winslow's wedding day has been a spectacular disaster. I write this between running around from person to person, side to side, trying to put the pieces back together. As things look at this moment, we, Diana and myself, will be leaving Kenya tomorrow. I can hear you asking what the hell has happened here and the answer is I don't know. Margaret, Buzz's wife as of yesterday, had the most appalling fight with Diana. Buzz himself laughs and hums loftily. But Margaret is *deadly* serious. She won't speak to Diana or allow her into the new marital home at Lake Naivasha. Diana is white-faced and tense; most of Buzz's friends mysteriously support Margaret's sense of grievance but will tell me nothing; Buzz continues to pretend nothing has happened whatsoever, and loftily hums his tunes from the operettas. This family is crazy. This whole damn *set* is crazy!

The day started this way. The position of best man had fallen to young Brick Taylor-Hammond, the Winslows' closest surviving male relative. In my role as chief usher, I was at the church in my tailcoat, gray top hat, and striped pants, ready for the guests to arrive. Promptly, I thought, given the hangovers everybody must have been suffering from the night before, the cars began to arrive from the direction of Nairobi at 11:00 A.M. With a couple of assistant ushers, young lads of sixteen or seventeen, I watched the first cars of the convoy bowl into the churchyard and begin to disgorge the wedding guests. Jake, my dear fellow, for this most solemn occasion they were all in fancy dress!

I guess I'd never been between pure rage and helpless laughter like this before. That poor parson! While he was busying himself before the altar with a few pre-wedding arrangements, the most ghastly pack of guests rolled down the aisle to take their places: Gypsies, Madame de Pompadours, native warriors, homosexual Roman emperors, neolithic hunters, gartered dancers from the Moulin Rouge, London bobbies, and a dozen more.

When Buzz arrived, he burst into laughter as he made his progress down the aisle, congratulating one, pretending not to recognize another as she leaped up pretending to sob inconsolably at the prospect of losing him. He assured her—and many others—that this was not to be so, and accepting a glass of champagne from Tom Boscowan, he took his place to wait for the bride.

The vicar, poor guy, was by this time completely distraught. It was by far the swankiest wedding ever held in his church, and he couldn't decide how to act. In the end he cravenly decided to ignore the fancy dress, but he did appeal to the congregation not to drink in church! In his nervousness he added "until the ceremony is over." This was greeted by a storm of laughter, stamping feet, hoots and whistles. Two or three champagne corks flew across the room before silence fell as music announced the bride's arrival.

Margaret was furious. She swept down the aisle, her mouth set, and stood beside Buzz. The actual wedding was a rather tense affair, but the moment it was over the guests, following the vicar's advice, popped champagne corks and spurted wine at each other across the aisle while Margaret dragged Buzz in fury into the vestry. It appears they left the church that way. There was indeed a wedding march played—but the couple had already left. As the music came to an end, Tom Boscowan, offended by some remark about Margaret made by a fellow guest, sent him sprawling in the aisle.

Of course Buzz planned the whole thing, and the utterly crazy party afterwards at the Nairobi racecourse. Margaret sees it as a deliberate attempt by Buzz and Diana to downgrade the wedding, to make it clear that he's marrying for money and not for love or any of those other things people get married for. And yet, behind even this, there's something else. It's Diana whom Margaret is so implacably angry with. Why? Was the whole wedding fiasco Diana's idea alone? Did Buzz even know about it? Sometimes these people are so tight you can't get the time of day from them.

Anyway, we're leaving Kenya and will be back in the world of comprehensible New York business decisions by Christmas. At least I will. Diana's going on to Germany, where she's spending Christmas with some of her new political and aviation friends. There's a certain Captain Hermann Göring pursuing her like mad. Remember him from the war? Took over the von

Richthofen Circus. Name ring a bell? Look forward to a large whiskey and a long talk when I get back in New York.

Charlie

One morning during the week after Buzz Winslow's marriage, Catherine Esterhazy looked out across the coffee plantation where she was working to see that she had a visitor. A car billowing red dust wound slowly up the gravel road from Nairobi and turned in to the long drive up to the farm. Rubbing dust from her hands on the seat of her corduroy breeches, Catherine walked slowly through the rows of coffee plants, watching the car circle the lake and stop in front of the house. She had no doubt about the identity of the woman who got out of the driver's seat and stood a moment shading her eyes, under the brim of her straw hat, against the sun.

She walked slowly forward, down the path where the *totos* were playing, touching their heads as they ran along beside her.

The woman in the straw hat and pale cream dress came toward her, smiling. Her face Catherine had seen in a hundred newspaper photographs. It was the way she moved, the angle of the head, that was only familiar to anyone who had met Buzz Winslow.

"I hope you don't mind me calling on you," Diana said. "I'm George Winslow's sister, Diana Chrysler."

Catherine stood before her. "Of course. I recognize you from your photographs," she said after what seemed to her too long a pause. "Come inside. It's too hot to sit on the veranda."

They walked together across the terrace and through the French doors. "You have a beautiful farm here," Diana said, turning to look out across the lake.

"Yes." Catherine walked to the end of the room. "Yes, it's beautiful. But it also has to pay."

"A great deal of very hard work."

Catherine nodded. She stood tall and sunburned. She wondered what Diana Chrysler knew of hard work. "I have seen so many photographs of you," she said, "getting into aeroplanes. Climbing out . . ."

"It's not roses, roses all the way," Diana said. "Engines have to be checked. Struts tightened by hand. Sometimes an oil line

[174]

blows and you're covered with warm, sticky oil. If you're unlucky, the windscreen's covered too."

Catherine smiled. "You're telling me we're both working women. We both get our hands dirty."

"Yes."

"But I can't begin to imagine you spattered with oil."

"You don't know me. Possibly don't want to."

"Yes." Catherine's lips twisted. "I want to."

"I'm not the fragile butterfly you imagine me to be."

Catherine pressed the bell, absorbed for a moment by the dust streaks on her hand and the broken fingernail on the bell button. "The lake," she said, "isn't natural. It's man-made. It was made by a man."

"I hope I'm not interrupting your work," Diana said.

"I always take coffee at about this time. Will you join me?"

The tension rose like heat waves around them. "You must wonder why I called," Diana said.

"No." Catherine shook her head. "Of course, I wasn't expecting you. But now that you're here I don't really wonder why. Please sit down."

"We have a friend in common." Diana gasped as if for air. "Someone who means a great deal to both of us."

"Yes." Catherine found she could do no more than agree.

"I'm leaving Kenya tomorrow," Diana said. "I came for my brother's wedding, of course."

"It's been the talk of the whole colony for months. I shall read about it in the newspaper this afternoon. Was it as glittering and spectacular as expected?"

Diana smiled, raising her eyebrows. "It was spectacular," she said. "The reception ended with my very drunken brother riding bareback, coattails flying, one of his best racehorses against three of his friends. Given that it was after midnight, I don't think even the Nairobi Racecourse has seen anything quite the equal."

The coffee arrived and they sat in silence as it was poured. "I would like to talk about Claus von Hardenberg," Diana said when the African servant had left.

Catherine gulped the scalding coffee and stood up quickly. "Sometimes when it's very hot I can't bear the thought of coffee," she said. "Will you have a gin fizz?"

"Why not?" Diana said. "When in Africa . . ."

Catherine mixed the cocktail and poured whiskey for herself. "Of course you know Claus was here during the war," she said.

"My brother said he stayed with you for several months."

"It was he who built the lake." She handed Diana the gin fizz.

Diana looked out at the flocks of birds circling the water. Then she turned back to Catherine. "He was a very young man then."

"Younger than I," Catherine said.

"I didn't mean that. I mean that he was still someone I feel I knew. I haven't seen him for a very long time."

"Longer for me," Catherine said.

"Does he write to you?"

"I write to him. Sometimes he replies. But I learn very little. He's not a very communicative man."

"But you liked him when he was here."

"I think you know," Catherine said, "I fell deeply in love with him."

"And he with you?"

Catherine eyed the other woman across her glass. "I think you know the answer to that, too." She emptied the glass in one movement.

"I did not come here as a rival," Diana said.

"No, we're not rivals."

"Perhaps you don't know," Diana said carefully. "After the war I discovered that Claus was in fact my half-brother. My mother found herself pregnant by Claus's father."

"He told me that. By letter. It was the last thing he really told me."

"The last thing?"

"I think it was the last thing that was really important to him. What was it you came to ask me?"

Diana got to her feet. "I've already asked," she said.

Catherine rose, standing beside her. "And I've already answered. No, he never loved me. Always you. Always you."

When Diana had gone, Catherine stood on the terrace, watching her car take the Nairobi road. Great masses of white cloud rolled from the four-peaked mountain of Ngong, casting areas of deep, fast-traveling shadow on the hillside. For a moment it seemed as if the hand of darkness, immensely swift, would engulf Diana and her tiny car, but at the last moment the shadows turned away and fled across the mosaic of square maize fields and the luxuriant forest of the Kikuyu Reserve.

She had drunk one large whiskey and was about to have another. She walked back into the house, poured herself the whiskey, and took her pen and writing paper from the ornate Swedish bureau. She had no taste for work this afternoon. She sat for a few moments on the terrace, thinking of the girl who had just called to see her. Even in their brief, awkward exchange, Catherine had recognized some quality—a sense of self, perhaps—that had been absent from the letters, barely more than a schoolgirl's, that Claus had once showed her.

She knew she was about to write to Claus. She always did in the more strained moments in her lonely life. She picked up her pen and began to write, still uncertain whether or not she would tell him that she had at last met Diana Chrysler.

My dear Claus,
    So few letters from you, I no longer know how to speak to you. I thought of you as my closest friend. I still do. Yet I understand how time and experience changes us all. What you have known in Germany has changed you. But I live under a different sky. Nothing supplants the memories of the coffee bags piled under the lantern lights, of us working together to gather in that first harvest.
    I would love to tell you that all is going well with the farm, but it would not be the truth. We are too high here in the hills, the ground is too thin or the rains too uncertain, to grow the sort of coffee crop that today's depressed prices make necessary. You remember when you were here we did almost eighty tons. In the last few years we have never exceeded fifty-five. Is it the soil that's exhausted, or my spirit?
    I wonder, will I eternally miss you? I traveled to London last year to consult a specialist about my sickness. No help. No hope. I mention it because I thought long and hard about coming to Germany to see you. I crept like a timid mouse as far as Paris, with the excuse, to myself, that I was buying much-

needed clothes and some books in French. But of course I was not. I was figuratively peering over borders for a glimpse of you.

So many things to tell you. Our beautiful Kenya has become political. Nairobi is now a town of many thousands, though probably not more than about six thousand Europeans. Scattered throughout the valley from Naivasha to Gilgil there are perhaps now some four thousand white settlers in an African population of two million. There is also a large but uncounted Indian presence on the coast and in Nairobi. Thus the politics. The settlers dream of completely separate development, Indians and Europeans together, Africans apart. The Africans (except for some, like Kum) simply dream. Sometimes I have no doubt they will wake. But for the moment they dream on.

Now, to the roll of fife and drum, enter the government in London. Its decree that Kenya Colony was held in trust *for the African* caused something approaching a rebellion among the settlers. Vigilante groups were formed; armed units threatened to march on Nairobi. But London smudged the ink on its decree and Lord Delamere, leader of the settlers, pronounced himself reassured that Kenya Colony was a land fit for heroes. Pale-skinned heroes.

In my crystal ball I see storms brewing. The late Lord Delamere and the vigilantes wanted nothing short of self-government. Independence from London. Freedom—to ensure that white Kenyans develop separately and in privileged security. The Indians are totally opposed. And the Africans still dream on.

We need, above all, Claus, men who see the *opportunity* here. Not just the opportunity to grow crops and lose some money in a good climate, but the opportunity to create something here in Africa *together*, white men, brown men, black men.

New men and women, Europeans, arrive daily now. Your friends who have mostly settled along the shores of Lake Naivasha make no good impression, I'm afraid. They are interested in neither politics nor farming. Trousers for the women, silk shirts that show the nipples, cocktails, dance music, parties, gin-slings, and morphine are the common report. How much truth there is in it I am not really in a position to say. Last week the marriage took place, at the Muthaiga Club in Nairobi, of your friend Lord George Amadeus Winslow to Lady Margaret

Ryder, a notorious divorcée, according to gossip. What do you, a man, see in this man? From a woman's view, of course, I understand the attraction. He is quite simply immensely beautiful, with his pale gold hair, his straight nose and perfect mouth. From a woman's view, a stupid woman's view, his astonishing arrogance and great elegance of dress are attractive. He is, I believe, clever if not brilliant and uses his wit to make dirty stories acceptable—a slow moral drip, drip on the forehead of any listening female. He is of course mad about women—cunt-struck as they used to say in the Middle Ages, as a man might be moonstruck or suffering from the sun. No woman in the Muthaiga Club is safe from that quizzical set of his head, that pale *doubting* glance.

But what is it you, Claus, a man, see in him? Is he good? Is he generous? Is he true?

His whole "set," known to some as the Happy Valley Pioneers, turned up for the wedding. There was, I am told, the usual quantity of champagne consumed, there were the usual rows and rowdiness, breaking of furniture, and dull-eyed settling of accounts with the club secretary next morning.

I was there in fact myself that next morning, lunching after doing a little bank business in town. Lord Winslow (Buzz, is he called?) and Lady Margaret had left for Cape Town on their honeymoon, but some exhausted revelers were still left. A fish-eyed fellow named Tom Boscowan I didn't take to at all. His bosom companion, Sir Harry Towers, I thought a reasonably amiable Toby Jug, and two pretty blond sisters named Mowbray who have left their husbands to "farm" at Naivasha were too deeply hung over to sit on their barstools.

I hope you don't think me too horribly rude about friends you once enjoyed. Of course I think all the time of Diana Winslow, Diana Chrysler as she has long been, but I have met your Diana. I have been trying to decide whether or not to tell you, but I will be conscience-stricken if I do not. She came here this morning to see me, to see the farm where you had once lived and to discover if I still wrote to you. What do I think? I think sullenly of how kissable her mouth must be to any man, how she would melt into her partner's arms. I felt broad-shouldered and broad-hipped. I felt mud-streaked and shabby. I tried to be rude to her but could not.

You will see that I have become fretful in my (approaching) middle age. I shall be forty-two on New Year's Day. Fretful, and not a little self-pitying. My London specialist, with all the charm of a puff adder, tells me I have only general paralysis of the insane to look forward to as a comfort in my dotage.

Your own letters have become so hideously factual. I know you live in Hamburg and you own a boardinghouse and a tugboat. But I know nothing of the poetry of your life. Give me some poetry, Claus, good or bad. Do you still love your half-sister? Stupid question! Do I still have syphilis? Do you still remember Kenya? As it was? Do you remember when we cut the timber to dam your lake and we worked late into the night because the water was rising at an alarming rate and threatened to sweep away (and did) the newly constructed barrier? Do you remember the June fireflies then, the green brilliance of a thousand tiny lamps flaring from tree to tree like children in a medieval masque playing silent hide-and-seek?

Syphilis, you see, makes one a romantic. Deprived of the opportunity to snuffle and snort and suck and savor a man, you dream of a walk in the woods to watch fireflies together.

That's all, darling Claus, until the next time I am drunk enough.

But verily I send my love.

Catherine

AN
EVENING
WITH
DOCTOR
SCHNEE

T E N

I had returned to Hamburg with nearly eight hundred pounds left of the money Buzz had given me. I had been changed by poverty. Not tempered or toughened as some romantics would assert, but changed. I had suffered enough the debilitating experience of homelessness, which reaches so much deeper into life than the simple lack of a dry bed. It means nowhere to keep your last possessions, nowhere to cook, nowhere to read, nowhere to keep clean. The descent is swift and certain the moment a man has no home. I therefore decided to buy with most of the remaining money a tall, rather battered house in the St. Pauli district. I made the top floor into a pleasant enough apartment and rented out the six remaining rooms to the most reliable of tenants, the prostitutes and transvestite performers from the bars and clubs in the streets below. Heini was a tall, essentially unfeminine creature who looked sensational in makeup and a dress. He had grown his blond hair to a woman's length. His problem, he told me early in our acquaintance, was that he visited his mother in Altona once a week, when he would leave the house in St. Pauli primly dressed in a serge suit, boots, and a bowler hat. But at his mother's house the hat never left his head. Beneath it his shingled but nevertheless luxuriant waved hair was concealed on the excuse that he suffered from one of those diseases that flake the scalp and destroy the hair. Coffee and cream cakes on a hot summer day, Heini told me, could make a person feel very foolish if taken in a bowler hat.

A prostitute named Ruby had taken two rooms on the floor above Heini. She was still quite young and energetic and worked a particularly profitable strip between the Kit-Kat Club and the Dancing Fenice. She was, I soon discovered, a considerable money manager. She paid on the dot and saved to buy a café-hotel in the Black Forest for her retirement from "the life" as all the girls called it.

These two, Heini and Ruby, were my principal tenants. Others passed through the house, staying a few weeks or months, sometimes leaving without paying, sometimes (not by any means always) returning weeks later to settle their debt. They were a kindhearted, friendly face of Germany that I could always remember later when the country's public face became harder and more frightening.

My remaining two hundred pounds were invested on the advice of an old Jew I had done some translating work for in the bad days just after the war. We were to take fifty-fifty shares in a harbor boat that was used to carry pilots, crews, and supplies back and forth to ships moored in the harbor. It was not much of a boat, but the concession was a valuable one and I gladly took up old Herr Hendel's offer. From time to time I would pilot the tug myself, until I became a passably well-known figure on the Hamburg waterfront.

I had one further source of income that came out of the blue. I received a letter from my old commander, Bitov, inviting me to dinner in Drexler's, one of the best of the smaller restaurants in Hamburg in those days.

I found it an immensely enjoyable meeting as we talked of our times in Africa and of Germany's plight after the war, and of the slow, slow climb back. Bitov, as a regular army officer, had been one of the very few invited to stay on, from the old Imperial Army, into the newly formed Reichswehr, the 100,000-man force that was all Germany was now allowed under the Treaty of Versailles. In terms of rearmament, Bitov explained, the Reichswehr, though small, would prove an excellent professional basis for officers and NCOs. When the time came, this force would be capable of training a German army ten times its number.

I was genuinely puzzled. "But why should Germany want an army of a million men?" I asked him.

"Ah, my dear fellow, don't pretend to be simpleminded. France, England, Soviet Russia, Italy, America, and Japan have all got military or naval strength to back their commercial negotiations or diplomatic demands. A strong army is not necessarily for war. It is the only way to put us on an equal footing in the world, with France and England in particular. We cannot be dominated forever. *That* will lead inevitably to another war."

I very much liked Bitov. In Africa I had found him the sort of senior officer it was not difficult to respect. He was considerate of his men, askaris and Germans alike. When he asked me if I would do a job for the Reichswehr, for Germany, I was certainly in a frame of mind to think about it.

"On this question of future rearmament," Bitov said, "there are two crucial issues. Both concern weapons developed in the last years of the war, the tank and the military aeroplane. Under the treaty, we have the right to develop or train with neither."

It was the best dinner I had eaten for a very long time, and I felt a compulsion to repay Bitov with at least my interest. "Without tanks and planes," I said, though I no longer had very much interest in things military, "no modern army can be said to exist."

"Exactly," Bitov said emphatically. "In the Reichswehr it has therefore been decided that steps must be taken."

"What can be done?"

"Officers and development engineers could train and work on these weapons *outside* Germany . . ."

"Which foreign country would allow that?" I asked, puzzled.

"There is one," Bitov said mysteriously. "One that needs our engineers as much as we need their freedom to work and maneuver."

"Am I allowed to ask which country this is that's so well disposed toward Germany?"

"The host country need not be at all well disposed to Germany. It must only need German skills. Soviet Russia needs German engineers. We need their fields and skies."

I was genuinely shocked. I could not conceive of the Soviets helping to rebuild a force that had defeated them at Tannenberg and imposed the crushing treaty of Brest-Litovsk on Russia in 1917.

"Will you help us, Claus?"

"How can I help?"

"You have a boat, a boat of reasonable size. Naturally the officers who visit the Soviets cannot take advantage of conventional transport. The railways have been excluded. By sea to Leningrad has been judged the best route."

Thus I made three illegal journeys to Leningrad in the early 1920s, until suddenly, without explanation, Bitov told me there were to be no more. I at least saw the first capital of the Soviets. And in addition, I was paid for the risk.

My financial situation, funded originally by Buzz, was thus reasonably secure in the late twenties. Personally, I lived a strange life. In St. Pauli, an essentially working-class part of Hamburg, I was seen, with approval, as a dropout from the aristocracy. I was mostly known as "the Captain" (more from my ownership of the tugboat than because of my wartime rank) and sometimes, rarely, as Count von Hardenberg. My friends were Heini the transvestite performer; Ruby, who would occasionally procure for me one of the more wholesome new arrivals from one of the local clubs; Karl-Hans, the barman of the Kit-Kat; an American painter named Josh; and a lady conjurer of formidable proportions who did striptease conjuring at the Dancing Fenice. Her name was Eva, and early in 1926 she became a long-term tenant like Heini and Ruby.

We would meet mainly in Ruby's rooms, with sausage and a few bottles of schnapps, and Heini would tell of his most embarrassing moments (there were many of these in his extraordinary life), Ruby would describe the more bizarre requests of her clients, and we would talk about the new posters and films and even books. But most of all we argued interminably about politics. All of us, in our different ways—even Josh, the American—felt the sheer weight of the problem of Germany. I could see that in one sense Bitov was right. Without an army a country was at the mercy of rapacious neighbors. The Poles had taken the lands my family lived on for five centuries; the French, when war-debt repayments weren't maintained, had simply marched in and occupied the Rhineland area of Germany. How did England and America imagine that any German government could withstand these body blows? What was left of the nation's prestige? They were opening the way to an army coup or, worse, a victory by one of the right-wing nationalist or national socialist parties that were growing in strength every year. Most of all, they were putting a rope around the neck of the German Social Democrats, the only real hope for a stable, decent government.

Eva, the striptease conjurer, agreed with none of this. She was a Communist, and she reveled in the certainties of her faith. She believed implicitly, in her generous way, and I knew my descriptions of life in Leningrad were painful to her. I was fairly restrained because I knew that her adherence to the faith sprang from a great, good-natured spirit rather than from a narrow need for faith itself.

Heini and Josh were both Social Democrats by vague inclination, but Ruby now proclaimed herself an anarchist. Her political views were so obviously the result of her bitter experience of the Great Inflation that it was difficult to take her anarchism too seriously.

She left my house (she was to come back later for several years) early in the twenties to buy the café-hotel she had worked and saved for. I cannot remember now how much she had in marks, but it was a substantial sum. The café-hotel would mean she would be reunited with her mother and her daughter, neither of whom had any idea of the nature of her profession. I believe she had told them she was a schoolteacher in Altona!

We had a party the night Ruby left. It was perhaps not an untypical St. Pauli party, but as from time to time I stepped back from it, it seemed a most bizarre happening. Heini had brought five or six friends, beautifully dressed, grave-mannered "ladies" to whom one automatically offered chairs and lights for their long-holdered cigarettes. Ruby had brought a selection of her St. Pauli colleagues and one or two of her more important regular customers. Josh had invited some Negro musicians. Eva's friends were a circus strongman and a dapper figure with a thin mustache. By the evening's end he had revealed that he was a lion tamer, and he finally demonstrated with a chair and a whip, while Eva played the lioness, how exactly he dominated the beasts. He put so much into the performance that when, at the end, Eva hurled her huge, tawny-haired bulk at him and wrestled him to the ground, he yelped with genuine and pathetic terror.

Ruby left the next morning. We were all more than a little

sad to see her go, but as the weeks passed and the Great Inflation increased the price of a kilo of potatoes from a few marks to a few hundred, then to a few thousand, and finally to a few million marks, we who either had no money or already had it invested in a boardinghouse or a tugboat thanked God or someone that Ruby had taken her "dowry" and invested in her hotel just in time. Around us, madness surged on. Men carried wheelbarrows of banknotes to buy quite insignificant objects. Anybody with pounds sterling or dollars was a rich man overnight. The profiteers profiteered. "Capitalism is settling its debts," Eva said darkly, massaging her huge breasts with olive oil to keep them supple, "and it's the workingman of Germany who pays."

The workingman, and even the lower middle classes, with a few thousand marks saved, certainly paid. Their life's savings were worth nothing—not half or a quarter of what they had been worth, not just a little of what they had been worth, but *nothing*. The sense of betrayal by the authorities, the state, was overwhelming. In another people it would have produced anarchic crime. In Germany it produced a deep desire for a new, stronger, more *trustworthy* state.

Ruby returned the following month. She came up to my apartment and placed her suitcase on the floor just inside the door. She said wanly, "Do you have a room?"

I could see from her face how much was wrong. "Of course I have a room," I said. "Two, if you like. Your old rooms."

She shook her head. "Just one," she said. "That's all I can afford at the moment."

She moved back into her old rooms at a temporarily reduced rent. The café-hotel, she told me, had never been bought. She had lodged the money with a local lawyer when she began to look for suitable premises. He had failed to warn her of what was happening, and she was unable to see clearly for herself. Like millions of other Germans, she believed the trend would reverse itself, that the mark would again become worth something. Germans have such a frightening belief in normality even when mutant beasts haunt the forests of their history.

In short, her life savings were worthless. She could buy nothing, not even a pair of shoes for the child. I have described her, on her return to the house, as an anarchist, but of course she was not. As soon as the Hitler party became known in the north, she attached herself to it. It was only the Nazis, Ruby proclaimed in our discussions, who could really be relied upon not to let the ordinary workingman or woman down.

I was happy in Hamburg. The sharper detail of the memory of Diana Winslow, or Diana Chrysler, as she was now, was fading. From time to time I saw some reference to her in a newspaper. As a beautiful, titled, and now immensely rich young woman she was perfect for what were just beginning to be called the gossip columns. She had, the newspapers reported, become a flier. I tried to tell myself I was interested neither in this nor in any other of her activities, but if a report appeared about her in one newspaper, I would inevitably buy all the others in the hope that I might find something more.

But in Hamburg, at least, there were few reports in the newspapers I read, and with the years, inevitably, the scars, the ridiculous scarring of my youth, began to heal.

Sometime in the winter of 1928, when I had just finished a profitable afternoon ferrying crew members out to a passenger liner that lay at anchor, I saw Lorelei again. She was sitting just outside the pool of lamplight on a huge cast-iron capstan on the edge of the dock, and by her slow smile I recognized that this was not a chance meeting. She sat there, as pretty as ever, a small, dark-haired figure in an old leather coat and a leather seaman's cap. As she stood up I kissed her and she kissed me back with what I took to be comradely warmth.

I put my arm around her. "Let's go and get some food," I said. "And a drink to celebrate."

She shook her head. "I don't want to be seen with you. Eva told me where to find you."

I frowned. "Eva?"

"She lives in your house," Lorelei said. "An entertainer. She said she knew someone who would let people stay from time to time. I laughed when I heard who it was."

We walked on down the quay. "Do you want to stay yourself?" I asked.

"No," she said. "Or at least not yet. We're thinking of comrades passing through."

"You mean Webel's thinking of other comrades."

"He's the comrade leader on the waterfront, you know that."

"These comrades, they would not have papers."

"No."

"Would the police be looking for them?"

"No, I can promise you that. They are travelers."

"Couriers."

"Yes."

"To and from Moscow? Russians?"

She nodded. "Some of them."

"At the first brush with the police," I said carefully, "any arrangement ends immediately."

"Agreed."

"Unless you yourself need to come, anytime."

She nodded, happy, like a young girl. "Webel will be pleased," she said.

"Fuck Webel," I muttered in English as she skipped off into the fog. In the following months I received an odd collection of morose or unbearably jovial Russians, a few steely British or German Communists, a Greek who got drunk and tried with no success whatever to rape Eva. But most of the comrades were quiet, friendly fellows with an awesome dedication to the cause. They were, in shabby twentieth-century form, soldiers of Christ, but I fear they would not have recognized Him if they had met Him carrying a cross. I mean by this to say that my short-term tenants were entirely devoted to the task at hand. They were not accustomed, and certainly not encouraged, to lift their eyes unto the hills.

One comrade was markedly different. It was a day of humid squalls sometime in the early summer of 1930. I had been out to load supplies for a pair of tramp steamers in the harbor and had returned about lunchtime. I was hungry and slightly irritable. I bought some cigarettes at a kiosk and decided against a beer in the Kit-Kat. Instead I bought a liter of wine at the Konditorei Pfalz on the corner, and took it back with some bread and cheese. I had decided I should listen to some music, get slightly drunk, and pass an hour or two in sentimental musing about the past.

But the past was waiting for me at home. I pushed open the front door and saw a figure seated in the farthest, darkest part of the hall. A man came to his feet and a deep, rich voice said, "Well, Captain . . ."

Kum came forward, smiling, and we grasped arms like Roman senators. It took me moments to sputter my surprise, and much more time, over the liter of wine, for him to explain how he came to be in Europe. I had heard nothing of him since Africa, with the exception of a paragraph in a letter from Catherine Esterhazy:

Kum has gone. It had to happen. In the years since you last saw him, he has changed so much. He read with truly African voraciousness, like a leopard devouring a buck. When I had answered all his questions, I found he began to answer mine. One evening, sitting over a drink together as had become our habit, I even confided in him the story of my sickness.

Not surprisingly, I have acquired a certain eccentric reputation. Some passing settlers who had spotted Kum ensconced on the veranda imagined he was ensconced in my bed too. I care nothing for speculations. I care that Kum has left, but I knew it must happen. There was a world to see that he had only read about. There was the art of politics to investigate, an art in which I believe Kum will excel. He came with me to London and supported me through all the disappointments of the specialist. We parted (tearfully on my part) in a Lyons tea shop in Trafalgar Square. I ache to hear from him. Next to you, he is my greatest friend.

"Catherine Esterhazy told me you were in Europe," I said to Kum. "That was many years ago."

He smiled. "Centuries even, for me." He wore shabby clerk's clothing and heavy boots, but his smile was as warm as it had been the first day I saw him in the swamp.

"Well?" I was intrigued and impatient to know so many things about him.

"I got a job first on the London docks," he said slowly. "It lasted a few weeks only. I was cleaning up in a canteen. I got to meet the English workmen. I began to talk to some of them and they invited me to meetings. We talked much about socialism and Karl Marx. I had information to exchange. I told them about my country, Kenya."

"What happened to the job?"

"I was dismissed. It appears I was incapable of washing dishes in the required manner," he grinned. "But I was there long enough to meet one of the local party organizers."

"The Communist Party?"

"They gave me a small job at their headquarters in King Street. They also gave much free time to attend the Workers' Educational Institute. Do you know it?"

"No."

"They have eminent men like Professor R. H. Tawney teaching there. Last year I took an external degree at London University."

"And you're now a full-time organizer for the party?"

"Lorelei said there was a safe house in Hamburg, run by a Captain Hardenberg. I nearly exploded with joy, although she did warn me that you are not a party member."

"My dear Kum, God bless the party," I said, "if it's brought us together again."

I got more wine and we talked through the afternoon and late into the night. We talked about Catherine and the Ngong farm and we laughed about the lake we had built together. It was odd to think that it was over ten years ago. We talked of our days flying together along the Uganda railway line and swooping with a sense of unbelievable freedom across the Great Rift Valley.

"You should go back, Captain," Kum urged me. "Go back to the baroness. A little capital could transform the farm." He laughed. "Advice from a Communist agitator."

Later in the night, drunker in the night, I asked him if he knew Webel.

"I know Webel," he said. "Why do you ask?"

I shrugged. I wanted to say that a cold, utterly ruthless man like Webel could surely not nurture the same dreams that people like Kum and Lorelei and Eva had.

Kum put his hand on my arm. "Such men are necessary," he said. "It will not have escaped you that Marxism is like one of those English chocolates with a hard shell and a soft center. The soft center, even in communism, is bourgeois morality. You can divide Communists between the two," he said. "Men and women of the hard shell or of the soft core."

"Can they not exist in the same person?"

He shook his head. "If that were possible," he said, "then

communism would be truly a faith in which all men could believe."

He stayed only two days. I asked him to write to Catherine, but he said it was difficult. He even preferred that I should not pass on the news of our meeting. I realized, I suppose, even then that he was not a Communist like Eva and her friends. Not even with the blind faith of Lorelei, but he was nonetheless, I thought, part of the party shell. At the time it seemed to me an insight. Years later it would simply be obvious.

The 1920s ended. The new decade was celebrated throughout Europe with bread and water for many as the capitalist world suffered one of its great sea changes. I had not married, although I had had one or two long-standing affairs of no real importance to me. I don't think it was Diana who created the barrier I was unwilling to leap. Certainly not in the sense that I had any expectation that in some ideal world we would come together. But she served as a measure of a very special type of womanhood, the measure of a certain type of *glamour*, as I would have said before Hollywood destroyed a word as elusive as scent.

Lorelei came to see me from time to time. She took many precautions, arriving always after dark and leaving only after checking the street below. Perhaps she was afraid that the police were keeping her under some sort of surveillance, or perhaps it was all part of the party mystique—adopted names, safe houses, mystery packages delivered, urgent messages relayed. Above all, as I learned from all my party guests, it gave them a sense of being involved, of a cause that could always call on the sacrifice of the individual. In this sense, politics is the only alternative to war.

On the occasions when Lorelei came alone, we fell into the habit of sleeping together, guiltily, as if she were a minor or perhaps a nun.

I came to believe that she was seriously afraid of Webel, and one day when we were talking in bed, I summoned up the courage to ask her if this was so.

She did not normally talk about Webel or the party, and in all the time I knew her I heard no more than a dozen names, all coded first names, connected with her work. When I asked her this time, she rolled out of my embrace and lay back, hands behind her head, looking at the ceiling. "It's not for me to criticize," she said.

I shrugged as best I could, resting on one elbow.

"It is not for me to criticize," she said in the rather formal German she used for party matters, "but I consider Comrade Webel on occasion to be seriously unrealistic."

I grunted sympathetically.

"For instance, he has ordered me to enroll you as a party member."

I laughed.

"It's not a laughing matter," she rebuked me severely.

"No."

"Within a year or two, a German government could be hanging or imprisoning all Communists."

"*If* the right comes to power," I conceded. "But why should Webel want me as a member of the party?"

"He wants to command your services. He doesn't like this informal arrangement."

"You know my answer," I said, rolling out of bed and beginning to collect a bottle of schnapps and two glasses.

"I have already told him. But he will not accept it. In other things, too, he is unrealistic," she added cautiously.

"What other things?" I poured schnapps for her and got back into bed with the bottle.

"He is one of six leaders on commissar level in Germany. His influence in Moscow is very great. His reports insist that the Social Democrats are the greatest threat to socialism in Germany. Not the Hitler party."

"Why does he write such reports?"

"Because he knows it is what Moscow wants to hear. For six months I was his secretary. I know all this is true."

I poured my schnapps and clinked my glass with hers. "Politics is a dirty business," I said unthinkingly.

She sat bolt upright, spilling schnapps across the sheet. "That's a weak, foolish thing to say," she said. "It shows you understand nothing of the *necessities* of politics."

"Probably you're right," I agreed quickly. I was beginning to want her again, and I was in no mood to squabble. "I don't really understand it."

She drew a deep breath. "Nevertheless," she said carefully, "I believe the Nazis are closer to power than we think. I believe it's the Nazis that the Communists should be attacking."

"And are they not?" I asked politely.

"I must tell you, Claus," she said, suddenly urgent. Her eyes darted across the room as if she were probing its dark corners for spies, "We are *not* attacking the Nazis. Sometimes we are even collaborating with them."

It seemed like Bitov's story all over again.

"I will explain," she said. "Each week it is my duty to visit Thorn."

"Thorn, the Brownshirt leader?"

"His SA unit commands a thousand men in Hamburg alone. In the Redcommando we have about the same number."

"Why do you have to see him?"

"We decide which Social Democrat meetings we are to smash up. Sometimes we both send squads to big meetings. Then Thorn and I work together with signals across the hall."

This time I didn't make the mistake of muttering about politics being a dirty business. Instead I nodded sympathetically and tried to ease her toward me. It would be two years yet before I understood the significance of her complaints against Webel.

In Hamburg, or at least in St. Pauli, despite all my protestations, I was still considered a gentleman. The café waiters would bow as I passed; the young whores on the street would be severely castigated by the old hands if one of them mistakenly approached me as a client.

I wore my English suits. I carried a stick with a broad silver band. I worked no more than one or two days a week. I spoke a German very different from that of the denizens of the greatest red-light district in Europe. I knew myself to be an exile, cut off from my own past.

As the last years of what came to be called the gay twenties were danced and drunk away, I had from time to time met up with an uncle or a cousin. I found it was only Wolfgang with whom I had any sympathy. A grenade had mutilated his face. He had lost both his arms and his right leg in one of the last battles on the Western Front. His left leg was badly damaged. He described having dragged himself like a one-tentacled octopus through the slime of the field of battle. He suffered from persistent vomiting as a result of unspeakable wounds in the stomach. He suffered, too, from a monumental bitterness. I had known him as a kindly, thoughtful German nationalist, secure in the Junker class to which we had both been born. But at the veterans' hospital in Paderborn, where I saw him just once or twice in those years, he was already placing his hopes and Germany's destiny in different hands. He urged me to read a book called *Mein Kampf*. The passages he read to me were full of hate and bitterness. I found it a sinister sight to watch my cousin, with his poor mutilated mouth, reading the outflow of ugly bile that was the thinking of Adolf Hitler.

During these days I read more and more of Diana. She was the pilot in a two-way flight across the Atlantic—not an achievement on the level of Alcock and Brown or Lindbergh, but the world's press gave it great attention because Diana Chrysler was involved. She was by now very definitely "news." Even the Hamburg newspapers carried stories or pictures about her. She did not pursue her life as much as thrust it in front of my eyes.

She visited Germany many times in the late twenties: "Lady Diana Chrysler attended the coming-out ball of Princess Olga-Marie of Hesse. . . ." "At Tempelhof Airport, Lady Diana Chrysler today inspected the new Junker aircraft with which Lufthansa hopes to capture the travel market of the skies. . . ." "Reports of a growing rift between Lady Diana and her millionaire American husband were dismissed as meaningless gossip by her as she landed at Munich for a motor-skiing holiday in Austria, which included the Prince of Wales, King Alfonso of Spain, Lord Louis and Lady Edwina Mountbatten, Lord Henry Holland and Lady Berrington. . . ."

It was still difficult, at whatever distance, not to feel drawn into the details of her life.

Sometime late in 1931 I received an invitation by telephone

to attend a discussion on Africa that was to be held by the German-East African Society in Hamburg the following month. I assumed I had been invited because of my war service there, but I had no real interest in a symposium on Africa and was preparing to decline when the voice on the other end of the telephone broke in. "The society is desperately anxious to appoint an Air Advisor," he said. "I have specifically been requested to make the point to you that we are not without funds to reimburse our consultants."

I agreed to go. For many seconds after I replaced the telephone, my hand lingered on the brass and green Bakelite receiver. The mere mention of flying and Africa after all these years flooded me with memories. I saw the sea of waving grass below me or the great acreages of scrub crisscrossed by a thousand animal trails, dotted with native villages surrounded by high thorn barriers. I saw the reflected flash of the zebra stripes on the underside of my Fokker aeroplane's wings as it dived across the calm surface of a lake. And I heard Kum shouting, singing, clapping with all that irrepressible spirit that only European education had repressed.

I think I mentioned to Heini and Ruby that I was to attend a symposium on Africa. Certainly I remember a long talk, the afternoon of the meeting, with Eva and the American painter, Josh. The future of what was once Tanganyika or German East Africa was the subject. Josh felt it only fair that the colony should be removed from Britain's control and returned to Germany. Eva, of course, believed in the immediate abolition of all colonial links. They had both drunk quite a lot, and the conversation was not conducted on the most exalted level. Powerfully built as she was, Eva could and did threaten the slenderly built American. "Germany's rights in Africa!" I remember her screaming. "Germany has no rights in Africa. Nor do England or France or any of the other colonialist cock-pullers!"

She had pinned Josh against the wall with one heavy forearm under his chin, pressing hard on his throat, when we heard Ruby's voice on the landing below. She was calling me in breathless, excited tones. As she ran up the remaining flight, I glanced at Josh to see that he had been released, and opened the door to allow Ruby to tumble into the room. "My God, Captain," she said, "you must hurry. They've sent a car for you."

As if in choreographed movement, we all crossed to the window to stare down into the street. A large brown and white Mercedes was parked outside the front door. "What makes you think the car's for me?" I asked Ruby.

She smiled, almost shyly. "The driver said so," she said.

Eva growled at her suspiciously. "What's going on, Ruby? Whose car is it?"

Ruby laughed nervously. "It's for the Captain. From these African Society people."

"Except?" Eva said menacingly.

"Except Herr Thorn's sitting next to the chauffeur."

"Thorn?" I pushed Eva aside. Thorn was the St. Pauli Brownshirt leader. "Are you sure, Ruby?"

"You're honored, Captain," Ruby said. "There's a truck with a dozen young chaps in SA uniform drawn up behind."

I went back to the window. Sure enough, a rather battered open truck, with young Brownshirts sitting along the slatted seats, was parked fifty yards behind the Mercedes.

"Don't go, Captain. Don't go with that rabble," Eva urged me.

Ruby looked on, impressed at the size of my escort, but silent now.

"Don't worry, Eva," I said. "I'm not about to become a Brownshirt."

She smiled doubtfully as I passed onto the landing and began to descend the staircase.

The symposium, when I arrived, gave me no pleasure. Worse, the meeting, held in a large private house in Altona, was chaired by a man I had hoped to have confined to the strongbox of my past, Dr. Schnee, the former governor of German Tanganyika, who had tried in vain to escape from the shadow of the great von Lettow. It was a Nazi Party meeting, of course. Dr. Schnee informed me proudly that Herr Hitler had promised to appoint him Commissioner for German African Colonies as soon as the party came to power. A more menacing figure, a very tall, fair-haired man of about my age named Zeitz-Apolda, hovered around the six or seven academics or ex-Tanganyika settlers seated around the table. I was, it appeared, quite literally the only German who had ever flown over East Africa. As such, I was invited to offer advice on the number of

German aircraft necessary to defend Tanganyika. Once Britain had been forced to return it to Germany, of course. I found the whole discussion ridiculous, and I believe that Zeitz-Apolda found it equally so. Schnee was as unctuous and irritating as ever. I asked him if he had invited von Lettow.

"General von Lettow declined our invitation," he said.

"Perhaps he believes that nothing short of another war will restore Germany's old African colonies to her."

"A negotiated settlement is possible," Schnee urged. "Britain needs the support of Germany in the colonies. We should never, never have fought each other in Africa. The European races must stick together. I am a man of peace, Hardenberg. A man of peace."

In the mirror I caught Zeitz-Apolda's look of amused contempt.

A geographer held forth on a new possible division between Germany and England, with the dividing line running south of Kilimanjaro; a geologist read notes on the possibility of discovering oil and coal reserves; an agriculturalist discussed the establishment of a vast chilled-beef industry based on new ranching methods. Zeitz-Apolda slipped into the empty seat beside me. "Of course you may be right," he said with his curious half-smile, "to claim that only a war will cause the British to return Tanganyika to us."

"I believe I am right," I said.

"But let us dream a little," Zeitz-Apolda whispered below the monotonous drone of the agriculturalist's statistics. "Let us imagine a free, independent British Kenya. Run by the settlers, for the settlers. Now would *they* not appreciate a German Tanganyika on their southern boundary? Would they not see the common interest of the white man?"

I shrugged. "Perhaps," I said. "In any case, it's more feasible than war."

Zeitz-Apolda seemed to be content that he had made his single point. "Diana's upstairs," he said. "I'm sure you'd like to see her."

"Hardenberg . . . the family comes from the Eastern Marches, does it not?" Zeitz-Apolda asked as we approached the broad marble staircase that led to the landing above.

My mind was entirely on the thought that within a few seconds I should be seeing Diana again. "We lost our land in the scramble at the end of the war," I said.

"Your home too, no doubt."

"A rundown manor house with more charm than comfort."

Thin and elegant in his pale gray suit, Zeitz-Apolda paused, one hand on the carved marble newel post, one hand held lightly inside his double-breasted jacket. "It is the policy of the party to return all such land to the original owners," he said. "Herr Hitler is not at present inclined to advertise this fact, but his deputy, Herr Hess, has given me his word."

"Your family had land in the East too?"

"Near Danzig. Now farmed by flat-faced Polish peasants."

He began to climb the stairs.

"And how does Herr Hitler expect to recover *these* lands for Germany? Is it to be like Africa? Is it to be through the extraordinarily powerful appeal of his calls for justice?" Above I could hear voices, a man's laugh, the clinking of glass on ice buckets.

Zeitz-Apolda's eyes narrowed. He did not look directly at me, but I understood I had gone too far. In truth, I was only passing the seconds as we mounted the staircase, crossed the hall, and entered the large ornate room where Diana stood among a group of men, in sunlight, at the terrace doors.

She saw me, but she gave no immediate sign. I was offered champagne or whiskey and soda by Zeitz-Apolda, and I stood watching her laugh and gesture to the men around her. She wore a gleaming sheath of green silk, the sleeves slashed to show her slender tanned arms, the back cut deep to the waist. In her shingled, thick blond hair an emerald tiara sparkled. Next to her a squat, powerfully built man laughed in short, impressive bursts of released energy.

"She is most beautiful, is she not?" Zeitz-Apolda said as he joined me with the whiskies. "She is much admired in the party."

"The man next to her," I said. "Is he not Captain Göring?"

"They are great friends," Zeitz-Apolda said. "Aviators, of course, both of them. Tell me, Hardenberg, is that how you first met Diana, through your common interest in flying?"

I was watching Hermann Göring as his hand reached across her bare back, rested on her shoulder, exerted a light intimate pressure. I shook my head. "No, I was a friend of her brother's. We were at the University together."

"Heidelberg?"

"Cambridge."

"I myself spent a happy year at Oxford," Zeitz-Apolda said. "If I were English I would say I was a Balliol man."

Watching Diana, I suppose I had barely heard him.

"You should, you know, reconsider your attitude to the party," Zeitz-Apolda said. "Like many members of our class, you probably believe that it is essentially a socialist party. That is of course its name, the National Socialist Workers' Party. The truth, old chap, is that the party is classless. There are opportunities for people of our type in it. Hermann Göring has seen that himself."

I heard the words, but they had no interest or meaning for me. Diana had detached herself from the group around her. She threaded her way toward me through importuning guests.

I left Zeitz-Apolda in mid-sentence. Advancing through the guests, I came to a halt a pace or two from her. By some exhilarating magic, neither of us spoke. She was smiling, her blue eyes fixed upon my face. Then she lifted both hands and grasped mine. "Claus, Claus, Claus," she said softly, in conscious echo of a letter long ago.

"I regret that we were unable to impress Hardenberg with our plans for Africa," Zeitz-Apolda said as he joined us.

Diana laughed. "Isn't Dr. Schnee the most frightful pompous ass?" she said.

Zeitz-Apolda smiled agreement. "Of course he is. You're not supposed to take him seriously." His face set again, unsmiling now. "But I fancy the problem is different for Hardenberg. I think it's the party, not Dr. Schnee, that fails to impress him."

I was desperate to speak to Diana alone. Waiters brought plates of canapés. I drank another whiskey and perhaps two glasses of champagne. Captain Göring came to tell Diana he was leaving. His face was cherubic, sly, and open at the same time. "Come with me," he was urging Diana. "I'm speaking in the Ruhr-gebiet tonight. We're expecting the Reds to turn up in force. It'll be a hell of a party."

Zeitz-Apolda was asking me about flying in Africa. I waited until I was sure that Diana had declined Göring's invitation before stumbling through a banal answer. Diana returned as Zeitz-Apolda conducted Göring to the door.

"When did you last see Charles?" I asked as Zeitz-Apolda left us.

"Oh, in New York a month ago. More, even."

"And he doesn't object to your being away so long?"

"Since I no longer share his bed, Charles has become tolerant of my absences in Germany."

"Is Captain Göring your lover?"

"No."

"He acts as if he might be."

"Many men act that way toward a woman. Charles believes I have a hundred lovers."

"And you don't."

"No," she said gravely. "None. None at all, Claus."

"Then why do you let Charles believe it? It seems cruel."

Her head turned from me. "No, it's not cruel, Claus. One single man would be impossible for him. That would be cruel."

"And there is no one man."

She smiled and touched my hand. "Come and walk with me on the terrace and tell me about your life."

We walked out onto the terrace. It was a mild late autumn day. At the end farthest from the drawing room a stone staircase led steeply down to the garden below. Although I could hear the distant signals of shipping, we seemed, looking down onto the informal English garden, to be many miles from the great, dirty, smoke-stained port. We walked along the flagstoned terrace and stopped within a deep, columned window space. Through the glass we could see an empty music room with two grand pianos, a half-circle of chairs, and music stands.

"Do you know why I asked Dr. Schnee to invite you today?"

"No."

She laughed. "I was conspiring," she said. "With Hugo Zeitz-Apolda."

I frowned.

"There will be such opportunities in Africa," she said. "Germany has such plans."

"Germany? You mean the Hitler party."

She nodded vigorously. "Two independent East African states, Kenya and Tanganyika. Imagine it, Claus. Two states populated by the best of English and German stock. True aristocrats. No, let me explain." She held up a hand to stop me from interrupting. "I conspired to get you invited today because you can see what this Dr. Schnee committee amounts to. Hugo is not part of it, of course. He is simply a courier. But those old duffers downstairs will never achieve anybody's dream in Africa. The way is wide open for you, Claus."

"For *me*?"

"Join the movement now," she urged, "and you will be the party's governor-elect in Tanganyika within a year. I promise you that."

I suppose I gaped at her in astonishment. But she had not yet finished.

"I've already spoken to Buzz," she said.

"To Buzz . . ." I stammered in an attempt to keep pace with her headlong, reckless imagination.

"Of course. Now that Lord Delamere is dead, the way is open for Buzz to take his place as the settler leader of Kenya. You see my dream, darling," she said, her eyes shining. "My two favorite and most gorgeous men, leaders of the new twin states of East Africa."

I knew she was utterly serious. "I don't want to rule a new German colony in Tanganyika," I said. "I want you."

I put my hand around her waist. The palm lay flat at that warm point where her silk dress opened to leave her back bare. The very slightest pressure brought her toward me. Her long legs brushed and pressed against mine. Her blue eyes were large and wide, as if in fear; her mouth trembled like a child's mouth, the pale shadow of her teeth shimmering between her lips.

She had reached up one hand and placed it on the side of my neck, caressing me, urging me toward her lips. I kissed her, and her mouth opened warm beneath mine. I had never felt so completely engulfed by a woman, or so much felt her as the receptacle of my body. A decade of forgetfulness flowed away from me. When we broke apart, I needed her as much as I had ever needed her. In seconds of softness and scent, she had recreated in my memory all that the dull years had obscured. "Will you leave Charles?" I said. "Will you come with me?"

She stepped back, her hand still trailing across my shoulder. "You can't have me, Claus," she said slowly. "And I can't have you."

She was staring down, one hand on my shoulder, at the

flagstones below her feet. "Walk in the garden with me," she said. "Then I must go back."

We descended the steps from the terrace and walked, hand in hand, along the grass alleys of the English garden. I almost imagined we would come upon traces of a long-abandoned monastery, as we had many years ago, in a tinseled past, walking together in the gardens of Lady Gorringe's house.

"I believe, Claus," she said, "that it can never be any different between us."

I took her hand. "Just come with me now." I knew I must be slightly crazed. "Leave all this," I urged her. "Just come with me."

Years later, when I thought of that moment, I could still see her hesitate. I *know* she hesitated, but of course then I did not know why. She stood before me, trembling. I did not know she was trembling in the presence of the truth. But then I could not guess at what the cost would be to her.

The moment's hesitation passed. She said with a dead finality, "We can never be together, Claus."

"Why not? It makes no difference between us what your mother told you. You feel no revulsion?"

She smiled. "No," she said.

"Then why not?"

"We could never face Buzz," she said. "I think he would kill you."

I put my arm around her, and for a moment she leaned toward me. Then she turned and moved away. "I must go back now," she said. "I had hoped today would turn out differently. I came not to make love to you, Claus, but to urge you to take part in your own future. There will be such splendid opportunities for a man like you in tomorrow's Germany. But I had not realized that we were still more to each other than onetime lovers."

Everything, the very seriousness of her face, the set of her lips, recalled Diana in that summer garden in 1914. She turned, reached up, and brushed her lips across mine. "I don't suppose we shall meet again."

"Tell me you love me," I said. "Will you tell me that?"

She paused, the blue eyes half-closed. "I love you," she said simply, and turned to walk quickly toward the house.

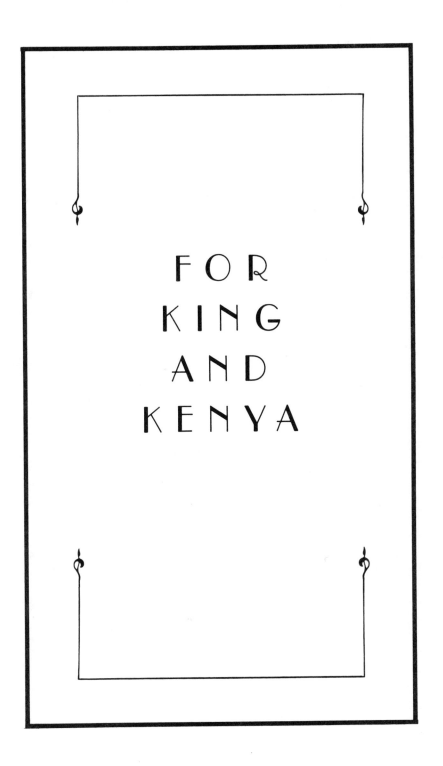

FOR
KING
AND
KENYA

ELEVEN

A small, bull-nosed Morris car bumped along the unmade-up road from Naivasha to the lakeside. It was early evening and the rays of the setting sun, bifurcated by the rising hillside, lit the dark lake's surface in two great, separate pools of gold. The attention of Mr. Hyrcano Rahvdi, however, was concentrated not on the lake and its vast, circling flocks of cranes and guinea fowl, but on the isolated houses, pockets of light in the fast-growing darkness along the lakeshore. Mr. Rahvdi was not a man much concerned with the natural world. He liked to think he was a philosopher, a humanist. Some, he knew, would add that he was an opportunist, and he gravely accepted the description. But he had seen so much of raw nature. He found the night frightening, the savage beauty of Lake Naivasha vaguely sinister, even in daylight. The brick and stucco houses built by the new English settlers along the lakeshore were far too isolated for his taste. The animals that commanded the night, the leopards, the jackals, the hyenas, filled him with alarm.

He carried no gun in his car, fearing to suffer the humiliation of the refusal his coffee-colored skin might provoke if he applied for a gun license in Nairobi. He drove, watching the dramatic shadows lengthen beyond his feeble headlights. He winced at the shriek of bird or beast that he neither identified nor wished to identify. His concentration was solely on the brilliantly lighted house on the road below him. He was already thinking of the horrors of the lonely drive back, the dark shapes in the headlights, the human-sounding screams of the bush.

The house Mr. Rahvdi was approaching from the final turn of the dirt road was lit by batteries of orange lights placed high in the acacia trees on both sides of the sloping lawn. Its façade was of brilliant white stucco, softened now by the lights. A dozen Greek columns supported the roof of a long veranda that overlooked the lake. It had been a wedding present to Lord George Amadeus Winslow from his new bride, and he had named it Corinth.

Beyond the Winslows' house it was over a mile to the next pocket of light. There the house was long and low, an inflated Surrey bungalow in style. It was the home of Gerald Longman and his wife, Pamela. From the huge drifting mountains of cumulus that daily floated across the sky as the rainy season came to an end, the Longmans' house had been named Passing Clouds. There were already other houses along the lakeshore. Boy Carstairs and Tom Boscowan rented a house half-built and then abandoned by an Italian settler; the Mowbray sisters were extending another house at the far end of a mountain lake. Within a few miles of Corinth lived Nancy Hofmanthal and Gloria Adams; Paula Upton-Mallet and her white-hunter husband, on the rare occasions he was present; and the recently returned Basil and Marjorie Bellamy. With Harry Towers and Brick Taylor-Hammond, this group formed the nucleus of the Winslow "set." The Brocklebanks, Fitzhamptons, Crackanthorpes, and Harcourts were perhaps within the next concentric circle of Dantean cosmology. Beyond them were visitors to Nairobi: writers and journalists like Evelyn Waugh; the American McMurton clan, who arrived at least once a year; the owners and trainers among the Nairobi racing fraternity; the unhappy heiresses circling the world as dangerously as moths around a candle.

Rahvdi switched off the engine. Freewheeling down through the open five-bar gate, he let the car roll to a halt about twenty yards from the house. He judged it a polite distance. Lord and Lady Winslow and their friends, should they be enjoying the evening on their veranda, would not, obviously, wish their view of the lake obscured by a dusty, bull-nosed Morris inscribed NAIROBI WATER DEPARTMENT on its passenger door.

The Winslows were nowhere to be seen. The veranda was lit, a drinks table was laid. Inside the house, dogs barked. Mr. Rahvdi came forward and stood admiring the elegance of the colonnade. Deep chintz-covered armchairs were grouped around low drinks tables. A glass double door was open, leading into a pale green hall from which an elegant chromium and brass staircase ascended. Mr. Rahvdi never ceased to admire the tastes of such aristocrats. He leaned forward to peer into the hall. The walls were pale green and lined with pieces of mahogany furniture, an escritoire, a semicircular card table. Mr. Rahvdi took a step or two forward. Double doors were open into a dining room. The table, also of mahogany, had been pushed against the wall. A thorn tree, decorated with lights and baubles to make an English Christmas tree, stood at the far end of the room, its base surrounded with wrapped and labeled presents.

Mr. Rahvdi turned and stopped. On the wall opposite hung a full-length portrait in oils of Lord Winslow in his House of Lords robes. And next to it hung another portrait, this one of a nymph, classical, naked. With a sudden shock of embarrassment, he realized it was an intimate painting of Lady Margaret. He stepped back guiltily, and at that moment a terrible voice bawled from the darkness beyond the veranda's colonnade.

"What the bloody hell d'you think you're doing?"

Mr. Rahvdi spun round, shaking with guilty alarm. He could see nothing, but the running footsteps across the gravel drive were clear and terrifying.

A tall man in riding breeches and polished boots burst onto the veranda from the darkness. His finger was stabbing toward Mr. Rahvdi. "Stay where you bloody well are," he shouted. "Move a muscle and you'll catch it."

Rahvdi stood petrified as the man took half a dozen rapid paces toward him. He could see a young, gaunt face, a thin line of mouth, a frightening energy with which the man crossed the space between them. Then he was gripped by the shoulder and dragged forward under a light fizzing with a million moths.

Prodding hard at Mr. Rahvdi's chest with his index finger, Tommy Boscowan thrust his darkened face forward. "And what's a bloody duka-wallah doing in Lord Winslow's house, eh?"

"Please sir, I am not a shopkeeper. Allow me to explain." Mr. Rahvdi tried in desperation to wriggle out of Boscowan's grip.

"You'll explain, right enough," Boscowan said with a hiss of anger. "And if you don't stand still, I'll smack you one in the mouth."

Mr. Rahvdi stood still. Crouched, breathing heavily, he stood absolutely still.

"That's better," Boscowan conceded. He released his grip on Mr. Rahvdi's shoulder. Slowly the other man straightened up. "You are making a great error, sir," he said cautiously. "If I may advise you, you are in error to believe that I am an Indian gentleman."

"You look like a bloody Indian to me."

Mr. Rahvdi lifted his hands, palms outward in protest. "I am of Turkish origin, sir. A European."

Boscowan twisted his lips in a smile of disbelief.

"Indeed, a British subject from the island of Cyprus, a former member of the college of Corpus Christi, Cambridge."

From within the house, footsteps diverted Boscowan's attention. He looked up to see Winslow and Lady Margaret coming out onto the veranda.

Mr. Rahvdi, his body tensely still, twisted his head around. "Ah, Lord and Lady Winslow," he sighed in relief, relaxing from the shoulders.

"What's going on here, Tommy?" Winslow asked cheerfully. "What's all the shouting about?"

"Caught this bloody Indian chap mooching around your veranda," Boscowan said. "D'you know him?"

"Of course." Winslow lifted a hand in greeting. "Hallo, Rahvdi, glad you made it."

"I was explaining to this gentleman, your friend, that I am not in fact an Indian chap at all. The unusual color of my facial skin is due entirely to my Turkish origins."

"Of course it is," Buzz said indifferently. He had already reached the drinks table and was pouring a large gin and tonic.

"On leaving town," Mr. Rahvdi said, "I was hailed by my intimate friend, Mr. Hopkins of the Post and Telegraph Office. Hearing through intermediaries that I was to make the journey to Naivasha tonight, he asked me to transport this package to you, my lord." He drew from his inside pocket a brown paper package and handed it to Buzz. The surface of the package was crinkled and cut by the strings. It was addressed in Diana's writing, and the line of pfennig stamps carried the face of Hindenberg.

"What is it?" Boscowan asked suspiciously.

"It's from Diana," Buzz said. He put in on the table, tapping it reflectively. "I think it must be her book."

"Well, are you not going to open it?"

Buzz shook his head. "Not yet, Tommy, no. I promised to pick up Brick and Harry." He scowled at Rahvdi, then looked up at Margaret. "You could take your bath before we get back."

She gently slapped his cheek. "What would be the point of that, darling?" she said. "I'm clean already." She smiled. "I don't know what you've done, Mr. Rahvdi," she said as she sat on the arm of a chair and stretched out her hand toward her husband, snapping her fingers for a drink, "but you seem to have upset poor Tommy."

"A simple misunderstanding. Easily resolved, Lady Margaret."

"How much did you bring?" She took the drink Buzz had mixed her and sipped it, watching Rahvdi over the edge of the glass.

"A hundred shillings' worth," Rahvdi said. "In Nairobi there are beginning to be some elements of a shortage." He looked quickly toward Buzz.

"A hundred shillings' worth is nothing," Margaret said sharply. "You know that. I've got a big party on tonight."

Buzz came forward and stood beside Rahvdi. "I told him," he said. "I told him no more than a hundred shillings."

"So there's no shortage." She looked past her husband toward Rahvdi. "You were lying."

"There is not a very *large* shortage," Rahvdi conceded uncomfortably.

She stood up. "Let me have it."

He took four small bottles of morphine and a yellow envelope of cocaine from his pocket, and handed them to her.

"You're a dear," she smiled. "It's only my husband who's a brute." She turned quickly and walked into the house. In a quick flutter of color he saw her run up the brass and chromium stairs.

Buzz Winslow turned back to the table and poured himself another gin fizz. Mr. Rahvdi watched him. In all his visits to Corinth he had never been offered a drink. He had seen others—guests, of course—walk across and pour themselves one without a word. Perhaps that was the style of a gentleman, he wasn't sure.

"One thing, old chap, before you go." Buzz turned to face Rahvdi. "My wife never orders anything I'm not aware of. That right?"

"Before your lordship's marriage, of course, she ordered frequently."

"Since our marriage?"

"Since your marriage it has been known for Lady Margaret to place one or two orders. Very small ones," he added as he saw the set of Buzz's mouth. "Very small, Lord Winslow."

Buzz nodded. "Understand me, Rahvdi," he said without animosity. "If I catch you letting her have anything I've not ordered for her, I'll give you the most fearful thrashing."

Rahvdi gulped and ducked his head. "I understand, sir."

Buzz nodded. "Do you ever take any of this stuff, Rahvdi?"

"No, sir."

"Very wise, I suppose. Plenty of people fall for it, the morphine especially."

"These drugs are of a very potent nature, my lord. It is even said that they will soon be on prescription only."

"Are you saying my wife takes too much?"

"It is not for me to comment, sir."

"All right, Rahvdi. I take your point. Now push off, there's a good chap. Our guests will be arriving shortly."

"No problems, I hope, Mr. Rahvdi," Margaret Winslow said. She had returned to stand in the doorway. The light from the room behind her, Mr. Rahvdi noticed, faintly outlined her long legs beneath her yellow evening dress.

"The only problem," Rahvdi said gaily, "is a slight misunderstanding between your friend and me. Understandable in view of the restrained lighting on the veranda here." He turned to Boscowan. "May I present myself, sir. Hyrcano Rahvdi, of the Nairobi Water Department."

Boscowan nodded dubiously.

"And your tormentor is Tom Boscowan." Margaret came forward and slipped her hand through his arm. "A very dear, but not very bright friend."

"Thanks a lot." Boscowan removed his arm. "Harry and Brick will be waiting."

Buzz laughed and rattled the ice in his gin fizz.

"Don't grump, darling," Margaret said. "Don't forget, this is the season of love and goodwill. If you're awfully good, I'll blow your feather in the direction of a new girlfriend."

Through the glass doors Rahvdi could see servants moving

back and forth with trays and bottles. "There is the question of the hundred shillings, my lord."

"Put it on the slate."

"There is also the question of an earlier one hundred and seventy-five shillings, which is already on the slate."

"So?" Buzz's head came up.

"So, to buy further stock, sir."

"Always the same excuse. The duka-wallahs use it all the time."

"I am of European origin, my lord," Rahvdi said in desperation.

Buzz walked toward the glass doors. "Course you are, old chap," he said absently. "Put it on the slate."

Mr. Rahvdi stepped back a pace. "Then may I wish you the compliments of the season," he said, accepting his defeat. "And Mr. Boscowan, too, of course." He half-bowed in the direction of Tom Boscowan.

"Very kind of you, old chap," Buzz said. "Now run along, will you?"

"If I may"—Rahvdi hesitated in mid-step like a baby ostrich—"I would be honored to show you a photograph."

"A photograph?" Buzz said, frowning.

"I am to be wed in the coming year," Mr. Rahvdi said. "A most beautiful bride." He drew a large photograph from his inside pocket. "It would give me great pleasure for you, Lord Winslow, to view her. And Mr. Boscowan, of course."

"I'll view her," Buzz said, taking the photograph.

"Her name is Mary. A very good old English name."

Buzz Winslow did not disguise his astonishment. The photograph, in poor hand-tinted color, was of a girl of sixteen or seventeen, dark-haired, dark-eyed, with full red lips. Her shoulders were bare, glistening brown in the photographer's lights. Her breasts swelled toward the cropped edge of the photograph.

"You've drawn the ace of diamonds there, Rahvdi." Buzz handed the photograph to Boscowan.

"How in God's name did you get hold of this?" Boscowan asked, holding the picture under the light.

"It is the careful work of a photographer local to her village," Mr. Rahvdi explained. "This is, of course, not the normal photograph."

"Nothing normal about Mary," Boscowan said.

"What's *abnormal* about Mary?" Boy Carstairs came out on the terrace. "Oh, I say!" He snatched the photograph from Boscowan's hand.

"Please to be careful." Mr. Rahvdi came forward, his hand outstretched.

"Just a moment, old chap." Boy Carstairs placed a large hand in the middle of Rahvdi's chest, pushing him backwards. "What a cracker!"

"Rahvdi's wife-to-be," Buzz said, smiling. "Lucky chap."

"Very lucky chap," Carstairs agreed. "You must have gone through quite a number before you chose her."

"Indeed I did, sir. She was not my very first choice."

"You mean you go through all these young girls until you get what you fancy?" Boscowan said. "You're a dark horse, Rahvdi, in more ways than one."

"It was a selection, of course," Rahvdi said uncertainly.

"And how was Mary?"

"She was my preferred."

"The choicest, eh?" Boscowan winked at Buzz.

"A nice *feel* about her, you thought," Carstairs put in.

"I never took you for a dirty old man, Rahvdi," Buzz said, laughing. "What a life! Feeling up hundreds of young girls until you find just the mushroom that suits your taste. And you a Cambridge man, as you tell us."

"Please, gentlemen," Rahvdi said, a high note of panic in his voice. "Please give me back the photograph." He lunged forward and met Carstairs's hand, hard this time in the middle of his chest. Carstairs tossed the photograph to Buzz.

Buzz smacked his lips. "Ace of diamonds."

"Lord Winslow . . ." Rahvdi came forward, but Buzz flicked the photograph like a playing card into Boscowan's lap. Boscowan stood up, towering above Rahvdi, holding the picture at arm's height. "Only if you promise," he said, "as a Cambridge man to an Oxford man . . ."

"If I may have the photograph."

"Only if you promise. Yes?"

"I promise," Rahvdi said desperately. "What shall I promise?"

"To give me first shot when you put her in the bazaar."

Mr. Rahvdi's lips trembled. He stepped back, leaving Boscowan standing, his arm in the air. "Keep the photograph, gentlemen," he said quietly. "If it gives you pleasure."

He turned away and walked down the veranda steps. Buzz

snatched the picture from Boscowan's hands. "Rahvdi," he called into the night. "Only a bit of fun."

They stood listening to the crunch of footsteps across the gravel, and the opening and slamming of a car door.

"I think we've offended him," Carstairs said, shaking his head.

"Worse than that." Buzz looked down at the photograph in his hand. "He'll probably call off the marriage."

Beyond the house, the engine of the bull-nosed Morris coughed and flared into life.

"Rahvdi!" Buzz plunged into the scented night. Racing down the drive, he skidded to a dusty halt in the headlights of Mr. Rahvdi's Morris. Then, walking forward he handed the photograph through the open window. Rahvdi took it silently.

"Terribly sorry, old chap," Buzz said. "The joke got out of hand."

"It was, in any case, Lord Winslow, not a joke I appreciated," said Rahvdi with dignity.

Buzz nodded. "Quite so, old chap. Heartfelt apologies, then. All right?"

"Thank you," Rahvdi said, without his ready smile. "Please say good night to Lady Winslow for me."

Buzz returned to the veranda.

"What did he say?" Boscowan asked, laughing.

"Funny chaps, these Indians," Buzz said, recovering his drink. "Their trouble is they're so awfully polite. Anybody else would have belted you in the mouth."

As Hyrcano Rahvdi started on his long night journey home, the party at Corinth began to gather. Paula Upton-Mallet, a petite, rounded brunette, arrived alone in a large, well-sprung Plymouth. She was particularly looking forward to the two-day Christmas *ngoma* that Buzz's invitation had promised. It was the first real Winslow thrash she would have attended alone. Her husband, Nick, had been engaged to take an Anglo-American party on safari for the Christmas holiday, partly in the expectation that Paula would join them. But she had claimed that she was not up to camping and marching in the Christmas heat, hinting at the possibility that she was pregnant again. It had been enough for Nick Upton-Mallet. He was convinced that only an almost unending line of children would really serve to make his wife adjust to life in Kenya. For almost the first time he had set off to lead his safari into the northern regions without a serious worry about the Happy Valley set with whom she seemed so much at home.

For her part, Paula felt a delicious sense of freedom as she pealed with breathless laughter after long kisses from Boscowan and Boy Carstairs under the mistletoe in the hall. "I haven't been here five minutes," she said, patting her hair, "and I feel raped already."

"There are worse ways to begin a Christmas party," Carstairs said. "So you managed to duck out of the old bugger's safari."

"You mustn't call him an old bugger," she said. "The word might spread."

"It spread pretty far at Eton."

"You're not serious."

"Young bugger," Boscowan said crisply. "Very pretty as a lad."

"You're not serious," Paula repeated. "Nick? Interested in other chaps?"

"We all were," Carstairs said. "Nothing else to get a handful of, turn to your own kind, don't you? Look at the amoeba."

"I'd rather not," Paula said. "And *is* there any champagne to be found in the house?"

Tommy Wandle, arriving with his friends the Harcourts, approached the coming thrash without enthusiasm. Like Towers, a founding member of the Corinthians, his circumstances had changed dramatically since his Cambridge days. Even then noted for an overtender temper, he had returned after the war to the family estates in the West of Ireland. His father, very far from the image of an Anglo-Irish landowner, had turned, in twenty years, gentile poverty into a considerable income from salmon fishing on his estate outside Westport. He had even succeeded in extricating himself from the political difficulties of the postwar years. When Tommy Wandle returned from war service in India, his father had arranged a will that would have kept Tommy and his younger brother in considerable comfort for the rest of their lives. But it was not the way Tommy Wandle saw the matter of inheritance. His younger brother was, in the first place, a younger brother. In addition, his lame left leg had excused him from fighting for King and Empire, ideas that, even though they no longer ruled Ireland, vaguely ruled the heart of Tommy Wandle.

Within a week they were barely speaking. Within a month there was open hostility that became even worse when it became apparent that Tommy Wandle was paying court to his brother's wife. The night had come when Wandle fought and knocked down his younger brother with enough viciousness to send him to the hospital.

The father had called the great, hulking, red-haired Tommy into his study. He had had, throughout his life, an un-Irish ability to control his emotions. "I'm not going to say anything, Tommy. I'm not going to talk about things I can't understand. What I do understand is that there'll be murder if you stay here. I'm proposing to you, Tommy, a lump sum of twenty thousand pounds, and I'm asking you to leave us forever."

He had accepted the offer. For the time it was a large sum. But two years in New York and a few more years in London had reduced it to almost nothing. He had telegraphed his father in Ireland to ask if he might come and see him, and received a brief answer: AN AGREEMENT IS AN AGREEMENT. SORRY TOM.

His correspondence with Buzz Winslow, sporadic but continuing throughout the years, had offered him a way out. Harry Towers, as rich as ever, was farming near Gilgil. He would be delighted for Tom to come out and help him. Of course, he already had an excellent farm manager, an ex-sergeant in the Loyals, who relieved him of the tedious day-to-day part of the life of the soil.

Tommy Wandle's agreement had been immediate, and since the beginning of last year he had lived in luxury and without friction with his friend at Gilgil. But in the last weeks he had, he thought, begun to detect an interest on the part of Anthea Mowbray.

The two Mowbray girls, divorced now by their husbands, had cut the marital knot together and sailed to Africa. The source of their fortune was mostly unknown but rumored to be South African or Rhodesian. They were, they sometimes claimed, simply bringing the diamonds back home. Certainly they were rich, and both of them were pretty enough. Anthea, slightly the elder, had had a long and public passion for Buzz Winslow. But in the last weeks or even months, Tommy Wandle thought he had detected the very beginnings of a change of tack. They had had some nice evenings together listening to the gramophone, talking, drinking a little wine. The real prospect of a new future suddenly loomed before Tommy Wandle. A future very different in quality from his present position as pseudo-farmer living on the charity of a friend. The easy atmosphere developing between him and Anthea Mowbray offered real hope for that future. But it was an atmosphere, as Tommy Wandle knew, that a real Corinthian *ngoma* could break in one single night.

Tom Boscowan's hopes for the evening were higher. But the possibility that they would be again painfully shattered he already accepted. He had come to Africa in pursuit of Margaret Ryder. He had no interest in her fortune, being adequately funded, as he put it himself. But he had made no effort and had never attempted to make an effort to disguise the fact that since he was first introduced to Margaret Ryder at Diana's Venetian wedding party, he had been in love with her. It was not that she had not allowed him frequent sexual contact since his arrival in Africa, but it was such as to reduce him to the role of a rather sinister lapdog, and his furious jealousy when Margaret was "won" by anyone in a game of feather football was a source of high hilarity.

Harry Towers was an altogether more simple man. He was in Africa because Buzz was here, and he was in Africa for a strictly limited period. To his family back home, he was sowing his wild oats sufficiently far away for the details not to attract too much comment in his native Shropshire. When he returned in a year or two, he was expected, and he himself expected, to marry one of the six girls of a neighboring Shropshire squire. In the meantime he had been inspired by the response of Paula to his mistletoe kiss, although the full-figured Marjorie Bellamy might, if what he had heard on the veranda came to pass, be unescorted by her husband over the next two days of the thrash.

The first marital disagreement of the night, between Basil and Marjorie Bellamy, had in fact begun long before the party got under way. The Bellamys, though quite recently married, were of very disparate ages. Sir Basil Bellamy, once considered the second-best-looking man in the Brigade of Guards, was in his late fifties, a widower, when he had met in London a round-faced, full-figured girl in her early twenties. Marjorie Crawford was lucky, as she often admitted, that she had missed the era when it was fashionable to be as flat as a plank door. She dressed carefully but with awareness of the new value of her charms. She played tennis at the right clubs and began to be seen at the right parties. She had, it was said afterwards, achieved the extraordinarily difficult feat of slipping into London society unobserved.

She needed Basil Bellamy as much as he, in his fifty-sixth year, needed her. She had received several offers to be the mistress of distinguished members of the aristocracy. The young Prince of Wales—Edward P., as he was known to his friends—had once taken her into the garden at Belvoir and attempted to feel her through her ball gown. He had been surprised and perhaps mildly amused when she rebuffed him. Thus she had had offers, but no offers of marriage. Until she met Bellamy.

They had met just once before, at a cocktail party, and Bellamy took the opportunity to take her hand and press the flesh of her upper arm. A few minutes of desultory conversation had been the prelude to the most remarkable exchange in Bellamy's life. They were standing together on the terrace of the House of Commons, where a mutual friend was entertaining his guests. "A pretty girl like you, Miss Crawford, should have pearls," Bellamy had said. "Lots of pearls."

She lifted her face to him. Her smile pouted her lips. Her raised eyebrows rippled her forehead.

Bellamy felt a tremor of excitement. "Nothing looks better around a girl's neck than a rope of fine pearls," he repeated.

She drew on her cigarette and exhaled through relentlessly pouting lips. Her eyes never left his. "Fine pearls," she said crisply, "cost a nabob's fortune."

"An arrangement is not out of the question," he breathed.

"I sense an offer coming," she said in a direct, disconcerting way that men were to find attractive.

He rubbed his chin, and was irritated to feel stubble from a badly executed shave. He knew that under strong light his face would be speckled with a grayness that made him look old and even somewhat scruffy. His fear of aging welled up as he looked down at the unlined face of the girl beside him. "If there were to be an offer," he said, backing away from the beam of the embankment light, "I wonder how it might be received."

"It depends," she said. "I shall never be a rich man's mistress."

"No. No, of course."

"I should want a proposal of marriage. A proper settlement. An agreement for separate beds. A cash sum in the event of divorce. And I should want to live at least three months of the year abroad, in the sun."

His hand dropped from the side of the face he was shielding. He had thought to set the girl up somewhere on a thousand a year and the occasional rope of pearls. Marriage had not crossed his mind. But why not? She was the right sort of companion for him, and pretty enough to carry off her slight air of commonness. Yes, he'd snap her up. He took her hand. "My solicitors will be in touch with you tomorrow, my dear." He bent down grayly into the lamplight and smiled at her, no longer the second-best-looking man in the Brigade of Guards.

The arrangement had initially delighted Marjorie. She spent three winter months of each year in the sun and nine months within range of her new lover, Dick Taylor-Arche. She had traveled to California, to the Bahamas, and, last year for the first time, to Kenya. Peripheral members of the Winslow set last year, it had still been enough to whet Marjorie's appetite and to make Basil Bellamy vow that he would not bring her to the colony again.

They had had several quarrels already about the desirability of the Winslow set. What Harry Towers had overheard tonight was in some ways little more than a repeat performance. The Christmas arrangements, as understood by Basil, had been simple. He and Marjorie were to call in at Naivasha for a glass of champagne before traveling on to Elmenteita, where an old Brigade of Guards friend of Bellamy's had invited them to spend Christmas Eve and Christmas Day. Perhaps it was no part of Marjorie's understanding. It was certainly no part of her plan. When Margaret Winslow had pressed them to stay for the party, Marjorie had accepted. What Harry Towers had heard on the veranda was Basil Bellamy's response. "A wife," he said, "should be spending Christmas with her husband. It stands to reason, Marjorie."

"A husband worth his salt should simply not have accepted an invitation to spend the whole of Christmas with two old fogeys. I'm just not going, Basil. Telephone them now and say we've been delayed here and will be with them tomorrow. That should be enough for anyone."

"It's not enough for me," he said furiously. "Don't think I don't know what it is. All these young bloods roaming around unattached is making you hot. I know it."

There had been a long pause.

Harry Towers, in the shadow at the far end of the terrace, had moved closer.

"Do you mean you don't deny it?" Bellamy asked incredulously.

"You must think what you think," she snapped. "Dirty thoughts and dirty old men go together. I'm staying here."

There had been nothing Bellamy could do to dissuade her. When he left to drive to his friends at Elmenteita, Marjorie was already dancing a very slow fox-trot with Harry Towers.

The guests' cars were rolling in a constant stream into the paddock by now. From all around Naivasha and from as far away as Nairobi or Gilgil or Elmenteita the Hope-Wallaces, the Brocklebanks, the Crackanthorpes, the Fitzhamptons, and the Pedersens burst from their cars calling greetings and carrying presents. The African servants scurried between the house and the paddock, carrying the colored boxes to the Christmas tree, themselves wondering and delighted at this strange white man's yearly rite. But they had seen other Christmases. They knew to be careful. Those who did not live in the outbuildings of the house would time their departures with care to the safety of their thatched-roof huts in the *shambas* halfway up the hill. They knew the bwanas and memsahibs could change when they drank. They could shout and shriek with a laughter that could turn like a cheetah into spitting fury. During such white men's *ngomas,* many had been beaten for no reason but to placate the spirit of the dance.

Before the party proper could begin, there was a rite to be observed. All Corinthian parties since the first meeting of the club in Cambridge had begun with Buzz's favorite word game, a ritual guessing of the authorship of entries in *The Oxford Dictionary of Quotations.* When he called for the book, it was expected that the guests would fall quiet and drift across to the veranda, where the teams would be chosen.

Buzz issued orders. "You know where the book is, Harry. One round of quotations to lift the intellectual level of the evening. A bottle of champagne to toast absent friends, and the party can go to hell and beyond after that."

The Oxford Dictionary of Quotations was placed reverently in Buzz's hands. Guests organized themselves in the veranda armchairs, or seated themselves on the low wall between the white columns of the colonnade.

"Quiet, please," Buzz said. "We'll have two captains, Mike Drummond and I. First choice to you, Mike, as a guest."

The teams were selected. Drummond, Margaret Winslow, Marjorie Bellamy, and Nancy Hofmanthal against Buzz, Harry Towers, Tommy Boscowan, and Paula Upton-Mallet.

"Margaret, your choice," Drummond said.

Margaret considered, fingers lightly touching the base of the chin, long legs crossed in front of her. "Page one hundred and twenty-eight."

Buzz flicked through the pages.

"Quotation seventeen." Margaret leaned forward eagerly now. "No Latin," she said. "I have little Latin and less Greek." She smiled at Drummond. "What is it, Buzz?"

Buzz got up, holding the book. He declaimed:

> "'He thought he saw a Rattlesnake
> That questioned him in Greek,
> He looked again and found it was
> The Middle of Next Week.
> The one thing I regret, he said,
> Is that I cannot speak.'"

Buzz lifted his fingers. "And another verse:

> 'He thought he saw a Bankers Clerk
> Descending from the bus:
> He looked again and found it was
> A Hippopotamus:
> "If this should stay to dine, he said,
> There won't be much for us."'"

Buzz beamed down at the opposing team. "Got it?" he said. "It's frightfully easy."

Margaret shrugged. Marjorie Bellamy frowned. "Easy enough for you, perhaps, Buzz."

"Ah, flatterer." He drew his free hand down the back of her head. "For that you'll get one more verse to see if that tells you:

> 'He thought he saw an Albatros
> That fluttered round the lamp

[222]

He looked again and found it was
A penny-postage-stamp.
"You'd best be getting home," he said,
"The nights are very damp.""

Buzz fixed the opposing team, each in turn, with his theatrical glare. "Not an idea in the collective cranium. Come now, English rather than American, a name known to all. His works, some of them at least, a household name."

They stared at him silently. A faint breeze from the lake disturbed the warm air trapped by the veranda. Marjorie Bellamy's skirt lifted. As she smoothed it down, Buzz caught her eye.

"Nobody has any idea?" Mike Drummond said. "Harry?"

"Not me, old chap."

"Marjorie?"

"I can only think of Hilaire Belloc."

"It's something." He turned to Buzz. "We'll say Hilaire Belloc."

"No," Marjorie said sharply. "I've remembered. It's Lewis Carroll, of course."

"Lewis Carroll. Brilliant, Marjorie. The first point to your lot. And now, Mike"—Buzz handed Drummond the book— "we'll begin with—what shall it be, Paula?"

"Page five hundred and fifty-four. Does it go that far?"

"Indeed. And the quotation number?"

"Twenty-seven," Paula announced.

"Well, Mike?" Buzz looked toward Drummond in keen anticipation. "What is it?"

Drummond frowned. "My Latin's not what it was, old chap," he said. "Not sure I can scan in the regulation manner."

"Try your best," Buzz said.

"'*Vestibulum ante ipsum primis.* / *In faucibus Orci,*'" Drummond read stumblingly.

"'*Vestibulum* ante *ipsum primis.* / *In faucibus Orci,*'" Buzz corrected him easily. "The caesura comes after *ante.*"

"What the devil does it mean?" Harry Towers said.

"Simple enough." Buzz smiled his angelic smile. "Caught in the vestibule with a fearful hard-on, he launched himself at her open legs."

"I say," Drummond murmured, "steady on, old chap."

"What does it say there, Mike?" Lady Margaret said soothingly. "In the book."

"Hard before the portal in the opening of Hell . . ." Drummond began.

The guests burst out laughing. Drummond forced a smile.

"The *Aeneid*," Buzz said. "By Virgil. Dirty bugger."

"Correct," Drummond said stiffly. "One point each."

It was not a game for most of the guests. Margaret Winslow failed to identify a Shakespeare sonnet. Marjorie Bellamy gathered praise for a verse she successfully ascribed to Longfellow. But it was Buzz Winslow's game: with only one lapse he identified John Donne, Macaulay, and two Shakespeare quotations. His finest moment was to pronounce Thomas Appleton the author of "Good Americans, when they die, go to Paris."

His team won by five points to two. The book was put away, the champagne glasses filled. Guests crowded onto the veranda or stood on the lawn below. Buzz jumped up on a chair. "To the Corinthians," he said. "Absent friends, wherever they may be. To Diana and Charles particularly. And to Claus von Hardenberg, our old gray forest wolf."

The guests lifted their glasses. "To the Corinthians!" they said. "Absent friends."

The party already had all the ingredients of success. The cold buffet, spread under an open-sided, floodlit marquee in the middle of the lawn, was surrounded by a great surge of white-dinner-jacketed men and colorfully dressed women. A band, hired from the Norfolk Hotel in Nairobi, played dance music under the acacias. A fireworks display on the edge of the lake threw arcs of red and green lights into the hills beyond.

Buzz Winslow moved through the guests like a commanding officer, giving orders to the band, chivvying servants, greeting late arrivals with shouts of "*Jambo! Jambo!*" and kissing wives with great lascivious kisses under his own personal sprig of mistletoe, which he carried in the buttonhole of his dinner jacket.

"Drugs, anyone?" Margaret cried from the top of the staircase. "Gentlemen only, come and get your sniff in my bedroom!"

African servants ran back and forth with ice buckets and bottles of champagne. Three or four guests had already fallen or been thrown from the jetty. Nancy Hofmanthal and the Brocklebanks had called for rifles and were shooting at what they swore was a hippo rising from the waters of the lake. By midnight, Marjorie Bellamy was hallucinating from an excess of alcohol and cocaine, running across the lawn screaming that there was a disembodied hand up her skirt. Already Margaret Winslow had achieved her own personal Christmas ambition by seducing the seventeen-year-old Fitzhampton boy, and was locked in her bedroom, with Tom Boscowan hammering desperately on the door.

In the dining room, Tommy Wandle lurchingly accused Mike Drummond of badgering Anthea Mowbray. Pushing his flushed face forward, he took Drummond by the lapels while Anthea shrieked that she was quite happy to be badgered.

Tearing himself free, Drummond struck out at the red face in front of him, and as Wandle reeled backwards, he struck him again with a wild swing.

While Anthea screamed, the two men circled each other, closed, pummeling at chest and face, and broke apart sweating, blood dripping from their noses. They were stumbling together again, grunting hoarsely, when Buzz hurled himself between them, broad-shouldering them apart. "Fight like gentlemen," he shouted angrily. "If you have to fight, make sure it's serious. Revolvers at fifty paces. How dare you fight like Welsh coal miners in my house!"

In the silence that followed, the two men brushed blood from their faces.

"Buzz is right," Wandle said finally. "It's not on, fighting like this." He held out his hand to Drummond, still sullen-faced.

Drummond took his hand and shook it briefly while Anthea Mowbray, among the half-circle of applauding guests, gave forth peals of hysterical laughter.

Beneath the acacia trees on the lawn, the band played furiously an approximation of Harlem jazz and then the slowest of slow fox-trots. Husbands searched for wives, while wives avoided husbands. On the coconut-mat dance floor, Margaret Winslow danced dreamily with her hand in the fly of the champagne-stupefied Fitzhampton boy.

At four o'clock, when some of the guests were already leaving, the first cries for feather football, where a bedfellow could be won or lost at the puff of a feather across a table, echoed across the lawn.

Thirty-six hours later, Marjorie Bellamy wrote to her lover, the London stockbroker, Dick Tyson-Arche:

Naivasha, Boxing Day, 1931

Jambo, darling, Jambo!

I got your inspired letters when we arrived at Mombasa. Of course I should have written to you immediately, but you must believe me when I tell you that the reason is not indifference, nor Matthew Arnold's cruelty, "composed and bland," but something quite, quite different. Darling, try to understand, coming back here again I wanted to catch my own little fistful of Africa, draw it to me and inhale it, sniff it, lick it, before the merest grain or scent escaped in half-formed thoughts, in letters, arrived-safely telegrams, wish-you-were-here postcards. Try to understand. For understand you must—if not you, who?

You ask me questions and I'll answer pat. Have I:

a. gone native? Going! Going!

b. started an affair on the boat? No!

c. met your cousins the Harcourts? Not yet.

d. been unfaithful to you in word? No.

e. or in deed? 'Fraid so!

This last answer, however, requires exegesis. On Christmas Eve I went to the most divine party, given by Buzz Winslow and his wife. Of course I'd met the Winslows before. Lord Winslow (everybody calls him Buzz) is the leader of the young set here. His wife, Margaret, is tremendous fun and thoroughly modern. A *ngoma*, the native word for a dance, at Corinth, their house, is an occasion!

The party was what Buzz calls a *thrash*. And a thrash it was. By dawn (the first day, that is) *le tout Kenya* was there, or so it seemed to me. On Christmas Day it was still going on, and the guests, fortified by an hour or two's sleep, unlimited champagne, and the sheer excitement of it all, were not—not a single one of them—to be seen to flag. By then I was hallucinating. Wherever I turned, Buzz Winslow's disembodied hand seemed to be up my skirt. Most of the male guests thought it was hilariously funny. Then, sometime later, when I was lying on a moonlit bank of lilies, I'm damned if the hand was not in the least disembodied after all. There you have it. He rogered me in a nonchalant, matter-of-fact way, hauled me to my feet, and said it was time I turned in. Which I duly did, for an hour or two. Buzz with me.

Basil knows, I'm sure, having arrived back here this morning after spending Christmas with some friends. But he is really too much of a gentleman to do more than grump about for an hour or two this morning. Margaret, Buzz's wife, who takes it all quite calmly, warns me that Buzz will be borrowing a fiver from Basil at the first opportunity. Apparently it's his way of signaling that he's had a man's wife—a rather charming way, I think, of admitting the whole thing and clearing the air without some dreadful man-to-man, middle-class confrontation.

So—I *have* been faithful—and unfaithful too. At least that's the view I came to this morning. Margaret and I sat under a great bush flaming with strange flowers and took our aperitivos *à deux*—the African boys here make the most superb gin fizzes—and talked the whole thing out. The way Margaret sees it, if I'd succumbed to a jolly roger at an English house party it would have been a clear act of infidelity to *you*. But Africa is different (of that, more later). As it is, in Margaret's philosophy, I've only been unfaithful to poor Basil— thus, faithful and unfaithful at the same time.

But really, darling, much more serious things have been happening to me than being set upon by a charming knave among the lilies. Serious things that are making me sit up and take a deep breath. Of course I can't talk to Basil about these things and don't really want to. You won't believe that Africa has, in a few short weeks, become part of the very weft and warp of me. And how could you believe it if I don't try to explain? So here goes.

What I see here in Africa, what I see before me, is nothing short of a new life, a new *hope*. Some things will be obvious to you, like climate and scenery. Some things will be less obvious, like the great, generous breadth of Africa's spirit. Anything goes here. Everything is forgivable.

The people are of course remarkable. Perhaps it's not too fanciful to talk of Darwin in these circumstances—an assemblage of more wit and wits, more concentrated good humor, tolerance, ability, talent, classical education, and sheer *joie de vivre* than you'd find in New York, Paris, and London combined.

You'll say I've fallen in love. And the truth is I have. With Africa!

And with this unique society completely without guilt or shabby sexual furtiveness. Without guilt? Why not! Since there's no working class here to thrust its grimy hand forward, rattling the begging bowl for higher wages. An African servant costs you a whole eight shillings a *month*!

Look, they all here think they're onto something. I don't want to exaggerate, darling, but there's something brave-new-world about Africa, the *real* brave new world, not Aldous's sick nightmares. Something Greek, even. Periclean Athens. Yes, I've said it. And what would Greece be without the noblest Greek of them all. Come out and join us. Sell up, cash in your expectations, beg, borrow, steal the price of the passage out. Under these wide skies we'll picnic at breakfast time and love the night away. Bring Laura and the children too, if you really *must*.

Love,
Marjorie

TWELVE

On Boxing Day morning, while Margaret Winslow and
Marjorie Bellamy were laughing together under the
acacia trees and Tom Boscowan and Boy Carstairs wandered morosely down to the water's edge, clutching large gin
slings in shaking hands, Buzz ordered his horse Achates to be
saddled up, a bottle of iced champagne to be packed in a wetted
leather saddlebag, and rode off alone toward the hills above
Lake Naivasha.

Other guests who had stayed over watched him going without surprise. After a big thrash it was known that he would ride
off for hours alone to sleep or drink champagne and read by a
rock pool in the native forest above the lake.

By midmorning he had dismounted and was leading Achates
through a grove of acacia trees above the dirt track that climbed
north from the lakeshore. The country was rough and broken
here, nearer the foothills of the Mau, with dark cones of old
volcanoes jutting strange and sinister into the sky.

Leading Achates through the acacia grove, Buzz Winslow felt
with pleasure the weight of the package in the pocket of his
bush jacket. At the rock pool he tied the reins to a branch and
unpacked sandwiches and the champagne from his saddlebags.
The cicadas shrilled in the shadowed woods around him. The
fall of water splashed into the rock pool. He tied the neck of the
champagne bottle to a string and lowered it into the water. The
rug he stretched on a flat rock, and kneeling on one knee, he
took the package from his pocket and began to tear open the
wrapping with its Berlin postmark. The book he held in his
hands seemed to him a marvel of production, its pale gray dust
jacket perfect in its restraint, the calculation of title and author's

name impeccable in yellow lettering: *Echoes from a New Century,* by Lady Diana Chrysler.

He turned the book into the flat of his right hand. His sister's photograph looked up at him, a beautiful and self-confident face, but somehow formally expressionless, like a royal head on a postage stamp.

The letter tucked inside the cover was in Diana's hand, postmarked Berlin.

My dearest Buzz,

You cannot imagine what these months have been like in Germany. The buildup to the next election has been the most exhausting, exciting time I have ever lived. The streets of every German town and village from Prussia to Bavaria are bedecked with swastikas. There are mass rallies, parades of Brownshirt storm troopers, blaring loudspeakers on the corner of every square, bonfires and torchlight parades through the villages at night.

As an international flying celebrity I have been traveling in Captain Göring's party. Sitting on the platform during one of these huge rallies is a massively intimidating experience. The roaring mass of faces below you, the chanting of *Sieg! Sieg!*, the arms raised on clockwork cue, leave me shaken and exhausted. Not so Captain Göring. Gentleman though he undoubtedly is by birth and education, he welcomes the hurly-burly of the election address, removing his coat, rolling up his sleeves, and roaring at them like an angry bull. A true Corinthian! The crowd, need I say, loves it all. Göring himself seems to have taken a great shine to me, and talks lots of frothy nonsense about my being the archetypal Aryan woman. Much more to the point, he is prepared to offer Charles all sorts of valuable airline contracts as soon as he is in control of Lufthansa, as is apparently his intention.

Am I for or against? Or simply reeling under the shock of so much color, so much noise, so much excitement, so strident a blast on the trumpets that beckon us toward the new century. As you will see, I am certainly not against.

Well, I have written a book and here is an advance copy. The timing, through no fault of my own, is perfect. An Englishwoman's account of the rise of Adolf Hitler is to be published on the eve of his triumph.

In your last letter you asked me for a true pen portrait of the man, not, repeat *not*, for publication. So . . . not as small as cartoonists represent him, certainly not as ugly, he has an Austrian shopkeeper's charm with women, always bobbing up and down as if he is about to show another couple of yards of dress material he has been keeping especially for you. Initially, Charles's view of the man was that he was the "commonest little dog" he ever met. But I hope that view is changing. What Hitler undoubtedly and mysteriously possesses is *power*. By this I don't simply mean the demonic energy he produces at his meetings, but much more, I think, the sudden glacial reserve he affects when any phrase, any gesture displeases him. The effect is that, for all his bobbing and bowing, you tend to treat him like the Pope at Rome. You are literally terrified of putting your foot in it. How he achieves this effect on people I simply do not understand.

Where will he take Germany? Where will he drag Europe?

According to Captain Göring the Nazi Party's anti-Semitism is ninety percent smokescreen. Smokescreen for what? Apparently for the party's intention to destroy their principal opponent, German communism. When this has been done and Germany's position in the world has been reestablished, we shall hear, according to Captain Göring, very little more of the Jewish problem. Do I believe him? More or less. I think more.

My book, as you will see when you read it, is more than an account of Hitler's rise. It is also an attempt to interpret this extraordinary Austrian to the British and Americans. If he is a power for good, which I have broadly indicated, it is an immense power for good—but if, as I know some believe, he is a power for evil, then he will rapidly bring the world to the crossroads. He is a man in a hurry.

It's terribly difficult to get over to you the intoxication of these days in Germany. As much as some people feel about Africa, we here feel we are about to experience a new world. I do so much hope this letter and the book reach you by Christmas.

My love to you, my brother dear, and a very happy Christmas,

Diana

Buzz put aside the letter and opened the book to its table of contents. The numbered chapters were titled "A Man of Destiny"; "To Capture a Nation"; "To Banish the Fainthearted"; "Analysis Even When It Hurts"; "*Mein Kampf,* a Blueprint for Victory." Then, finally, "Echoes from a New Century," the title chapter.

He turned to the last chapter and read:

If Adolf Hitler should die tomorrow, the National Socialist movement will still triumph in Germany. To some Englishmen and Americans the Nazi movement might seem to have a raw, feral quality, uncomfortably *working-class!* And of course it *is* working-class. Like its blood brother and life enemy, communism, it believes that the working class is the repository of all virtue, racial in the case of *National* Socialism, economic in the case of *International* Socialism. So far there is no difference between the dictatorship of the proletariat and the dictatorship of the Germanic peoples. Both believe that the structure of capitalism should be dismantled. Both believe that an elite— self-appointed, it is true, but who else can appoint an elite?— should then rule the body politic. Hegel and Plato would have joined in approbation. Of course the democrat in Britain or America or France would see problems. Much depends on the sheer *goodwill* of the leadership elite. Much depends on its trenchant honesty. The Soviet Union has fallen short of its own ideals. It is becoming fast the most *bourgeois* of societies. But in Germany, the flag of revolution is still flying and will fly higher. Socialism, National Socialism, is admittedly more philosophical than the economic socialism of Russia. But both believe in a view of the past, in a historically depressed class, in the ability of that class to establish its own destiny. Where Stalin is already falling by the wayside, Adolf Hitler will raise the banner. We Europeans must understand the concept of the elite. Only in this way will we free our millions from their chains.

He stood up and walked through the acacia grove toward the edge of the steep fall of rock. He let his mind drift over the chaotic events of the last two days of the Christmas party. Diana had found her course. But he was still so driven by the rage in his blood that the consumption of women was like food, an end in itself. In the dozen years since the war had ended, he had had nothing else. Even his marriage to Margaret, a woman as possessed as he was himself, had been aimed to allow his ruling passion to continue. He was most uneasy in times like this, when he began to feel that he was not a serious person, when he began to doubt that he could ever cast off the role of a playboy.

He felt seared, burned out by the excesses of the last two days. Below him he watched an old box-bodied car bounce its way along the dirt track that cut between high ground crowned with rocks and scrub and thickets of gray-green wild olive.

He knew it would be his neighbor, Gerald Longman's car, carrying seed or meal or oil or dung, a farmer's load. Lighting a cigarette, he watched the dust plume from the car's rear wheels as it ran for a steep slope, smiled at the wild, swerving attempts to reach the crest, and saw, rather than heard, the engine die.

It was Pamela Longman who, after a few moments, got out of the car and stood looking at the steam rising from the radiator. She was obviously alone. Her jerky gestures of despair were not meant for a companion. He finished his cigarette, considering. He could return to the rock pool at the end of the acacia grove and settle down with champagne and book. Or he could go down and offer assistance, although he knew nothing about motorcars and their greasy, spluttering engines. He was turning away when, in that brief second, he glimpsed a movement that intrigued him. The woman below reached into the top of her shirt, easing the strap of her bra away from her breast. He hesitated, watching her change hands, this time cupping the breast to separate silk from overwarm flesh.

The simple movements decided him. He parted the branches before him and slithered down the rock face toward the track, calling greetings as he burst into the bright sunlight. He had never before noticed what a pretty woman she was, large-eyed, brown-haired, dressed in a pale blue cotton shirt and khaki shorts. Flustered by his sudden appearance from among the rocks, she smiled toward him.

"Some trouble, Mrs. Longman?" He stopped with a concerned look at the hissing radiator of the car.

"Lord Winslow," she said, obviously at a loss.

"I was out riding," he said, hands on hips, still looking hard at the radiator. "Just a matter of time before she cools down. Not in a hurry, I hope."

"No. But in this heat . . ."

He agreed. "Slow business. I think you and I had better cool down too. Let's get up into the trees. If we can't get it started in half an hour, we'll set off on horseback."

She hesitated. Gerald had forbidden her to do more than pass a crisp good-morning with any of the Corinth set if she met them on the road or at the club. "Perhaps I should just wait here," she said.

"You'll get awfully hot."

"I suppose you're right," she said despairingly.

They climbed up into the acacia grove and walked through it following the stream that trickled into the rock pool. Where the shrubs closed on the track, she walked ahead. She had long slim brown legs that pleased him.

"What a lovely spot," she said. "I must have passed here a thousand times. I had no idea it was so pretty up here."

"It's beautiful," he agreed, watching her scramble down to the edge of the pool.

She patted Achates's neck. "It's a long ride from Naivasha."

"I come up here to be alone," Buzz said. "Sometimes I find it necessary." He felt no need to mention which times. "What are you doing out driving by yourself on Boxing Day? Trying to be alone too?"

"Goodness, no," she said. "The farm animals still need tending. Boxing Day or not."

They sat on a flat rock, dangling their bare feet into the water. "I'm sorry we don't see you at Corinth, Mrs. Longman," he said, staring into the water. "I've sent invitations over, of course, but apparently you and your husband have always been too busy."

"There is so much to do on a farm."

"That I would know nothing about?"

"I didn't mean that, of course."

"But it's true that's the way your husband thinks about us at Corinth, is it not? As newcomers. Not quite up to scratch?" He smiled pleasantly.

"I'm sure he doesn't," she said, distressed.

He pressed a single index finger on her bare thigh. "That was very naughty of me," he said. Lifting his finger, he left a white fading mark on the brown skin. "I wasn't trying to upset you. Just sorry you don't come over."

"Perhaps next time," she said without conviction.

He splashed at the surface of the water with his bare foot. "Where do you come from in England? Are you a country girl?"

"No," she said. "I come from the East End of London. Deptford. My father was a policeman there. When my mother died just after I was born, my father accepted a posting out here and brought me with him."

"I'd forgotten your father was Inspector Lusk," Buzz said. "So you're from Deptford. What about your husband's family? Where do they come from?"

"They're from south London. Battersea. The nice part, near the park."

"Yes," he said thoughtfully, "Battersea. Of course. Near the park."

"May I ask you a question, Lord Winslow?"

He looked into her eyes, smiling suddenly. "Only if you call me Buzz."

"No, really." She squirmed on the rock ledge. "I couldn't."

"You could. And will. Repeat after me. Buzz."

"Buzz." Her face colored.

"Was it so difficult?"

"No, . . . not really."

"Now pose your question, Pamela. What was it you were about to ask me?"

She looked down. "Something you said earlier about wanting to be alone sometimes. It was just something of a surprise, that's all."

"A surprise? Why? I ride into the forest to read, sometimes even to write a little. Mostly perhaps to think. There's a great deal of thinking to do in Africa, I find. We who are conditioned by Europe, be it Deptford or even Battersea, are naturally struck thoughtful, to say the least, in the immense presence of Africa."

He gestured up through the dark canopy of trees above their heads. "Beyond this tent of bough and leaf the skies of Africa are vaster, more liberating, or more menacing than anything you and I have ever seen before, Pamela. In terms of the natural world, to come to Africa is the transformation from croft to castle, from hovel to hall." He looked down again toward the water, shaking his head. "Who can be surprised that any of us Kenyans, men or women, find the need, just sometimes, for solitude."

"When one knows you, even a little," she said haltingly, "you're very different from the person people imagine you to be."

"Am I such an ogre?" he asked slowly.

She was silent. "Would you mind awfully," she said after a moment, "if I answered yes?"

His head tilted to one side. "I would think, on the contrary, that it might just be the beginning of a friendship between us." He considered, but judged the moment too early to place his palm on her cool brown thigh. "Do you think that's possible?"

"Friendship?"

"Yes. Between you and me. Do we come from such different worlds?"

"We do, of course."

"We did, perhaps. But Africa has changed all that."

"I'm not sure . . . " she said uncertainly.

"About our being friends, you and me?"

"It would be awfully difficult," she blurted out.

"I'm not sure you're being candid with me." He looked at her appraisingly. "We meet by chance for a few minutes in an idyllic spot like this—I think that deserves candor."

"Any real friendship between us would be impossible."

"Gerald."

"I'm afraid so."

"Can we not simply be good neighbors?"

She shook her head. "Not even that."

He nodded somberly. "Then we shall be reduced to meeting on those rare days when your car breaks down on the Mau road and I am ruminating in these hills." He smiled at her.

"You must have had an immense party on Christmas Eve," she said. "We could see the cars arriving from the farm."

"It's a time to be among friends," he said. "What about you? Did you have people over?"

"On Christmas Day the Hodsons dropped in."

"The Hodsons, yes. An extremely pleasant couple. I like Sheila Hodson particularly, although she's not our generation, of course."

"They're Gerald's friends, really. But it was nice having them. Naturally at Christmastime one wants a little company. We could hear the sound of your band, you know. At night it carried right up the hill."

"It didn't disturb you, I hope."

"Of course not." She hesitated. "Gerald got a little grumpy."

"He's not a man for parties, perhaps?"

"Not *really*, no."

"And what about you, Pamela? Do you enjoy parties?"

"It depends," she said, flushing. "I suppose it depends on the party."

He laughed. "I think you've heard some wild rumors."

"Perhaps."

"As far as I know, nobody at any party I have given has ever done anything he or she didn't want to."

"I'm sure you're right."

"When I hear stories repeated back to me," he said, "I'm frequently hard put to recognize the occasion."

"I suppose we all gossip too much," she said.

"And why not? Gossip can be fun. Here," he said. "I've a bottle of champagne hanging on this line. Let's have a glass."

"Champagne?"

He hauled up the bottle. "You won't mind sharing a glass?"

"Of course not." She shook her head. "Who would have guessed half an hour ago that I would be sitting by a pool drinking champagne with Lord Winslow."

"Buzz," he said firmly.

"Very well. Buzz."

He opened the bottle and poured champagne into a tumbler he took from his saddlebag. "I'd like it frightfully," he said, "if we *could* be friends."

She shook her head.

"I mean Gerald too." He poured more champagne.

"No. It's really not possible."

"Then just you and me."

"I couldn't."

"But we *are* friends," he laughed. "We're sitting here in the cool of a mountain forest, paddling our feet and drinking champagne. We're not *enemies*, surely?"

"No."

"Then we're friends. You mustn't feel disloyal, Pamela. My

[237]

wife, Margaret, has quite a number of friends that I don't necessarily approve of."

He reached out and held her arm lightly. "It is agreed? That we're friends?"

She was not sure whether it was the heat of the journey, the champagne, or his smile, but she knew she was in danger of conceding something that could be important to Gerald. She got to her feet. "The car," she said, "it must have cooled down by now."

"Very probably, I'm sorry to say."

They scrambled down the broken hillside hand in hand. He released her hand the moment they reached the road.

"I have very much enjoyed talking to you," he said as they walked toward the car.

"But I've hardly said anything," she protested.

"You listened," he said. "You spoke when you wanted to. It was not a drawing-room meeting."

"We must thank Africa for that," she said, and felt immediately bold.

"Yes," he agreed. "We must thank Africa for that."

She climbed into the driver's seat and turned the ignition. The car shook and started.

"When we meet publicly," he said, "it will of course be Mrs. Longman."

"And Lord Winslow."

"Yes. In any case, we meet so rarely. By then we shall have forgotten this strange interlude."

She nodded slowly. "Perhaps. But I shall never be able to think of you in the same way again. In the way many people think of you."

"As an unrepentant playboy?"

"You invite people to consider you that way. Why?"

"We all use the most improbable armor," he said, "to conceal ourselves from others. Good-bye, Pamela."

Framed by the open window, her face clouded, cleared, and seemed to cloud again. "It's become rather established," she said slowly, "for me to visit the north farm on the first Friday of each month."

A silence fell between them.

He smiled. "Strangely enough," he said, "it's a day I usually reserve for riding in the hills."

THIRTEEN

The settlers' meeting at Gerald Longman's house at Naivasha took place on an afternoon in February. The subject to be discussed was the rumor that agitators were in the district, visiting native villages at night to spread the word that if the local laborers acted together they would be able to ask for higher pay and benefits.

The idea was not entirely new. Last year at the coffee harvest several villages were said to have withdrawn their labor until a higher rate was agreed upon. To many settlers on the edge of bankruptcy, the agitator slipping silently from village to village was a potent image.

The Longman house was a low, three-sided bungalow set in the wooded hills above Lake Naivasha. Like so many other settlers' houses, it had only in the last few years had its corrugated iron roof replaced by tiles. On the veranda looking onto the dusty courtyard, Gerald and Pamela Longman served beer and directed new arrivals where to park cars or tie up horses. There were about thirty visitors, none of them, Longman was pleased to see, from the official sector of Nairobi life. In particular, he had no wish to see his father-in-law, Tom Lusk, there. "Agitation" was not against the law of the colony, and seeking out agitators was a vigilante practice that could easily bring them into conflict with Inspector Lusk.

Jack Nyquist arrived with his neighbor Alfred Pedersen, both on horseback. The Billington family came in their old box-body—father, mother, three grown sons, and two powerful, white, pink-eyed English bull mastiffs.

"Stick those bloody dogs in the backhouse," Gerald Longman called cheerfully to Frank Billington. "They'll tear the throats out of my curs if they get near them."

There were a few women there. Pam Longman carried a tray of teacups out onto the veranda for them. Dogs were locked away, the hill road scanned for further possible visitors, and Gerald Longman jumped up on a heavy toolbox at the far end of the veranda and called for silence.

The women sat in the few easy chairs with their teacups poised; the men, bronzed or red-faced, in shorts and khaki shirts, sat along the veranda rail or squatted Kikuyu fashion, their backs against the wall. As her husband began to talk about reports of native meetings being held at night, Pamela picked up the empty teapot and carried it into the kitchen. From the moment the meeting had first been discussed, Gerald had insisted that all the house servants be sent to work outside for the afternoon.

Pamela put the teapot down on the big kitchen table and refilled the kettle from the hand pump. She frowned as she swung the iron kettle onto the stove. She was deeply troubled by this meeting her husband had called, and even more troubled that she had been instructed to keep it from her father.

She roamed around the brick-floored kitchen, her arms crossed over her breasts, occasionally releasing one hand to fling back the heavy tress of hair that had fallen over her eyes. Personally she doubted that there were agitators. Certainly not "paid agitators." And if they did exist, she was not happy with the way her husband and his friends reacted, in the ferocity of the belief that these were *their* natives. From her upbringing with her policeman father, she was deeply uncomfortable with the idea that anyone had rights to another human being. At twenty-one she thought in terms of settlers and natives. She did not yet fully understand that she equally disliked the idea when applied to herself.

Outside in the forest, the sunlight picked up movement. Pam Longman crossed to the window. The bushes parted to reveal a horseman. And a moment later she saw that it was Lord Winslow in the saddle. For an instant her stomach churned guiltily as she watched him tie his horse to the fence, climb the back gate, and saunter through the sunlight toward the kitchen door.

She drew back from the window and glanced quickly into the mirror hanging next to the stove. Then she crossed the room and opened the door to Buzz.

He removed his safari hat. "Good afternoon, Mrs. Longman," he said. "Forgive my coming over the back fence, but it's much the quickest way from my place. I understand there's a meeting here this afternoon."

"It's a settlers' meeting."

Buzz smiled. "Perhaps I don't count as a settler?"

She flushed faintly. "I'm sure my husband will be very pleased you've come, Lord Winslow."

"Buzz," he said, looking around with exaggerated caution. "Buzz, when we're alone."

She smiled, caught again in the warmth he exuded. "Shall I take you through?" she asked.

"Good God, no. Not yet. I'd much sooner talk to you."

He watched the tall young woman in khaki slacks and shirt as she emptied the teapot and washed it out at the hand pump. He knew she was on the very edge of finding an adult confidence. In another year she would be a woman, even more attractive than she was now.

"You *do* know what the meeting's about?" she asked him.

"Vaguely. I believe there's some talk of agitators up in the villages. Personally," Buzz said, "I don't believe a word of it. I think it's white man's paranoia."

"You don't suffer from it because you don't employ native labor," she said firmly. "And if you're not worried, what are you doing here?"

He spread his arms wide. "I came to see you, of course."

The confidence left her.

"You didn't stop in the hills last Friday," he said.

"No." She glanced involuntarily behind her. From the direction of the veranda on the other side of the house she could hear raised voices.

"I was there," Buzz said. "I watched your car go sailing by. I don't think you so much as looked up."

She swallowed. "Yes," she said. "Yes, I saw you."

He moved across the distance separating them. "Why didn't you stop, Pam? Just for a few minutes, even. I don't mind telling you, I was awfully disappointed."

"You should go through to the meeting," she said hurriedly. "You'll miss it otherwise."

He came half a step closer, to stand at her shoulder. "To tell you the truth, Pam," he said, "I'm not terribly taken by all this vigilante business. I'd sooner hunt foxes than men."

"I agree," she said vigorously. "It's probably very disloyal to Gerald, but I do agree."

He touched her warm neck with the back of his fingers, then immediately removed his hand and circled the table away from her. "You give a great deal of thought to being loyal to Gerald, don't you?"

"I wasn't aware of it."

"He's a lucky man." Buzz crossed back toward the kitchen door and opened it. "Perhaps we'll meet, one of these days."

"Aren't you going to the meeting?"

He shook his head. "No. Vigilantes, not my brand. Truth to tell, I only came to see you anyway."

She stood irresolutely, both hands flat on the kitchen table before her. "Will you be riding on Friday?"

He cocked his head. His eyebrows lifted. "Indeed."

"Then . . ." She shrugged.

He nodded gravely and closed the door behind him.

For a few moments she watched Buzz cross the yard and climb the fence. From the top bar of the gate he leaped onto the back of his horse and began to ride up into the hills.

There was a commotion behind her. The noise level from the veranda was rising steadily. She hurried along the corridor and through the sitting room to stand at the veranda doors. Young Henry Jones, red-haired and red-faced, who farmed some land over at Gilgil, stood in the middle of a dozen questioners. "One of the village elders owes me a favor, that's how I know."

"He told you himself?" Jack Nyquist asked. "He told you there would be an agitator there tonight?"

Jones pushed Nyquist aside and reached for his bottle of beer. "You've been in this country long enough to know it doesn't happen like that. The man came up to my place with some old leathers to sell, rough stuff he knew I wouldn't buy anyway. We squatted down with a roll of tobacco outside and he told me about some sort of meeting being held at Kasambu tonight. People from this area are going is what he said."

Gerald Longman had abandoned the dominating height of the toolbox. He stood with the other settlers now in a tight male group around Jones. "Did he say there'd be an agitator up there tonight?"

"He said men would be talking."

"What did he mean by that?"

"He said they would be talking to a stranger."

"A stranger," Pedersen said. "What would they be talking about?"

Pamela Longman stood at the veranda door, watching Henry Jones.

"If they're talking to a stranger, that's good enough for me," Jones said. "And this old chap owes me a favor. I once botched up a story to the District Officer on his behalf. They don't forget a good turn."

"What d'you think, then, chaps?" Longman asked.

The men drifted back to their positions on the veranda rail or chose the slanting angle of shade. "No harm in riding up there tonight," Nyquist said. "Half a dozen of us. Just to take a look."

"You're not going to be able to just take a look, Mr. Nyquist." Pam's voice sounded high and nervous. The men looked toward the veranda door. "I mean," she said carefully, "that to find out if anything's going on, you'll have to ask questions. There could be lots of strangers there. They'll all have to be checked up on."

"You mean whatever happens, we're going to have to break up tonight's party."

"Yes. That could cause a lot more trouble than a couple of so-called agitators."

Gerald Longman turned angrily on his wife. "Since when have you been a native-affairs expert?" he said. "I thought you were a town girl. I thought you grew up in Nairobi."

"It's common sense, Gerald," she said. "But I didn't mean to interfere in your meeting. I'm sorry." She stepped back into the sitting room, and for a moment the men were silent as they listened to her footsteps crossing the board floor.

Margaret and the two Mowbray sisters emerged from the water, wrapping themselves in white terry robes. "God, you are a bore, Buzz," Margaret said, laughing. "Are you still lusting after that Longman girl?"

"It's now or never, Bunty darling," Buzz said lazily. "I can see the uncertainty in her eyes. In a year's time she wouldn't look at me. She'd think of me as what I am, a rather sordid old reprobate. But not yet!" He leaped up and swung his wife in a bear hug. "Suffer little children to come unto me," he said, wrestling Margaret to the ground.

Gerald Longman put the old Austin into gear and moved the car forward slowly through the scrub. Without lights, he was dependent on the moon, which slipped from behind purple clouds. With the window down, he could hear an African voice from time to time rising above the steady hissing of the wind through the thorn bushes. Flames rising from the village fires made a small dome of warm light above the scrub ahead.

"You've only got Henry Jones's word for it that something's going on tonight," Pamela Longman said from the passenger seat.

"Good enough," her husband said shortly.

"But you know how much he likes to come across as the old Kenya hand."

"It's the best information we've had," Gerald Longman said. "If you think, in your wisdom, that it's a waste of time, you shouldn't have come."

Pamela slid farther down in the seat, without answering.

Her father, Tom Lusk, had sent a message during the day saying that he was up visiting the Naivasha police post and would like to spend the night with them. She had no intention of facing him alone. Gerald could give his own explanation when they got back.

The dark column of cars was only a few hundred yards from the village now, and the high arch of thorn, blocked by a lattice of thorn branches that served as its single entrance, was directly ahead. Kasambu was larger than many of the villages of the region, a collection of almost fifty huts within a thorn fence woven thickly enough to deter wild animals from attacking the cattle inside. The huts themselves, varying greatly in size, enclosed a large, roughly square-shaped piece of land where by day children played, old men crouched in the shade of a huge acacia tree, and women shuffled forward in line to collect water from a source that broke bubbling through the rock. By now, few Africans were still awake. The thorn gate had been drawn across the entrance to the village. Old women were shoveling damp earth to bank the fires for the night. A group of old men, slightly drunk from illicit beer, were drifting along the side of the square arguing in a desultory, half-interested manner some point of ancient Kikuyu marriage practice.

The headlights of the settlers' cars, suddenly switched on, illuminated the village like a flash of lightning.

As Gerald Longman's car burst through the lattice gate, the women shrieked and the old men crouched in terror. Jack Nyquist, in the second car, hit the horn and swung around behind Longman's Austin so that his headlights covered one group of huts. Pederson and the Billingtons, their horns blaring, drove across the square and stopped, headlights fanned out across the village.

In the Austin, Pamela felt sick with shame. Africans tumbled from the huts, rubbing their eyes, cowering in the beam of the headlights. Nyquist was already out of his car. He held a short police baton in one hand, a powerful flashlight in the other. He was waving the baton and shouting to the men to line up along the edge of the square. Pederson and the four Billingtons were running forward, shouting orders into the dark huts.

Gerald Longman got out of his car and stood in the middle of the square. Pamela slid across into the driver's seat and started the engine. As she reversed and turned, her husband came running toward her. "Keep those bloody lights on the huts," he called angrily.

She stopped the car. "I'm going home, Gerald," she said. "You can get a lift with Jack Nyquist."

He stood uncertainly. "Going home?"

"I'm having no more to do with it. You can see there are no agitators here."

He hammered on the roof as she put the car in gear. But she shook her head violently, her dark hair flying, and headed the car back across the square. Passing over the crushed thorn lattice fence, she swung the car onto the track that would take her along the outside of the village and eventually down to the gravel road, which would bring her back to Naivasha. It was then that she saw the figure in the headlights limping away from the village.

He could not escape from the car. Even when he stumbled off the road into the scrub, she had only to turn the wheel to bring the Austin alongside him.

She had already decided to continue down the track as if she had not seen him when he collapsed and rolled over in the dust.

She stopped the car and got out. As she walked forward, the African got painfully to his feet. His shirt and khaki slacks were bloody and torn to ribbons. He wore canvas shoes covered with blood.

"Don't be afraid," she said in Kikuyu. She knew he had burst through the barrier surrounding the village. The long thorn spikes could deter an animal more easily than a determined or desperate man. "Do you speak English?"

The man nodded.

"You will need treatment for the cuts," she said. "You're losing a lot of blood."

Behind them, wailing voices rose from the village. The African was swaying now. Without answering, he lowered himself into a crouching position.

"I don't care why you wanted to get away from the village," she said. "It's no concern of mine. But you need medical help. I'll take you to the hospital post at Naivasha. Get into the car."

The African shook his head. "Not Naivasha," he said.

"Believe me," Pamela said earnestly, "you must have help."

He nodded. She saw that his lips were gray. "Will you take me in the car?"

"Yes, of course."

"To a farm a long way from here?"

"Where is this farm?"

"In the Ngong Hills," the African said. "It's owned by the Baroness Esterhazy."

My dear Claus,

These last days had a familiar ring to them. In what seemed the middle of last night, Pamela Longman, one of the settlers' wives, drove in with an injured African in the backseat of her car. Not only injured but on the run. It was Kum.

He is mostly delirious and weak from loss of blood, his legs torn as he fought his way through a thorn fence while being pursued by settler vigilantes. It is of course a political business.

I am writing briefly because looking after Kum takes much time. But I am sure, as is Pamela Longman, too, who is a trained nurse, that Kum will recover. In moments of clarity he sends his best wishes to you.

Pamela claims she met you during the war. She is the daughter of the man who interrogated you, and a very remarkable young woman. Her independence is such that, though her husband was one of the vigilantes pursuing Kum, she spirited him away here from under their noses.

I will write more later. Kum will stay only until he recovers. After that, I have no doubt he will go again.

Write to me. Write to me.

Catherine

FOURTEEN

During the period of the long rains of 1932, Buzz and Margaret Winslow returned to England. The biggest passenger aircraft disasters ever had claimed fourteen lives, one of them that of Charles Chrysler. The aeroplane he had chartered to bring friends from Paris to London had disappeared in the Channel. There were no survivors, and not until a week after the accident was any wreckage found. Telegrams had been sent to Diana in Berlin and to her brother in Kenya. A team of six lawyers had boarded the *Queen Mary* in New York and would be in London in a matter of days. There were already rumors of intricate financial trusts and conditions that would control Lady Diana's access to Charles's vast fortune. A senior member of the Chrysler family expressed dismay at Diana's current political views. It was revealed for the first time that there was a previously undisclosed Jewish background in the Chrysler family.

Two memorial services took place, one in Long Island and the other in London. At St. George's Hanover Square, Buzz Winslow escorted his sister to the church, Diana pale and half-veiled, Buzz grim-faced at her side.

There was some difference, during the next two weeks, in the way the London press treated each of them. While the reporting and photographs of Diana were clearly sympathetic, the attitude toward Buzz was harder.

He was made particularly angry by the press, who ran frequent stories on the Corinthians as a modern Hell-Fire Club translated to Africa. Nairobi stringers of the Fleet Street newspapers were required to produce photographs of his house at Lake Naivasha, and of Marjorie Bellamy, Nancy Hofmanthal, Gloria Tate-Adams, and the Mowbray sisters. In the grim Depression London of 1932, suggestions of aristocratic nymphs and satyrs under an East African heaven were seen by editors as the stuff of salable copy.

What was an irritant to the Winslows had an altogether different impact in Nairobi. The *Banner-Post* ran a weekly résumé of Fleet Street stories on life in Kenya. Settlers, themselves struggling against bankruptcy in the depressed condition of commodity markets, raged over cocktails on their farms in the White Highlands. In the legislative council, Gerald Longman went so far as to propose that Lord and Lady Winslow should be informed that they were persona non grata in the colony of Kenya, and the governor was forced to spend a difficult afternoon explaining that such a decision was beyond his powers.

Unaware of these developments, Buzz sought—and found— new diversions until the time arrived for them to return to Africa.

Clare Debenham was eighteen when Buzz Winslow first met her in London, brown-haired, reasonably pretty, consciously wild, and the niece of a royal duke. From the beginning it was obvious that she was immensely flattered by the attentions of someone with Buzz Winslow's reputation, and when they met she made no effort to disguise her interest.

Margaret considered her simpering and totally dull. But she also knew Clare Debenham was rich and dangerous. It had not escaped Margaret in the last few months that her husband exhibited all the signs of restlessness that might have suggested, in most marriages, an imminent departure from the marriage bed. But Buzz Winslow's married life was one long departure from Margaret's bed. This restlessness, she realized, was of a different order. She found it difficult or even impossible to make sense of the problem because Buzz refused categorically to talk about himself. A gentleman, he said, should walk, drink, gamble, shoot, or screw himself out of his problems. He should not load them upon his unfortunate wife.

Thus Margaret Winslow approached the question of Clare Debenham with some care. She knew that Buzz was urging Clare to accompany her kinsman Edward, Prince of Wales, on his safari trip to Kenya planned for next year, and she affected to encourage the idea. "Cannon fodder for the Winslow Beast," she described it in cheerfully mixed metaphor. But there was little that was cheerful about her real concerns. She was now well into her forties and needed no reminding from her mirror that when careful makeup was removed, she no longer looked the agelessly attractive woman who had sailed through her thirties in a shower of male compliments. She drank relatively little and exercised regularly, but she knew Buzz was increasingly angry about her drug habits, and he had not been slow to allege that the morphine was leaving its mark on her face.

Before they had left for Kenya, Buzz had accepted an invitation to spend a weekend in a party that had included Clare Debenham. For Margaret, her own weekend at another country house had passed in a narcotic stupor punctuated only by bouts of intense anxiety. When Buzz had returned on Monday morning, she had asked him, as casually as she could, about the party.

"Good," he said dismissively. "Not up to Kenyan standards, but good."

"Did you get her?"

"Get her? Get who?"

"Clare Debenham, of course. That's who you went for, wasn't it?"

"My dear girl." Buzz paced the room in the newly built Dorchester Hotel, puffing on his cigarette. "I went after Mollie Sarjeant, not tiny Clare Debenham."

Margaret sat on her dressing table seat and swiveled to face him. "And did you get Mollie?"

"Mm, no, not actually."

"What went wrong? She's mad about you."

"So I thought, old girl. Turns out she isn't. Or so it seemed to me."

"Bad luck."

"It was. All the beauties were more or less spoken for."

"Except Clare Debenham."

"Please, Margaret. Clare Debenham, Clare Debenham. You sound like a suspicious wife."

Margaret swung back and forth on her stool. "I would be less suspicious if you told me you'd done nothing but roger her all weekend."

"Well, I didn't," he said petulantly. "I partnered her at tennis, but that was as close to coupling as I got with her."

"Why was that?"

"I don't know, for God's sake," he flared.

"Did you try?"

"No, I didn't. Look, I'm going to my club for lunch. This inquisition breaks the rules, you know that."

He picked up his hat and stick.

"You could take me for lunch," she said.

"And submit to another round of questions with the cheese. No, thanks." He walked toward the door.

"Buzz . . ."

He paused, turning back toward her. His eyebrows lifted. "Yes?"

"Is she going after all?"

"To Kenya? With Edward P.? I rather think she is."

"You'll get another chance, then."

"Chance? What for?"

"To have another stab at her. That's your interest in the child, isn't it?"

"Oh, for God's sake, Margaret," he said, and let himself quickly out the door.

She knew she had done the wrong thing. As she prepared her silver syringe, she knew she had done wrong. She had revealed far too much of her hand.

When, back home in Kenya, the long rains ended and the great, high, silent billows of cloud sailed clear across the Rift Valley and vanished into the blue air beyond, the Winslows returned to Naivasha. Three days of frantic celebration passed before Buzz applied himself to his mail. Then another day before he came to open the letter from the secretary of the Muthaiga Club.

Dear Lord Winslow,

I believe you will appreciate how distasteful it is for me to write this letter. Equally, I hope you will understand that I am speaking as secretary of the club and at the request of a significant number of members.

At an Extraordinary General Meeting on June 1, it was proposed by Mr. Gerald Longman and seconded by Mr. Henry Myles that Lord George Winslow and Lady Margaret Winslow be refused continuing membership of the Muthaiga Club.

The committee, of which you yourself are of course a member, though absent on this occasion, declined to vote on the proposal on the grounds that the reasons given were not relevant to the question of club membership. These reasons, I must inform you, were conduct, on your part and on the part of Lady Winslow, likely to bring the good name of the white community into disrepute.

As secretary I was happy to rule that such reasons were altogether too vague. And I endorsed the committee's refusal to vote on the issue.

A regrettable demonstration then took place, involving a significant number of upcountry members. As a result of this demonstration I felt obliged, as secretary, to propose an Extraordinary Meeting for October 10, and to ask you to speak on the issues involved.

I am fully aware that I am acting outside the strict bounds of the Club Rules. But as secretary I have the power, indeed the obligation, to call an Extraordinary Meeting to discuss issues of concern to a significant number of members. You, in turn, are under no obligation to be present, although I do most sincerely ask you to attend. In so doing, I assure you that you will be given adequate opportunity to answer any comments from the floor.

A reply was telegraphed that same evening from Naivasha:

MY FIRST KANGAROO COURT! NOTHING WOULD KEEP MY WIFE AND SELF AWAY. LOVE AND KISSES. WINSLOW.

In the early morning of October 11, 1932, Catherine Esterhazy sat among broken chairs and rolling champagne bottles in the empty ballroom of the Muthaiga Club and wrote to Claus von Hardenberg:

My dear, dear Claus,

Forgive what is about to be a long, long letter. You will see from the writing paper that I write from the Muthaiga Club. I am alone in a ballroom awash with champagne, the litter of broken chair legs, empty bottles, and smashed chandeliers. It is four, possibly four-thirty in the morning, and from time to time I am disturbed by a member incapable of speech and sometimes locomotion, reeling out to the gardens where a party continues. Young girls in evening dress run past, sobbing wildly. Laughter comes in shrieks and shouts from the darkness beyond the mostly broken windows of the ballroom. From time to time a club servant hurries through, carrying brandies on a large tray. The steward, Ali, has looked in, surveyed the chaos wryly, and withdrawn.

What a night we have had!

It began in the late afternoon with something approaching Kenya's first traffic jam on the Nairobi road. I had not, since Lord Delamere's funeral, seen so many motorcars on the road. The dust was quite unbelievably horrible. The *totos* playing by the roadside ran screaming from the great column of vehicles. And at one point when, inevitably, we broke down, I was asked by an apprehensive (yes, apprehensive) looking old man if all bwanas and memsahibs were leaving Africa forever, it looked so much like a pell-mell flight.

But it was no mass evacuation. It was instead a Special Meeting at the Muthaiga Club! Can you believe that nearly three hundred people would drive, some of them over a hundred miles from farms at Gilgil and Elmenteita, even from Nanyuki, for a Special Meeting of the Muthaiga Country Club? But then, this was no ordinary Special Meeting. It was to be the public debagging of your friend Lord Winslow. The banning from the club precincts of the devil incarnate and his aristo doxy!

By chance I had booked a room for that very night, having yet more bank business to do in town. I was fortunate. Most rooms were organized as group changing rooms, and members were resigned, if that's the word, to a long, sleepless night of drink and excitement.

It was provided for them in ample measure. Let me try to paint the picture for you. The Muthaiga Club you don't know, of course. It was built a few years ago, an English country club in the middle of town. It is a pink, pebble-dashed nonentity of a building with metal-frame windows and stunted Greek columns to add a touch of class. Even to enter it makes me feel very American. I mean, of course, it is so entirely *British*, although saying that I am aware that many millions of Englishmen would shrink from the dread rituals of the place with as much horror as I do myself. And the rituals are many. It is of course an institution devoted to that desperate and pathetic snobbery which the British, it seems to me, created after the war. Perhaps, understandably, their certainty of superiority was no more. Perhaps they became more frenetically anxious to *demonstrate* it. What happened to effortless understatement? The British in Kenya Colony at least are more likely to be loudmouthed yahoos or shrieking memsahibs. Once yearly they have an Eton Ball. That and the Nairobi races bring them to the Muthaiga in droves. But never in droves so large as the Winslow Trial brought them in last night.

The ballroom was utterly packed. From somewhere the club secretary had organized hundreds of chairs, cane-backed, leather-backed, metal-backed, all manner of shapes, materials, and colors. The members filed in to take their places at seven o'clock. The men wore dinner jackets, the women long dresses and pearls. Lord George Amadeus Winslow was evidently to be dispatched with style.

The same Lord Winslow entered a few moments later with Lady Margaret and a group of friends, "toughs" like Tommy Boscowan, Harry Towers, and "Boy" Carstairs, looking as mean as gunslingers at a revival meeting. The ladies, I admit, were beautifully dressed: the Mowbray sisters, silently haughty; Marjorie Bellamy, pretty but sharp-nosed; Paula Upton-Mallet, statuesque and educationally subnormal; and Lady Margaret herself, looking strained I suspect by too much cocaine, but genuinely beautiful and, I must confess, genuinely nice—for all her outrageous ways.

Lord Winslow, in white tie and tails, led the group in. Yes, I'll say it again. He has presence, even beauty. He is of course irredeemably lecherous. On an afternoon at the races last year he cornered me in the Owners' Bar and began to allegorize about Beauty and the Beast. I found him, I must confess, not uninteresting as he developed his theme of a necessary attraction between Beauty and the Beast, between aestheticism and the lusts of the flesh.

Later, when he tried to afternoon-bed me in his trainer's flat, I discovered his mood to be less allegorical: *I* was cast in the role of Beauty, and the Beast was making visible efforts to jump out of his trousers. Poor Buzzy, or whatever ridiculous name it is that everybody calls him—he doesn't know how lucky he was that afternoon not to get *my* feather in his cap!

Back to last night. Winslow strode down the central aisle at the head of his chums. Heads turned to follow them. In the front row, ten or a dozen places had been left for the Winslow set, hard upright chairs facing comfortable club chairs from which secretary and committee and the proposer and seconder of the Act of Attainder would address the members over the heads of the accused.

You can imagine the stunned reaction, then, at the sheer arrogance of the man when he strolled straight on past the front row of uncomfortable uprights and threw himself casually into the secretary's chair, his cohorts taking the other committee members' places.

The secretary and committee, with Gerald Longman and Bunny Myles, entered a few minutes later. Reaching the end of the aisle, they saw their seats already taken by lounging aristos, male and female. Meekly the secretary accepted their right of place and led his committee to the empty uprights in the front row.

Yet I have known Gerald Longman many years. I know him to be angry and capable. If he was to take over Lord Delamere's role as leader of the white community, he needed a success tonight.

Silence fell as the secretary rose like the dinner-jacketed compere at a boxing match. If he'd begun by announcing Lord George Winslow in the blue corner, I would hardly have been surprised. In fact, as the cigarette smoke rose like steam toward the ballroom ceiling, the secretary made a short, decorous introduction—a proposal had been made and seconded, etc.— and sat down.

When Gerald Longman rose to speak, a brisk outbreak of clapping rattled across the room. It was neither too long nor too warmly enthusiastic, but it offered support from nearly everybody there. Gerald is a well-respected member of the community.

I made notes on his speech, and indeed on Lord Winslow's reply. Allowing for not more than a little editing, this is what Gerald said:

"Members of the Muthaiga Club, I believe that this is the first time since the club's foundation that it has been proposed that a member and his wife should be banned from the precincts. That that member should bear the name of one of our most distinguished families and that he should be a member of the Club Committee is an additional source of pain to us all."

At this point a loud and unreal snore broke from a recumbent Lord Winslow. His friends entered into the spirit of the farce. Tommy Boscowan tried to "wake" him. Boy Carstairs shouted to him to open his eyes. "Wake up, my dear fellow," he bawled. "You can't take forty winks while they're trying to put your head on a platter!"

The ballroom of course was in chaos. Even those shouting *for* Gerald Longman seemed to succeed only in putting him more and more off his stride. When eventually the secretary re-established order, Gerald continued, but I felt there was now more apprehension than anger on his face.

"My point is perfectly straightforward," Gerald began again. "Lord Winslow, I very much regret to say, over the years he has been among us, has increasingly drawn upon himself a considerable notoriety."

The Winslow chums clapped and stamped, shouting, "Hear, hear!"

"His reputation," Gerald continued, white-faced, "whether or not entirely justified . . ."

"*Justified*, entirely justified," shrieked Paula Upton-Mallet gaily.

"Whether or not justified," Gerald forced himself on, "has been widely commented upon, first in the Nairobi newspapers and more recently in the home press. I can't tell you, ladies and gentlemen, what a disastrous effect these stories could have on the reputation of the rest of us. We are, all of us, not far from being tarred by the same brush. How can we expect to receive consideration and, more important, subsidy from the government in London if they are led to believe we do nothing but fritter our time away in parties, drugs, and champagne? More important, how are we going to progress toward self-government if London sees us as fundamentally unserious playboys? Now I do not intend to speak at length. But my final point is this: We must make it utterly clear that we disapprove of these endless parties, these rumors of drugs and free love. To make it clear, I can think of no better way than to require that Lord Winslow be no longer a member of this club and that he be unwelcome as a guest of a member. That will make our position clear. It will be a decision that will be widely reported in the London newspapers. It will have the desired effect."

He sat down as something at least approaching a storm of applause passed through the ballroom. Bunny Myles then said a few words as Lord Winslow yawned, stood up slowly, turned his chair around, and languidly supported himself with the back. Folding his arms, he pouted his bottom lip and stared silently down at Gerald Longman.

"Peculiar chaps, you do come across," were his first words. Gerald, I swear, squirmed in his seat. Pamela sat next to him, head down, hands folded in her lap.

"What champagne I drink and how I drink, how much and with whom, is a matter between me and my liver," Winslow said slowly. "Whom I roger and how I roger and why I roger and where I roger is a matter between me and my companion." He paused theatrically. "Or possibly her husband," he added, to the first real laughter of the evening. "Dear old friends," he said suddenly, expansively, "I think the whole matter is complete balls." One arm outstretched, he pointed an index finger at Gerald Longman. "The chap comes from Battersea," he said. "Family of shopkeepers. Thinks it frightfully posh *not* to drink out of a saucer."

He paused. "I consider his allegations to be gross and purely impertinent. It would be devilishly insolent of him to expect a reply. His motives are envy . . ."

"Personal vendetta," Tom Boscowan shouted. "The whole thing's personal. Dismiss it for what it's worth."

"Personal matter. Exactly." Boy Carstairs echoed.

A low whisper swept the audience. The club secretary rose and said mildly, "If this is a personal matter, perhaps we should know the details, Lord Winslow."

"There are no details," Winslow said haughtily.

Boscowan and Carstairs were smiling broadly.

"I would strongly suggest you at least confirm or deny the existence of a personal animosity between you and Gerald Longman."

"Confirmed. And why not? The man's a Battersea shopkeeper."

We could all see that Winslow's anger was mounting. He had refolded his arms across his starched white shirt front. He stood bolt upright like a stage magician, his eyes on Gerald. I think we all saw he was in a dangerous mood.

Gerald's mood was merely reckless. Or so it seemed in the retrospect of a few awful minutes. "It is suggested that my proposal to ban Lord Winslow is personally motivated. I challenge Lord Winslow to explain how."

He did not see that his wife, Pam, was sitting wild-eyed with terror.

Winslow remained standing, cataleptically still. Whether an act or genuine, it was effective. Gerald Longman repeated his challenge.

Very slowly, Winslow lifted his head to look now over Gerald's head. "As a gentleman," he said, "I am not prepared to answer Longman's challenge."

"Because there's nothing personal in this at all. You call yourself a gentleman, so admit it."

"I call myself a gentleman. I am a gentleman. I can do nothing, Mr. Longman, to infringe my own code of honor."

"I demand an answer or a withdrawal," Longman said, feeling he was on the edge of triumph.

"You shall have neither."

"Then let one of your cronies speak for you."

"Willingly, old chap," Tom Boscowan said, leaning forward, his dark face no more than three or four feet from Pamela's. "I would, old chap, if there weren't a lady involved."

A sob burst from Pamela Longman. It seemed to silence the whole room. It had come from her in the sheer tension of the moment. It was then, I think, that Gerald Longman realized he was about to be destroyed. He turned frantically to his wife. "The filthy cad, Pam, he's slandering you."

He was begging her for a denial. But there was none to come. Pamela Longman stood and walked quickly from the room. Poor Gerald stumbled after her while Lord Winslow looked on, head cocked to one side, lips elegantly twisted in theatrical surprise at the way it had all turned out. Dear, dear Claus, am I really the only woman in Kenya Colony your friend Buzz has not yet had?

But we were far, far from finished yet. An opportunity had presented itself, and Lord George Amadeus Winslow was not about to pass it up, as I could see. Here was an audience of an important part of the settler population of Kenya. Had he already prepared the lecture that followed? God knows!

"Friends," he began quietly, "I have, as you know, just recently returned from London. It is appropriate, I feel, to give you some impression of what is happening in our home country and indeed further abroad in Europe. I don't have to tell you of the increasing power of the Soviet Union. Or of the steady growth of the envious ideas of Karl Marx in our factories and on our farms. Don't misunderstand me. An empty belly cares little about the *ism* that is feeding it. But here we come to the curious success of Soviet, European, and American communism. It is feeding no one. It is filling *no* bellies. Not even in Russia, where the greatest famines ever have destroyed hundreds of thousands of lives. It is feeding no bellies," he said with emphasis, "but it is nevertheless successful in feeding minds. Middle-class intellectuals in New York tell us how it will cure American overproduction. And I've no doubt it will, given the chance. The communist system has been spectacularly successful in curing overproduction. University students at Oxford and Cambridge wear red ties and proclaim the arrival in the hungry squares of unknown Moscow, of a new era of the love of man for man."

He paused, looking down at the rows of puzzled faces. "You're surprised, I see, at the serious turn this evening has taken. Why, you ask yourself, does that notorious pouncer, Lord Winslow, choose to address us on the distant issue of the growth of communism? Lord Winslow chooses to address you because it is *not* a distant issue. Today in London we have a coalition government run by a socialist Prime Minister. Tomorrow we may have a socialist government with communist ministers in a new left alliance of the popular front. And where will that leave you, here in imperialist, colonial Africa? Will you still have a right to your farm? Will you still, as the white community, control the legislative council? Will the tenant-laborer ordinances, on which your supply of African labor depends, still be law?"

The rows of settlers listened in silence. Some already, in a matter of a few minutes' speech, saw the shape of a new Lord Delamere arising. Perhaps to the women especially this new seriousness was appealing. Perhaps they saw it as providing an argument in the defense of George Winslow.

"There is in England," he said, his voice low, "a new resolution, growing among some of the most forward-looking and the best of our compatriots. It is a resolution to face the future and to brave its perils. It is a resolution to which I have decided to devote myself. In the form of a political party, it is called the British Union of Fascists. Its leader, as you no doubt already know, is Sir Oswald Mosley, a politician of extraordinary talent and energy and, above all, honesty."

For an hour or more, your old friend Buzz Winslow described the Fascist attitude to colonies. In London the Blackshirts are, it appears, prepared to give us settlers a free hand if they should gain power. There will be no more talk of the paramountcy of African interests, even if it is only, for the most part, talk. Lord Winslow made a powerful impression with one single point: there is no likelihood, unless Fascism triumphs in Britain, of an independent government of the white community in Kenya. The present British government is committed to an attempt to establish a mixed-race Kenyan legislature; future Labour governments will be even more so committed. And that will mean a legislature dominated by Africans, one in which even the Indian traders will outvote the European settlers. We must send out a message to London and to the rest of the world, a message that we, the white community in Kenya, will not surrender our rights and duties; that we, the white community, are determined to live, and live greatly. My dear Claus, what manner of man is this Winslow? How can he change from buffoon to visionary at the clap of a hand? You must tell me, is he dangerous as he appears to be? Is he stupid when he dismisses as "mostly lies" the accounts of Adolf Hitler's Nazi Party in Germany? Is he naïve or careless or infinitely calculating when he says casually that his sister, nothing less than a glamorous celebrity to us poor farmers, has met Adolf Hitler and finds him charming?

So many times, in my letters to you, I've begged for poetry. Now I beg for facts.

How did the evening end? My fellow settlers, hardworking and mostly fond and reasonably careful of their Africans, came to their feet to applaud Lord George Amadeus Winslow, he whom they had come to crucify.

Gerald Longman's political career is finished. Pamela Longman is seen as simple bed-fodder for the Beast. The farmers are interested, some are exhilarated. There is talk of forming a Kenya Fascist Party with Lord George as *leader*. Is he just playing? God knows.

The lecture over, the games begin. Lord George orders three hundred bottles of champagne (at thirty-five shillings a bottle; he recently, it appears, sold a house in London) and commands his audience to their enjoyment.

They need no persuasion. Within an hour the ballroom echoes to the whoops of the Highland reelers. In the dining room a great crowd gathers around Lord George. He is the man of the moment, and, some of us suspect, the man of many future moments. He holds court, gives opinions on A. Hitler and B. Mussolini, on the balance-of-trade figures for the colony, on the possibility of a rise in sisal prices, on the wisdom of planting a back-up acreage of pyrethrum. Where has he acquired this knowledge? We took him for a buffoon, a playboy. And in any case, a dictator can't be known as Buzzy to his friends, can he?

I try four or five times to escape to bed. But my room is locked to prevent its use for casual adultery by passing club members, and I cannot find Ali, the steward. I return to the ballroom. Lord George is sober among a jostling phalanx of drunken guests. The ballroom temperature is over a hundred. While the band plays American dance music, "Chimp" de Warren does his celebrated act of swinging like an ape along the metal beams high above the dancers' heads. In the gardens, fights break out and are quelled. Women shriek with surprise or misery. Drinks are spilled over dinner jackets and ball gowns as men push and thrust their way through the throng. "Boys" have been dispatched to scour Nairobi for motor-bicycles. There is to be a speedway race in the ballroom at midnight. In the squash courts, a ladies' nude squash competition. The young bloods line the gallery, hooting and cheering and betting more than they can afford. Tommy Boscowan has struck one of the African servants and then compensated him with a half-crown at the club secretary's insistence.

The motor-bicycles arrive long after midnight. Six dust-covered, oily machines, each to be ridden by a man with a girl pillion rider. The "off" is arranged as if it were Race Week. They are under Starter's Orders; the ballroom is thunderous with the din of their engines, acrid with the explosion of blue exhaust smoke. Bets are placed again. Ball gowns are hitched over thighs, clear of the wheels. The starter brings down the flag. The machines leap forward. At the end of the room the turn throws two riders and two girls sliding hopelessly across the floor. Boy Carstairs is in the lead, his pillion rider screaming to him to pile on more speed. Anthea Mowbray is thrown from the back of Harry Towers's machine, strikes her head against the band dais, and is carried off with a concussion. I escape into the garden and find so many couples lying on top of each other in the bushes that one small clearing seems to undulate in the moonlight. I return to the dining room. Jake Parsons-Hurst, one of Lord Winslow's friends, has challenged all comers to a chair-throwing competition. The rules are loose, but require hoisting a chair through the dining-room windows at twenty feet. Most miss the open windows and shatter the panes of glass. Chimp de Warren still swings across the roof. What am I seeing? Is it Götterdämmerung or just good clean fun?

Then, toward five o'clock in the morning, silence falls. Except, as I said for the occasional reveler, incoherent or in tears. A husband missing or a wife misplaced. I have recovered from Ali the key to my room, but the bedroom is intolerable at the moment; the rows and recriminations preclude sleep even for those of us who have beds. I will finish this long, long letter and leave for Ngong. I don't have to be there to see the morning sunlight purpling the hills, the *totos* up and running about the lawn. By midday I suppose the great columns of motorcars will start back to the farms at Naivasha or Nanyuki, and perhaps, who knows, the myth will enter Africa's spoken history of the day the white men left the hills and were persuaded to return only by the eloquence of Lord Winslow-bwana. History has been made of much less.

My love always,
Catherine

FIFTEEN

By the evening of March 5, 1933, the German election results were known to the world. Adolf Hitler's National Socialist German Workers' Party had polled 17 million votes, an increase of 5 million over the last election. The Social Democrats were second, with 7 million. The Communists gained less than 5 million. Adolf Hitler was now Chancellor and Führer of Germany.

He had made his last election speech the night before, in Königsberg. Among flaring torches and chanting SA men, the Austrian had mounted the platform in the square outside the cathedral. Arrangements had been made by Goebbels to broadcast the event live to every city in Germany. Newsreel cameras mounted on tripods were positioned to scan and record the German and international celebrities in the stand to the right of the podium. Bankers and industrialists sat among fur-caped film stars. Diamonds glittered under the camera lights in the cold March air. Generals sat among academics and their wives. The *trahison des clercs* had begun even before the first votes in the election had been cast.

Diana Chrysler shared a bank of red-colored benches with an international group of aristocrats, politicians, and sportsmen. The cameras, constantly closing on her, picked out her animated face deep in the collar of her fur coat, her breath rising in the cold air as she leaned forward to exchange remarks with the people around her.

Her cousin, Toby Gorringe, had supplied himself with a pair of opera glasses and was scanning the half-circle of men behind Hitler on the podium. "I can make out Göring there," he said, passing the glasses to Diana. "And Rudolf Hess. But who's the little chap on the right of Hess?"

Diana took the opera glasses and focused on the podium. Hitler was wearing a pale gray double-breasted suit to catch the searchlights playing on him. He leaned forward, staring out across the massed banners waving below.

"On the right of Hess is Heinrich Himmler," she said.

"Who is he?"

"He's a second-ranker. Runs the black uniforms, Hitler's bodyguard, the SS. Now quiet, Toby, he's about to begin."

Magnified by loudspeakers placed around the square, broadcast by radio throughout Germany, Adolf Hitler began his final bid for power. In a low voice he covered the familiar ground of Germany's humiliation: the Versailles Treaty; the threat of international and domestic Bolshevism; the need to put Germany's unemployed millions back to work. For an hour he spoke on the old themes, then by a verbal sleight he proclaimed the morrow's election as won. His voice rose in triumph as he spoke of the revolution achieved, the suppression of Bolshevik power complete. Throughout his audience the formality of tomorrow's vote was forgotten. In the arms of the leader they rose ecstatically into the future. "Now hold your heads high and proud once again!" he screamed into the microphones. "Now you are no longer slaves and bondsmen. Now you are free—by God's gracious hand!" And as the last words echoed across the square, ten thousand SA men burst into the final stanza of a hymn to victory while the bells of Königsberg Cathedral pealed the triumph of Adolf Hitler.

After the speech, the reception at the Königsberg city hall maintained the fiction of an election already won. Some two hundred guests drank champagne and ate canapés in the great vaulted council chamber. At the far end, Adolf Hitler, surrounded by Göring, Hess, Himmler, and Schacht, drank coffee and talked to chosen guests. Adjutants in black uniforms and white gloves moved smoothly among the guests, inviting them to meet the Führer. Diana was among those selected early.

She had met him only once before, but he seemed to remember a great deal about her. He clicked his heels and bent low over her hand and told her how pleased he was to see her present at this particular moment in German history. Her German, much improved in the last year, enabled her to answer without the help of an interpreter who stood at her shoulder.

"Tell me, Lady Diana"—Hitler took her by the elbow, turning her away from the interpreter—"you are so wonderfully slender, I am bound to ask you. Do you enjoy cream cakes?"

"I adore cream cakes," Diana said in surprise.

Adolf Hitler nodded gravely. "So do I. But my doctor informs me I shall grow as fat as my friend Benito Mussolini." His blue eyes looked up at her from a somber face. "All around us they think we are discussing political developments in Great Britain. What would they think if they were to learn that our subject is cream cakes?"

She laughed.

"Maintain a serious expression, my dear Lady Diana," he said, his eyes twinkling, "or you will give away our secret."

He returned her to his SS adjutant a few minutes later. They had talked of cream cakes, mille-feuilles, and Black Forest cherry cake. Ladies in peach-colored satin dresses, blond hair crimped into perfect permanent waves, had watched with open envy as Adolf Hitler paced beside the tall Englishwoman or stopped and, with a playful touch on her elbow, made some remark that caused him to jump back a step, fingers locked across his pale gray jacket, head thrown back in relaxed laughter.

During the course of the next half hour, ten or so other guests were introduced. It was estimated by adjutants and disappointed party wives alike that none of them had received half the attention he had devoted to the Englishwoman.

At just after nine o'clock, the SS adjutants moved through the press of guests, informing them that Herr Hitler was about to leave. Champagne glasses were put down and the guests moved forward to form two long lines facing inward and leading to the door.

The room fell silent as Adolf Hitler, with his entourage of party leaders a pace or two behind him, took up a position at the far end of the room at the beginning of the two lines of guests. For a moment it seemed possible that he would address them, then, seeming to decide against it, his face grim, his hands clasped almost awkwardly in front of him, he began to pace slowly between the double line of guests toward the doors at the far end of the room. From time to time he stopped and shook hands and his somber expression would change so that the brief smile that illuminated his face seemed all the more friendly, more human, in contrast. As he approached Diana, stopping to nod gravely to one guest, courteously shaking hands with another, Diana felt some sense of the unpredictable nature of his personality. When the set look and the unseeing blue eyes were suddenly lit by an almost playful smile, the whole room seemed almost to rustle with relief. It was inconceivable, even to her now, that his mind was ever occupied with the problem of his love for cream cakes.

As he drew opposite Diana, he stopped and bowed. *"Gnädige Frau,"* he said, then passed on quickly toward the door, his entourage hurrying behind him.

She flew back to Berlin that night, arriving exhausted at Tempelhof at three in the morning. In the lobby of the Adlon Hotel she said good night to her cousin and turned wearily toward the concierge for her key.

"Lady Diana," the man said, seeming almost embarrassed, "there is a gentleman to see you."

"At this time of night?"

"I told him you were not expected back until late. He insisted on waiting."

"Who is he?" she said, frowning. "What is his name?"

"He declined to give his name. He has been here several hours."

Diana looked in the direction the concierge indicated. In the far, darkened end of the long lobby a figure in a topcoat was rising from an armchair. It was only as he walked forward under the lights that she saw that he was Claus von Hardenberg.

As a reflex, to reassert her control, she ordered coffee from the concierge. Then she walked slowly forward under the lights and stopped before him.

It could not have been an ordinary meeting, with shaken hands or kisses on the cheek. They stood before each other until he reached forward and took her arm. "Come and sit down," he said. "I'm sorry to arrive here like this."

"To arrive here?" she said, brittle-voiced. "It's I who am the visitor."

"Talk to me properly, Diana. We haven't just met at a cocktail party."

She looked at his hard features. Buzz's phrase leaped into her head, "the German forest wolf." Maturity had hardened his mouth, brought his dark blond eyebrows down protectively over his eyes. "I'm sorry, Claus," she said. "I was just babbling. From shock."

He smiled slowly. "That's better. My God, it's so good to see you. I've seen lots of photographs, of course. Some of them in dubious company. But none of them do you justice."

They sat down together, on the edge of a sofa, half-turned toward each other. "You're not in trouble, are you?" she asked anxiously.

"No, I'm not in trouble."

"You didn't just decide that it was safe to meet each other again."

"No, it will never be safe."

He felt some tremor pass through her. "I want to ask about everything, Diana. I want to ask you about Charles. I want to say how sorry I am."

"But you have no time."

He nodded.

"You would not have been waiting for me here in the middle of the night if you had had time. Tell me what you've come to tell me, Claus."

"I've come to *ask* you," he said. "For money. Quite a lot of money."

"You *are* in trouble."

"Not yet. Perhaps I shall be able to avoid it. But many of my friends need help. And many others, who are not even friends at all."

She reached out and held his hand. "You must explain, Claus."

"I have many friends," he said, "who are sitting through this dreadful night in stark terror."

She withdrew her hand slowly.

"Not all of them Jews," he said. "Not even most of them. But they all believe that if Adolf Hitler wins this election, they and their families are bound to be arrested."

"But why?" she said. "What have they done?"

"In the Nazi paradise that will start tomorrow, it's what you are, not what you've done, that will put you in jail. Or worse."

"That is what your friends believe."

"Yes."

"And you believe it too."

"Of course."

He was aware that she seemed to be making a terrifying effort to keep calm. The concierge brought coffee, setting the tray with a silver pot, a milk jug, and two cups on the table between them.

Carefully she lit a cigarette. He could see that every controlled movement concealed, barely, a desire to throw her hands in the air, to stand up, to run from the room. He knew their paths had parted.

"These friends, Claus," she said. "If they felt in danger, why did they not leave Germany before?"

He shook his head. "Diana, you live in a different world. Why did Frau Bartelmann in the corner shop not leave for the South of France when she knew her trade-union husband could be at risk? Because she's hanging on to their one asset in the hope that the danger will go away. Like all the others I'm talking about, she's staying because she thought she can't afford to move. It's only now that she and the others realize they dare not stay," he said in a distant voice.

"But what makes them think they'll be arrested?" Diana said wildly. "Do they imagine that if the Nazis come to power tomorrow, there will be hundreds of random arrests?"

"Not hundreds, thousands. Tens of thousands. Perhaps even hundreds of thousands."

"That's ridiculous."

He sat away from her, perhaps a fraction of an inch only, but perceptibly. She reached out a hand to him. "Please God, Claus," she said, "we mustn't argue like this. Tell me, what is it you want the money for?"

He held on to her hand, but it was cold in his. "I am the part owner of a boat," he said slowly. "My partner is an old man. A Jew. The Nazis have stated that they will confiscate all Jewish-owned property. Motorcars and boats will be first."

"So you will be able to buy your Jew partner's share from the state for a song."

"That would be wrong."

"Claus, it's the sort of thing that happens all the time in business."

"I wanted to pay my partner in full. This will be the only money my old friend has. That's why I came to you."

Their eyes met and held. "I cannot believe it's necessary," she said.

"You don't believe they'll do what they've threatened? Hitler, Göring, Goebbels, the rest of the diseased gang?"

Her mouth tightened. She removed her hand from his. "I think you and your friends are wrong, Claus. I believe you are forgetting that the Nazi Party is made up of politicians, like any other party. When they say that they will sweep away the Marxists and even the Jews, they mean that they will deprive them of power, the excessive power they feel they have had in the past. That is all."

"Frau Bartelmann would enjoy knowing how and when she wielded this excessive power."

"Her husband is a trade-union organizer, you said. I assume he is a Marxist too."

"He votes for the Social Democratic Party. His life's work has been to try to improve the conditions of the laborers in the asbestos plants in Hamburg."

"Then why should he be arrested?"

"Because he is a Social Democratic Jewish unionist! By tomorrow or the day after, or the day after that, it will be enough. We have to believe that these Nazis mean what they say. I've seen them in the streets—the back streets, I mean, where no foreign journalist is likely to be watching. They shout and kick and beat people. They do it not because they are simple sadists but because they *believe*. The leaders believe even more than their uniformed street gangs. Germany is about to enter a Dark Age."

She put out her cigarette. "I was at Königsberg tonight," she said quietly. "I should have told you earlier. More than that, I've written a book about the Nazi movement. It's called *Echoes from a New Century*. It is already published in England. Soon it will be published in Germany too."

"*Echoes from a New Century*," he said bitterly. "Tell that to Frau Bartelmann tomorrow." He stood up.

"Don't go, Claus," she said.

"Why should I stay?" His tense face looked down at her, the brows knit even closer across his bright, angry eyes.

She stood beside him. "How in God's name can I answer that

in a sentence or two?" she said. Tears were starting from her eyes.

"I would have to tell you day to day about everything I've done and felt since that night in Venice. To make you understand, I would have to recount every single moment of the last thirteen years."

"We don't have time," he said brusquely. "Frau Bartelmann doesn't have time."

"For God's sake, don't quote Frau Bartelmann to me," she blazed. "She's hysterical, she's wrong. Above all, she's no excuse for you to leave me now."

"I need no excuse," he said, turning away from her.

"Dear God." She grasped his sleeve. "I'll find the money you want. I think it will be a total waste, but that doesn't matter. I'll find it."

He removed her hand from his sleeve. "No," he said. "Not now." He paused. "It's too dangerous."

She burst into tears and collapsed on the sofa. When she recovered and looked up, it was the concierge who was standing looking down at her.

"The gentleman has gone, madame."

She got to her feet, fumbling in her purse for a handkerchief. "Yes," she said. "Of course."

She walked back through the darkened lobby, trailing her fur coat. Outside she could hear the tramping feet, the singing and the kettledrums of the marching SA formations. In her room she sat at the open window, smoking cigarettes and watching the most desolate dawn she had ever known rising over the rooftops of Berlin.

SIXTEEN

The two men sitting at lunch together under the acacia trees at Corinth looked remarkably alike. Like Buzz Winslow, Hugo von dem Zeitz-Apolda was tall and improbably blond. They were within a few years of the same age and shared a blue-eyed handsomeness that could have proclaimed them brothers. Marjorie Bellamy, driving over from the house she rented in Naivasha, was headed off by Margaret Winslow only just in time. "Margaret, darling," she said, and kissed her friend's cheek, looking over her shoulder toward the newcomer. "Who is he? What a splendid, splendid new find."

"Listen, Marjorie, control your juices," Margaret said. "He's just arrived from Germany, and he and Buzz are talking business."

"Well, take me over and introduce me."

"Absolutely *verboten*, darling. Buzz is being awfully stern."

"You mean I can't meet him?"

"Certainly not yet. It's business, dearest, political business. Come onto the veranda and have a drink. We can drool at him from afar."

Under the acacia trees, Zeitz-Apolda had declined a cigar in favor of an American cigarette. "Philosophically," he said, "what is interesting about National Socialism, or Fascism as you call it, is that it succeeds in combining revolutionary and conservative elements to a remarkable degree. Thus it has strained, that is to say distilled, some of the timeless elements of European aristocratic culture, and yet at the same moment it can exert a total appeal to the Hamburg dockworker, or, as I would like to suggest, to the London dockworker."

Buzz lit his cigar and watched his doppelgänger through the curling smoke. "What I had not appreciated was the pan-

European aspect of National Socialism," he said slowly. "Naturally enough, I had assumed its wellsprings to be national."

"Ah, just so, they are. The source of our strength is *national*, as the source of an individual's strength is personal. But that strength can be increased in brotherhood, and we in the SS see that brotherhood as one to which all the Northern European nations have free and most welcome entry."

"Some of your politicians, nevertheless, seem to take an exclusively nationalistic line."

"That, Winslow, is for immediate political reasons. *Raisons d'état*. If you listen carefully to the Führer's speeches, however, you will detect no hostility to the European ideal. To us in the SS, the dividing lines are racial, cultural. You need look no farther than this lunch table to understand the concept of Anglo-German consanguinity. Here in Kenya your problems are even more frankly racial than ours in the Reich."

"My sister's letter," Buzz said, "indicated you could be of help. I don't imagine she meant solely in terms of exegesis."

Zeitz-Apolda laughed. "Your sister is not only an infinitely charming woman, but a woman of discretion at the same time. May I explain to you our thinking on the colonial issue?"

"I've some rather fine port, Taylor '12." Buzz signaled to a servant standing at a distance from the table. "You do drink port?"

"Indeed. Although it's a long time since I have drunk Taylor '12."

"The colonial issue . . ."

"Yes." Zeitz-Apolda sat back in his chair. The sunlight caught and sparkled in his hair. He knew this to be the most delicate part of what he had come to say. He watched the African servant cross the lawn bearing a decanter of port on a silver tray, and wondered whether, with this particular Englishman, a blunt approach would be most effective. He decided, as Buzz pushed the decanter toward him, that he would take the risk. "The German nation," he said, pouring the rich red-black liquid into his glass, "has never accepted the total loss of Tanganyika, your neighboring colony."

Buzz pursed his lips. "Defeat in war, old chap."

"Magnanimity in peace, old chap," Zeitz-Apolda responded.

"Perhaps."

"There is the additional fact that Germany was *never* defeated in East Africa. You recall General von Lettow?"

"Very well. I was present when he marched his *Schutztruppe* into Abercorn."

"Exactly." He paused. "It is the Führer's irrevocable decision to recover Tanganyika for the Reich," he said.

"That will bring Germany inevitably into conflict with Great Britain."

"Conflict is not inevitable," Zeitz-Apolda said. "Germany would be prepared to cede the Kilimanjaro area to Kenya. You, the British colonists, would have the assurance of a new surge of white immigration into the colony from Germany. If you see the future with a clear eye, Winslow, it must be in terms of a conflict between the white and nonwhite races in East Africa. Germany can offer support for your somewhat precarious position here. I revert to the idea of Anglo-German consanguinity."

"As you well know," Buzz said carefully, "it is London that rules here. Not us."

"That could change. *Must* change. 'For King and Kenya' is not an ignoble aspiration."

"I see you've done your homework."

"Typically German," Zeitz-Apolda laughed. "Now listen, Winslow. Your sister's letter of introduction talked of help. The Führer has already appointed a minister to deal with the colonial question. He is Herr Schnee, did you ever meet him at Abercorn?"

"He was the governor of German Tanganyika," Buzz said, remembering. "Von Lettow carried him around in his knapsack for four years."

"Not an impressive man," Zeitz-Apolda agreed. "But with an English wife, probably the right man for the job. Funds have already been assigned to his ministry. Large funds."

"This is the help you are offering."

"A Kenya Fascist Party, with you as leader, would never lack financial support."

"I'm beginning to understand you, old chap."

"Do you like what you hear?"

"I would like to think about what I hear."

"Excellent."

"Finish your port," Buzz said. "I think it's time for us to join the ladies."

In Germany, two days after Adolf Hitler's election victory, an ordinance had been issued authorizing the extension of prison facilities in an open-site camp form. The new prisons were to be known as concentration camps. Within a week, SA murders were commonplace: five Communists in Chemnitz, the editor of a Saxon Social Democratic newspaper, a lawyer in Kiel, an anarchist, a clairvoyant. . . .Meetings were broken up and their participants whipped; Jewish businesses were harassed; a grenade was thrown through a Reichstag deputy's window. Before the March winds had blown themselves out, over three hundred Germans had been murdered in their homes or offices. Many thousands more were openly beaten on the streets. In the next month the terror grew. With the coming of spring, a hundred thousand prisoners were crammed into the old prisons or the makeshift concentration camps.

SEVENTEEN

n the wild olive grove above the Naivasha road, Buzz Winslow tied his horse and walked slowly down toward the rock pool. He knew well that he was at a crossroads, perhaps the first real crossroads of his life. He had learned something about himself, something that his whole background and upbringing had conspired to disguise. He knew now that what he sought was significance, a sense of importance that went beyond having been to Eton and Cambridge and bearing an ancient title. The world had so much changed since that world before the war, when only those things were important. It was his ego, smarting at the accusation that he was nothing more than a playboy, that had made him construct, virtually on the spur of the moment, that first Fascist speech at the Muthaiga Club. Of course, Diana had been there in spirit. In some ways she always was. Every man, every woman acts out his or her life to an audience. For most, it is an audience of one. That one can change, of course—Richard, Claus, Diana—but he was acutely conscious of no longer living in a world where the dilettante, the playboy, impresses. We need, he felt, to offer something more substantial, an act that defines our existence. A definitive act that raises us above the ordinary, as riches and titles once did.

Buzz Winslow stood looking down into the green depths of the pool. Margaret, he knew, was part of the past he would have to shed. The playboy past had no part in this harder future. Margaret was a liability. She was no longer young enough, or rich enough.

Clare Debenham, eighteen years old, rich, and well connected, would help to carry him over the crossroads. Zeitz-Apolda had offered funds and the support of the new German government. In Kenya it was time for the whites to bid for the power that the settlers had earned by their own efforts since Delamere had arrived in the Rift Valley. He knew he could lead this movement for King and Kenya. Within a year, Marjorie Bellamy had said, Buzz would be dictator. She was a fool, of course, a stupid woman. But stupidity sometimes breeds simple insights.

Somewhere above, the branches of a candelabrum tree rustled. Then a footfall crunched rock and dust. He turned to see Pamela Longman looking down at him. She was dressed in a cotton aertex shirt, a flowered skirt, and sandals. "I saw you riding along the ridge," she said. "I thought you would be here."

For the first time he realized that today was the first Friday of the month.

"You haven't been here since," she said. She was leaning forward like a schoolgirl, hands behind her back.

"Since?" he frowned.

"Since that dreadful evening at the club."

"There didn't seem to be much point," Buzz said carefully. "I didn't imagine you'd be here."

"I was." Her mouth was tight. Her hands were still clasped behind her back, and it occurred to him with a start that she might be carrying one of the farm revolvers with her.

He walked a few paces to her left and began brushing Achates's flank.

"I'm terribly sorry about what happened at the club, Pam," he said. "But I don't think in fairness you can really blame me."

"I can't?" she said.

"No. After all, it was Gerald who started the whole business. He's the one who set the ball rolling with his complaint to the club secretary." As he spoke, Buzz had taken a pace forward, but she had adjusted her position. He was now more than ever concerned that she held something behind her back.

"I tried to persuade Gerald to withdraw his complaint," she said. "But he insisted we had to clear the playboys out of Kenya."

"Do that and you'd lose half the white population," Buzz said wryly, forgetting for a moment the possibility of the revolver behind her back.

"The white trash is what Gerald calls you and your friends."

Buzz grunted. "Yes, he would."

"You told them all about me, of course."

Buzz shrugged.

"You *must* have told them. That awful Boscowan person must have known."

"Tom Boscowan, yes," Buzz said. "He's the only one, though."

"Liar! They all knew."

"Just Tom Boscowan, Pam. Had to tell someone." He took a rapid pace forward now, and she backed off. "Look, what is it you've got there, Pam?"

"They all knew," she repeated. "The women too." She was punctuating her statements with short, angry breaths. "You'd even told your wife. That's when I broke down—when I realized that you'd told everybody, the whole dreadful set of snobs, that you'd even boasted to your wife! Well, Gerald's right," she said slowly. From behind her back she drew a native ox whip.

"Put that thing down," he said in alarm.

"Gerald's right," she said, advancing on him. "You're all ugly snobs, decadent, ugly snobs."

She flicked her wrist expertly and the whip cracked. Hard, knotted leather, flying through the air, caught him across the arm.

He felt an intense, stinging pain, saw a torn shirt and bleeding torn flesh before the whip curled away and came hissing back toward him. Her fury was backed by the skill gained from five years behind an ox team. This time the leather thong slashed across his neck, curled, uncurled, and came spitting back at him, wet with blood.

The whip sang around his head, flaying his cheeks, burning across his shoulders. He was terrified for his eyes. Then she changed the movement of her wrist and drove the thong again and again, to crack and spit and tear between his legs. In mortal fear, he now ran at her, arms outstretched before him. When the hard leather knots wrapped around his wrist, he knew it was his last chance. He snatched at the thong, grasped it, lost it, and grasped it again. Then with a sharp jerk he brought the handle of the whip flying from her hand.

She turned to run. "Stand still, you bitch," he roared at her. "Try to run and I'll flay you to death."

She turned slowly back toward him. Her anger was unabated

as she looked at his bleeding face and the torn flesh on his arms. With astonishment he realized that she showed no fear.

"You murderous little bitch," he said quietly. One hand cupped his genitals, the other held the whip. He stood, trying to understand the different elements in the anger that was rising in him. He trembled with satisfaction at the thought that he would thrash her as she had thrashed him. He walked around her, twitching the whip through the dust at her sandaled feet. But there was a flimsy thread of caution in Buzz Winslow. He had been humiliated, and that must be avenged; but if he beat her now and she lost an eye, as she might, there was still a law in Nairobi. Worse, the immediate representative of that law was her formidable father, Tom Lusk.

He watched her flinch as he played the whip around her legs. She had no control over her knees as she tried to press her shaking thighs together. But it was the expenditure of energy that made her tremble. It was still not fear.

Lust swelled through him. He sent the leather singing and cracking over her head. But she still stood her ground, flinching certainly, but refusing to cringe, refusing to try to run.

With a quick, disgusted movement he hurled the whip away from him into the pool. His clothes were torn, his cheek streaming blood. Yet he was aware that he could not beat her. He thought of abusing her for her common background, but that seemed suddenly inadequate. Instead he took a few steps toward Achates, released the reins, and swung himself into the saddle. "You're too good for Longman," he said, "but then I'm sure you know that already."

He shook the reins and pressed Achates forward. As the horse picked its way through the rocks, Pamela Longman watched the sun on the horse's rich chestnut flank and on the rider's gilt hair.

EIGHTEEN

The convoy of American cars rolled down the narrow dirt track from the direction of Thika, slowing almost to a halt to take each bend, spurting stones and dust as each cautiously accelerated again.

From the tents of the safari camp pitched beside the stream, African servants came running to stand watching the eight cars reach the bottom of the gorge and move slowly across the grass, rocking like coracles until they stopped in the deep shade of the forest's edge.

The Europeans, men and women in khaki drill, emerged more slowly from the tents and formed up around a slight, fair-headed figure in safari shirt and shorts. Edward, Prince of Wales, opened his eyes in amused surprise as car doors opened and his guests emerged into the sunlight. "Good Lord," he said, "can we really feed and water all these people?"

"The tables are already laid under the trees, sir," his aide-de-camp said. "Lord Winslow was invited to bring up to twenty-five guests."

"He looks as though he's brought half of Kenya."

The A.D.C. smiled wanly. Buzz Winslow came forward with Margaret.

"Glad you could make it, Winslow," Edward said. "Hope you're not going to eat up all our stores."

"The ship's biscuit's perfectly safe, sir," Buzz said easily. "I can't vouch, however, for the grog. You know my wife, sir."

Edward moved forward while Margaret Winslow curtsied. "Lady Margaret. At Ascot, I believe."

"When Bluebottle won at seven to two. We shared a hundred guineas on it."

"Of course," he said distantly.

On the dusty track behind them, the other guests had formed a line. As they moved forward, Buzz presented those who had not already met the prince. Nancy Hofmanthal thought him remarkably slender, like a child. Both of the Mowbray girls remarked afterwards how easy he had been, paying them compliments and puffing at his cigarette in a short black holder. Tom Boscowan said he had a limp handshake. Marjorie Bellamy thought he might just have stepped from a storybook.

Champagne was served from glistening silver ice buckets, and the guests circulated slowly beneath the trees, the new-comers greeting members of the safari party with kisses and small cries of pleasure. Smoke from the field kitchen drifted through the trees, heavy-scented wild olive wood spiced with the odors of grilling guinea fowl. In the background the Kikuyu ridges led up to the twin peaks of Mount Kenya, dark purple in the clear air and capped with snow.

"I knew your brother Richard well," Edward said, one foot resting on the trunk of a tree that grew tortuously from the bank of the stream. "No country can afford the loss of a man like that. I've heard it said often that there would have been a great political future for him after the war."

"Politics was one of his ruling passions," Buzz said. "Although Lord knows what he would have made of the world today."

"Quite so," Edward said. "At home the level of unemployment is appalling."

"And the international situation menacing."

The prince ejected the end of his cigarette into the stream and immediately took another from a gold case.

"Your sister, of course, has spent a great deal of time in Germany."

"I must arrange for you to have a copy of her book, sir."

"She approves, I understand, of Herr Hitler."

"In general, yes."

"She speaks German?"

"Rather well, I believe."

"And is personally acquainted with most of the leadership of the new government."

Buzz nodded. "Her connection was originally through Captain Göring. There's an exclusive international flying set that seems to be rather centered on Germany."

"But she's not met Herr Hitler."

"Not for any serious discussion. Indeed, I think last time his chosen topic was cream cakes."

"Cream cakes! He likes them?"

"Overmuch is his worry."

Edward laughed. "A human enough failing." He accepted a light for his cigarette. "And what about you, Winslow? What do you think about the German question?"

"I think," Buzz said cautiously, "that in Europe we have to live with Germany as Germany has to live with us."

"You mean an accommodation is necessary."

"I believe it's vital if we're to avoid the maelstrom for the second time in our lives."

Edward puffed his cigarette without inhaling. "And do you think there's something in Germany's new creed? All these new ideas?"

"I doubt if any philosophy can be translated from one nation to another, just like that. But the politicians at home have not shown themselves so entirely successful that we shouldn't at least consider the possibility of learning something elsewhere."

"Open mind, you mean?"

"An open mind," Buzz agreed.

The Prince of Wales nodded thoughtfully, then turned back toward the clusters of guests under the trees. "Idyllic spot," he said. "Beautiful women. Who could ask for more?"

They began to walk toward the other guests. "Lovely thing young Clare Debenham has turned out to be," Edward said. "Seems only yesterday she was in pigtails and ankle socks."

"When a young woman begins the maturing process," Buzz said, "it can be disconcertingly quick."

"Disconcertingly?" The prince's youthful face turned toward him.

"One day you lift them onto your lap to read them a story . . ."

"And the next day . . . quite so!" The prince chuckled. "Even so, I think these bright young things rush into marriage too much these days, do you not?"

The hairs lifted on the back of Buzz's neck. It was said that King George and Queen Mary had approved Clare Debenham's marriage to John Seymour. Was Edward hinting that he felt differently?

"When the difference in age between a man and a woman becomes the subject of drawing-room gossip," Edward was saying, "I'm not sure it's entirely decent."

"With age comes wisdom, so it's said, sir."

"With age come a lot of things, Buzz, my dear fellow. But most of all loss of *attack.*"

They had reached the trees now. The prince stopped and inhaled deeply the scent of woodsmoke. "In America," he said, "I've had the most amazing lunches *alfresco*. Barbecues, they call them. Of course, you probably know, with your American connections." He touched Buzz lightly on the arm. "You won't forget what I said about young girls marrying."

"No, I won't, sir."

"Never does harm to leave it a year or two."

"A year or two."

"Time enough for things to settle down."

Luncheon was served at a long table beneath the trees. The prince sat between Lady Palewell and Elizabeth Cadwallader. It escaped no one's notice that as the wife of Buzz, Margaret Winslow might have expected to sit next to him.

Buzz, sitting beside Clare Debenham, kept up a stream of Kenya stories. But his mind was racing with excitement. He was sure that he had just been discreetly given the royal approval to marry Clare Debenham. The terms, if terms they were, were clear enough. Time had to be allowed for a divorce from Margaret to fade into history. But a divorced suitor was acceptable. At least it seemed acceptable to Edward P.

At the end of lunch a gramophone had been produced, and coconut matting rolled out under the trees. The prince had already invited those who wished to dance to do so, while he himself sat back with a glass of port and a cigarette, laughing with Lucy Palewell, who may or may not have been his current mistress, and several others from the safari party.

Buzz, who was leading Clare Debenham toward the improvised dance floor, suddenly saw Margaret leave the table and walk with quick, angry steps toward the bank of the stream.

He squeezed Clare's arm. "I'll be back in a moment," he said.

She leaned against him. "What is it, darling?" she said in a stage whisper.

"Go and talk to Boy Carstairs a moment. I'm just going to head off a scene."

He walked quickly across the grass toward Margaret, slowing as he approached her. "Hallo," he said. "This is no time for soulful meditation."

She turned on him. "Isn't it?"

"There's music. Come and dance."

She shook her head.

"But you love dancing."

She looked at him. It was so seldom he looked worried. "Are you trying to ditch me, Buzz?" she asked calmly.

"Good God, Margaret, what are you talking about?"

"I'm talking about your aging wife and your nineteen-year-old mistress."

"She isn't my mistress."

"Then what are you interested in her for? Her skill at the quotations game?"

"For God's sake, Margaret," he turned his back to the table under the trees, "pull yourself together. We're guests at Edward P.'s party."

"Some of us more clearly than others. I made a mental note to check with you. Was I actually invited?"

"Of course you were invited."

"Then perhaps someone should inform His Royal Highness," she fumed. "He has not addressed a word to me since I arrived. At least not a civil word. What was he talking to you about for so long?"

"Politics."

"You're planning to ditch me, Buzz," she said, her face flushed. "But I'm not going to let you do it. You understand?"

"I've no intention of ditching you."

"Even though the money's running out? My money?"

He shrugged.

"Even though my forty-eighth birthday is fast approaching?"

"You're being stupid. I told you, these are all wild imaginings."

"Good," she snapped, and walked past him back toward the trees. "Because if they aren't, Buzz," she said loudly over her shoulder, "I'll drag you through the dirtiest divorce case ever."

She laughed. "And that's even including my own first experience."

At the end of the luncheon table, a bread-roll fight had developed. The missiles flew back and forth as the heir to the throne ducked below the level of the trestle to rise, aiming at Lucy Palewell, who fell back defenseless with laughter.

On the dance floor, Tom Boscowan clasped Margaret in his arms. "My baby," he said, "I'm mad for you, you know that."

"I know that, Tom darling," she said indifferently.

"If Buzz wants to chase jailbait, so what?"

"So what?" she said, looking past his shoulder to where her husband was dancing with Clare Debenham.

At the table, a well-aimed bread roll struck Lucy Palewell between the eyes. "You devil!" she shrieked, and, taking the edge of the cloth, jerked hard, sending decanters and half-filled glasses tumbling over the crouching prince.

As the record ended, Margaret pushed Boscowan away from her. "I've had my fill of men for today," she said. "Nancy," she called, and reached out and hauled Nancy Hofmanthal onto the coconut matting as the music rose again. "Come and dance with me." She wrapped her arms around Nancy's slender body.

"Margaret, my dearest, what's come over you?" Nancy gasped.

"I've decided I loathe men after all," Margaret said, laughing hysterically. "That's what's come over me, *loathing*." And she closed her lips over the other woman's mouth and hung on to her, rocking them both back and forth to the music.

"For Christ's sake, Margaret!" Buzz pried them apart. "What the fucking hell d'you think you're doing?"

"Providing evidence," she shrieked at him, "for the divorce!"

"We're guests, for God's sake!"

"And we must not behave in an unseemly manner." She waved her arm toward the table beside which the Prince of Wales lay sputtering with laughter, port wine trickling into his open mouth from a decanter that rolled back and forth on the bare trestle above his head.

On the morning of the Prince of Wales's safari party at Thika, the *Banner-Post* property section, already heavily subscribed as depressed commodity prices bit into settler profits, carried a full-page advertisement for the sale by auction of the farm of Mr. Gerald Longman at Naivasha. A date was given and the sale announced to take place at Pearce's Nairobi Auction Rooms. The settler community knew that this sale was one of the few not prompted by the Depression. Gerald Longman had some time ago announced his intention of moving to the Union of South Africa. He had waited in the hope that land prices would rise again, but as the summer of 1933 passed he had become reluctantly convinced that he should sell this year.

Pamela Longman had moved back to her father's police bungalow after her humiliation at the Muthaiga Club. She had found that not just his love for her, but his immense common sense had buttressed her against the lip-licking insolence of the young Nairobi administrators and civil servants. Tom Lusk's presence in any bar or hotel restaurant was enough to ensure her safe conduct. And as the months passed and she completed an advanced nursing course and was seen traveling the Nairobi area, bandaging wounds and applying iodine to the heads of the farm children, her fast reputation faded to a distant notoriety.

Tom Lusk placed the advertisement in front of her. "Gerald's selling up," he said. He watched his daughter as she stood at the table, leaning forward to read the newspaper, her dark hair curling down past her face.

She had made a determined effort to drive Buzz Winslow from her mind. She had seen him a few times since, usually in the road outside the Norfolk, and he had greeted her with a wry and wary smile before entering his political offices next to the hotel.

She herself was no longer the young wife of Gerald Longman, walking in his shadow, unable to resist the practiced blandishments of a Buzz Winslow. She knew now that she had been seduced in an outrageously skillful manner. Buzz had played on her awe of aristocracy, had gradually separated her from her husband's hopes and aspirations, and had reserved the final compliment, the final lie that he loved her, for a moment when they were lying together beside the rock pool.

She smiled now when she thought how easy it had been for him. But she had no smile left for Buzz Winslow himself. He had humiliated her; he had ruined her husband. Her father had in many ways been the most difficult to deal with. She had had to beg him not to intervene, and it was only her account of the whipping incident that had stilled his hatred of Winslow. But she knew he would never forget.

She stood up from the paper. "I'm going up to Naivasha," she said.

"You're going to see Gerald?"

She nodded. "It's almost a year, you know."

"He's kept away from Nairobi," Lusk said. "I can't blame him." He paused. "Why do you want to see him?"

In the shaded room she smiled, her teeth white in her brown face. Leaning forward, she kissed her father on the cheek. "I have to see him, Dad, before he goes."

She drove up to Naivasha that afternoon, her small District Nurse's box-body trailing red dust behind it.

She had thought a lot about this first meeting. For months she had ached to see the farm, to know how many pair of oxen the season had produced, and if the sisal was a success, or the new pyrethrum. She had, after all, been happy on the farm. But did that mean her marriage had been happy? Certainly at no time, even at the beginning, had it been as exciting as her brief affair with Buzz. But she told herself, as she drove through the drab little town of Naivasha and on toward the lake, that Gerald was a more solid personality, a man from whom other very real satisfaction might flow, but probably not sensual excitement.

She knew the extent of the changes in herself. Of course, she had no idea of the changes, if any, in him. But she knew that she had struck him, almost casually, a desperate blow to the pride that had dragged him from a lower-middle-class home in Battersea to one of the more prosperous farms in the colony and a position of respect among his fellow settlers. If he was to go to South Africa to start again, she felt she should go with him. If he wanted her.

The long, low bungalow was no longer tin-roofed. A covering of bright red tiles led the eye down to new metal-framed windows. The track along which she had fought to drive teams of oxen in the rainy season was now gray, dusty concrete.

Gerald Longman stood on the veranda in bush shirt and khaki slacks. He watched the car approach, and continued slowly filling his pipe, making no move to go out onto the drive.

She pulled the car to a stop and got out. She felt the prickle of heat on the nape of her neck and the place in the center of her back where her dress had been pressed against damp skin. She walked forward and stood in the full bright sunlight, opposite him.

He stopped filling his pipe. "Come in out of the sun," he said, and pulled a chair out for her. As she sat down, he leaned over and pressed a bell button. "Bring a couple of beers," he said to the African who appeared almost immediately.

She noticed he had not asked her what she wanted.

"Dad showed me the auction notice in the *Banner-Post* this morning," she said.

He nodded. "It's not a good time to sell," he said, "but who's to say next year will be better?"

"You're going to South Africa?"

"Yes. You know where you stand there."

"Politically, you mean."

He pursed his lips and reached up to scratch the short stubble of his cheek with the stem of his pipe. It left a faint brown mark, like the trail of a snail. "There *are* agitators about, you know. Mission-school boys who are talking to the natives. They come at night. My man Mboro told me. My God, if I catch them at it . . . "

The beer was brought and opened at the table.

"There's talk of an African Party, did you know that?"

"No."

"And a secret trade union for Kikuyus."

She took her beer. "I came to talk about us, Gerald," she said.

He struck a match for his pipe, broke it, and struck another. "What was it you wanted to say?" he asked after he had the pipe going strongly.

She shook her head. "I'm not sure. I felt we should talk, that's all."

"No point in aimless talk," he said. "You're the guilty party, of course," he said reasonably, "but if you want to come back, if you want to come with me to South Africa, you've only got to ask."

She took a deep breath. "I want to talk to you, Gerald. That's all."

"Things haven't been too good, living with Dad in Nairobi,

eh?" he said with a sudden strange savagery. "Your aristocratic playboys didn't want anything more to do with you, eh?"

She sat looking down into the bubbles rising to the surface of the golden beer.

"Well, you can come if you want," he said. He chuckled suddenly, a mask for his anger. "But if I catch you up to any of your tricks . . ."

Her head came up slowly. He was disconcerted by the flinty look in her gray eyes. "I came to wish you good luck, Gerald," she said. "I know how much harm I've done you. Harm you didn't for one moment deserve." She stood up. "We hurt each other so casually, don't we? Like children at play."

"Hang on," he said, "you haven't finished your beer."

She held her hand out and took his, feeling it knuckled and thin and already old. "You were not vindictive when it all happened," she said. "I shall always be very, very grateful for that." She leaned forward and kissed him on the stubbled cheek, where the brown mark gave off a faint tang of tobacco.

NINETEEN

t was night, and Catherine Esterhazy sat on the terrace of
her farmhouse at Ngong, watching the moonlight throw
quicksilver reflections across the lake. She had just written
one letter to her mother in Nebraska, and another, more difficult, to her sister, who proposed bringing her three children to
stay in Kenya for a month or two. She had been obliged to say
no. She had not seen her younger sister since she had left for
Africa, and couldn't bear the thought of all the American
optimism that poured from her sister's letters, translated into
night after night of conversation. She had told her sister she
was likely to be leaving for Europe for a holiday, but the truth
was that she feared a family visit would irrevocably destroy the
barrier of solitude she had built around herself.

She was sealing the letter to her mother when she thought
she saw the pattern of moonlight ripples change at the far edge
of the lake. Someone, or perhaps some animal, had moved the
branches of the young acacias growing there. She sat for a
moment watching without fear. A minute or two passed before
she saw a shadow, this time clearly a man, move across an open
stretch of grass and stop not fifty yards away in the moonlight.

The figure raised a hand in greeting and came on across the
lawn. Only when the house lights caught his face did she see
that it was Kum.

"Baroness," he said as he came up onto the veranda. "It is I,
Kum."

She got to her feet and came to meet him, holding out both
hands in greeting. "Kum," she said, tears starting to her eyes,
"what a marvelous, marvelous thing to have happened to me
now."

For Kum it was an unimaginable shock. He knew she was

drunk from the effort she had made to raise herself from the table, from the unsteadiness of her walk as she crossed toward him, but most of all from her face, puffed and coarsened around the eyes, the muscles slack with sudden emotion at her mouth.

"My dear Kum," she said. She held him at arm's length, looking at his pressed khaki safari jacket, the faint flecks of gray in his wiry hair. "We're both older," she said. "Come and sit with me."

He sat down beside her and accepted the whiskey she poured him. For a moment they looked at each other, then he raised his glass.

"You must tell me everything," she said unsteadily. "Everything."

He nodded slowly.

"You're wondering what has happened to me, Kum. Is that it?"

"It is nearly two years since Pamela Longman brought me here from the village," he said. "We have both changed since then."

"Yes." She poured the last of the bottle of whiskey into her glass. "I drink too much, Kum. I could give you a hundred reasons for that one simple fact, but there's no point. I drink too much to run the farm properly any longer. I drink too much to be able to keep the confidence of my bank manager in Nairobi. I simply drink too much." She laughed. "I can write letters when I'm drunk. Better letters than when I'm sober. My life is lived through letters—written and received. Therefore I drink to expand the arena of my life. Q. E. D. ..."

Kum nodded. From his pocket he took a pack of Chesterfield cigarettes. He tapped one from the packet and lit it with a Zippo lighter. "The captain," he said, breathing smoke from his wide nostrils, "he has written to you over the years."

"Mostly I've written to him," she said. "I've poured out my thoughts and feelings, my regrets, to him. Possibly I have severely embarrassed him with the raw honesty of my friendship."

"But he has written to you, too."

"Yes. Mostly facts, details." She finished her whiskey and, fumbling under the table, produced a new, unopened bottle. "Mostly facts," she said, "when what I wanted was poetry."

Kum reached across the table and, taking the bottle from her, twisted the cap. She held her glass out for him and he poured a careful half-measure.

"Tell me, Kum, tell me about yourself. All about yourself."

"In some ways," he said, "there's too much to tell, Baroness."

"Will you call me Catherine?"

"Yes." He paused. "I have been in Kenya most of this year. I don't need to tell you what is happening here."

"I am not happy at the way some of the white people are behaving. Some, not all."

"The African peoples see less romance in Africa than the Europeans. It's not surprising."

"Don't go too fast, Kum. Don't hurt them," she said drunkenly, "don't hurt your own people."

He lit another cigarette. "The world's changing fast," he said. "The lines are being drawn. In Germany, Adolf Hitler is in power. This year I returned to Germany."

She put her glass down on the table, misjudging the distance so that the base banged down heavily on the metal tabletop. "You're still a Kikuyu, Kum. You still move in circles. You've come to tell me something. I can feel, drunk as I am. You've come to tell me bad news."

"I was in Hamburg," Kum said.

"Don't make me work for it, Kum. Don't be cruel. You were in Hamburg. You saw Claus. The bad news is about him."

"I was in Hamburg, but this time I did not see the captain," Kum said. "The Brownshirts were everywhere. Jews they hated more than men of my skin. No, I did not see the captain."

"But you had news of him."

Kum reached forward and poured whiskey for both of them. "Yes, I had news."

She sat silent, not even reaching for her glass.

"When the Nazis came to power," Kum said, "they sent their Brownshirts to find all who had spoken or written against them. I am told they never found some because they had been taken away in the night by people like the captain. Sometimes a whole family—mother, father, children—had gone, disappeared from their rooms. The captain took some, perhaps not many, in his boat to Denmark. For a month or more he did this."

"For a month or more?"

"Until the Brownshirt police arrested him."

"He is in prison now?"

"Yes. He is in prison at Moabit in Berlin."

"At his trial he was given a sentence?"

"There was no trial. There will never be a trial."

"You mean he's in prison for as long as the Nazis want him to be."

"He will die there," Kum said. "Unless you can find help, he will die there."

"How did you learn all this? Are you sure it's true?"

"It's true. He's in prison now, Catherine. It was in this way that I learned the facts. In Amsterdam I met a young comrade whose name is Lorelei. For a month or two we lived together, doing the same party work in the docks. She told me that many years before she had met an aristocrat who had served with von Lettow's *Schutztruppe*. It was the captain. The party had soon required her to stop seeing him."

"She obeyed the party?"

"Yes. She was more in love with the party than she was with the captain." Kum smiled. "She was more in love with the party than she was with me."

"Had she kept in touch with the captain all those years?"

"No, it was more or less by chance that she heard he was smuggling people onto his boat. One or two of them were party members. It was through the party underground in Berlin that Lorelei heard what had happened."

Catherine poured herself another drink. "I am naïve in these matters. Is the captain a Communist?"

"No."

"But you are?"

"I am not afraid to tell you that I am."

"I don't pretend to understand why."

He slid his cigarettes slowly into his jacket pocket. "Nazi Germany claims back its former colonies," he said. "Adolf Hitler has already appointed a minister for Tanganyika."

"It's not possible."

"Von Lettow himself says it would be in all ways wrong. The man Adolf Hitler has appointed is former Governor Schnee. His deputy is already in Nairobi."

"Do you have to be a Communist to fight against the Nazis recovering Tanganyika? The British would not accept it."

For a long time he was silent. "Many inducements could be offered to the settlers of Kenya to accept these changes."

"But it's not up to them to agree. It's up to the government in London."

"Many people, like the captain's friend, Lord Winslow, believe that should be changed."

"You are a very well-informed person, Kum."

He smiled briefly and got up, standing by the table. "I will go now," he said.

"You know, of course, that you can stay if you choose."

He smiled. "I will come and see you again," he said. "Do something quickly, Catherine."

She watched his slender shape move from under the veranda lights into the whiter moonlight of the lawn. Then he reached the young trees beside the lake and was gone.

She took a bottle of whiskey with her in her old box-body motorcar and set out a little after ten o'clock on the journey north to Naivasha.

A small incident occurred on the way back from the prince's party. On one of the last bends before Naivasha, the car Tom Boscowan was driving had skidded across the loose gravel surface of the road and come to rest in a tangle of shrub and bushes. Harry Towers, fondling Mollie Mowbray in the backseat, had been thrown forward. Boy Carstairs, in the front passenger seat, had lightly bumped his head against the roof. They had climbed out to inspect the damage, Tom Boscowan swearing and muttering under his breath. The taillights of the rest of the convoy were already sweeping around the next bend ahead of them.

"Told you you'd never qualify at Brookwood, old chap," Towers said.

"Not my bloody fault," Boscowan said fiercely.

"Sorry I spoke," Towers chanted. "What's the damage?" he asked in a normal voice.

"We're going to have to lift the front wheel clear." Boscowan was leaning over the hood of the Oldsmobile, his head almost lost in the bushes. "I could smash the axle if I try to drive her off," he grunted, straightening up.

Carstairs, bending from his great height, pointed into the

tangled shrub. "There's a broken branch through the wheel hub," he said. "The three of us will never manage it."

"The four of us," Mollie Mowbray corrected.

Harry Towers patted her backside. "It's a couple of miles, but I vote we walk."

"Wait," Boscowan said. From somewhere in the darkness on the road below came a faint chatter of African voices. "You there!" Boscowan bawled into the darkness. "Hey, you there!"

The voices ceased.

"Oh God, Tom, you're enough to scare off a rhino. Let me talk to them. *Jambo*," Mollie called. *"Jambo."*

There was a shuffling of bare feet on the road and about twenty Kikuyu *morani*, the young warriors of the tribe, and a group of maidens stood in the Oldsmobile's headlights. Their bodies, blonded by the red chalk with which *morani* and *nditos* alike rub their bodies, stood out pale against the night, the young men naked but with chalk-mud extending and teasing their coiffures into spectacular shapes, the girls in tanned leather skirts and thick bands of beads. They stood in silence, looking into the bright headlights.

"Jambo," Mollie Mowbray said, walking forward. "What news?" she asked, following the ritual of Swahili greeting.

"Good," a young man said, "and yours?"

"Good," Mollie said. "Why are you walking so late?"

"We are on our way to the *ngoma*," the warrior said proudly.

"What in the devil's name are they going on about?" Boscowan said as he stomped from the darkness behind the headlights. "Tell them we want them to lift the car free."

"Oh, quiet, Tom," Mollie Mowbray remonstrated. "They're on their way to a *ngoma*, a big dance. They take an age to get all dressed up for it. We have to ask them nicely."

"Dressed up for it!" Carstairs said, emerging into the light. "Those fellows haven't got a stitch on them. Girls not much better."

"Our car is stuck in the bush," Mollie said.

Two or three *morani* nodded gravely.

"It was not stuck when other *morani* passed this way?" the spokesman asked.

"No," Mollie said patiently. "The accident has just happened."

"It is a misfortune," the spokesman said.

"I have known similar," another young warrior said, coming forward.

"During the long rains the motorcar of Longman-bwana is often fixed in the mud near his house," a third young man observed, nodding knowingly.

By now they had moved slightly forward so that they were scattered along the edge of the road, the thick bush behind them.

"What's happening?" Towers asked.

"They're discussing the problem," Mollie replied, turning to him.

"We *know* what the bloody problem is." Boscowan's voice rose angrily. "Just tell the blighters what we want them to do about it."

"Hey, just a moment," Carstairs said.

Mollie swung around. Six or seven of the group had already slipped into the bush behind them. Others disappeared with a single deft movement backwards.

"They're legging it!" Boscowan roared. "Come back here!"

The roadside was empty. Twenty figures had disappeared in as many seconds.

She could see Lake Naivasha below her now, iron-gray in the black encircling night, sinister, it seemed to her, under the metallic reflections of a waning moon. Her own headlights danced before her eyes, bounced, probed, and jumped on every rise and fall of the track. Then a glimmer of light showed through the trees, was lost again, and reappeared. She was too tired and of course too drunk to be sure, but as she took a steeply banked bend, she had the impression that the glimmer was not where it had been before. That there were two lights.

She was driving on the straight now, a length of road that was almost even, before the plunging track led down to the lakeshore. As if by some strange trick of the earlier twisting path, she now saw the light as if it were on the hillside to her left. She shook her head and turned the wheel to direct the car down the narrowing track. The light clearly *was* up on the hillside above Corinth—it was no trick of drink or tiredness. And there was another, and a third nearby.

The outline of the Winslow house lay clearly below now. From a scattering of outbuildings at the back, a few lights shone. She let the box-body run down the last few hundred yards, turned through the gates, and stopped in front of the darkened veranda.

She got out of the car. Her legs ached from the long drive. She walked stiffly up the veranda steps and stood for a moment looking through the glass doors into the hall. A single pair of shaded wall lamps threw a cold green light across one wall. She peered in through the French doors. It was the first time she had been here. The brass and chromium staircase intrigued her with the modernity of its style. Imported from Europe, of course. All the other houses she knew in the colony had wooden staircases, built by Indian carpenters from local wood. Her eye traveled down to a chair at the bottom of the staircase. A painting stood against it, left not for display but casually, as if on its way to some other resting place on a landing or study wall. It was a portrait. She looked again and saw with a shock the glowering features of Adolf Hitler.

She brushed aside her dismay. It was, after all, what she was here for. As she stood there, a door opened and Buzz emerged into the hall wearing a silk dressing gown and carrying a glass of whiskey.

She rapped urgently on the pane in front of her. He turned, frowning, then came forward rapidly to open the door. "Catherine Esterhazy," he said. "Come in." He pulled the door wide. "Is anything wrong, Catherine?"

"I'll tell you about it." She was surprised to note that she sounded breathless.

"Come into the study. I'll get Ali up to make some coffee."

"A drink," she said, "would do as well. Better."

She followed him into the study.

"Brandy?"

"Whiskey." She dropped into a leather armchair. "A large whiskey."

He carried a glass and a decanter to her. "Say when."

He began to pour, glanced at her, lifted an eyebrow, poured again. She watched him expressionlessly. He poured yet again. The tumbler was over half full. "Soda? Or water?"

She shook her head and reached for the glass.

He collected his own whiskey and sat on the arm of the chair opposite her, watching as she tipped the glass to her lips and drank as if it were water.

She nodded. "I drink, Lord Winslow."

He smiled. "So do we all. What is it that brings you here at this time of night, Catherine?"

"Your friend Claus. He's in prison."

"In Germany?"

"Yes."

"What for?"

"Does it matter?"

"Yes, it matters," he said slowly. "Of course it matters."

"I'm sorry, yes. He hasn't stolen an old lady's purse or murdered a pimp. It's for political reasons."

"He was arrested by the new government?"

"Yes. For helping some people to get out of Germany."

"When was this?"

"Shortly after the Nazis came to power."

Around his mouth she saw the muscles tense. He was looking down at the carpet. "Oh my God," he said. "My poor Claus."

"They are your friends who have put him there," she said, and immediately regretted the harshness of her voice.

He stood up. "And they will be my friends who get him out," he snapped. "If it's possible to get him out."

She handed him her almost empty glass. "I'm sorry," she said. "I think I'm sorry."

He walked slowly to the side table and refilled both of their glasses. "How do you know about this?"

"A letter," she lied. "From a friend in Germany."

"The telegraph office at Naivasha is closed. I'll go first thing tomorrow morning and send a message to my sister in Germany."

She took her second glass of whiskey from him. "I thought I was going to have to persuade you," she said.

"To do something for Claus? What sort of man d'you think I am!"

"I don't know. I suppose I simply don't know."

"For God's sake," he said. "This is of no importance. Do you know where Claus is in prison?"

"No. I know no more than what I've told you." She began to get to her feet.

"You can't go now," he said. "You must stay the night."

She fell back wearily into the chair. Her eyes were half closed. "There are fires on the hillside," she murmured. "You're not clearing land, are you?"

"The natives are holding a big *ngoma*," he said. "Somebody's daughter's just married somebody's son."

"You don't take much interest in your Africans."

"They're not *my* Africans," he said, shrugging. "I don't run a farm, I don't need native labor."

"You must employ a number of them here at the house."

"Of course. God knows how many, my man Ali sees to that. But there are usually a dozen or more sloping around, not even pretending to look busy."

"You don't think they'll ever have a real part to play?"

"It's a white man's country," he said. "We're here by right."

"The *droit du plus fort*."

"Much more than that. We're here because we represent a civilization. A way of life that has not been equaled since Classical Greece. Might may be right but it doesn't *confer* rights. Nor does the wishy-washy settlers' belief that their rights are based on their ability to produce three coffee beans where the native can only produce one. Our right is based on the pure, unsullied confidence of our class and race. I'm not prepared to indulge in maudlin discussion about anything less."

Outside the study window there was a sudden thunder of horses' hooves. Men's voices whooped and shouted Buzz's name.

"What the devil's that?" He put down his glass. "Tom Boscowan and the boys playing silly buggers," he muttered.

The door from the veranda was thrown open. Riding boots stomped heavily across the hall. Tom Boscowan stood laughing in the study doorway, his face flushed and sweating. Boy Carstairs ducked to peer in, grinning. Behind them, Harry Towers looked sheepishly pleased with himself.

"What the devil are you about?" Buzz said, more indulgent than angry.

"We're about teaching these uppity natives a lesson, that's what we're about. We've just fired their *shambas*."

Catherine Esterhazy sat up. "You've set fire to the huts?"

The three men erupted into the room, filling it suddenly with the smell of leather and the sweat of horses.

[298]

"Swept straight through their *ngoma*," Boy Carstairs said. "They ran like madmen, screaming like banshees."

"Hid up behind the village, watching," Harry Towers said, his eyes glowing. "Then we lit our firebrands and galloped down on them like an Apache raiding party."

"Let's have a drink, Buzz," Boscowan said. "You should have been there."

Catherine was watching Buzz Winslow as he waved his hand toward the drinks table. "You made bloody sure there was no one in the huts, I hope," he said.

"For Christ's sake," Boscowan said, "they were all at the *ngoma*."

"There could have been *totos* left to sleep."

"They carry them with them," Carstairs said as he handed around drinks. "Nobody hurt. Just a bit of fun."

"And a bloody good lesson at the same time," Boscowan said, and turned to Catherine. "Baroness Esterhazy, forgive me. The manners of the rude soldiery," he knelt down beside her chair. "It's not often I ignore the presence of a beautiful woman. Let me get you a drink."

"I was just going to bed," she said heavily. She looked, her eyes hard with detestation, into his flushed face.

Boscowan waved his arm, spilling whiskey. "It would be ungallant to thwart a lady's wishes."

"Ungallant, yes."

Buzz had turned and was talking urgently to Towers and Carstairs.

Boscowan rested a hand on Catherine's arm. "You and Buzz," he said, opening his eyes in mock surprise. "He never told me a thing about it."

She shook her arm free. "There's nothing to tell," she said. "It's late. He invited me to stay."

"Then," Boscowan thumped down his glass on the carpet, "I will escort you to your room."

"Thank you, no," she hissed.

"You must allow me to insist." He half fell across the arm of her chair. "I insist, I insist."

The other three men were laughing at him. "Come on, Tom," Buzz said. "You should know when you're not wanted."

"Wait!" A sudden change came over Catherine Esterhazy's

face. "Perhaps it would be wrong to decline so gallant an offer."
She looked at him, her expression softening into a smile.

Boscowan knelt before her uncertainly.

"If you insist," she said, "then I accept."

He burbled an incoherent phrase and gave her his hand to
raise her from the chair.

Buzz watched, frowning.

"Which room, Buzz, shall I escort the lady Esterhazy to?"

"The corner front," Buzz said, still frowning.

Boscowan slipped his arm around her waist. "Then the corner
front it is." He pressed his face against hers.

She threw an arm around his neck. "Mr. Boscowan may take
some time to find his way back," she said to the room at large.

"Quite some time." Boscowan nuzzled her cheek.

"Come along." Her arms clung around his neck. "Bring your
unsullied confidence in class and race," she murmured to him.
"Come and love me, Mr. Boscowan. Promise me that you will
love me, love me."

TWENTY

I n his office at the Central Police Station in Nairobi, Inspector Thomas Lusk looked up from his desk as Sergeant Henderson came in.

"There's an African to see you, sir," the young sergeant said. "Chap named Kum."

"What's he want?" Lusk finished signing his latest cattle-rustling report. The Masai were responsible, as ever, but he knew that precious little could be done about it. It was a way of life.

"He didn't say. Just that it was important. Very good English. If he'd been your ordinary customer, I should have dealt with it myself, of course."

"Kum . . ." A memory was coming back to Lusk over the years.

"Says he was once employed by Baroness Esterhazy up at Ngong."

"That's the one," Lusk said. "Strange how old birds come back to roost."

"What's that, sir?"

"Doesn't matter. Show him in."

Henderson left the room and returned a moment later with Kum at his side.

"That's all right, Henderson," Lusk dismissed him. He looked at the tall Kikuyu in front of him, noting the well-pressed shirt and trousers. "Well, Kum, it's a long time since you worked for the baroness."

"It's a long time, Inspector."

"And even longer since you flew as observer for the *Schutztruppe*."

"You know I never did that, Inspector."

"Your English *has* improved. What's the problem, Kum?"

"The baroness, Inspector. She's missing."

"Missing?" Lusk stood up, his back to the window.

"I called at the farm this morning. Her Somali told me that she had been to Naivasha two days ago and had not returned."

"Naivasha."

"To visit Lord Winslow on business."

"So perhaps she stayed a day or two."

"She *had* returned. I found her car on the edge of the small wood behind the farm."

Lusk began to fill his pipe. "Why didn't you say that before?"

"I've said it now, Inspector."

Lusk tamped down the tobacco with his forefinger. "Could she have returned from Naivasha this morning, left the car behind the farm, and, for whatever reason, gone off for a walk across the hill?"

"The *totos* at the farm say the car has been there since yesterday morning."

Lusk eyed him. "Just give me the *full* story, Kum."

"That's the full story as I know it."

"I see. If the *totos* are right, she returned yesterday but she did not sleep the night at her farm."

"That is so."

Lusk banged on the partition wall. "Henderson," he shouted.

Henderson's fresh face appeared around the door.

"Get someone at Lord Winslow's place on the phone for me. Lord or Lady Winslow themselves, if possible."

"Right, sir." Henderson's head disappeared.

"What had you gone up to see the baroness for, Kum?"

"As a friend I went to see her."

"As a friend."

"Even when she was my employer I counted her as a friend."

Lusk grunted. "What do you think might have happened? Any ideas?"

"A misfortune, Inspector. An accident."

"Well." Lusk scratched his cheek. "It certainly seems strange. Just get this call through, and I think we'd better go up there, Kum."

The telephone jangled. Lusk picked up the receiver. "Lady Winslow? Inspector Lusk, Nairobi, here. I'm sorry to trouble you, milady, but I wonder if you could answer a couple of questions about Baroness Esterhazy's visit to you the night before last. I'm trying to discover what time she left."

He listened for a moment, then covered the mouthpiece and looked toward Kum. "The *totos* were probably right. She left very early Wednesday morning." He removed his hand and spoke into the telephone. "What was the reason for Baroness Esterhazy's visit? Captain von Hardenberg in prison?" he said after a moment. "Well, let's hope something can be done."

When he had finished the call, he picked up his linen jacket and, pipe clenched in his mouth, swung the coat over his shoulder. "Captain von Hardenberg is in prison in Germany. Did you know that?"

"Yes."

"You knew, then, why the baroness had gone to Naivasha?"

"Yes."

Lusk blew air through closed lips. "Very well, Kum," he said. "But you know in my business silence isn't always golden."

At Catherine's farm a cluster of Africans stood on the lawn as Lusk's car drew up. The field workers had abandoned the fields, the houseboys had left the kitchen, the *totos* stood watching, large-eyed, wondering why the baroness was not there for a schoolday.

Forsan, her Somali headman, came forward. He cupped his hand rapidly from chest to forehead in greeting. "I have found some letters in the baroness's car, Inspector," he said. "Many letters, sealed, ready to be posted."

Lusk stood in the burning heat. "Oh Christ," he said.

Kum looked at him. "Perhaps you give the letters too much significance, Inspector."

"And perhaps I don't. I've been in Kenya too long, Kum. You see a lot of this business."

"What business is that, Inspector?"

"You know what I'm talking about, Kum," Lusk said. "A woman who lives alone. Too many debts. Too much whiskey."

"What should we do?"

Lusk began to walk toward the house. "We should draw up a rough map of the property. You can do that. And then we organize all these lads into search parties." He turned to Forsan. "Send the *totos* off home," he said. "This is not work for little ones like that."

*　　*　　*

Kum found her body in the early afternoon, facedown among the reeds on the edge of the lake. The inspector came in answer to his call, and they both stood for a moment looking down at her.

Lusk nodded. "You'd best push off now," he said. "You know why."

"Have I committed a crime, Inspector?"

"You don't need to, I'm sure you know that."

"Will you shake hands, Mr. Lusk?"

"No, Kum." Lusk shook his head. "I don't believe in all that silliness, old chap. We're natural enemies, you and me." He smiled. "Let's behave like it, eh?"

For a moment they stood watching Catherine Esterhazy's long skirt as it billowed out around her, undulating with the reeds. Then Kum turned and walked along the track that led out to the high fields.

APPOINTMENT
AT
NAIVASHA

TWENTY-ONE

I never knew I was in Berlin's Moabit Prison until the night I left it. I was arrested in Hamburg and taken to the local Fuhlsbuettel Camp. There I was questioned with much random beating, and after three or perhaps four nights I was thrown into an enclosed prison truck and taken on a journey of many hours. For some time I slept; I have no real idea for how long. When I was dragged from the van I was in a prison yard. Which prison yard seemed of no great importance. I would have asked, certainly, if I had ever met another prisoner in circumstances that made asking possible. But no such circumstances arose.

Moabit had achieved, by the time I had been there for a month or two, a certain degree of administrative order. My first camp, Fuhlsbuettel, or KLF (Konzentrationslager-Fuhlsbuettel), as it was known, was an unruly hellhole where we, the prisoners, were the galley slaves to the SS whip-masters set above us. At KLF, tiny vignettes chilled the blood of the new arrival: three prisoners, chained together, tumbling and falling as they were made to "race" each other down the steep wooden steps from the railway siding; a fat blond girl throwing herself to the floor in a reception hall and scrambling to her feet in wild-eyed terror before throwing herself down again as a guard chanted, "Up . . . down . . . up . . . down. We'll teach you to open your legs to Jews"; an old man pinned against a wall by a snarling dog while a guard laughed every time a bloodstained strip of clothing was torn from the prisoner's trousers.

And yet, in these days, I talked to one young SS guard who offered me a cigarette and explained that once the rotten apples had been cleared from the barrel, Germany would become a kind of paradise. He was a slim, good-looking boy of twenty.

Before the National Revolution, he said, homosexuality had been rampant in Hamburg's St. Pauli district. He himself had twice been chased by gangs of homosexuals. I accepted his cigarettes and agreed gravely that we were moving into an altogether better era.

In Moabit my interrogation was conducted by a Gestapo inspector from Inspektion 6, a special anti-Comintern squad, it being believed that I had smuggled out only Communist agents. I don't believe that the inspector was ever convinced of this himself, but he was prepared to go through the painful motions until he gradually persuaded himself that he was wrong, that I was doing what I had confessed to, smuggling anybody and everybody who, I happened to know, desperately needed to leave Germany in the days after the Nazi victory. Because of my willingness to confess and to give names of people who were by now beyond the reach of the Gestapo, I received little more than kicks and slaps around the face, although I could hear, from other cells on my corridor, the terror-stricken screams of men and women, which showed clearly enough that the Gestapo had no lack of further resources. Perhaps the fact that I had earlier decided I would tell them that I exacted high fees every time I smuggled anyone out to Copenhagen or Amsterdam helped my case.

In truth, there had been no Communists left in the house by the time the election results were declared. As the campaign seemed to point more and more decisively to a Nazi victory, all the professional Communists seemed to melt away. Eva was still there, and as far as I know she managed to disguise her beliefs with the help of Ruby, who was now a committed Nazi election worker but still a faithful friend.

Two days before the election results, I had returned home to find Lorelei in my apartment. She sat with her leather worker's cap on the back of her head, her hands hanging between her knees.

I came in and poured her a beer. She accepted morosely. "Webel has ordered me to stay in Hamburg," she said.

I looked at her, shocked. "But you're known to every Nazi here," I said. "You told me yourself you've been involved in arrangements with the SA man Thorn."

She nodded, sipping her beer.

"What's Webel up to?" I asked. I was frightened. I suddenly realized she was too. "Where is he? Here, in Hamburg?"

"He left for Holland this morning."

I was silent. She gave me a wan smile and lifted her eyebrows.

"It's a death sentence," I said. "If the Nazis win this election, it's a death sentence."

She gave a small, uneasy shrug.

"Come down to the docks now," I said. "I can take you across to Amsterdam as soon as it gets dark."

I could see she hesitated. But she sat silently, baffled by the enormity of what Webel was doing to her, yet unable to condemn it.

"I've got to stay," she said after a few minutes. "If I don't stay I lose everything."

We argued for almost an hour and I still failed to persuade her to leave Hamburg.

"At least," I said finally, "come and stay here."

"It's too dangerous for you," she said.

"What is Webel doing?" I said. "You must know."

"He is cleaning out his opponents. He was proved wrong about the Nazi threat. Those of us who opposed his reports in the past have now to be liquidated. As martyrs. I have been too full of pride, Claus. I have brought this upon myself."

"For God's sake," I said, "you speak like a nun. Not even a twentieth-century nun!"

"I must stay in Hamburg until my task is completed."

"What task?"

She paused. "It will not help you to know too much," she said. She stood up and kissed me. Warmly, for once.

"If you ever need somewhere . . ."

She nodded and turned toward the door. Hatred for men like Webel surged through me as I listened to Lorelei go down the stairs to the front door.

But fear of the coming election results was not confined to members of the Communist Party. My neighbors along the street were in varying states of nervousness. Because I had a boat, and—God save me—because I was a gentleman, they approached me for help. They were small Jewish businesspeople, mainly. Some were simply Social Democrats who had shown their faces on streetcorners collecting for their party.

In the next few days before the election results, I began to make inquiries at the dock and found to my horror that a scale had already been decided among the trade-union convenors: cooperation to smuggle Jews was fixed at 250 marks per head.

I now urged people to leave while they could still do so freely, but many hung on in hope.

On the election night itself, I did something I now deeply regret. I approached Diana for money. What happened? I remember the fluttering nervousness of waiting. The wireless was giving special election-night commentaries. Nobody doubted that the Nazis had done well; some foresaw a spectacular victory.

I had no means of raising money immediately, and old Mr. Mendel's need was immediate.

I think it was the saddest night of my life. The Hitler party was winning. Men like Thorn, who strolled through St. Pauli like a petty princeling, would now be in control. And Diana, who had written to me once about a decent chance for all of us in Europe, was blindly supporting them.

It took prison to reduce the pain of my visit to Diana at the Adlon. For days after my meeting with her, I formulated a reasoned denunciation of Nazism, from Darré to Rosenberg to the arch-hypocrite-believer himself. But then I would feel sick with the hopelessness of the idea, and days would pass when I would push it roughly from my mind, thinking of her with a kind of manufactured distaste.

The day at Moabit began at 5:00 A.M. with a visit from the young Gestapo guard. As the door opened I was required to spring from my mattress, stand at attention, and shout, as though at the ceiling above my head: "Prisoner Hardenberg, Claus Thomas, 5709. No complaints."

This pointless ritual began a day of solitary confinement broken by periods of questioning and further random beatings. In those early days of the Nazi victory I had the impression that there were far too many new prisoners for all to be dealt with efficiently. Certainly the inspector in charge of my case carried a permanently worried air. I could hear the footsteps along the corridor as he hurried toward my cell, and from time to time I could hear him ask for reports on other prisoners unknown to me.

"Klosterman?" the inspector would ask. "Is he conscious yet?"

"Recovered this morning," the guard would report. "We gave him another ten lashes but he still had nothing more to say."

"Take him all the way," the inspector would say fretfully. "Take him all the way. He *must* know his brother-in-law's address."

Or, on another occasion:

"Sylvia, has she added to that list yet?"

"No, Inspector, we dunked her last night for half an hour, but she insists she has nothing more to tell us."

You could almost see the inspector's face nodding in concern. "Try cigarette ends." His voice came through the grille in my cell door, as concerned and thoughtful as a doctor prescribing. "Cigarette ends on the lips can be very effective with women."

I had the impression that Inspector Beck, as I eventually discovered was his name, was constantly pressed by some superior to produce longer lists of traitors from the prisoners in his care.

After a week or two, a few days would elapse between sessions, and on those days, after reporting my name and number and adding that I had no complaints, I was free to lie on my mattress and think what thoughts I chose until soup time.

If I now sound somewhat overrelaxed and casual about my first weeks in Moabit, it is perhaps that I was still suffering from the shock of my arrest. But in truth I think that I was far more sustained by my wartime memories. Compared to the horrors of some of those long weeks on the Somme, life in prison was both more comfortable and very much less dangerous.

Toward the end of the summer of 1933 I was assigned a cell with another man who was equally unaware of the whereabouts of our prison. He was a Communist named Ladecker who had been badly beaten in his early interrogations. His arm, which had been broken, remained unsplinted, and his right eye had been damaged to the point of blindness. But none of this meant anything to him against the fact that he had finally given the Gestapo interrogator a list of comrades, some of whom might not have had time to flee. At night he would sob like a child at what he had done until I awoke and assured him that his friends

[311]

would have all taken the first opportunity to flee as soon as they heard of his arrest. Then he would go to sleep and the night might pass with no more than a whimper.

We lived in conditions of desperate filth and, as the winter drew on, increasing cold. Our prison uniforms were striped cotton jackets and trousers with wooden sabots. Our heads, which had been shaven on induction, were now covered with odd sproutings of hair. We were, of course, bearded.

The food was not food for a man. The soup that was delivered at 6:00 A.M. and midday was a water gruel with perhaps some vegetable. A slice of bread seemed to depend on whether or not the guard had remembered to bring it. A curious part of the ritual, which may or may not have predated the Nazis, was "eating-up time." This was now a matter of perhaps thirty seconds that a prisoner was given to finish his soup before the removal of the spoon and bowl. On the days when the soup was cold, this was no serious problem, but we soon discovered that if the soup was hot or near boiling as it sometimes was, then a mug of water from the lavatory flush was necessary to be held in readiness. The alternative of leaving any portion of the soup unconsumed was unthinkable.

Our guards were of two types. The older men had been warders before the Nazi victory and would, I believe, have been different men if the younger, Nazi guards were not watching them all the time. I believe this because of one or two simple kindnesses I received from the older men from time to time. Once, one smiled at me. Two or three times we were given, poor Ladecker and I, an extra few seconds for our soup. I believe we always had a slice of bread when an old warder was on food delivery.

For all these minor comforts, I was losing weight rapidly and I feared the onset of scurvy, although I was ignorant of when it might strike. I had no hope of release, and that in itself induced a curious resignation. Perhaps I had simply accepted my total defeat.

I think I broke down only once. It was the practice of prisoners to commit to memory the names of other prisoners they had seen alive or dead. Lists of names were passed back and forth in whispered seconds in the night. For those men involved in long interrogations, it was sometimes vital to know a comrade was dead. Then, at least, he could be relied upon.

On one very cold day I was ordered to take an overcoat to Inspector Beck, outside in the exercise yard. Wrapping the warm coat around my numb fingers, I savored the moment and dawdled along the corridor that led to the door to the yard. The voice that stopped me hissed out of the darkness. A cell's spy-hole had been left open. Peering in, I could just make out a filthy, bearded face.

"With my own eyes, comrade, with my own eyes, remember . . ."

"Yes," I said uncertainly.

"Executed by guillotine in the main yard: Ralf Silbermann, Heinz Dietzel, and two girls, first names only, Sylvia and Lorelei. Pass it on."

I delivered the coat and returned at the regulation dogtrot to my cell. I was bursting with an anger I could not control against all the scheming Webels of this world. As I was slammed into my cell, I looked across at the bundle of rags that was poor Ladecker. I knew that if it had been Webel, I would have fallen on him and torn him flesh from bone. Ladecker told me afterwards that I howled like a wolf intermittently through the night. Those parts I remember, I was crying like a child.

Then, one evening in November 1933, Inspector Beck had come down to the cell. He had opened the door himself, though two of his henchmen were with him. To my astonishment, he *invited* me with a wave of his hand to enter the corridor. But much more significantly he had used the polite form in German to address me, when prisoners were *always* spoken to in the manner used with children or dogs.

I was taken to his office, where I was again *invited* to sit down. A cup of coffee was placed before me, and a woman secretary gave me a pack of cigarettes and a box of matches.

"I would be grateful if you would sign the document before you," the inspector said.

My intelligence was perhaps so blunted by prison that I never even considered the possibility of some sort of obscure trick. I read the document, inhaling my first cigarette for months, and saw that it was, in written form, what I had in fact been affirming every morning since I had been imprisoned—that I had no complaints against the staff of Moabit Prison, Berlin. There, their secret was finally out.

I hesitated over signing, and saw the inspector's face cloud over. But instead of a fit of furious shouting, he asked me if there were any specific points that concerned me.

I suppose the truth is that all we prisoners were a little mad. Perhaps living so close to death or casual mutilation makes a man unhinged in his recklessness. But like some predatory animal I had smelled blood. I told Inspector Beck that there were no specific points I was prepared to discuss, and I would, of course, not dream of signing the document.

He stood in the room, alone with me now, stroking the side of his face and nodding in an understanding manner. "It is in the nature of our work that unfortunate incidents occur from time to time," he said.

"Broken arms, smashed teeth."

"No, no," he said hurriedly, "that's all perfectly legal under Gestapo Handling Instructions. No, I was referring to an error by the arresting officer, which of course indirectly was myself."

"An error?"

"So it appears." He took a deep breath. "I have this afternoon an order from Gestapo headquarters at Prinz Albrechtstrasse informing me that your arrest was in error. I am instructed to obtain from you a no-complaint certificate."

"Why, if beatings are perfectly legal?"

He lifted his eyebrows in incomprehension. And fear.

I thought of a soft September morning when we were walking in pairs on weekly exercise around the cobbled inner courtyard of the prison. I had been paired with a stranger, a small, middle-aged man with a gaunt face and the last traces of a once-plump belly. Through the corner of his mouth he had asked me my name. The four young guards, talking in the center of the slowly circling, shuffling prisoners, had seen nothing. But Inspector Beck, standing unseen by us in the shadow of a stone doorway, had seized upon the moment. He had ordered me and the other man—Milsen, I think he was called by the guards—to face each other in the middle of the yard. It was a procedure I had witnessed before. Punishment by prisoners. Milsen was ordered to strike me. With no more than a moment's hesitation, looking me straight in the eye in the most abject apology, he did as he was ordered. A blow of most unexpected violence, high on the cheekbone. I reeled back under the impact and was ordered up immediately to face him. On the word of command I struck Milsen, openhanded, across the face.

I was judged by Inspector Beck to have used insufficient force. I was ordered to strike again and again until blood ran from Milsen's mouth and he stood unsteadily before me, crying like a child.

It was the sickness and shame I felt that morning that came back to me as I looked at Inspector Beck now. "Rely on it, Beck," I told him, "I have powerful friends in Prinz Albrechtstrasse. I will make a full report to them as soon as I am released."

I had more powerful friends than I knew. Beck was certainly convinced. "Revenge," Sir Francis Bacon had said, "is a kind of wild justice." But there was no justice in German prisons in the days of the Third Reich, and I doubt that my bold threat served to alleviate even one prisoner's treatment for one single hour. And though I believe it desperately frightened Inspector Beck, he still refused to cringe and instead took on a hurt expression, as if to say there was, after all, no justice in this world. In that, at least, he was right.

He tried again. "In the circumstances of your arrest," he said, "it is difficult to see how the error occurred."

I could not understand what he was saying. All I knew of the circumstances of my arrest was the thunder of sledgehammers as my apartment door flew from its hinges, the rush of men in damp overcoats, the pinning of my arms, the manacles, and Inspector Beck nodding benignly the first time I was kicked to the floor.

"What was unusual about the circumstances of my arrest?"

Beck looked at me warily. "The order, Herr von Hardenberg, the order to arrest you, came from this very same department that has now rescinded the order."

"The Gestapo headquarters on Prinz Albrechtstrasse."

"They countersigned it. The order was issued by the office of the Minister-President of Prussia, General Göring."

I think I came close to fainting with dismay. I took another of his cigarettes. "I wish to see the document," I said, lighting my cigarette. "There must have been some sort of deposition signed by someone, which led to my arrest."

It was only now, as I tasted again the mere *possibility* of freedom, that I felt astonished at my former lack of interest in what Beck called the circumstances of my arrest. Perhaps it is so deeply irrelevant in a Gestapo prison, where innocence and guilt are apparently considerations of no interest to your tormentors. But now, as I felt myself escaping from the coils of fear and submission that had embraced me for the last months, I desperately needed to know the answer.

Beck was looking down at me, his mouth twisting first left, then right as if he were clearing it of a handful of dry breadcrumbs. "I think," he said at length, "that we could be helpful to each other, *mein Herr.*"

"If I sign your documents . . . ?"

"I will show you the depositions concerning your arrest. Yes." His dark eyebrows moved up and down like Groucho Marx's. It was only with effort that I could remember Milsen crying like a small boy as I punched his face. "Does your wife know what you do for a living?" I asked him.

His eyebrows dropped. "She knows I am an Inspector of Police, of course."

"Do you tell her what you do to people here?"

He looked at me, baffled. "A miner or a steelworker doesn't go home and tell his family all the jokes and stories that pass between men."

I felt too weak and sick with hunger to do anything but mutter into the cloud of cigarette smoke. "I suppose there are people like you in every country," I said.

He grunted. "Like me?"

"Do you come from some sewer at the heart of the human race? Is that the answer?"

He smiled. "Count von Hardenberg," he said, "you are an aristocrat. Naturally you don't think highly of men with my background."

I gave up. "Get me more coffee," I said. "And the depositions you promised."

An hour later I was given my identity documents and a pack of (opened) letters that had arrived at my flat since my arrest. A black leather jacket, a shirt, trousers, and a pair of shoes were provided, the latter secondhand like the other items, but of outstandingly good quality, having been handmade by Bronstein in Berlin, and I was escorted to the main gate. The prison clock struck nine as the sounds and smells of Moabit fell behind me. Outside, a cream and brown Mercedes was waiting, with Diana Chrysler at the wheel.

She told me afterwards that she had managed to retain control as the prison doors closed behind me, but that as I approached the Mercedes and she saw that under my expensive dead man's shoes I had not been issued socks, she had broken down.

As I reached the car she was crying uncontrollably. She moved over and I took the wheel and drove toward the center of Berlin while she wiped her eyes and lit cigarettes for both of us.

"Just tell me what you want to do, Claus," she said, her voice thick from the tears in her throat.

"I want to stop at the nearest *Bierstube* and eat sausage and sauerkraut," I said without hesitation. "Then I want to be out of Germany by dawn."

She nodded agreement. "You're safe," she said, "if you want to pick up anything from your flat."

I shook my head. "There'll be nothing left. There's nothing left in Germany I would waste an extra ten minutes on."

At the station *Bierstube*, I found that the first mouthful of sausage made me sick. I pushed the sausage aside and asked the astonished waitress for a plate of plain boiled potatoes, and Diana sat and watched me while I wolfed it down, prison-fashion.

"You're looking at me," I said, "as if I haven't had a bath for six months. Which, since in point of fact I haven't, I suppose is quite reasonable." God knows why, but I felt like laughing.

She sat, starkly red-eyed, opposite me. "Oh my God," she said, "what have we done to you? What has my bloody family done to you?"

I lit a cigarette. "I'm only concerned now about getting out of Germany by tomorrow. I need help for that. Nothing more."

"Please, Claus . . ." she said. "Please . . ."

"No, I'm wrong." My anger was bubbling up inside me. "I'm concerned about other things too. About the other people I *may* have been able to get out if I hadn't been arrested."

"Please . . ."

Trains hissed and shunted out on the platforms.

"About a little dancer in the Kit-Kat Club named Maria Stollmitz whose Jewish student boyfriend had already been arrested for defiling the race. And who was waiting for me with her bag packed the night I was arrested. Where is she now? In Moabit or KLF or Papenberg? You can't pull strings for all of them."

She was silent, her eyes on the cheap oilcloth covering the table. One perfectly manicured finger circled a large cigarette burn. "It was not deliberate, believe that at least," she said.

We had moved a world apart. "What possible, earthly difference does it make?" I said.

Her head came up. "I'm going to tell you whether you like it or not."

"Tell Maria Stollmitz," I said. "She's the one with blood running out of her ears. Tell Bartelmann the trade unionist, who was hoping to follow his family to Amsterdam. Better still, tell his wife and children when the letters come back marked 'address unknown.' I've read the depositions," I said. "I know why I was arrested."

"You *don't* know!" Her voice was as taut as a stretched wire.

"Cocktail-party talk," I said. "I don't believe you left the Adlon the next morning after the election and went down to Gestapo headquarters. That would have been too un-English for words. But you had to tell someone what a frightful surprise it had been to see me at the Adlon that night. And you chose Hugo Zeitz-Apolda to chatter to."

"I never thought for a moment Hugo would do anything about it."

"In London or New York it would of course have been unthinkable."

"Of course," she agreed hurriedly.

"But how in God's name did you imagine that Hitler's new Berlin would be like London or New York? How crass and blind can you all be, for God's sake?"

"I can't ask you to forgive me." Her face was crumpled with tears. "I can't ask Maria Stollmitz or Frau Bartelmann. But I can beg you to try to understand."

"What is there to understand?"

"Can't you understand that any of us could have done this to you? Buzz, Margaret, even poor Charles had he lived. We were all pickled in a special sort of arrogance. A certainty."

"Your brother Richard—do you think he was the same?"

"No." She shook her head over the scarred oilcloth. "You know he wasn't."

I pushed my chair back. "I'm going," I said. "I don't want to talk."

She fumbled in her purse. "I brought money with me." She placed a pad of new marks on the table. "And these." She was holding three small leather volumes. "I want you to have them. I want you to know the truth about me."

I took the money.

"These too. They tell you all I have dared not tell you," she insisted.

"What are they?"

"A diary," she said. "A journal I've kept since we first met."

I shook my head, pushing the volumes back across the table toward her. I had nothing else to say. I stumbled out of the café toward the platform for the Vienna Express.

TWENTY-TWO

I read the letters from Africa on the night train to Austria. Diana had bought a first-class ticket and I sat opposite a primly correct young couple, unshaven, smelling of prison, without socks, and the tears filling my eyes.

I read the letter from the firm of Nairobi solicitors first. It told me that Baroness Esterhazy had left her land and all property in the Ngong hills to me. It warned that there was a large bank loan to be settled, and various small debts. If I wished to farm the land, it concluded, an injection of capital would almost certainly be necessary. If, on the other hand, I intended to sell, a number of property companies in Nairobi might well be interested in developing it as a housing area close to the growing city. The solicitor could, of course, recommend one such company. The price for Catherine's six hundred acres would probably be in the region of fifteen thousand pounds.

I saw the young woman opposite looking at me with alarm. Catherine was dead. It was fifteen years since I had seen her, but the picture was still as clear as a Kenya morning, as she stood in the high fields in her long skirt and wide-brimmed hat bound with a leopard-skin band.

The young couple got up and left to find another compartment. I opened the next letter. It was from Kum.

Dear Friend,

You will only read this if certain efforts have already been successful on your behalf. I will therefore keep it short. Catherine Esterhazy took her own life yesterday. She was the victim of an illness that could not be vanquished and a loneliness and a sense of failure she could no longer sustain. She has left you her farm. Write to me, if you are able, Poste Restante,

[320]

Nairobi, and send me your instructions. I am at your service as you have so often been at mine.

Kum

I read Catherine's last letter again and again over the weeks that followed. Much of it was drunken rambling on what might have been. She could not face, she said, telling her African servants and farm boys that the property was to be sold and that there would never again be farming on the land. It was the destruction of their homes at least as much as her own. What she had chosen to do was somehow an attempt, however futile, to assure them of that.

There was also a passage about Buzz. "Perhaps," she said, "there is little that is personally evil in him. He confuses by his qualities of charm and friendship. But we must not be confused. His new Kenya National Party is to put up candidates for all the European seats in the next election. From somewhere he has found backing. The party offices in Nairobi are hung with a Nazi-type flag. There are new cars available, and secretaries. Buzz Winslow himself tours the country, talking to groups of settlers. His line is simple. For the European to survive in Africa, he must rule. Not the government in London, but a new independent government in Nairobi. New economic links with Germany are also confidently proposed. I would not by any means be surprised if, behind our backs, he already had an agreement with the Nazi government about the return of Tanganyika to Germany. The motto for all this devildry is 'For King and Kenya.' Well, neither King nor the Kenya African will see much benefit."

I crossed the border into Austria near the fantastic fairyland castle of Neuschwanstein, built by mad King Ludwig of Bavaria. In the long line before me at passport inspection was a Hitler Youth Choir that had just sung in the great wooden hall of the castle and was now going into Austria to spread the word. They looked healthy and happy and in every way an advertisement for the future. I stood behind them trembling as I approached the frontier inspection of my documents. I was still a young man, not yet forty, but I shuffled along with that furtiveness and pathetic anxiety to please that allows any experienced policeman to identify an old lag. The frontier guard's head came up sharply when he saw my papers. *"Jawohl, Herr Graf,"* he said in answer to no question I had put, and he pointed me to the head of the line, holding back the Hitler Youth choristers with one peremptory arm. It was only in the train through Austria that I examined the signature on my exit visa. It read Heinrich Himmler, but in those days the name meant nothing to the world beyond the tiny frontier post at Fussel.

By week's end I was in Genoa with a passage booked on the *Michelangelo Buonarotti,* which was to sail across the Mediterranean, through the Red Sea to Italian East Africa, then on down to complete its voyage at the Kenya port of Mombasa.

On long, hot nights on the Red Sea I would sit on the bow deck, looking out, it seemed, across half of moonlit Africa. I could feel the peace of these nights gradually restoring my mind to some sort of balance. After prison a man is afraid of anything, of banging into the edge of doors, of dropping a book. We apologize to everyone, fearful of offending. We compliment waiters and clerks for trivial services, concerned they will forget us. Strangely, we don't so much fear loneliness or, at least, being alone, because the fear of being with company is greater.

On one evening I was joined by a Frenchman who was on his way back to Indochina. He offered me a *digestif,* and when I declined he ordered an Armagnac from the waiter and took the deck seat beside me. He introduced himself as René Lacoste, merchant in ivory, and handed me a card that gave his address as the Rue Catinat, Saigon. I gave my name in return, and he must have been studying the passenger list because he wagged his finger as he corrected me: "Monsieur le *Comte* von Hardenberg, is it not?"

I agreed reluctantly. In Africa I had resolved to drop my worthless title, and I regretted now having allowed it to be taken from my passport for inclusion on the ship's list. We exchanged trivial snippets of information, most of it perhaps no more true on his side than it was on mine. He told me of a shrewish wife and three ungrateful children in a village west of Paris, and a beautiful and compliant Annamite mistress in Saigon. "My home is there, in the East," he said with conviction. "Every night my girl prepares my pipes of opium and offers herself for my pleasure. I have friends among the French administration. I attend dinner parties. From time to time I fondle, a little drunkenly, the wife of one of the guests. But I am not attracted to European women, Monsieur. I fear not just their independence, but their greed. Perhaps it is we men who, by consigning women to an indeterminate position in our society, have encouraged their voracious appetite for the life of the male. Do I make sense to you, *Monsieur le Comte?*"

That night he made no sense to me at all, though I assured him he did. Later, Monsieur Lacoste, ivory merchant of the Rue Catinat, Saigon, would, in retrospect, make a greal deal more sense.

The *Michelangelo* sailed on through the Red Sea and out into the ocean beyond. I began to feel well again as we turned between the Horn and the island of Abd al-Kuri and began to run south along the East African coast. I was now in all ways much fitter. The steward in the second-class dining room, I remember, had counted it a triumph the night I had finished a full plate of pasta and *fegato* and called the chef out to receive his due credit. Before we left the Red Sea I was drinking wine again, and my ferocious prisoner's desire for cigarettes, stronger by far than for food, had abated. On these nights of soft splendor as I sat alone on the deck, I thought constantly of my first visit to Africa over fifteen years ago as the old *Francken* had churned toward my rendezvous with the ragged soldiers of von Lettow's *Schutztruppe*. Of course I was thinking of Catherine Esterhazy. But mostly of Diana Winslow and the words that had held me captive through my adult life: Oh, what fool was it who invented kissing!

There was some talk in the newspapers about the Chrysler Trust. The family, it seemed, would go to law on the issue of the very large sums of money that were to go to Diana. Unfortunately for her, Charles had written in, or his family had insisted, that the recipient of the Chrysler fortunes should be a patriotic and worthy representative either of the United States or Great Britain. It was vague enough in the drafting, apparently, but once it was widely known that the Chryslers were a part-Jewish family, the intention was clear. Did Diana's known enthusiasm for the Nazi cause mean that in the United States courts she would *not* be considered "worthy"? The newspapers throughout the world speculated endlessly and published photographs of Diana in every fashionable city, but her life was no longer a simple round of beach and cocktail parties.

During my voyage to Kenya she was visiting Italy as a guest of Mussolini. There were audible ruffles in the Berlin dovecotes when she visited the annual maneuvers of the Italian army and posed with the beautifully uniformed officers of the elite armored division "Trieste." A week later she was at Sennelager in Germany on the dais at the march-past of the Führer's bodyguard SS *Leibstandarte Adolf Hitler.*

Bizarre parties were held nightly. The rats on board seemed to be diminishing in number as the voyage continued, but during nightly dances on the lower deck they still scuttled between the feet of the uniformed Italian legionnaires grasping close the tall, beautiful whores of Somalia.

I disembarked at Mombasa. The long quayside was ringing with cheerful shouts as black porters raced one another with trolleys piled with luggage. Settlers meeting family or friends smiled and waved up to the high decks of freighters lining the quay. In the bright sunlight I felt very far from the wet cobbled yard of Moabit, the dawn chill and the shuffling click of the prisoners' wooden sabots. But I knew that some things in me or about me had been irrevocably punctured. I had been a gentleman in England long, long ago. I had played an eccentric Bohemian gentleman in the red-light district of Hamburg where I had chosen to make a home. I believed I would try, now, to play no more.

I left by train for the capital that afternoon. But my euphoria was clouded by a double front-page picture in the *Banner-Post* of Diana and Buzz. They looked toward the camera, sleek and blond and impeccable in the black uniforms of the SS, in which they had been promoted to honorary field rank.

I spent as little time as possible in Nairobi. It had changed vastly since those days during the war when it was so obviously a frontier town. There were still plenty of corrugated iron roofs to be seen, but more substantial government and commercial buildings dominated the townscape. The roads were paved, and the pall of light dust that was a feature of the old Nairobi seemed to have disappeared. As a town it was still small, but there was a sense of bustle and growth. On the street, upcountry settlers hailed acquaintances with shouts and whoops or long blasts on the horn of a dusty motorcar. Women emerging from the shops looked young and tanned. It was a town, indeed a country, in which the Europeans had not yet had time to grow old.

I was shown into the office of Mr. Claud Dexter, Catherine's solicitor, and was greeted effusively by a short, round, middle-aged man with a brick-red face. I had somehow imagined he would be dressed in a black coat and striped trousers, but like everybody else he was wearing a safari jacket and khaki drill shorts.

We spent the first ten minutes pushing papers back and forth across his desk. I signed my name a dozen times or so, and at last he proclaimed himself satisfied that the formalities were complete.

"Time for drinks," he said, ringing an electric bell on his desk. An African arrived at the door and we ordered gin and tonics, which were produced while Mr. Dexter gave me an account of the new developments in Nairobi.

"The truth of the matter is, Count von Hardenberg, I could have saved you the trouble of coming all the way to Africa. You could have stayed comfortably in Germany while I dealt with the whole business for you."

"Comfortably."

"Now you've seen the situation in the documents there. The bank is owed five thousand five hundred pounds sterling. As agricultural land the baroness's farm wouldn't, I regret to say, clear that sum with more than a thousand or two to spare. Even that money would be eaten up by incidental expenses, some small debts to the garage here and the wine-and-spirits merchant. No, the situation, as I've said, is crystal clear, I regret to say."

I didn't like his small, pale eyes, red-rimmed like a ferret's.

"All that having been said and done"—he gulped at his gin and tonic—"the Esterhazy property does have one very significant plus. In terms of distance from Nairobi, it can very nearly be considered a suburb. This means that as land pure and simple it is a lot more interesting. Indeed, one or two far-sighted companies have already, as I told you in my letter, indicated that they are prepared to start talking."

"I'm not, Mr. Dexter," I said.

His face clouded. The line of his mouth became suddenly thin and petulant. "You mean you don't want to dispose of the property?"

"Certainly not yet."

"Then I can only assume you have considerable capital you are prepared to invest. Or, not to put too fine a point on it, to waste."

"What's the name of this far-sighted company that is willing to start talking?" I asked.

"Of what possible interest can that be to you, if you are not going to sell?"

"What is the company?"

He considered. "The company is called Nairobi Colonial Land Holdings. They have mentioned a figure of fifteen thousand pounds. A handsome profit."

"That would be your advice."

"Most certainly."

"To take this particular offer."

"In the circumstances, yes. As I say, there's a handsome profit in it."

"Who for?"

"You, of course."

Prison had not disposed me to indulge in social niceties with someone like Dexter. "Are you on the board of this company, Mr. Dexter?"

"No."

"But you have shares."

"I am acquainted with the directors, of course." He was worried.

I was suddenly reminded of an English version of Inspector Beck in Moabit. Perhaps my face showed the images that were passing through my mind. "Do you have shares, Mr. Dexter? Or does Mrs. Dexter have shares? Or does Aunt Agatha Dexter have shares?" My voice was rising.

He reddened, hesitated, and then pursed his lips. "I have a small shareholding, yes. Control of a small shareholding."

I stood up. "All right," I said, "now that I understand the gentlemanly level on which we're conducting this business, you can send someone up to Ngong to talk to me if you like. I'm not selling yet and I'm not selling for fifteen thousand pounds, but we can talk. And," I added, "if I thought it was any earthly good I would report you to the Law Society in London."

I left Dexter and asked directions in the street to the police station. I remember still the warmth I felt, the sense of being not entirely alone, when I discovered that the Senior Inspector was a certain Thomas Lusk.

He greeted me with a formidably strong handshake. He was as big and powerfully built as I remembered, but gray now, his hair cropped short at the sides in the manner of the British working class. He was pleased to see me.

"Well, Captain." He sat me down opposite him. "A very sad business. I suppose you know she was drinking heavily."

"I should have realized from the tone of her letters sometimes. I didn't."

"And of course she was a very lonely woman."

"Yes, I know that."

"She was something else, though, Captain." Lusk ran his tongue between lower gum and lip. "Don't know quite how to put it, but she had a special way with Africans. No, that's wrong. Plenty of settlers here get on well with their Kikuyu. It was more than that."

"She had," I said, "some vision of a future. Is that it?"

He nodded. "That's the word." He fiddled with his pipe. "Every white man in this country thinks he knows what the future should be. Trouble is," he said, "it's always a white future only. Talk to your old friend Kum. He's got more than one idea in his head."

He took me upstairs to the canteen and we had sausage and mash and a bottle of beer. "Are you thinking of staying here, Captain?" Lusk asked.

"I'm thinking of it."

He nodded. "No wish to go back to Germany?"

I knew what the question really meant. "I was in prison," I said bluntly.

He smiled. Of course he knew. "Anything interesting?"

"I was smuggling people out. Very amateurish."

"And very dangerous."

"As I discovered."

"Kum's a good fellow," he said, as if changing the subject. "I'm not sure he'll ever get to join the Muthaiga Club," he grinned. "But he's a good fellow."

We finished our sausage and mash and I took leave of him, inviting him up for dinner when he next had a free night.

We stood on the steps of the police station in the brilliant sunshine. "Watch out for advice from that toad Dexter," he said. "He's got his thumb in every pie in Nairobi."

"Including the Nairobi Land Holding Company," I said.

He laughed explosively and turned back into the deep shadow of the station entrance.

I hitched a lift up into the Ngong hills with a taciturn young settler named Jones. Mr. Jones had worked his acres of coffee outside Thika for ten grinding years. He believed now that he was just turning the corner. He had two fears in his life, a renewed plague of grasshoppers and the government in London. But there was one real hope for Kenya, he told me. If we all rallied behind Lord Winslow we could turn this country into a self-governing paradise in ten years. Faith and hard work, he said, had seen him through the bad years, and now the time had come to get something in return.

I had one heavy knapsack as luggage, and I hoisted it onto my shoulder when I left Mr. Jones and began to walk up the long driveway toward the farm. Of course it seemed that nothing had changed. The sun browned the rippling grass as it always had. The peaks of Ngong rose black along the ridge, and as I got closer, the lake sparkled. My lake. It had water birds on it now, ducking and shuffling and preening themselves, and thick green reeds along the bank where Catherine had been found. The house had a forlorn, decrepit air, like the house of a maiden aunt whose pension would not run to regular repairs. The thatch was black-brown with age, and bald in patches where the rusting corrugated iron showed through. There were no servants, no *totos* playing on the lawn. The tiny schoolroom had lost part of its grass wall, and the timber structure was visible, rough carved boughs of the blue gum trees that had once covered the area.

On the veranda I dropped my knapsack on the table ringed with the marks of many glasses. There was no grave. Catherine's parents had ordered the ashes to be scattered on the lake. I lit a cigarette and sat against the edge of the table, looking out toward the high fields of coffee. A man can break his back on coffee or on the blue flowering fields of flax that so delighted Catherine. And worse than breaking the back is breaking the spirit. I was not such a romantic that I would farm this magical land until suicide was the only acceptable end. I must not invest my whole life in these acres of hill and lake and forest, as Catherine had done. There were too many broken hearts in this country. I would sell, even to the toad Dexter, and take the small profit to New York or California.

Somewhere beyond my line of sight, somewhere to the side of the house, I heard a faint shuffling. It was a sound I had not heard for nearly fifteen years—the sound of bare feet moving through the dust.

The Africans came in ones and twos, in larger groups of women and silent, wide-eyed *totos*, and stood before me, perhaps twenty yards away, on the parched lawn. After a few moments one or two of the older men in their blood-red blankets eased themselves down onto their haunches. Others gathered around them in a *tableau vivant* of black skin glistening with an application of sheep fat. Some of the men wore shorts, and the young wives stood silently watchful in oiled leather skirts, their bobbing spatulate breasts now at rest.

We faced each other without embarrassment for the long silence. I had learned from Catherine that the pause, the rumination, was a form of communication in itself in an African debate. It was used to give weight and significance to all that followed.

I believed I recognized one or two of the faces. A tall, slender man in tattered shorts and singlet I was sure was Njomo, who had been the young oxen-boy when I was last at Ngong. One or two of the glistening girls, it seemed to me, evoked memories of *totos* I had taught in the schoolhouse fifteen years ago.

I lit another cigarette. Patience, or perhaps feigned indifference, is another part of the gavotte. I exhaled smoke and watched it tumble gently across the veranda to become suddenly blue in the sharp sunlight. I raised a hand in greeting. "*Jambo.*"

Njomo, the onetime oxen-boy, nodded his head. Very slowly, as if expecting reproof from his elders, he came a few steps forward. "*Jambo,*" he said. "What is the news, Captain-bwana?"

"Good," I answered. "And yours?"

"Good," he affirmed.

He dropped on his haunches, took a piece of stick from the ground, and stirred rough circles in the dust. We were still ten yards apart.

I came forward to the edge of the sunlight. "I have come to take the memsahib's farm," I said in a low voice.

The Africans at the back shuffled forward a yard or two. Njomo continued to describe circles in the dust with the twig.

"I say again that I have come to take the memsahib's farm."

"Yes." Njomo looked up briefly.

"Many years have passed since we last met, Njomo."

"Many years," he agreed.

"Now that the memsahib is dead, you must talk to me."

"Yes, bwana," Njomo said.

"My name is Hardenberg. Perhaps you remember."

"Yes, Captain-bwana."

"So be it," I said. I turned back to the house, feeling that I had accomplished all I possibly could with the Africans for that day. Of course they wanted to know if there would be work on the farm. They wanted to know if they would be allowed to keep their *shambas* on what was, according to land law, *my* land. But they had learned all that they needed to know for today. As the heat rose they would drift away with the unspoken questions. My problem was that I was uncertain about the answers. The toad Dexter could be right, that the farm was impossible to run. Certainly Catherine had been unable to make flax or coffee pay. I looked out over the heads of the group of Africans, toward the high fields. I knew from Catherine's letters, and even from my own experience in that year long ago, that Ngong and its people could become for me the same trap that they had become for her. Impossible to live on and impossible to leave.

I went into the house and walked through the dusty rooms. It was nearly two months since Catherine had died. There were no supplies in the kitchen, and no oxen left in the stalls. I ate a sandwich I had brought with me, and drank a small whiskey from the half-finished bottle in the cupboard. Then I set out on a long walk into the high fields.

The coffee plantations were in sad condition. The leaves, desiccated by the wind from the Athi Plains, were limp and yellow. Some of the acreage beyond the ridge seemed to be suffering from coffee disease, thrips or antestia. In some fields the young plants were almost all dead, a sign perhaps that the taproots had been broken at planting or had not been properly positioned.

It was impossible not to feel the sadness of Catherine's last years here. Africa is extreme. The symbols of my friend's decline had no subtlety. They were the collapsed rest house, the abandoned flax fields, the raw scar on the hillside of a failed coffee plantation over which the eagles of Ngong soared.

A farm like this was too much for a woman like Catherine, with her own special burdens to bear. But was it too much for me too?

I watched the car come up the Nairobi road and turn into the drive. The Africans on the lawn, I saw, began to drift away as the three men got out. I began to walk down through the plantation. Mr. Dexter had lost no time in talking to his partners in the Nairobi Colonial Land Holding Company.

There were two young men with Dexter, similarly dressed in bush shirts and shorts, their foreheads sweating under their brand-new pith helmets, which seemed too big for them. Dexter introduced me. Mr. Jackson, tall and thin, shook hands eagerly. Mr. Hopcraft licked his reddish mustache and eyed me warily through steel-rimmed spectacles.

I took them into the shade of the veranda but decided against offering the last of the precious whiskey. The Africans had gone, except Njomo, who crouched by the lake, glancing toward the veranda. How much did they already know of the plans discussed in the shaded solicitors' offices in Nairobi?

Hopcraft began the discussion. "Mr. Dexter," he said, "has told us that you might consider our offer, but would like some time to think it over." He had removed his helmet and he now brushed back his thinning red hair with the palm of his hand. There was something hard and aggressive about the gesture. Jackson smiled uncomfortably.

"Is that what Dexter said?"

"More or less." Hopcraft's eyes never left my face.

I thought of the dusty fields, the crackling leaves of the coffee plantations, and that huge overdraft at the bank. But I was aware too of Njomo, crouched by the lakeside, and his occasional glance toward the white men on the veranda, who, whether he knew it or not, were discussing his future.

"At the price you've offered," I said, "I'd sooner keep the land unfarmed. In ten years anybody can see Nairobi will be four times the size it is now. This farm will be prime building land. Fifteen thousand pounds is robbery."

"Since we're not mincing words," Hopcraft said, "I'll ask you directly if you can wait ten years. There's a heavy bank loan made against this property, I understand."

"Professional confidences?" I looked at Dexter.

"In a small town like Nairobi, everybody knows everybody else's business," Hopcraft said briskly. "The point is, can you clear the debt?"

"Yes," I lied. "Not with ease, but I can clear the debt."

Hopcraft nodded slowly. "Then you are saying that you are going to sink your capital in a farm that the baroness has already found unworkable."

"I'm saying I'm not selling it to you, Hopcraft, or to your greasy partner, Dexter. If you want to offer a hundred thousand pounds, I'll think about it."

Jackson smiled wildly. Dexter was sullen and silent. Hopcraft pursed his lips.

"I'll put it another way," I said, inspired by anger. "There's a hundred-acre field beyond that woodland between us and Nairobi. Give me ten thousand pounds for that and guarantee the money will be in the bank by the end of the week."

"Done." Hopcraft reached across and shook my hand. "I'll give you a letter of intent before we leave."

Inevitably, my sense of triumph was reduced by his alacrity. When they left I stood on the veranda thinking that perhaps I could have asked fifteen thousand. But I had bought time, and as I looked toward Njomo, I realized I had bought responsibility too.

There seemed to be no point in further delay. I walked down to the lake. "Njomo," I said, "will the baroness's people come back to work for me?"

"They will," he said.

"Work will begin tomorrow," I announced.

He stood up, grinning. "Is it true that there will be no houses on the hills?"

"There will be houses beyond the forest," I said. "In the low fields. There will be none in the high fields."

"Long ago Kum told us you came out of the sky. It is true. You come like the rains."

Later in the afternoon, Njomo returned. He sought permission to hold a *ngoma* the following night. The village would, he said, send far and wide. It seemed a fitting moment for a *ngoma*, and I believed that Catherine would have approved. "There will be snuff," I told him, "for our own farm women. And sugar for the *totos* as in the baroness's time."

On the night of the *ngoma* I had a visitor. Inspector Lusk brought beer and a piece of ham, bread and a bag of oranges.

It was a cool, pleasant evening as darkness came upon us, and we sat on the veranda with Catherine's last bottle of whiskey, watching the Africans build the huge fires on the rough grass area surrounded by trees and lake that had always been called the lawn. Beyond the flames, the darkness chattered with cicadas and the voices of young girls. I had just recounted to the inspector my business deal with Hopcraft.

"So you plan to stay with us, Captain," Lusk said.

"If I can, Inspector."

In the light of the kerosene lamp, shadows formed and dissolved quickly over Lusk's face. What had seemed craggy in the bright sunlight now appeared softer and more mobile. Or perhaps it was just the difference between his on-duty face and his off-duty one. "This is not Thika," he said, "where coffee can be a success. It's not ranch country, either."

"You mean you think I'll go under?"

"I can't see how you'll avoid it if you try to grow the same crops as the baroness. I doubt there was ever a year here when she turned a real profit."

"There wasn't," I said. "I went through the books last night. Most years were indifferent, a small, not-too-serious loss. But when the grasshoppers came or the rains failed it became a bad, bad year."

"Friend of mine came out here a year or two ago," Lusk said, puffing thick pipe smoke toward the bugs that hurled themselves suicidally at the kerosene lamp. "We were on the beat together in London. Name of Fred Lawton. Quick-thinking sort of chap. Cockney born and bred, like me. But I'm not so quick on the feet. Anyway, Fred came out to set up as a builder's merchant. Took a pasting in the first six months."

"A pasting?"

"Sorry, Captain. Suffered a heavy financial loss," he mimicked my own English accent. "But Fred's not one to sit on his backside. He went home and was back here within four months. God knows how he got onto it, but he now signs up farmers to grow pyrethrum."

"Pyrethrum?"

"It's a plant, not that difficult to grow, as I understand it, and it's shipped to London and used in the manufacture of insecticides. Price is good and, according to Fred, the insecticide industry is on the way up in Europe."

I was interested. "Can I talk to your friend?"

"Of course. I'll get him to come up and see you."

Dark figures were closing around the fires on the lawn. The snuff and sugar for which I had sent down to the Indian duka during the day was to be distributed by Njomo. We ourselves, Lusk and I, had no part to play in the proceedings, but we had, sitting on Catherine's veranda, a grandstand view. As we began our supper, the young guardians of the dance moved through the gathering crowds, the morani in cock-feather spurs and ostrich-plumed headdresses, posing with proud, swift movements of the head to the sound of drums and flutes announcing the arrival of ever more visitors.

"I came to Africa in 1913," Lusk said meditatively. "The first Europeans were just trickling in. All upper-class people. Aristocrats. Strange thing that, isn't it, Captain? The British working class went off to Australia and New Zealand." He smiled. "It was only the nobs that came here. And me."

"What made you come to East Africa, Inspector?" The thud of heavy drums out in the darkness, stopping and restarting like European musicians tuning up, was the recognized prelude to the real dancing. The squeals of delight from the maidens became sharper, the laughter of the young morani higher.

"Why did I come out here?" Lusk tapped with the stem of his pipe to the rhythm of the big drums. "My wife died, shortly after our daughter was born," Lusk said. "Run over by a brewer's cart. Broke her back. Less than a year later she was dead." He stopped tapping to the time of the music. "I suppose I could have got someone to take her on—young Pam, I mean. Or I could have given her to be brought up somewhere by the Charity. But I didn't want that, Captain. I was, what, thirty-three years old, a sergeant at Whitechapel police station. One day I read an announcement asking for police volunteers for the new East Africa Force. Your own servant, it said, to look after the children. So that was it. I applied, was accepted, and I brought young Pamela out here, three years old she was."

"I met her once," I said. "She'd been singing 'Salvation Army, all gone barmy' outside your office window."

Lusk smiled. "I suppose I couldn't really complain, since I taught it to her myself." He paused. "She's had a spot of trouble, you know."

"Catherine wrote me."

Lusk nodded. "She's come through it now all right. She was young at the time and very flattered, of course. But she's tough, you see, Captain. She's a cockney at heart."

As the dancing began and the noises of approval and delight mixed with the thrumming music and the thin, clear notes of the visiting singers, Lusk and I left the veranda and moved inside to the dining room. Through the glass doors we could still see the movement out on the lawn and still hear the drums, but somehow it seemed right, with Catherine no longer here, not to place ourselves too prominently as overseers of the *ngoma*.

Perhaps it was the ceremonies in full flood beyond the glass doors that reminded Tom Lusk of his own youth, and he began, warmed as we both were by beer and whiskey, to talk about the tribal occasions of his own past in the East End of London, the funerals and the marriages, the street parties for Queen Victoria's Jubilee or the Coronation of King Edward. It was an English world I knew nothing of, a world limited by a desperate poverty that made the Kikuyu seem rich in comparison. There was no land, no cattle, no trees to cut for heat. Some winter nights, he told me, when he was a child, his mother would rule that they sat in darkness, laughing and giggling and singing songs certainly, but in darkness all the same, until his father arrived home from work at nine or ten in the evening, when a candle would be lit and the supper would be laid out on the kitchen table.

He had lived in a house on Flower and Dean Street in Spitalfields, where Jack the Ripper had committed one of his murders and the inspector's uncle, another Thomas Lusk, had organized a vigilante group. He was immensely proud of the fact that the Ripper had singled out his uncle to write him one of his sinister letters in red ink. It began, he said, "From hell, Mr. Lusk . . ."

To me, whose view and knowledge of England was so exclusively Corinthian, the inspector's stories held a special fascination. Lusk told me that for the people of Spitalfields, Jack the Ripper was, at one and the same time, a fearful death-dealer and a figure of heroic proportions. It was the first time that I had seen him as a terrorist-anarchist, someone who might have assassinated a Tsar or placed a bomb in the Café Terminus in Paris. The people of London's Spitalfields, the women particularly, feared him as you might expect. But there was also, at the same time, a degree of admiration for his ability to elude the police and all the established authorities of the realm. Inspector Lusk was ten years old when the unknown assassin padded the mean streets of Spitalfields and Whitechapel. But he believed that it was the Ripper who had focused the attention of that other, richer London on the life of the poor. It was for this reason that he was referred to in the Spitalfields area for many years as "Dear Old Jack."

The faint drumming that came from the *ngoma*, the eerie reediness of the flutes and the occasional wild shriek of a girl, made a strange counterpoint to Tom Lusk's stories of fog and fourpenny doss houses and a maniac "down on whores" as he had written Lusk's uncle.

I learned that night that the inspector had given these matters much thought. One theory that had developed in the rowdy pubs of Whitechapel and Spitalfields at the time was that Jack the Ripper was a sort of aristocratic protector of the poor, that he was pointing with each murder to the inadequacies and indifference of his own class. Tom Lusk, I was to learn, was something of an expert in matters of class.

I invited the inspector to stay the night and he accepted readily enough, but with a slight embarrassment visible on his big, craggy face. For a moment I was at a loss to understand. Then he pocketed his pipe and stood up. "You know," he said, "it's the first time I've ever been asked to stay the night in a gentleman's house."

He spoke without irony, although dust shifted gently across the floor and our beer bottles stood in plebeian ranks on the table before us.

TWENTY-THREE

n the week after the *ngoma*, I set to work. I transferred Catherine's bank loan to my name and extended it on the basis of Hopcraft's letter of intent. I paid off the garage and the liquor bill and I bought four pairs of oxen from one of the farms beyond Ngong. I appointed Njomo my cook and general factotum and, through him, hired laborers to clear the ailing coffee plantation. With Fred Lawton, Inspector Lusk's friend, I signed a pyrethrum contract that included planting and growing advice from his company. I seemed to have developed energies I was unaware of. I worked late on plans for the future and rose early to smell the cool air of the mornings, which, Njomo informed me, told of the coming rains.

A letter from Kum arrived in the first day or so. It was brief and enigmatic as to his whereabouts, but it wished me well and promised that he would be at the farm as soon as he possibly could. I had asked Lusk about him and he had said, in his blunt manner, that Kum was storing up trouble for himself. "Even the baroness"—he had allowed himself half a smile—"thought of them as 'my Africans.' The truth's on Kum's side, not on ours," he added. "The African is less dependent on us than we like to believe. He's his own man. Your friend Kum is just a more than usually educated version of any boy in the Manyatta."

Buzz came at the end of the first week. He wore riding breeches and polished boots and a perfectly pressed white safari shirt. It was more than ten years since I had seen him, and I could not help being struck by his unselfconscious swagger and his confident, blond good looks.

"Claus, you dreadful jailbird," he yelled from the veranda. "Come out here and turn your pale face to the sun." He grabbed me in a great hug and spun me around to the edge of the veranda. But he saw immediately that I could not respond. He dropped his arms and took a step backwards, his head assuming that theatrical angle I knew so well. "*Lasciate ogni speranza, voi ch'entrate . . .*" he intoned. "Is that it? Abandon hope, all ye who enter here?"

"Come in, Buzz," I said.

He jerked his thumb over his shoulder. "Tom Boscowan and a couple of the ladies are in the car. I just called in to welcome you back and ask you to drive up to Naivasha for dinner tonight." He spoke slowly, almost menacingly, awaiting my reply, awaiting my refusal.

I knew that it would all have to be said now, in these next few minutes. I walked over and sat on the veranda rail, his eyes following me, a half-amused smile on his face. I had seen that smile before, too. When he was uncertain of an outcome.

"No, Buzz," I said. "No dinner invitations."

"Shall we be forced to meet by midnight, then, cloaked against discovery?" He flung an arm dramatically across his shoulder and dropped his face to stare narrow-eyed across his forearm. "Shall we meet thus?" His voice was low, the faint American accent thrumming.

"Buzz," I said, "we're on different sides of the mountain. We probably always were."

He let his arm drop. "You talk like the former inhabitant of this place. A noble soul certainly, but given to a certain literary imprecision."

"Then I won't be vague. I've seen more than you have. More than Diana even. In Germany the scum has risen to the top."

"Not in Kenya, old boy," he said, again with a faint menace in his drawl.

I knew how much pain I was giving him. I took out a cigarette and lit it. From somewhere down the farm drive, Tom Boscowan was shouting up to Buzz.

"No two gentlemen," Buzz said, "have ever been seriously divided by politics."

"Don't quote me worthless aphorisms, Buzz. Our paths have divided."

"Yours and Diana's too?"

I felt a surge of bitterness.

He shrugged. "It's said of the lower classes that they lack only the capacity for gratitude. Did you know that in Swahili there is no word for 'thank you'?"

"Get out, Buzz," I said, gently enough. "Push off. The call of Corinthianism doesn't work any longer. What you stand for I have come to hate."

There were no theatrical movements of the head. No blue, ironic glances. He looked down. "I would have wished it otherwise," he said. He turned and stood for a moment on the veranda step, then vaulted across the rail and ran down the drive to where Tom Boscowan was waiting in the car.

My leg had been injured for a second time in Moabit, and a doctor in Nairobi told me that it would require twice-weekly stretching exercises. A few days later a small car turned into the drive and stopped in front of the house. The girl in the white uniform who got out was in her twenties, tall, just slightly more strongly built than was strictly fashionable, with a bright smile that reminded me immediately of her father.

"You've changed," I said, shaking hands with her. "When I last saw you, you were playing hopscotch in your father's outer office. You must have been about nine or ten at the time."

She frowned. "When I told my schoolfriends I'd seen a real, live German, they wouldn't believe me until I said you had narrow, evil eyes and a cruel smile." She took off her white sun hat. "In case you get worried about it, you haven't. Shall we look at this leg?"

"When I've arranged a drink."

She came up from Nairobi regularly after that first visit, and we would engage in a hilarious push-and-pull that was the stretching exercise.

We talked about the farm sometimes over a drink. I was astonished at her knowledge of farming, which went far beyond mine and indeed beyond that of anyone I had met since my return to Kenya, with the exception perhaps of Fred Lawton. But I did not feel as yet that I knew her well enough to talk about the farm at Naivasha that she had worked with her husband.

One morning a week or so after her first visit, she climbed

from her car with something less than the smile or wave I was accustomed to.

I came down the veranda steps to meet her and she stood, fingering the brim of her white hat in circles.

"I have a message from Dad," she said. "I'm afraid a close friend of yours has been killed in a road accident. It's Kum, the African."

I stood, shocked, in the hot sunlight. After a moment I took her arm and guided her up the steps and onto the veranda. "Tell me what happened," I said.

We sat down, her wide-brimmed hat between us. "He appears to have been killed by a motorcar on the road from Thika."

"When did it happen?"

"Dad's not sure yet," she said. "Kum was found by a coffee farmer named Jones as he drove home from the railway station last night."

"The accident," I said. "Your father thinks it was an accident?"

She shrugged cautiously. "You know him where police work is concerned. He's slow and careful and never speaks until he's sure. At the moment, as far as he's concerned he's calling it an accident. But I notice he's gone up to Thika himself. He didn't send Robbie Henderson."

"What was Kum doing up there?"

She looked at me evenly, then her eyebrows rose slowly. "You know what Kum's been up to since he came back from Europe. He's in politics, Captain. A very dangerous end of politics. There are many settlers who do not take kindly to an attempt to organize an African trade union."

"You're saying he might have been killed?"

"Dad said his mule was found in the bush. It had been grazed along its flank. The local district officer who telephoned Dad this morning said he thought Kum had been struck more than once, from different angles."

"Murder," I said.

"You won't get my father to say so yet, but it's obvious what he thinks."

I drove down to Nairobi early the next morning to see Tom Lusk. Pamela was in the bungalow, preparing breakfast before she started work. I leaned against a cupboard, watching her as she made coffee. When I had first met her I was struck by a sense of something missing, certainly compared to Diana or Margaret Winslow, but even when compared to Catherine. It took me some moments, as I watched her moving around the kitchen, watched the precise, confident movements as she took cups from cupboards and placed milk and sugar on the table, to realize I had been wrong. In these small, insignificant acts she communicated a directness, a lack of the pretension that even Catherine sometimes showed, in perhaps a literary sense. But this girl lacked that self-consciousness. It was not to say that she was not, from time to time, self-conscious, but a consciousness of herself would never rule her life.

"You're thinking hard," she said, smiling. "Coffee's on the table. Or hadn't you noticed?"

I sat down as Tom Lusk came in from his shower. He was wearing a white bathrobe, and his dark hair was wet and ruffled, showing a bald spot.

We shook hands. "Where is Kum to be buried, Tom?" I asked as he sat down next to me.

"Not here. In his village. Best stay away, Captain."

"You think he was murdered?"

"I think he was knocked off the mule. Then, as he crouched, dazed, he was struck again by the car reversing and probably again as it came back. I've already spoken to every farmer in the Thika area. Nobody admits being out that night. Except Jones, of course, the one who found him."

"You've examined his car?"

Lusk gave me a grim smile. "It wasn't him. Or rather it wasn't his car. We don't have the facilities here to do real tests, and I don't really see myself sending back whole cars to Scotland Yard."

"So the investigation will go no further?" I knew Pamela was watching me.

"No," Lusk shook his head. "There won't be an inquest. I've already had a word with the Commissioner. There'll be an *ex gratia* payment to his village."

"You take it so damned easily," I said, still aware of her watching me.

"No, I don't, but it's the system, Captain," Lusk said. "It's not justice, but it could be worse."

Mr. Hyrcano Rahvdi was checking the drinking water in the farm cistern, drawing out samples in a long-handled tin jug and pouring them into a series of small labeled bottles he had lined up on a wooden bench.

"I will be back in a day or two, Captain, when I have completed the tests. In the meantime you would be well advised to be especially careful to boil all water for human consumption."

I thanked him as he fitted his sample bottle into a rack in a wooden attaché case and we turned toward the house. "You talk to a lot of people, Mr. Rahvdi," I said. "What do you think happened to Kum?"

"You know as well as I do, Captain. He was murdered, of course."

"And by whom?"

"One could become philosophical, Captain. Poetically, one could say he was murdered by the Colony of Kenya."

"And less poetically?"

Mr. Rahvdi shrugged. "He was killed by one of the members of one of the many settler vigilante groups. You do not need me to tell you that, Captain."

"You have no more information than that?"

"I would not give it to you even if I had. I consider you a friend. It would not be an act of friendship to give you information that would compel you to take steps in vengeance."

"Is that what you think I would do?"

"You would respond to the promptings of your class and culture." Mr. Rahvdi smiled. "We all do."

"You think it best I put aside the memory of Kum."

"Yes. Others will mourn him. More appropriately than you can."

"And will others avenge him, do you believe?"

"Of that I'm certain," Mr. Rahvdi said. "Although it may not be for many years."

I bade Rahvdi good-bye and turned back toward the veranda. Standing under the acacia tree was a tall Kikuyu, a young man dressed in a tattered Fairisle pullover and baggy shorts that accentuated the extreme thinness of his legs.

Njomo was standing next to him, but at that half-pace behind him that is a mark of respect or deference.

I greeted the newcomer.

"*Jambo*, Captain," he replied.

"Is your business with me or with Njomo, friend?" I asked him.

"My name is Milton Moturu," the young man said. "I am passing on my way to Kum's village."

"You know I was a friend of Kum's," I said.

Njomo nodded with a series of rapid, jerky movements like a bird pecking berries. "Moturu knows many things," he said.

"Does he know who killed Kum?" I asked.

Moturu shook his head.

"Does he believe that a few shillings compensation is justice?" I asked savagely.

Moturu shrugged. "No, Captain," he said. "But if justice does not contain compensation, is it not simply revenge?"

I smiled. "Perhaps," I said. "You do well to remind me."

"If you would come"—Moturu shifted from one matchstick leg to the other—"if you would come this afternoon, it would be good."

"Come where?" I asked him.

"Njomo will bring you. And perhaps you will bring Mrs. Longman with you."

He saluted me and loped off across the lawn, his long, thin legs covering the ground at a remarkable pace.

As the late-evening sun cast long tree shadows across the waving grasses, I stood with Pam Longman looking down the slope of the hillside to where a long column of Africans moved toward a rock mound set in the plain.

On that mound, some half a mile away from where we were standing, Kum was being buried.

"Do you know what we're watching?" Pamela asked me.

"I know we two are honored beyond the rest of the colony as the only white people to be invited. Catherine would have been here too, had she lived."

"Why do you think they asked us?"

I shrugged.

"It's not sentimentality, you know," she said. "Not just because we were friends of Kum. They are using us to pass a message to the white world."

I frowned, not understanding. Beneath us, Kikuyu, many more than could have come from just Kum's village, shuffled patiently toward the burial mound. A trailing cloud of dust rolled away toward the watching herd of zebra.

"What we're watching," she said, "is a parody, a deliberate parody of an event that has already taken place. This is a signal to Nairobi that the spirit of Kum has assumed the leadership of the Kikuyu."

"How in God's name do you know that?"

"What we're watching," Pamela said, "is an African re-creation of Lord Delamere's funeral."

TWENTY-FOUR

I seldom drove into Nairobi, and when I was there I made efforts to avoid the Norfolk or the Muthaiga Club. So it was with surprise and no pleasure that I saw Tom Boscowan and Harry Towers standing beside my car one morning soon after Kum's funeral.

Early as it was, they were both pretty drunk and greeted me with an effusiveness that I found particularly distasteful in the case of Boscowan.

"We've just bought ourselves a pair of sporting rifles," Harry Towers said. "New German Mausers. Beautiful things. Come up to Naivasha, old boy," he urged. "A day's shooting and a night's wassailing, what could be better?"

I shook my head. "No, thanks, Harry," I said.

"Look, old chap," Towers said, "politics shouldn't be part of a fellow's life."

Boscowan lounged against the car. "He's too busy for his old friends now, Harry. He's become a farmer. Inherited a patch of land, don't you know." He laughed. "She should have left it to me, of course, after all I did for her."

"What did you do for her?" I asked slowly.

"Forget it, Claus," Harry said. "Tom's been boozing all night."

"What did you do for her?" I repeated.

Boscowan smiled his dark smile. "I gave her her last one the night before she killed herself. 'See Boscowan and die,' as the travel posters say."

The loathing I felt for the man was mixed with an unfulfilled curiosity about the last hours of Catherine's life. I knew he wasn't lying. "She slept with you the night she died? Where?"

"She came up to see Buzz at Naivasha," Harry said quickly. "To tell him you were in prison in Germany. We were all drunk, old chap. Catherine Esterhazy too. Truth is, we'd just made fools of ourselves with Buzz's Africans."

"We'd taught them a lesson, that's what we'd done," Boscowan said.

"And afterwards Catherine agreed . . ." I began.

"Pushed herself at me, old boy."

"I see."

"Well, what's so bloody strange about that?"

I shook my head slowly. "You'd best pass by the farm some day soon," I said. "There's an address in her notebook you may find useful."

"What the devil are you talking about?"

"A doctor in London. A specialist. Not, as I understand it, that there's a lot to be done."

Boscowan came forward from the car and grabbed the front of my shirt.

"Steady, old chap," Towers said. "Hear him out."

"I'll hear him out, by Christ," Boscowan said. "What doctor? What the hell are you talking about?"

"A specialist," I said, "in venereal diseases. Best man in London. Not that he was able to do much for poor Catherine."

He hit me with a blow to the side of the head and, still holding my shirt with one hand, leaned back to strike out again. But in the old days I had taken part in too many brawls in the Hamburg docks to fight like a Corinthian any longer. I brought my head forward so that the hard side of the forehead struck the bridge of his nose. As he reeled backwards, I brought my knee up into his crotch. As he jackknifed forward, I kneed him again, full in the face. As he fell to the ground, I kicked him twice between his sprawling legs.

Harry Towers stood appalled, his fists clenched. "Don't do anything, Harry," I said.

"You shouldn't have kicked him," Towers said, kneeling next to the squirming, doubled figure of Boscowan.

"Why not?" I said. "What better way is there to give notice that I'm no longer a gentleman?"

An hour later, Margaret Winslow's car drew up on the gravel outside the veranda. She had heard in the Muthaiga Club about the incident with Boscowan, and I think she was offering covert congratulations. It was so many years since I had seen her. I stood opposite her and thought of Buzz as I had seen him in all the vigor of his late youth. Margaret, who had been slender, was now almost frail. Small pouches of flesh had formed on either side of her mouth. She was an attractive woman, but no longer young enough to be called pretty. "Everything's changed, Claus," she said desperately. "Everything's gone sour."

"Between you and Buzz?"

"He's planning to ditch me, Claus. I'm already part of his past," she said. "I'm already a millstone around his neck. An old wife with an unsavory reputation."

"Is there someone else?"

She laughed, a wild note in her voice. "There always has been someone else. George Amadeus Winslow has rogered a *remarkably* high proportion of the lady members of the Muthaiga Club. Of course, it was a condition of our marriage. Perfectly overt. We should both sleep with whomsoever we wished."

"But now it's different."

"The girl is Clare Debenham. She's young, rich, very well connected, and not in the least unsavory. For me, Claus, the writing is on the wall. In big, bold, black letters."

"What will you do?"

Her face crumpled suddenly. "I will be cut adrift, I know that. Outrageous behavior was all right under the umbrella of a husband with an ancient barony. But I know what's in store for me, Claus, as the *former* Lady Winslow. And it's not bloody much."

We walked down to the lake in the late afternoon sun. "I saw it happen with Poppy Broadstairs when Frank began to direct his gaze elsewhere," she said. "Nobody condemned Frank. Nobody said, 'He's just looking for younger prat'; it was Poppy they tore to pieces. 'There was always something just a little bit common about Poppy,' Mary Cadogan said to me when we were in London. 'You know I always found she had pretensions.' As if she were already dead!"

"I'm sorry," I said, "if you think the same things will be said about you."

She looked at me sharply, the bitterness evident in her grimace. "Why should you care?"

I could find nothing to say, no reason to give. Why *should* I care? The first forty or more years of her life had been buttressed with privilege: of class, wealth, physical attraction, and beyond all that, the political privilege that the twentieth century was just, perhaps too late, beginning to value. Why *should* I care? Because I had once thrust myself at her many years ago, on the eve of the vast European bloodletting we call the Great War?

We had stopped at the edge of Catherine's lake. Toward Ngong drifted enormous puffballs of white cloud. The sheer mass of these African clouds still, after years in Kenya, made me uneasy, released some feeling of vertigo. I had almost forgotten Margaret was standing beside me when she spoke again. "Are you completely finished with Buzz?" she asked me.

"With all of you," I said.

"With me too?"

"Yes."

"And Diana?"

"Diana especially."

I took her back to her car. "You're hard," she said. "I don't understand it. You've become so terribly hard."

Early in 1934 I received a letter from Webel. I had never met the man, but I thought I knew enough about him to be sure that he was covering his own decision with the party chiefs. Even with the sting in the tail, I believe the letter was for the Moscow record rather than for me. He wrote:

Dear Hardenberg,

Party member Lorelei left instructions for you to be informed in the event of her arrest. I regret to inform you of the following sequence of events:

1. Party member Lorelei volunteered late in 1933 to undertake a party mission in Germany.

2. Word has reached us that she was arrested by the Gestapo in Flensburg sometime in December of that year.

3. We have information that she was imprisoned and executed in Moabit, Berlin, at the end of last year.

She was an honored comrade and we are confident that she

did her duty to the end. Regrettably, we lacked the influence in high Nazi circles necessary to procure her release.

Webel

Influence in high Nazi circles to procure her release! Unlike myself. I have no idea what I thought about Lorelei's death. Perhaps if I had loved her more, or even at all, I could have weaned her from the party. Or at least from the activist section that people like Webel controlled. But she herself had in some way chosen to go into the darkness, and she was just one of the many thousands who were now being imprisoned and tortured and executed by a regime that Buzz and even Diana saw as some sort of model. I drank a few glasses of whiskey that night and went to bed and read Goethe until late. But I dreamed of prisons and execution yards and Inspector Beck and punching the prisoner Milsen in the face again and again until the shape of the features changed and it was an amalgam of Lorelei and Diana I was punching.

It was the next morning when I first heard of the air race. Nairobi Radio broadcast an early-morning news program, and I had developed the habit of listening to it while Njomo served breakfast. I was drinking excellent home-grown coffee when the announcer began to describe an African air rally that was to take place the following month. The interest for Kenya was that it was to finish in Nairobi. Some of the world's best-known aviators were to take part in the grueling three-day race, which would prove a massive endurance test for pilots and their single-engined machines.

I had by now forgotten my coffee as I waited for Diana's name to be mentioned. More than thirty aviators were expected to take part, flying as individual competitors. Several new airplanes would be on show for the first time. Lady Diana Chrysler was to fly the new German prototype, the Messerschmitt XB . . . Harry Logan, for the United States, would fly the Lockheed . . . Henri de Cressensac . . . I switched off the radio.

I went out of the house and headed for the high fields. I walked hard until my leg ached so badly I was forced to stop. A pair of eagles soared high above the ridge. Lorelei had been executed in some squalid, high-walled yard; Catherine and

Kum were dead; and Diana was flying a Messerschmitt prototype for the Third Reich.

I had no intention of going to the air rally. More than that, I had every reason to stay away. Hyrcano Rahvdi, who had passed by on one of his interminable journeys, had been at a loss to understand why I would not attend what could be the finest event of the year. He himself, he said regretfully, had not been invited to the racecourse itself where the landings were to take place, but he was full of enthusiasm for the event. The racecourse buildings had been repainted for this coming Sunday, and the marquees were already going up all around the track itself. "It has already, Captain Hardenberg," he said, waving his glass of gin dangerously, "a certain medieval air. One cannot help thinking of a tournament to which the finest flower of chivalry is to be invited. I see it as a moment like the one before the Battle of Poitiers, where the French knights met the English in manly sport before the next day's battle."

"You're a dreadful romantic, Mr. Rahvdi," I said. "I'm not sure the world of chivalry ever existed as the storybooks would have us believe."

"Perhaps not," he grimaced. "But surely that is not so very important. Surely what's important, Captain, is that the ideal exists. Men will always tarnish the ideal. They will make it trivial, even brutal. But it is the ideal that leads us on." His finger jerked upward. "Not *ideals*, you understand. They, I believe, have always been dangerous."

"Did you learn that at Cambridge, Mr. Rahvdi?" I asked him.

He smiled wryly. "I feel safe to tell you, Captain, that I was never *at* Cambridge. I was in Cambridge for a month and I had the great pleasure to attend a summer school in water engineering at Downing College." He shrugged. "It was a great pleasure. One doesn't forget such things."

I was silent.

"When you are a person of color, Captain, as I am, you develop a selective memory. It's a defense, of course. If not, you develop a rage, like Mr. Kum. A rage to prepare for change. He was, of course, before his time."

Mr. Rahvdi sat back in his chair and caught out of the corner of his eye what I had already seen, a car approaching along the farm road. "You have a visitor." He stood up hurriedly. "And I myself must be on my way."

I remained seated. "I was hoping you would stay to lunch."

"But your visitor . . ."

"Will you stay?"

He considered. "No, Captain. Thank you, but no. I do not have the courage of Mr. Kum, the African knight perhaps in the *Chanson de Roland*."

The car belonged to Lusk. He got out heavily and strolled across the gravel to greet us.

Mr. Rahvdi consented to stay, and we all went into the shaded dining room where Njomo was setting lunch.

"What brings you here in the middle of the day?" I asked Lusk.

He sat down. "I wondered if you'd heard the news," he said.

"What news?"

"Diana Chrysler has recanted," he said. "That's the word, isn't it?"

"That could be the word," I said carefully.

"You mean, Inspector," Mr. Rahvdi said, leaning forward, "that Lady Diana has denounced the German government of Adolf Hitler?"

"The planes were due to leave Nice this morning on the first leg of the air rally to Khartoum. They've just received a telegram at the *Banner-Post* office saying Lady Diana refused to fly the new Messerschmitt prototype. She's flying some old string-and-canvas kite instead. She doesn't have a chance, of course. But she's made a stand."

I leaned back against the sideboard. "What made her do it?"

Lusk shrugged. "The *Banner-Post* telegram quotes her as saying she no longer believes in the goodwill of the Nazi leadership. She says she's severed her connection with Germany for as long as the Nazi Party is in power."

"And where does that leave her brother Lord Winslow and his new Kenya National Party?" Mr. Rahvdi said excitedly.

They both looked to me, but I found I had nothing to say. I should have been swamped with pleasure and relief, but instead I felt uncomfortably suspicious of such a grand gesture at the beginning of a highly publicized air race.

"For us in Kenya it is great news," Mr. Rahvdi enthused.

I knew Lusk was looking at me. "Yes," I said. "It's great news."
"You will now attend the finish of the race," Rahvdi pressed me.
"Yes," I said slowly. "I'll go down to Nairobi for the finish."

Pamela Longman came up to look at my leg that afternoon. I
didn't think it was really necessary, but she insisted, giving
further instructions for treatment to Njomo in her beautiful and
fluent Swahili. We had tea on the veranda afterwards, and she
sat staring out across the lake. "You know, of course, that I was
Lord Winslow's mistress for some time a couple of years ago?"
As she spoke, she turned back slowly toward me.
"Yes," I said.
"I was very young. In many ways. Buzz Winslow was the first
aristocrat I had ever met."
"Are they different from other men?"
"Very different," she said. "When you come from a working-
class, East End family, aristocrats have a very special glamour."
"You mean he seduced you?"
She laughed. "Most certainly. He set out to charm me. In
that he succeeded. Then finally he flattered me into doing what
he wanted. He's a very experienced pouncer."
"What happened?" I'm not sure why I felt free to ask, but I
did. "What happened after that night at the Muthaiga Club?"
"I went back home with Gerald. I suppose it took a few hours
for him to emerge from the terrible humiliation of the evening.
He was much older than I, nearly forty when we first married,
and I had simply always looked on him as someone who knew
what to do next. He was a good farmer, hardworking and
sensible with the little money we made. But all this, of course,
was something different. I realized that, alone, without the
other settlers, he was *afraid* of the Winslow set. Perhaps really
afraid. Or perhaps only afraid that, even though they weren't
proper farmers or real settlers in any way, they could still make
life impossible for him in Kenya."
"You mean that he was prepared to accept what had
happened?"
"Many other husbands had. I remember he used those words.
He collapsed that night. Not that he fell down or got dreadfully
drunk or anything. It was just as if he had nothing to say. Just as

if in some way he felt Lord Winslow had a right to me, if he chose."

"And how did you feel?"

"I don't think I believed what was happening. I expected a husband who would threaten to kill me or Buzz Winslow or anyone who got in his way. He had always had so much anger in him. And then suddenly, as I said, he collapsed. He decided then to sell up and move to South Africa or Rhodesia."

"And Buzz? Have you seen him since?"

She smiled slowly. "Yes. I took an oxhide whip and I waited for the right opportunity. And when the time came I horse-whipped Lord Buzz Winslow to within an inch of his life, as they say." She laughed. "I didn't entirely succeed, but I think I still taught him a few things about Deptford and all the other places he so much despised."

We sat on the veranda rail and looked over the still water of the lake.

"Are you happy?" I asked her.

With one hand she tossed back her dark brown hair. "Getting happier," she said.

TWENTY-FIVE

Mr. Rahvdi was right about the medieval feeling of the Nairobi Race Course. While the central area was left clear for the landing aircraft, the surrounding grass track itself was filled with colorful marquees from which pennants snapped in the brisk breeze. Indian candy stalls and coconut shies for the children lined the far side of the white rails along one side of the track. Large tents striped red and yellow had been erected for private parties. The Muthaiga had taken an enormous gaudy marquee from which the arms of the club flew from a masthead set before the entrance. A band of the King's African Rifles played selections of swing music; Africans in red shawls sold rally souvenirs to the arriving guests.

I stayed away from the privileged section of the track where the hotels and clubs had erected their marquees. Instead I wandered among the Indian stalls, listening to the reports on the loudspeaker system. The Messerschmitt prototype was in the lead, as had been expected. But of course Diana was not the pilot. Now flown by a man I had vaguely known during the war, a Major Hans Goerdeler, the single-engined monoplane had been first to land at Khartoum and was now reported to be over fifty miles ahead of the competition and passing just south of Mount Kenya.

Diana's aeroplane, an ancient De Havilland, had performed creditably enough to arrive fifth in Khartoum. The spotter posts arranged at telegraph stations by the Nairobi *Banner-Post*, which was sponsoring the loudspeaker announcements, reported that she was now in fourth place some eighty or ninety miles behind Goerdeler. In that sense the race was over. There was no chance that she or indeed any of the other competitors would catch him now. Göring would have his victory. But it was not the victory it might have been if Diana had climbed out of the Messerschmitt's cockpit on the Nairobi Race Course.

I saw Rahvdi with his pretty Indian wife and waved to them and then met up with Tom Lusk and his sergeant, both impressive in starched khaki uniforms and black peaked caps as they patrolled through the crowds. I could see Pamela talking to a group of people nearby. As she saw me she turned from them and walked—sauntered, even—toward her father and me. She was wearing a pale blue print dress, which, as she walked, fluttered around her knees. She reached us as Goerdeler's aeroplane appeared as a small speck in the northern sky.

The crowd began to surge toward the rails. The rally officials emerged from the single official tent and the announcer raised his voice to a new pitch of excitement, inviting us to guess whether it was indeed Goerdeler or perhaps some other craft that had miraculously passed him.

But there was no doubt in anybody's mind that it was the Messerschmitt. It came roaring down from the sky, the black-and-silver crosses glinting on its wings. A gasp was drawn from the crowd as Goerdeler released streams of black, white, and red smoke, then banked to circle the racetrack and bring the aircraft in, bumping across the rough grass.

He was only fifty or sixty yards from where I stood with Lusk.

"One up for Adolf Hitler's Germany," the inspector said, watching Goerdeler climb down in his white flying suit, the swastika a brilliant flash of color on his left arm.

The officials came forward. Goerdeler threw his arm up in the Hitler salute and stepped forward to meet them. The K.A.R. band played "Deutschland Über Alles" and the hooked cross was run slowly up the flagpole. As a German, I felt vaguely sick. As a man, I wondered what I would have felt if the figure in the white flying suit with the swastika armband had been Diana.

It was proving a good afternoon for the Fascist dictatorships. An Italian entry came in second, and not far behind that, another Italian. The crowd was now on edge, searching the blue northern sky. If Diana had maintained her fourth place, she would be next to appear.

A small and very distant smudge in the sky was greeted by a

ragged cheer. "According to our latest report," the announcer was saying, "this will be Lady Diana Chrysler approaching in her De Havilland D6 trainer. After nearly sixteen hours of flying across some of the most inhospitable terrain in Africa, Lady Diana is now at last approaching the finish line. On the last stretch our post at Gilgil picked up her aircraft as she met the railway and turned west to follow it down past Naivasha. We can only speculate what it must feel like to be at the end of sixteen hours in a cramped cockpit. The only woman in the Nice-Nairobi Air Rally has certainly shown herself on this occasion the equal of the world's best."

It was, I reflected, easy to imagine from the announcer's tone that Diana rather than Hans Goerdeler had won the race. The speck had become an indistinct blob in the sky as the plane came in under a high, drifting tumble of cloud.

"That's not Lady Chrysler." Lusk's sergeant had a pair of binoculars up to his eyes. "It's a monoplane. She's been pipped by one of the Frenchmen. That's probably her just behind."

I peered into the haze of heat, but the announcer was already confirming what the sergeant had said.

"No!" The metallic voice was charged with excitement. "No, it's not Lady Diana! Just one moment while we get identification. . . ."

There was a crackle from the loudspeakers, and then silence. I could just see a second aircraft behind the monoplane.

"The other one's not either," the sergeant said. "They're both Frenchmen."

For a few seconds my attention was diverted. I saw Buzz duck under the racetrack rail and begin to walk quickly toward the official tent. Then the announcer's voice came on again. "Coming in now is Baron Henri de Cressensac in his Breguet, and his teammate Jean-Pierre Rostand is close behind in fifth place. It looks as though we have a few moments to wait for Lady Diana. In the meantime here comes Baron de Cressensac. . . ."

There was a quick flurry of applause as the Frenchman brought his aeroplane down and taxied toward the official tent.

Buzz, I saw, was the first to reach him as the aircraft stopped. He was talking hard as de Cressensac climbed down and began stamping the feeling back into his legs. Then, as the officials arrived, Buzz turned away and stood staring out across the racetrack in the direction of the highlands. A girl had joined him, and Boscowan and Wandle and Harry Towers. Taking a pair of binoculars from one of the men, Buzz lifted them to his eyes. Even at sixty yards or more, I could sense his anxiety.

"Lend the captain your binoculars," Lusk said to his sergeant. The sergeant lifted the strap over his cap and handed me the binoculars. Focusing them, I swept the line of hills. There were rain clouds clear enough, beyond the heat haze, but no sign of an aircraft. I lowered the binoculars. "How far is Gilgil?"

Lusk raised his bushy eyebrows. "Say a hundred miles. Is it serious?"

"If she doesn't show up in a few minutes, yes."

"Could she have run out of fuel?"

"If that's all it is, there are plenty of places to land. But there's cloud forming up there too."

Lusk nodded. "Some of the old upcountry hands have been expecting the rains early this year."

I handed the binoculars back to the sergeant. "I'm going over to the officials' tent," I told Lusk.

I threaded my way through the crowds still drifting along the track. Ducking under the rail, I made for Buzz, who was standing apart from his friends, scanning the sky to the northwest.

He glanced at me as I stood beside him, and again clamped the binoculars to his eyes. "The weather's broken over Gilgil," he said.

There were several specks in the sky now, but it was noticeable that the loudspeaker was silent.

"Any of these?" I asked Buzz.

He shook his head. "There are some more behind, though." He let the binoculars drop onto his chest and turned to stare at me, lips pursed, head cocked with the old theatricality.

"Stop playacting, Buzz," I said shortly. "The time for that is long past."

"Playacting, my dear fellow? What makes you think I'm playacting?" He thrust his hands deep into the side pockets of his white shirt. "Not a word of reproach has passed my lips. Nor shall it."

"I've flown the whole Gilgil-Naivasha area many times. In cloud it's dangerous. Very dangerous."

He nodded, as if dismissing what I had said, and again lifted

[357]

the binoculars. The announcer was reeling off names now as, one after the other, the aircraft came in.

"She could have simply lost the line of the railway," I said. "In that case she might be out in clear weather again, but still well off course."

"Perhaps." He turned back to me. "You are aware that she made some schoolgirl statement in Nice."

"I understood that she withdrew her support of Adolf Hitler."

Another four or five aircraft were identified on the loudspeakers as they approached the racecourse.

"She's behaved like the most insufferable bitch, of course," Buzz said.

"It's your chance to speak out too," I said. "If she can see it, so can you."

He swung around on me, but before he could speak, the loudspeaker claimed our attention. "Ladies and gentlemen, I am afraid there must be some cause for concern about Lady Diana Chrysler's aircraft. We have now identified all the aircraft approaching Nairobi, and there is no sign of Lady Diana's De Havilland."

A silence fell on the crowd. Buzz was standing upright, aware, I'm sure, that half the guests at the racecourse were watching him. Or perhaps not. Perhaps the image really had got to him of Diana alone in that cockpit. Perhaps he really felt, as I did, the panic of being lost in a small aircraft in a gray, wet bank of cloud.

In those seconds the first fat drops of rain hit us. The sunlight fleeing across the hillside left the whole racecourse drained of color. "She's crashed," Buzz said, already moving away from me. "She's crashed somewhere north of Naivasha."

"I'm coming with you," I told him as I brushed rain from my eyes. Around us, women in printed silk dresses were squealing and holding on to hats as they ran for the shelter of the marquees. Buzz rounded on me with a ferocity that made his white teeth stand out from drawn-back lips. "Stay out of it," he said, his voice hissing through the sheets of rain. "Stay out of my family affairs once and for all."

As I started on the road to Naivasha, I was no more than a

few minutes behind Buzz. The rain had stopped and the late-afternoon sun now blazed down, releasing tiny rising vapors from the rough grass on either side of the road. But I had been warned by Tom Lusk. The rains, having once started, would continue. By the time I reached Naivasha, he said, roads in the whole area could be reduced to mud slicks.

At first I could see Buzz's car ahead, taking the bends at a speed that threw mud and stones from beneath the back wheels, but his Buick was much more powerful than my own box-body Austin, and the gap between us opened until I could no longer see him even on the straightest section of road.

Other cars had left the racecourse shortly after mine, and if I looked back I could see a long line of roadsters and box-bodies bouncing along behind me. It was impossible not to feel that a sense of carnival still dominated the event. In the rearview mirror I could see girls standing high in passenger seats of open cars, waving and calling to friends behind. I don't really think it had yet occurred to most people who were at the racecourse that Diana had crashed. They thought of forced landings. The sense of sport so deeply rooted in their culture rose easily to the surface. It was a game called "Hunt Diana." "Find the Landing Site." No one thought in terms of splinting broken limbs or treating gasoline burns.

Except perhaps Buzz. When he furiously pushed me aside, there had been something demented about his anger. The perfect white silk tussore suit was already yellowed with rain as he turned and raced for the car park.

I had seen enough theatrical performances by Buzz to know that this was not one. He had reached the rail of the track and taken it in one leap, stumbling among the guy-lines of the marquees, swearing with fury as he tripped, fell to his knees, and scrambled up again. I remember Margaret calling to him from the opening of a tent, but he had taken no notice. The Buick, its engine bursting into life almost as soon as the door slammed, leaped forward, smashing aside an Indian candy stall, and keeled on its American suspension as he drove recklessly for the exit.

But as I took the road northeast to Naivasha I was no longer thinking about Buzz. Every moment I could spare from watching the road ahead I scanned the sky in the hope of seeing a single-engined aircraft appear out of the banks of gray clouds. It was, I suppose, just possible that she still had enough fuel to remain airborne, but as I had to admit, it was a forlorn hope.

It began to drizzle again as evening advanced. I was no longer leading a carnival procession. I occasionally caught a glitter of headlights in my rearview mirror. But they were settlers returning home from the air rally. I did not think that there would be any serious search for Diana's aeroplane conducted before morning. Except, I suppose, by Buzz and myself.

It was after nine o'clock that evening when I passed along the road above Lake Naivasha. There were many more houses, their veranda lights gleaming, than I remembered from just after the war. I had no idea which house belonged to Buzz.

I left the lake and crossed the railway line into the tiny township of Naivasha and stopped outside the still-lighted telegraph office. The aging Indian clerk was helpful and well informed about the situation. The District Officer, he told me, had ordered a company of King's African Rifles from Nanyuki, and they would begin a search of the area on both sides of the Gilgil-Naivasha section of railway at dawn. A police unit consisting of a sergeant and six askaris was already out somewhere in the hills. In addition, light aircraft were standing by in Nairobi and Nanyuki in the hope that the cloud would clear for a few hours tomorrow.

"But I have not yet related the most important event," the Indian said. "While Lord Winslow was here a half hour or more ago, a young man, an African named Mkutu, came in to report that he had been returning from a journey to visit his wife-to-be when he had heard the sounds of an aircraft in the clouds."

"Which side of the railway track was he on?"

"On the mountain side," the Indian said. "He was returning from the village of Soykuru. Let me show you."

The Indian took a telegraph form and turned it facedown. On the back he sketched out the line of the railway and the unmade roads leading into the mountains to the west of the town. "Mkutu was returning along this road." The clerk's long brown finger traced the journey. "He was himself in thin cloud as he walked. I calculated he heard the sound of the aircraft at about five o'clock."

"But why should we think it was Lady Chrysler's plane?" I said. "There were a dozen aircraft in the air at about that time."

"This is true," the old man said. "But Mkutu described an aeroplane that came down low, then climbed quickly and circled several times before the sound disappeared."

"The sound disappeared. You mean it faded away?"

"No, sir," he said gravely. "Mkutu says it stopped suddenly."

The muscles seemed to have set around my mouth. "Has the District Officer been informed?"

"I informed him myself," the Indian said. "But our own police are searching far south of where Mkutu describes. And the company of K.A.R. will not reach us until morning."

"What about farmers in the area?"

"All farms with telephones have been asked to help. Several search parties are being arranged at this moment."

I paused. "You've done marvelously well," I said. "I will make sure Lady Diana is aware of all you've done when she is found."

"Thank you." He seemed genuinely pleased in his grave, dignified manner. "There is one thing before you go."

"Yes?"

"When I was a younger man, I delivered the post in the area Mkutu speaks of," he said. "I have been thinking of the terrain."

I stood in the doorway, waiting.

"Mkutu said the aeroplane passed twice above his head. From his description the noise disappeared completely just as it began a third circle of the hills."

He gestured me back and used the reverse side of another telegraph form to draw in a hillside rising from the track Mkutu had taken. "I would look there for the aeroplane." He marked a cross on the thin paper. I took the form and buttoned it into my breast pocket.

I thanked him again and left the telegraph office. The scent of the night after the first arrival of the rains is somehow fresh and heavy at the same time. It is as if the earth and all the vegetation on it were making a swift yet unfamiliar adjustment. Like a country in the grip of a short but violent revolution.

I climbed back into the car, and took out my map. If the African Mkutu was right, it would mean that Diana, having successfully reached the railway line at Gilgil, had chosen to leave the line of the track that would have taken her straight to Nairobi. Reading the map by flashlight, I thought I saw why. In fact, if she had followed the track south, she would have arrived in Ngong. To reach Nairobi by the railway she would have been forced to turn almost back on her flight line. I believed she had chosen to cut the corner by flying by compass straight from the rail line at Gilgil over the east slopes of the Rift Valley, in a direct line to Nairobi. And when the cloud had descended, she might well have been in just the position Mkutu described. I had once or twice faced the cloud in these uplands myself. I remembered the cold and the loneliness and the sickness of cloud disorientation. And most of all the terror that at any moment a great wall of rock was going to rise before you.

Across the main street a girl was running toward me. I could see in the sparse lamplight that she wore a short rainproofed jacket over her dress. For a moment it seemed to me that it was Diana waving as she ran, then she passed by the lighted window of the telegraph office and I saw it was Pamela Longman.

I got out of the car.

"Claus," she called as she slowed and walked the last steps toward me. "I wondered," she said, pushing her hands deep into her pockets, "if you would like me to go with you." She paused. "I doubt if any of the search parties has trained medical assistance. If Lady Chrysler *has* crashed . . ."

I stood before her, trying to think. "Where is the nearest doctor?"

She shrugged. "There's Dr. Taylor in Nakuru. There's old Dr. Sampson in Njoro. The local man here is on holiday in England."

"Could you stay here tonight, in Naivasha?"

"Of course," she said, "if you think that's best." I could detect a faint disappointment in her voice.

"If one of the other search parties finds her, rather than me, they'll bring her back here. This is where you'll be needed."

"Yes," she said slowly. "That makes sense. I'll take a room at the hotel." She turned away, then turned back suddenly. "Good luck," she said. "Good luck."

I got into the car and switched on the engine. Pamela Longman reached the boardwalk that ran along the line of low, corrugated-roofed shops and, turning, lifted her arm to wave.

The road from Naivasha, a dust track in dry weather, had already been converted to a few inches of thin, treacherous mud by the onset of the rains. More rain would penetrate the harder level of compacted earth beneath and could, in a few hours, render some parts impassable. But if Mkutu and the Indian in the telegraph office were right, I would not have more than a few miles to drive. After that I would be climbing the hills on foot.

As I drove, hunched forward to peer into the drizzling darkness, I tried to run over in my mind the equipment I carried in the back of the car. A first-aid kit was always there—bandages, splints, iodine, a half-bottle of whiskey, and a little morphine. An ax, a length of rope, an old British Army groundsheet and weatherproof cape combined. A blanket roll. A powerful Zeissman torch. A reserve four-gallon can of petrol, half full. Mostly it was the sort of equipment I might have chosen. But there was no compass. And no food.

I drove on for an hour or more, and the rain seemed to be increasing steadily. As I got higher in the hills the cloud swirled around me, cloaking the way ahead, then lifting and tumbling around me again as if in some wild ballet. The road, winding upward, had by now reduced to a thin track between rocks and heavy shrub. Huge overhanging trees pressed down above me, and the car's headlights cut only a small hole in the surrounding darkness.

TWENTY-SIX

had lost all reasonable track of time. Rain poured down until it seemed more effective to still the windshield wipers; the tires spun and bit and spun again and the Austin advanced with a jogging movement that might have been fifteen miles an hour or, equally likely, five. Several times I was forced to get out and use my ax to cut branches to pack under the rear wheels. A tree trunk that had been washed across the road delayed me for almost an hour as I hacked it in two while the rain streamed down upon me, glittering like glass columns in the car's headlights. After that, only by threading the rope through the spokes of the wheels, like improvised snow chains, was I able to continue forward at all.

I now drove with the open whiskey bottle propped upright beside me between the two seats. Exhaustion came not in waves, but insidiously creeping upon me until I drifted into some bizarre reverie: I was racing Buzz along a bright seashore, or I was back in the schoolroom at the Schloss Hardenberg, where my mother was teaching me English words I already knew. I would wake from these moments with a shuddering jerk of my whole body, and the car would slew and slide while I fought to bring the wheels around again.

By some miracle, I found the track at the overhanging rock that the Indian clerk in Naivasha had described. I had already turned along it and crept forward perhaps fifty yards when I heard what seemed an odd honking sound of geese or perhaps buffalo. I stopped the car and got out to stand in the rain, listening. With the engine switched off, it was easy to identify the noise of an automobile horn being pressed at regular intervals. Even more, it seemed to me that somewhere farther along the road I was traveling, a faint luminosity glowed through the black night.

Then I saw, high on the slopes of the hill, not a mile from the point where the Naivasha postmaster had put his brown finger on the map, a small leaping flame that rose and died and leaped up again. It could equally have been a distress signal or the dying moments of a burning aeroplane. I gave no more thought to the car horn calling through the darkness. I took my ax, flashlight, and length of rope, packed the first-aid kit in my knapsack, and started up the hill.

My flashlight seemed powerless to roll back the darkness; around my head the clouds burst like water-filled paper bags at a fun fair. Streams became torrents almost as the beam of my flashlight touched them; trees bent and sighed and creaked in the wind; dislodged stones made a sudden rush through the undergrowth like an attacking animal.

I was mercilessly scraped and clutched and torn at by the dark rocks and the waving trees. Nature, erupting in malevolence, placed itself between me and the girl on the hillside, forcing me to climb, slip, hack my way forward, to fight for every yard of ground.

And then the rain stopped with that extraordinary African suddenness. As quickly as the storm sounds ceased, they were replaced by a quiet singing of water moving through tree roots and dribbling across the rocks.

I had climbed several hundred feet and now reached a narrow track leading upward. I had not seen the leaping points of light since I left the road below, and across the dark hump of the hillside I had no point of reference. But the flashlight beam, now that I was out of the thick undergrowth, pushed far into the darkness. And suddenly I heard a voice calling.

It was a release of tension like the act of sex. And as my light caught the white-clad figure running down the path toward me, I experienced a related, almost postcoital wave of tenderness. I called her name and she called mine, then I dropped the flashlight as she ran into my arms. I kissed her with the fury of a lover, and the anger of a parent who at last finds a lost child. I felt her tongue in my mouth, battling with my tongue. She was seized with violent bouts of trembling.

She repeated time after time, between kisses, "Claus, Claus, I knew it would be you."

I recovered the flashlight and we climbed the path to stop and stare silently at the burned skeleton of the De Havilland. The rubber wheels still gave off thick, bitter smoke, and from time to time the flames would rekindle for a moment, then die away.

"Half the colony is out looking for you," I said. "There's a K.A.R. company searching the hills, police askaris, every settler family within fifty miles."

"And Buzz?"

"He can't be far away."

"But *you* found me."

"I saw the flames."

"And what did you think?"

"I thought, 'She's mad. She tried to cut a corner through the cloud cover.'"

"Did you think I was dead?"

"I don't know."

"Did you think I deserved to be dead?"

Her white flying suit was streaked with mud, but there was no swastika on her arm. "No," I said slowly, "not now."

I kicked a few pieces of wooden strut, shredded canvas still attached, onto the burning remains of the aircraft, and the flames immediately came to life.

In the rock face there was a deep indentation, not a cave perhaps, but an *abri*. She led me by the hand and we sat together, our backs against the rock on the dry, pale grass beneath the overhang. I asked her now, at last, if she was unhurt and she nodded vehemently, like a schoolgirl, and said "Oh God, yes."

I handed her the bottle of Scotch and she drank, sputtering and smiling.

"I have a car down on the road," I said.

She nodded without interest. In the night air, humid but not cold, her hair had dried tight to her head. I ran my fingers through it and it came to life, blond and soft to the touch. Then I laid her in the thick yellow grass and began to unbutton her flying suit.

"If you thought of me," she said, "just as a woman you'd

picked up in the Savoy Grill or whose horse had bolted on the hunting field or something, could you just roger me without thinking about all the other things?"

"How can I possibly think of you as someone I just met in the Savoy Grill?"

"Do you mean you don't want me?"

It was a confidence bred of too many films, too many novels, too many years of fantasizing about this very moment. I had dreamed a thousand times of our coming together, and perhaps she had too. We direct these waking dreams and they follow their course, mostly as we would wish. But just occasionally one of them turns on a perverse tack, different from intention, shattering to the carefully constructed moment. Below me, I saw the struggle going on in her face. "You really don't want me," she said.

"It's what I've always wanted," I told her desperately. "I don't care what relation we are to each other."

"Then do it," she said, "for God's sake. Just do it."

As best I could, I did.

The barrier of fifteen years rose yawning before us. She pulled away, clutching her flying suit to her breast. "Well," she said, "that's it. After all these years." And she began to cry with huge, frightening sobs that made her gasp for breath in panic.

The beam of Buzz's powerful American flashlight found us there.

His voice was a strange roar from the darkness behind the beam. "You unspeakable slut!" he screamed. "You unconscionable slut!"

He hurled the flashlight toward the *abri* and Diana cowered as it struck above her head, the glass shattering over her. It dropped to the ground, the bulb intact, to light the figure of Buzz, his shirt open to the waist, his trousers torn around the ankles like the white canvas ducks of some Pacific castaway.

He was mad with anger and whatever other emotions were boiling within him. I think I was getting to my feet when he hit me a wild blow that threw me back against the rock. He was by now out of any control, shouting accusations of disloyalty at Diana for her renunciation of the Nazi cause, turning on me, raving that I was an insufferable swine, a common brute who would descend to fucking his own sister. And this was grati-

[367]

tude, this was what I offered in return for his family dragging me out of a German peasant village and showing me a world beyond it.

I made attempts to quiet him, but he was mad with rage. "By God, don't smirk at me," he yelled. "Don't imagine your beloved Diana has suddenly seen the light. She wasn't converted by you, you soft-centered nobody. She was converted by the thought of a fortune slipping through her fingers. The Chrysler family laid their counterclaims in the court of New York yesterday. That's why she recanted! I'm taking her with me," he raved on. "I'm out of gasoline. I'm using your car. I'm taking her back in *your* bloody car!"

I stood in front of him, my face still aching from his blow. "We'll go together," I said.

He came forward. "You treacherous bastard," he said, much more quietly. "I should kill you, you treacherous bastard."

Diana was beside me. "Please, Claus," she said. "Let me go with Buzz. . . ."

I could see she was shaking with terror. "I'll siphon some petrol into your car," I said to Buzz.

Now, of course, in hindsight, I can say I never regretted anything so much in my life, but in fact it seemed the best thing at the time. Buzz was blind with fury, certainly directed against Diana, but more against me. To have stayed with them or to have tried to take Diana to the road myself seemed a pointless incitement to his anger.

Diana herself seemed in no danger from him. I very clearly was. Was I afraid? Of course. Was it through fear of Buzz that I had let him take her? Perhaps. Certainly, to admit to it was not important to me now. That far, at least, I had traveled since my Corinthian days.

Or so everything seemed to me that night as I started down the hillside. I was now, beyond everything, intensely miserable. I did not understand what had happened between Diana and me, whether it was inevitable given the years and the taboos that stood between us. I had never felt brotherly toward her. To feel half-brotherly was something I refused even to consider. I had loved her since I was a very young man at war. The announcement that we were related within the forbidden limits of love and marriage had made no difference to how I felt, but only, until tonight, to how I acted.

I felt the sickness of fatigue and of failure. When I reached the road, I drove until I came to the Buick. As I began to siphon petrol into the tank, I could hear their voices as they made their way down the hillside. From time to time I saw a light through the trees.

With gasoline stops almost nonexistent outside the townships, most Kenyan settlers carried crude siphoning equipment in their cars for a fuel transfer to a stranded vehicle. I siphoned three or four gallons, enough to get them back to Corinth, climbed back into my car, and drove off along the Naivasha road.

I was driving slowly, trying to piece together the night's events. Had I forced myself on her? I could not believe so. She had led me to the *abri* in the rock. She had responded as I began to make love to her. And then, suddenly, pain and bewilderment had taken over.

Across the ridges toward the Rift Valley the thunder rolled, and occasional lightning flickered across the southern sky. I knew I had been naïve to imagine that one single act of sex could resolve what the last fifteen years had created. Or perhaps that was exactly what had happened, perhaps that one act of sex *had* resolved everything.

I had already decided that I would call first at Naivasha to tell the postmaster that Diana was safe, but I was uncertain how far I had traveled from the town. Perhaps I had been driving less than half an hour when I saw in my rearview mirror the headlights of a car approaching at speed. It seemed to me certain that it was Buzz, although of course I knew there were many other settlers out scouring the hills.

He passed me, his horn blaring, swerving back into the middle of the narrow road. The rear wheels of the Buick spat mud and pebbles that rattled against the side of my car. I could feel the anger and aggression in him as he accelerated the big Buick into the night.

For a mile or so its taillights were visible, riding the undulations of the road, then they disappeared completely into the distant darkness.

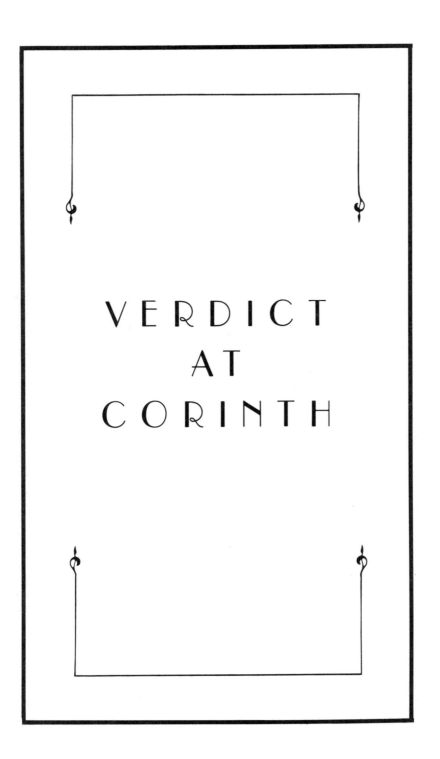

VERDICT
AT
CORINTH

TWENTY-SEVEN

S hortly after dawn on April 10, 1934, two young Africans
drove an oxcart along the narrow, waterlogged track that
would eventually lead them to the railroad of Naivasha, to
which they intended to deliver the four hogs in the back of the
cart. It had stopped raining and the sun was rising over the
distant peaks of Mount Kenya when the two men came across a
motorcar blocking the road. Handing the reins to the other
African, the driver jumped down barefoot into the mud and
sloshed along the track. Looking in through the side window,
he at first thought the car was empty. It was a moment or two
before he realized that he was looking down on the slumped
body of a man.

The hogs were abandoned in the oxcart. On foot the two
Africans covered the fifteen miles of mud-covered track in less
than three hours. By 9:00 A.M. the Indian telegraph clerk, the
sole authority in the town, had informed Nairobi that a European man had been found dead in a car on the Naivasha-
Soykuru road.

It was past noon when Inspector Thomas Lusk and Sergeant
Henderson arrived by train at Naivasha. From there, after a talk
with the Indian telegraph clerk, they drove in a borrowed car to
the point just beyond the crossroads where a group of people
stood around a large, mud-spattered, dark green Buick. Several
Africans squatted on the rocky slopes above the track. Two
Europeans and four police askaris stood beside the car. One of
the Europeans, he saw, was resting one foot on the running
board.

His first reaction was anger. All his experience told him that
already valuable evidence would have been trampled or mis-
handled. He told Henderson to stop the car well short of the

Buick, and climbed out. Beyond it, he saw, other cars were parked on the roadside.

He recognized Gerald Longman and Alfred Pedersen as he approached. "Deal with the spectators," he said to Henderson. He walked past them with a brisk nod to Gerald Longman, and stood a few yards from the car. He recognized it, of course. The Africans watched him with absorbed interest. The door on the driver's side, he noted, was pushed to, but not completely closed.

He took out his notebook. Starting from where he stood, he circled the Buick, examining the muddy road. There were too many footprints to sketch effectively. He called Henderson and told him to take photographs of every part of the road surrounding the car and then to start on the car itself.

While this was being done, he slowly filled his pipe and lit it. He could feel the impatience of the Europeans behind him. The Africans on the bank continued to watch with undiminished interest.

When the photography was completed, he stepped carefully to the door of the car and hooked it open by inserting the stem of his pipe under the handle. The body inside was slumped sideways into the deep well in front of the passenger seat. Blood caked the head, which was turned away from him, hanging down. A .38 service revolver lay on the carpet directly below the steering wheel. He called Henderson forward and told him to take photographs from the open door. As Henderson was working, he stood just behind him, drawing on his pipe. He could see, over Henderson's shoulder, that the dead man's wrist had a broken leather strap hanging from it. Glancing up, he saw that the arm strap above the passenger door had gone, the mounting twisted, leaving an exposed metal rivet.

When Henderson had finished, Lusk stood again, tamping and relighting his pipe, looking down at the body. From time to time he clamped the pipe between his teeth and made an entry in his notebook. The white trousers of the dead man were covered with mud; his left leg was tucked under him as if he had been half turning when the bullet entered his skull just behind the ear; the leather strap, he noted, was on the man's left wrist, whereas someone sitting in the passenger seat, or even reaching across from the driving seat on the left-hand-drive Buick, would have naturally engaged the strap on the right wrist.

He continued in his cautious, deliberate way to examine and note. The rear seat of the car contained a thick folded tartan blanket. There was no sign of mud on it, or on the carpet in the back. But on the center of the front bench seat there was a smear on the dark green leather that looked different in texture from the mud that streaked the rest of the seat.

He placed his pipe carefully on the ground and leaned forward, stretching out his hand. The man's neck above the damp collar was blue and congested in appearance and cold to the touch, but the body under the armpit was still faintly warm. He leaned forward farther, one knee resting on the driver's seat. Looking down at the shadowed face in the passenger well, he confirmed that it was that of Lord George Winslow.

At the Naivasha Hotel, Sergeant Henderson sat with Gerald Longman and Alfred Pedersen and a third man, Jack Nyquist.

They felt happier now, sitting in the hotel bar, drinks before them, no longer excluded from the process of investigation. Lusk too, having joined them from the telegraph office where he had arranged with the Indian clerk to call the government pathologist from Nairobi, seemed less self-absorbed.

Ordering himself a beer, the inspector sat down and laid his pipe and notebook on the low table in front of him. "I take it you gentlemen have all heard that Lady Diana is safe. The clerk at the telegraph office says that she was found unharmed during the night."

"We had heard," Longman said. "A couple of hours ago we ran into a squad of police askaris who told us that we could call off the search."

"Perhaps you'd like to tell me what happened?"

"We were on our way back from the hills when we came upon Lord Winslow's car," Longman said. "We immediately sent Jack on ahead to report it. At the time we thought we were the first."

Lusk turned to Jack Nyquist. "When you got here and discovered the car had already been found by two Africans, did you do anything else?"

"I telephoned Lady Margaret Winslow down on the lake. I told her there had been an accident."

"A fatal accident?"

"I told her that Lord Winslow had shot himself."

Lusk took up his notebook. "Did you discover where Lady Diana was?"

"She was at the house, Corinth. Lady Margaret said she would have to wake her up to tell her."

"How did Lady Margaret take the news?"

"As any wife would, I suppose. Shock, long silences." Nyquist waved a hand in front of him. "Don't ask me to be accurate. I was more concerned with trying somehow to put it over as gently as possible."

"Do you know who found Lady Diana?"

"Captain Hardenberg, apparently."

Lusk hunched forward over the beer that had been placed before him. "Now I want you to think about this very carefully. You approached the Buick, which was presumably blocking the road . . ."

"We were each of us in his own car," Pedersen said. "Jack was in front. Then myself, then Gerald. It had started to drizzle again at that point, if I remember correctly. Gerald came up and stood in the rain beside my car as Jack went forward to see what was happening. There was a flattish space on one side of the Buick where we could have driven around, but I suppose we were thinking about our springs."

"You went forward alone," Lusk said to Nyquist.

"I could see, or I thought I could, that there was no one in the car. I think I just assumed it was another search party who had climbed up into the hills. I knew it was Winslow's car, of course."

"So you reached the car. Go on."

"I still did not see him," Nyquist said. "I think I looked around a bit, among the trees."

Lusk nodded.

"I was turning back to my own car when I saw the gun."

The inspector looked at him under his eyebrows. "The gun." He repeated slowly. "Where was the gun?"

"In the mud beside the car."

"And?"

"I picked it up. There was no reason not to. I had no idea anybody had been hurt."

"Of course. What then?"

"I opened the door and dropped the gun inside. That's when I saw him."

Lusk took his notebook and scribbled with a pencil stub.

"How far was the gun from the edge of the running board?" he asked.

"A foot or two."

"And directly beneath the car door? Or forward or backward of it?"

"Beneath it."

"When you tried the door, was it firmly closed? Or was it pushed to, resting against the tongue of the lock?"

"I couldn't say for certain. Perhaps I have the impression that it was not fully closed."

"Did you do anything else? Did you touch the body?"

"I think I shouted to the others."

"And when they came?"

"We didn't open the car again. It was quite obvious he was dead."

Lusk looked toward the other two men. "Do you confirm Mr. Nyquist's account?"

They nodded. "Yes, it's about right," Pedersen said.

"What I want to know, gentlemen," Lusk said, "is whether it's *exactly* right."

Longman stuck out his lower lip. "It's accurate," he said.

"Now did either you, Mr. Longman, or you, Mr. Pedersen, see Mr. Nyquist pick up the revolver?"

"We both did," Pedersen said.

Lusk scowled. "Please answer for yourself."

"All right, I did," Pedersen said.

"And how far was the gun from the car?"

"As Jack says, a foot or two. No more, I'd say."

Lusk turned back to Gerald Longman. "And you? How far would you say?"

"No more than two feet from the edge of the running board."

"It's a very great shame the gun was moved, sir," Lusk said, turning to Nyquist. "Although I appreciate that at that moment you still thought the car was empty."

Jack Nyquist shuffled his shoulders. "I don't see what difference it makes," he grumbled belligerently.

"It could make all the difference, sir," Lusk said, pocketing his pipe, "between suicide and murder."

Inspector Lusk saw Diana that morning. She was sitting on the veranda at Corinth with a light cotton blanket around her knees. She wore a yellow silk shirt and some makeup, but her face was pale and tense. It had begun to drizzle again, and the air was cool.

"Are you sure you wouldn't like to move inside?" Lusk asked.

Diana shook her head and lit a cigarette with quick movements.

"You could still be suffering from shock, you know."

"Oh, for God's sake," Diana said, "just get on with it, will you, Inspector."

Lusk took out his notebook and sat on the low wall between the Greek columns. "I want to take you through the whole thing, Lady Diana," he said slowly. "I want you to start in Nice."

"Is that necessary?"

"Yes."

She shrugged. "I'm sure you know more or less what happened."

"Only more or less."

"Very well." She puffed rapidly on her cigarette. "I had originally agreed to fly the new Messerschmitt. This was an arrangement made, I would think, over a year ago between General Göring and myself. We discussed at length which of the various air races and rallies we should go for, and it was finally agreed that the Africa Rally, Nice to Nairobi, would be the one."

"Why was that, Lady Diana?"

"I really can't remember anymore. We discussed so many different possibilities."

"I'm asking," Lusk said in his still faintly cockney accent, "if your decision to fly this aeroplane in the Africa Rally had anything to do with your brother's political position here in the colony."

"Why should it?"

Lusk pursed his lips. "Your brother was of a particular political persuasion and known to be. I've no doubt the arrival of his celebrated sister in a German aircraft, a Nazi aircraft if you like, would have gained a great deal of publicity for his views."

"Perhaps."

"Conversely"—Lusk took out his pipe—"the cancellation of the Messerschmitt flight was bound to reap some adverse publicity for those views."

"I'm not a politician, Inspector."

"Why did you make the statement you did at Nice?"

"I had personal reasons for doing what I did, when I did."

"It could be very helpful to know what those reasons were."

She paused. "I came to believe," she said after a moment, "it was high time I cut my losses with the Nazis."

"Cut your losses? What does that mean?"

The flash of irritation reappeared. "It's a racing term, as you well know, Inspector. One doesn't continue throwing good money after bad."

"Did you inform your brother that you were about to do this?"

"I sent him a cable the day before the race."

Lusk grunted. "Tell me about the race itself. From the time you left Khartoum on the second leg. The aircraft was performing satisfactorily."

"The D.H. is a beautiful old thing," she said. "Very reliable. It banged its way across the desert without a single hitch. I knew Goerdeler and the Italians were ahead, of course. But I did hope to make fourth place. The Frenchman was just behind. That's why I decided not to follow the railway from Gilgil and to risk it through the cloud. By cutting the corner, I saved fifteen or sixteen miles. That is, I *would* have saved fifteen or sixteen miles."

"The cloud was thicker than you anticipated."

"Much. I was almost immediately thoroughly lost. I circled, trying to get my bearings, and by good fortune there was a flat strip of grassland. I knew I was out of the race. I took what Lady Luck had handed me and put the D.H. down on the side of the mountain. It upended. I climbed out and it began to burn."

Lusk lit his pipe and drew on it. "What happened then?"

"I fell asleep. Strange as it may seem, I fell asleep."

"You had been flying for sixteen hours or more, I don't find that strange. When did you wake up?"

"It was dark. Sometime after midnight. I could see from my position, high up on the mountainside, motorcar headlights in the hills. I thought it would not be long before I was found."

"And in fact?"

"I heard someone calling. A light was flashing somewhere below. I called back and recognized the voice as Claus von Hardenberg's."

"What then?"

"I couldn't believe it at first. He had a bottle of whiskey with him and we drank some of that."

"What time did you start down the mountain?"

She sat looking at him for a moment, then she threw aside the cotton blanket. "I must get myself a drink," she said. "I don't usually drink before lunch."

"No . . ." Lusk watched her pour whiskey and soda. She came back along the veranda, stopping once or twice to sip at it. "Do you mind if I have one of those?" He pointed with the stem of his pipe.

"A drink?" She shrugged. "Help yourself." She waved an arm toward the drinks table.

"Go on, Lady Diana." He got up and crossed to the table.

She turned to face him. "We had been talking for some time, trying to decide whether to wait it out until the morning, when we heard a voice calling and saw a light below. My brother had taken another path up."

Lusk stood waiting, his thumb on the lever of the soda siphon.

"He was in an extraordinary state, I'm afraid. He said I had ruined his standing here in Kenya." She paused. "He was in a very, very excited state."

"You all three went down the mountain together?"

"No, no, we didn't all go down together. I left with Captain von Hardenberg."

"You left your brother there?"

"That's not the way I would describe it, Inspector. My brother was utterly furious. He was shouting at us as we started down the hillside. It was obvious that he was terribly drunk. What wasn't obvious, I regret to say, was that he was, more than anything, terribly hurt."

"Hurt?"

"I freely admit that I'd been utterly beastly."

"The statement you made in Nice."

She nodded.

"Your brother, Lord Winslow, took a different path down the hillside?"

"Yes, I gathered his car was some distance from Count von Hardenberg's."

"And that was the last time you saw him."

"Yes. Count von Hardenberg and I came down in patchy cloud. We could hear my brother for a few minutes as he made his way down to his own car."

"Captain Hardenberg brought you back here."

"Yes."

"Were you not surprised when your brother Lord Winslow didn't arrive back?"

"I was in bed, Inspector. Within minutes I was fast asleep. I don't think I even heard Count von Hardenberg leave."

Lusk pressed the arm of the siphon and squirted soda into his whiskey. "I won't trouble you any longer, Lady Diana," he said. He drank, almost finishing the glass. "But just try to tell me this. Given the state of your brother's mind, or the apparent state, how would you think he died?"

Her head came up sharply. "How did he die? I understood he shot himself. What are you saying?"

"I'm asking about Lord Winslow's state of mind last night."

"I've told you. He was furious, bitter, very resentful."

"Thank you." Lusk finished his whiskey. "One last thing. Does Captain Hardenberg know about Lord Winslow's death?"

"Of course, I telephoned him immediately. I can't resist the feeling, Inspector, that some of these questions are not strictly necessary."

Lusk stood before her, nodding as if he accepted the rebuke. She was a most extraordinarily beautiful woman. He enjoyed looking at her. "All the same," he said, "I'm afraid I shall be back here. I've got a job to do. All policemen say that in the course of an investigation," he smiled. "I might as well say it at the beginning."

From where he stood he could see Margaret Winslow descending the staircase. At the bottom step she paused, glanced at herself in the long mirror, and came toward the veranda.

"I was very sorry to hear what had happened, Lady Winslow," Lusk said.

Margaret nodded without interest in his commiseration. "You have some questions to ask me."

"Yes." He paused. "In the past week or two, had Lord Winslow behaved at all unusually?"

"He always behaved unusually."

"In any way," Lusk said carefully, "to suggest to you that he was under very great stress?"

"No." She was looking ahead, past Diana, out across the veranda rail toward the lake.

"What was his reaction when he read Lady Diana's telegram announcing that she had decided not to fly the German aeroplane?"

"Fury. He was absolutely furious. Are you surprised?"

Diana looked up at her sharply, but Margaret kept her eyes fixed on the lake.

"Angry rather than depressed?"

"If you are trying to suggest that my husband committed suicide, the idea is ridiculous." She walked across the veranda and began to pour herself a drink. "He was murdered."

"You seem very sure."

"I am very sure. I believe your investigation will confirm it, Inspector."

"Lady Margaret is convinced he was murdered," Tom Lusk said as he got out of his car and began to walk with Claus toward the farmhouse at Ngong later that day. "Of course, her evidence as to Winslow's general mental state will be very important at the coroner's inquest."

Claus nodded, glancing sideways at Lusk's set face. "Who else did you talk to, apart from Diana and Margaret?" he asked.

"I talked to Longman and a couple of friends of his. They came across the Buick early this morning, not long after some Africans on their way to Naivasha."

"Could they throw any light on what happened?"

"I'm not sure yet," Lusk said. Small children skipped past them. For a moment Lusk stopped watching the children as they disappeared around the side of the farmhouse. "I spoke to

Pam too," he said at length. "I didn't know she was working up in the Naivasha area last night."

"She wanted to come with me," Claus said. "But I thought it better that she should stay in Naivasha in case one of the other search parties brought Diana in."

Tom Lusk nodded heavily, his lips pursed. "Yes," he said, as if he might have said much more.

"Will you stay for some lunch, Tom?" Claus asked as he led the way into the drawing room.

"I'll have a sandwich and a beer with you," Lusk said, "while I ask you one or two questions."

Claus rang the bell and asked Njomo to bring some sandwiches. "A shocking business," he said. "I suppose this is the time we bring out all the old clichés."

"What did you feel when you heard he was dead?"

Claus shrugged. "God knows. I suppose I could write it down for you, but I don't think I could tell you. He exerted an extraordinary influence on everybody he met. He could be rude, subject to unbelievable snobbery, childish, spoiled. And a lot of other things too. Loyal, I suppose, beyond anything else. It's hard to forget that."

Lusk took two bottles of beer and opened them. "When you left Naivasha and headed for the mountains, did you meet up with any search parties?"

"No. It was a foul night. There may have been others quite close, but I could see no more than a few yards ahead for most of the time."

"You were very lucky to have found the plane, then."

"It wasn't entirely luck. The telegraph clerk at Naivasha achieved an extraordinarily intelligent piece of deduction."

"I should invite him onto the force," Lusk said dryly. "Had Lord Winslow also talked to the clerk?"

"I believe so."

"He mentioned it when he arrived at the scene of the crash landing?"

"I think so," Claus said. "A lot of things were said. Hard, bitter things. I remember them. I'm not really sure I remember him saying how he got there."

"This beer's hot," Lusk said, grimacing. "Lady Diana describes her brother as furious."

"An understatement. He was demented. He stood there in the rain, raving like King Lear. He felt she had betrayed him."

"And then?"

"He went off down the mountain in a fearful state."

"A suicidal state?"

"I can't tell you that, Inspector. When I was in prison in Berlin I was often suicidal. That's to say I planned to kill myself. But I never did. Perhaps I was never really serious about it."

"Was *he?*"

"He stormed up and down, he swore, he accused his sister and myself of unbelievable ingratitude. I don't know if that's a suicidal state. I suppose it is. He had a quite massive pride, I expect you know that."

"He was an aristocrat. From an old family, Eton, Cambridge, the Greenjackets," Lusk shrugged. "You mean he had more pride than most?"

"Much, much more, I would say. A gargantuan pride."

Lusk nodded gloomily. "Yet I don't really believe people commit suicide because their pride's hurt."

Njomo came into the room and placed a plate of pork sandwiches on the table between them.

"Are you saying you don't think it's suicide?" Claus asked, pushing the sandwiches toward Lusk.

"It could be."

"There'll be an inquest, you said."

"Standard practice." Lusk munched a sandwich.

Claus watched him. "What is it, Tom?" he asked after a moment. "Something's worrying you."

"I think you should get yourself a lawyer to represent you at the inquest. I think Lady Diana should get one too. Maybe the same one. Maybe not." He took out his pipe and began filling it from his oilskin pouch. "I have to ask you not to leave the farm until after the inquest. Shouldn't be too much of a hardship."

"No."

"And Lady Diana will, of course, not be free to return to Europe."

"Do you mean that Diana and myself are suspects?"

Tom Lusk's face was creased with misery. "You know what I mean," he said roughly. "Just pray the inquest calls it suicide."

The Nairobi coroner, Colonel Fitzgerald, was informed by telephone during the afternoon of this same day, April 10, that the body of a European had been discovered in such circumstances as to require that an inquest take place. The facts he had before him at this point were scant. A leading member of Kenya Colony's society, Lord George Amadeus Winslow, had been found dead on a lonely road between Naivasha and Soykuru. He had been shot by what was believed to be his own registered revolver. The weapon had been found *one or two feet* from the car door. One foot invited the possibility of suicide; two or more feet indicated murder.

Colonel Todd Fitzgerald had been in the colony since the war. He was, in 1934, a man in his fifties, dignified by his unusual height and bearing. His face, framed by brushed-back iron-gray hair, might have been carved from a dark, hard wood. He had been a Grenadier Guardsman in the service of Queen Victoria, King Edward, and King George. He had paraded at the Trooping of the Color and had led his soldiers at Loos and the Somme. He was in Kenya because he had paid off his elder brother's debts and could not afford to live in England in what he considered an appropriate manner.

He was a bachelor because he believed he could offer no woman less than complete financial security. He was respectful of Africans and devoutly Christian. He was also the only man in Kenya known to have declined an offer of membership in the Muthaiga Club.

As further reports came from Lusk in the late afternoon and early evening, Colonel Fitzgerald began to feel the first real churnings of alarm. His clerk had informed him that the Nairobi telegraph office was on the edge of a complete breakdown, such were the numbers of inquiries from the London and New York newspapers. Fitzgerald notably lacked the cast of mind that might revel in a society murder. Instinctively he felt suicide would be the quieter, more decorous verdict. But one piece of evidence troubled him. Lusk had, it appeared, established that during the search for his sister, Lord Winslow had run out of fuel. Someone, therefore, had given him petrol. The colonel's mind was less than incisive, but he knew Inspector Lusk understood these things. And since Inspector Lusk clearly thought the issue of the motorcar fuel to be important, Colonel Fitzgerald considered it a question that required resolution if a verdict of suicide were to be recommended to the coroner's jury.

That evening, Pamela Longman called on Claus Hardenberg. For a few moments she stood awkwardly on the veranda, her hands thrust deep into the pockets of her white nurse's uniform.

"What is it, Pam?"

She closed her eyes for a moment, her face in deep shade. "I've done something, Claus. The last thing in the world I wanted to do. But I didn't know."

"Come in," he said.

She shook her head. "No, it's cool outside. Walk with me a bit."

She turned away, and as they walked among the *totos* playing in the dust road and listened to the older ones chanting nursery rhymes that Catherine Esterhazy had taught them at the school, Pam Longman told him about the night of Buzz's death.

"Sometime after midnight," she said, "an army doctor, an RAMC captain, arrived in Naivasha where we were all waiting at the hotel for information. There seemed to be no reason, no need to stay on there, so I decided to drive. The road passes the Naivasha-Soykuru junction. It had just stopped raining, I remember. I drove along with my window down and I heard, somewhere along the Soykuru road, a car horn hooting a Morse SOS."

"It was Buzz, of course," Claus said.

She nodded, looking down at the puffs of dust they kicked up as they walked. As the yellow dust rose and trailed past her ankles, she said, "I drove along the road. I think I thought it was you. I thought you'd found her injured and needed medical help. We're always so arrogant, aren't we? Why should it have been like that just because it was what I wanted? Instead it was Buzz Winslow waving his arms in the headlights, telling me he needed petrol—gasoline he called it, of course."

"What did you do?"

"I put my hand on the horn and my foot on the accelerator.

The last I saw of him, he was rolling in the mud where he'd jumped for his life. I wasn't sorry."

"You told your father this?" Claus said slowly.

"Yes," she said.

"And what did he say?"

"He puffed his pipe and said it was strange that although no one seems to have given Lord Winslow any petrol, he still managed to drive another five miles on an empty tank *and* end up with nearly three gallons left. Then he told me your account of what had happened."

"I see."

She turned, touching the heads of the *totos* who danced and played around them. "You saw Buzz that night, of course."

"Yes."

"And gave him petrol."

"Yes."

"Did you kill him?"

"I believe he committed suicide."

"What do I care, anyway?" she said. "He was a hateful man. Shallow. A bully. And of course a dreadful, dreadful snob. It's funny, I thought gentlemen were never snobs. I thought it was supposed to be only the lower classes."

They had reached the house. "I've caused you most awful trouble," she said. "I would have done anything in the world to avoid that. Did he really commit suicide?"

"God knows."

At Tom Lusk's apartment, Pamela sat opposite her father, eating supper in silence.

"Anything wrong, Pam?" he asked, looking at her from under his heavy eyebrows.

"I want to change my evidence, Dad."

He stopped eating, knife and fork poised above the plate.

"As I approached Lord Winslow's car, he waved me down. I stopped and he told me he had run out of petrol. I lent him my siphon and let him take a few gallons from my tank. Then I got back into my car and drove on."

Tom Lusk put down his knife and fork, got up from the table, and began to pour himself another beer. "Who are you trying to protect, Pam?" he asked, carefully tipping the beer bottle to control the level of the froth at the rim of the glass.

"I'm just changing my story, Dad. Witnesses do that, don't they?"

He grunted and lifted the glass to his lips. "You think Claus killed him," he said, putting aside the beer bottle.

"I've no reason to think *anybody* killed him. As far as I know, he committed suicide."

Lusk sat down at the table. "You don't normally get quite so many people with a motive for killing a man. By changing your evidence, you're placing yourself among the suspects, you know that."

She was silent.

"If it comes out that someone else gave him petrol—some farmer, for instance, who hasn't yet come forward—you'll be opening yourself to a serious charge of attempting to pervert the course of justice. You'll be finished in the colony, Pam." He reached across the table and took both her hands. "Claus comes from another world," he said. "He's not like the rest of them, but he still comes from their world."

"What are you saying, Dad?" She released her hands from his and got up to get a cigarette.

"I'll do all I can to help him," Lusk said. "I promise you that."

"I asked you what you were saying, Dad. What did you mean?"

"What I said, Pam. It's a different world."

"You mean he'll never look at me. No more than Winslow really did. Is that what you mean?"

"Pam, my love." Tom Lusk sat forward in his chair. The muscles in his forearms were bunched and tense. "Your evidence has already been written into the record by Robbie Henderson. It's not just a matter of changing it in my notebook."

"I know that, Dad."

"There'll be an inquest. And I personally believe the jury will find for murder. You must be a suspect, with a change of evidence like that. You've lived down all that Winslow business. You fought your way through it, and I can imagine what it took to walk through Nairobi with every man pointing the finger.

But changing your evidence could bring the whole thing to the surface again."

She lit her cigarette. "I've thought about it, Dad. I stopped and gave him petrol, okay?"

He nodded slowly. "Tell Robbie tomorrow morning, love." He stood up and put his arm around her shoulder. "Now I'm going to have a whiskey. Will you join me?"

"I'll join you, Dad."

"It's a good drink," he said, "when you're heading for rough water."

The funeral of Lord George Amadeus Winslow was set for the morning of Tuesday, April 12. He was to be buried at Limuru, just outside Nairobi. The Nairobi *Banner-Post* reported that nearly two hundred people attended the funeral. Attention was focused at least as much on Lady Diana as on the widowed Lady Winslow as they walked together behind the coffin, which was carried through the churchyard by six of Lord Winslow's grim-faced friends.

Claus von Hardenberg stood with Pamela Longman at the back of those gathered ten deep around the grave. He had received from Margaret Winslow an invitation to a lunch for close friends at the Muthaiga Club afterwards, but, as Inspector Lusk later noted, neither he nor Lady Diana attended.

The burial service was marked by one unusual incident. As the coffin was lowered, a heavily veiled woman pushed through the mourners and threw a bunch of red roses into the grave. Sergeant Henderson, dispatched by Lusk to discover who she was, reported that she had left alone in a car registered to Miss Clare Debenham.

"Tell me, Inspector," said the coroner, Colonel Fitzgerald, "what do you think about this whole business?"

Lusk pointed to the mourners leaving. "About the funeral, sir?"

"About Winslow's death," Fitzgerald said testily. "Of course he was a bad lot. One doesn't need a coroner's inquest to establish that."

When he retired, Lusk had long thought he would buy a place in Southend, near his sister's. For a few seconds he let his mind dwell on the thought of retirement.

"I've had word from on high . . ." Fitzgerald was saying.

"You mean the Governor, sir?"

Fitzgerald hesitated. "No names necessary," he said. "But it's felt that there's no real need for all the unsavory details to come out, the parties, the promiscuity, the drugs. It'd only be snapped up by the press-hounds in England. It's not felt it would help the colony's relationship with London. There are plenty of Members of Parliament already who are quick to ask why it's necessary to spend money on Kenya. India's different. But East Africa's not highly regarded at home, you know."

"Really, sir?"

Fitzgerald shook his head. "Apparently not. So no point in providing our enemies with ammunition, eh? Not if we can help it, I mean. For the sake of the colony." Fitzgerald paused. "And of course there's the recent visit of the Prince of Wales. He saw something of Winslow while he was here, I gather."

"I believe he did, sir."

"Most unfortunate." He grunted· unhappily to himself. "Of course Winslow had masses of enemies. Anybody could have done it, I suppose. If it was murder, that is. Personally, I think the fellow's mind just gave out. Influence of half a dozen things—the life he'd been leading, drugs. And he must have been worried sick about his sister, of course."

Lusk nodded. "Must have been, sir."

"The only thing that bothers me is this question of the petrol for Winslow's car."

"That's all cleared itself up, sir. Some confusion in my daughter's evidence there. She was a bit overwrought, sir. But last night she was able to confirm that she gave him petrol."

"First class," Fitzgerald said, relieved. "So what do you make of it all, Lusk? Same as me? I can guide my jury tomorrow? Simple suicide. Balance of the mind disturbed. You've no reason to think any different?"

"No, sir," Lusk said. "No reason to think any different."

*   *   *

"Forget the lawyer," Lusk said to Claus that evening. "On second thought, at a little inquest like this it might look as though someone had something to hide."

"So it'll go through as suicide?"

Lusk shrugged. "Whatever happened, it was not entirely the way you recounted it. But I'm thinking of Southend, Captain. If it was murder, I don't give a damn who killed Lord Winslow. The old aristocracy is dead, Captain. At least the one I used to know."

"You think so, Tom?"

Lusk nodded somberly. "This new lot are parasites. They've nothing to give and deserve nothing in return. The war killed it, I suppose. I believe they lost faith in themselves. They saw they were on the way out and they've decided to dance and sing as they go. Never change your story, Captain. Never tell me that *you* siphoned petrol into Winslow's car."

"I won't, Tom," Claus said. "I won't tell you that."

"And if you or Lady Diana ever decide to boast a little . . ."

Claus nodded. "I know," he said. "You told me once before."

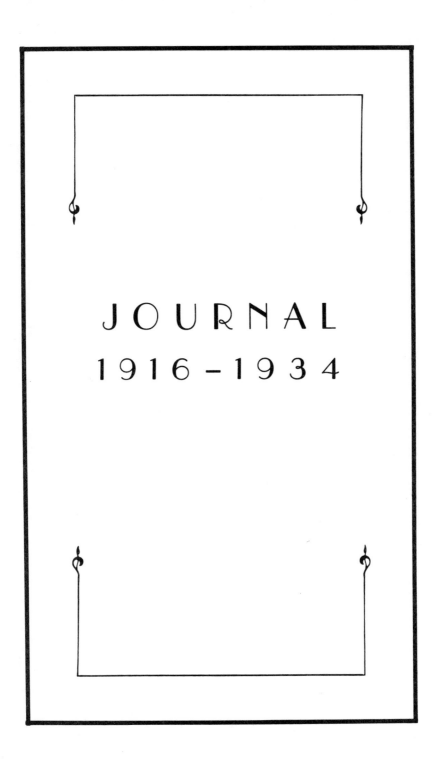

JOURNAL
1916 – 1934

TWENTY-EIGHT

held the bulky brown paper package in my hands. It was
addressed to me: *Claus von Hardenberg, Ngong, Private and
Confidential.*

The package had been delivered by Harry Towers to the
farm in the Ngong Hills the morning before the liner *Astoria* left
the port of Mombasa for Europe.

"I won't stay," Harry had said awkwardly. "But Diana asked me
to give you this. There's a letter that goes with it."

I took the package onto the veranda. Opening it, I found it
contained five or six leatherbound volumes, Diana's diary from
sometime in 1916 to the present. The envelope tucked inside
the first volume was crested with the arms of the liner *Astoria*. I
opened the envelope and read:

So *I* am to be allowed to leave. And *you* are no longer a murder
suspect. It's all so terribly, terribly sordid! I am sending you my
journal. It is my way of apologizing, far, far too late, for
involving you (and Buzz) in a monstrous romantic lie. I believe
you have every right to the enclosed. Drown my book when
you have read it. It is the first time I have been parted from it in
ten years.

Did you know that the morning after the crash it was Mrs.
Longman who came to tend my cuts and bruises? She seemed
quite unable to stop talking about you. So touchingly, so simply
in love with you. I suppose she is your mistress, or very soon
will be.

What do you think now, I wonder? Have you quite seen
through me? Do get on with that Mrs. Longman creature. Nice
enough face, but the superb body of the Chaste Huntress
herself. (Oops! Her name was Diana, wasn't it?) Poor Buzz. Poor

Buzz. One of the very *nicest* things about him was that he *never* meant well. He found people who mean well so frightfully common. And now he's gone from me. And you too.

You will be too stunned by the mountainous trivia of my life and thoughts to wade through it all. But you will know which days to read of, which to discard. I've written my account of the last week for you. I suppose, in truth, it's all you *need* to read.

I'm getting older, Claus. I can't tell you the panic that thought sets up in me. And I'm dirty. Terribly, terribly dirty.

Kiss Mrs. Longman for me.

All at sea on the good ship *Astoria,*

Diana

It was just afternoon when I began reading Diana's journal. When I had finished, the cloudy darkness had gathered around the Ngong hilltops and Njomo had silently placed a lamp and a whiskey and soda on the table at which I sat.

Between the worn leather covers a spiral clip system allowed extra pages to be added. Each volume was marked with a date; in some cases a clutch of years were bound together. There were, I noticed, some missing years in the mid-twenties. Flicking through the pages, I saw that it was not a product of the devoted diarist. Sometimes a month would be covered with the most cryptic of entries: March—Zermatt. June—Brioni for the polo. November—New York. Yet again it seemed that a letter or a comment by a friend might be accorded a full page or two. The whole seemed jumbled and confused and as redolent of Diana as the perfume that clung to the soft leather binding. First I was given, as on the flickering frames of a silent film, a picture of her life that I had never had. I read with astonishment of the frenetic traveling in the first few years of her marriage to Charles. From London to Budapest for a party. On to Egypt for a wedding. To Algiers to see the visit of the British Mediterranean fleet, then back by boat and train and boat-train to London in time to see a first night of Noël Coward or to be present at the opening of the new Dorchester Hotel.

Everywhere she and her friends wrote and received letters, four or five a day were not uncommon. And when traveling, Diana would beg her close friends to write *in advance* so that though she might arrive in some strange hotel, she would be greeted with letters awaiting her. At first I saw the letter-writing as a curious addiction; only later did I see it for what it was, a prophylactic against loneliness and despair.

Many men had fallen in love with her. She seemed to treat them with some regard and some effort to spare them humiliation. A vice-president of the United States had asked her to be his mistress, and she had received offers from figures as diverse as ministers of the new Soviet Union and King Zog of Albania. It was a life perfumed, wrapped in silk, and decorated with diamonds and pearls. It was a life informed and limited by that unshakable confidence I had known at Cambridge before the war. Perhaps it is the destiny of all Bourbons.

There was a great deal about her friendships with men. She was so obviously proud of their devotion. Yet I do not think she was able to offer any of them physical satisfactions. Several versions of the same question surfaced each year. "Am I frigid?" she asked herself. "Not just physically, but is there some cold black hole in the spirit to which I retreat?"

The cool air, crossing from the Ngongs, lifted tiny ruffles on the surface of the water. Being this close to Diana aroused in me an extraordinary intensity of excitement. I could not explain it even as I turned the pages, avoiding for the moment what were to me the crucial, the final days, tasting instead the flavor of those other incidents in her life in which I had played no part.

She talked so frankly of Buzz. And of his marriage to Margaret:

> I am ashamed of the way I have behaved toward Buzz in the past. Every girl he has introduced me to as a possible Lady Winslow I have heartily disliked. And this even when I knew the girl beforehand and felt rather fond of her. The worst was Mary Poole, whom Buzz was planning to take with him to live in Africa. I suppose we had known each other for almost fifteen years, as children and adolescents. We had even worked in the World's End Hospital together. And yet when I saw Buzz getting keen on her, I felt quite disapproving. I suppose it's not difficult to see why. A wife would cut all those extraordinary threads that bind brothers and sisters together. What is difficult to accept is the way I combated the threat. My God, I swear I began again to *flirt* with him as I had when we were children. I sat in corners

with him and exchanged new confidences. I pressed against him, knowingly, at dinner tables. I danced with him just more often than a sister should. And I saw poor Mary Poole pushed further and further into the background.

Charles is right in everything he says about me. He ranted for an hour or more the day Mary broke off the engagement. I shall always remember one phrase. The evil of the class system, he said, was that it substituted power for everything, for marriage, friendship, gratitude, love, and even sex. Strangely enough, as he said it I could only think of Claus.

In November 1931 she arrived in Africa for Buzz's marriage to Margaret Ryder:

Charles with me. Africa changelessly beautiful. Buzz has temporarily suspended the wild parties, apparently out of deference to old Lord Delamere, whose funeral, a punishing trek across the veldt, I attended yesterday with the rest of the white population of Kenya and a good representative sprinkling of Masai warriors (Lord Delamere's favorite human beings, everybody assures me). That anyway is what Buzz claimed yesterday. No parties until a suitable period of mourning for East Africa's Grand Old Man has passed! But then, as one knows, Buzz is *never* sincere.

How do I feel about his marriage to Bunty? Well, of course I can't really take it seriously. Buzz needs money. He needs to lay his hands on some of Bunty's fortune *and* retain his freedom. Bunty, for her part, is now closing on forty-five and drugs on morphine far too much. (The fact that she claims to have been rogered by every available gent in Kenya is, I suppose, neither here nor there.) How *do* I feel about the marriage? Well, the truth is, a lot better than I did about the engagement to Mary Poole anyway. Frankly, I don't want Buzz to be in love. He would become (he *has* become, on the odd occasion when he has been smitten) so much less fun. One can dwindle into a husband too, you see! But there's more, of course, much more. I have ambition for Buzz. I want Buzz to *be* something. And here in Kenya it would be so natural!

November 20. The wedding! A day of unbelievable hilarity and madness. The result, I fear (although truthfully I do not fear it too much), is a split between Margaret and myself. How did it all come about?

First the ceremony. Unknown to Bunty, Buzz had arranged for most of the guests to arrive at the church in fancy dress! Of course it imbued the whole event with the spirit of the carnival, or, worse, of the *théâtre grotesque*. We sometimes talk about the wedding as the bride's day, or the bride and groom's day. But this day belonged to Buzz alone. The day went from madness to madness. After the ceremony the guests paraded through the streets of Nairobi, shouting, drinking champagne, and firing revolver shots into the air. There were, I must admit, several scuffles during the church service and at least one actual fight during the carnival parade through Nairobi. Charles, on Margaret's side, is utterly furious at Buzz. Buzz of course is terminally drunk. He wears riding boots, white jodhpurs, a cutaway hunting coat, and a cravat. He reels, red-faced, champagne bottle in hand, from one table to another at the wedding luncheon, which is set in a huge marquee at the Nairobi Race Course. Afterwards we dance to a most marvelous swing band brought up from South Africa. Buzz is utterly, utterly outrageous. He insists I sit beside him. He keeps his arm around my waist and throughout the afternoon he keeps hauling me onto the dance floor as if I were the bride. Horseback riding—bareback, on real racers— is next. Then back to the marquee for a new band and the serious dancing.

Drinks, drinks, drinks follow—and then one cheek-to-cheek dance with Buzz in a circle of somewhat shocked guests. Happily, Charles has temporarily passed out somewhere; Margaret simply storms off! I feel an exhilarating sense of triumph.

This morning at my hotel I receive from Buzz a charming little verse. It is definitely *not* the sort of thing to show Charles. It reads:

> Oh, sister of most feminine quintessence
> Who can drive the fellows distrait with a glance,
> Please forgive the quite unbrotherly tumescence
> During the syncopated rhythm of our dance.

I am bound to admit that I hastily pen a reply:

> Brother Buzz, there's not the slightest need to mention
> Our terpsichorean revels of last night.
> I protest there was no increase in dimension
> And in this, please note, the lady's always right!

"As far as Margaret is concerned," Diana wrote the next day, "I have revealed my hand. She knows, with that quite deadly instinct for survival which she has, that I can *never* let Buzz go. Nor he, me."

It would be wrong to say that I was beginning to see Diana in a different perspective. I was seeing her now rather as a perfectly beautiful marionette—as Corinthian as Buzz and his friends, certainly. A guiltless perpetrator. I began to feel, as perhaps a sop to my own vanity, that the young girl I met at Lady Gorringe's and the girl who had begun to write to me in the trenches in France lived for a few short years before the lying mirror was placed before her face, making it impossible from then on to see the ugly, compulsive movements of the marionette.

I lit a cigarette. I wondered how much freer I was than she. I wondered above all why she had sent me this journal to read. Was it her first untutored movement since that summer of 1916? Or was it something else, yet another attempt to hide from herself the puppeteer's strings?

As the moths wheeled around the lamp, or crackled in the hot cone of air above the glass, I turned to those final pages that I knew now would release me from a lifetime's thrall.

Diana was in the South of France. Her Messerschmitt had arrived. The great Nice-to-Nairobi Air Rally is to begin at noon tomorrow. With the new German monoplane she knows she will win. Then:

> The most shattering news. First a telegram from my London solicitors. A Mr. Johnstone, an American lawyer, is leaving Paris tonight. He will arrive at 6:00 A.M. at St. Raphael. They urge me to meet him. Importance cannot be overstressed. Race or no race, I must be there, it seems.
>
> Tired and far from gruntled, I meet the train at St. Raphael. It is warm but it is raining. Mr. Johnstone is tall. He wears a pale gray suit, gold-rimmed spectacles, and a hat whose brim has been crushed during the night, making it look like the hanging wing of an injured bird. He looks so ridiculous I want to laugh. He is carrying only hand luggage and recognizes me as quickly as I guess at his identity.
>
> We go to the station bar. He prefers this to any decently comfortable hotel because he announces he is intending to catch the next train back to Paris. Only there, in Paris, he says

ominously and incomprehensibly, he is one hundred percent sure of his power base. He gives me a withering smile and I begin to wonder if all this is a dreadful hoax perpetrated by the French fliers.

It isn't. Mr. Johnstone begins to speak in a soft, cultivated American accent. All around us, weary travelers from Paris are ordering coffee and cognac and croissants. Mr. Johnstone tells me there have been the most serious possible developments in New York. The Chrysler family has been advised to initiate an action against me. The grounds are that, given the Jewish origins of the family and in particular of long-dead Sam Chrysler, who made the bulk of the money, no substantial sums may be inherited, under the terms of the trust, by someone who supports an openly anti-Semitic government such as that of Adolf Hitler.

These damned interfering Jews, with their Jew lawyers prodding them into more and more expensive actions! I am beyond fury. Charles has left the money to me. Me as I am! I require Mr. Johnstone to fight his way through the travelers and order me a very large cognac and more coffee. I ask Mr. Johnstone what it is he has come all the way from Paris to advise me to do. He is patient and blunt and his mind is crystal clear. But I can never forgive him his hat. His advice is devastating. He wants me not to fly the Messerschmitt in the rally. He wants me to make a short, dignified statement saying I feel that flying the Messerschmitt might be interpreted as a commitment to German government points of view. And that while I will always greatly admire the people and culture of Germany, I am unable to endorse all of the new government's policies.

I have to admit it. I plead with him. I feel I shall never be able to bear the humiliation of such a recantation. Could I not just withdraw from the race, claiming I was unwell?

The severe gray head shakes. The Chrysler family must be undercut before their case goes to court. There must be no ambiguity in my views.

I am shattered, shattered, shattered. I stand to lose all my friends and high connections in Germany. I *will* lose them, and if I fly the Messerschmitt, Mr. Johnstone, who has returned with more coffee and cognac and just sat on his hat, assures me that I will be deprived of a fortune and left, after legal fees (a wintry smile goes with that one), to live at no more than a reasonable, a *comfortable* level. Oh God!

I ask him does that mean Claridge's when I stay in London? He shakes his head. Eden-Roc when on the Riviera? Again the wintry smile. What are his views of comfort? Devastatingly, I think I know. Very wearily I ask him to draft a suitable statement to the press.

I think how Claus will read it. And Buzz. I make the statement, say good-bye to Mr. Johnstone, and watch him walk back along the platform with one brim of his ridiculous hat flopping against his ear. I have lost a creed. But gained a fortune.

The end of the journal had been written in the last day or two, and obviously with the knowledge and intention that I should read it. It described the flight in the De Havilland and the crash landing through dripping cloud and the moments of paralysis as she sat in the crazily angled cockpit and flame began to spurt from the engine. I had flown enough to know the fear. And to understand the need for sleep afterwards as an escape from all that had happened.

She had awakened to see, at the high points in the hills, car lights moving back and forth along distant roads. She assumed they were cars looking for her. When the rain stopped for a few moments, she collected dry leaves and twigs from under the overhanging rock and managed to set fire to the wood and rubber of the De Havilland wheels. These were the leaping points of light I had seen.

I read the next passages with pain. Pain greater than from the failure of our hasty act of love. Unconsciously echoing her first letter to me in 1916, she wrote:

My darling, darling, darling Claus, forty-eight hours that began with Mr. Johnstone ended with my brother lying dead across me in the front seat of his car. Across me, Claus!

He was driving like a madman. He had drunk more whiskey. He was crying when he talked about what he had seen up in the hills—you and me, I mean. He began again to call me the most appalling names. He was shouting, shouting, shouting. He stopped the car. He said—he said, Claus, that if I would go under one brother, why not under the other! He tried to make love to me!

It was such an inexpressible shock. I was so shocked, Claus, although I shouldn't have been, perhaps. All those years of flirting with him, inciting him, all those jokes and letters about Lord Byron and his half-sister Augusta! Do we always reap what we sow? God, I hope not!

But that night I did. He turned on me, Claus, his trousers torn open, one hand gripping the arm strap above me so that he was crushing me down on the seat. The gun was in the glove compartment. Did I seek it or did my hand fall on it? God knows. His mouth was crushing mine. I screamed for breath. I screamed in a revulsion I could not possibly, possibly have felt as he tore open my flying suit. I shot him and I dragged myself from under him and I told him as I buttoned his trousers neatly, one button after the other in correct sequence, that I had lied to you both. That I had involved you both in a monstrous, romantic lie.

Trembling, half crazed with what I had done, I sat beside him. I thought back to where it began in the shame I felt on the night before my wedding, in the shame I felt as I discovered that my mother was right. That I was willing to abandon all I had so stridently claimed that youth stood for, in order to marry wealth and position. That night in Venice, I could have left everybody and run through the dripping halls of the Palazzo Bellini, laughing with madness. I watch you, Claus, I watch you, gaunt, a touch of the dark forests in the blue eyes that wander constantly in my direction. I know you love me. But Charles is good and rich and undemanding. With him I will float and fly the world. I will meet kings and princes and Gary Cooper. And will I still be able to laugh at myself, even if a little wildly? Perhaps. Perhaps.

I was too ashamed that night in Venice to tell you the pedestrian truth, darling Claus. Too ashamed and too fearful of losing you forever.

Before Mama died in June, she told me a little of your mother and her time in England. She was even honest enough to tell me something about your father, Thomas Winslow. A terribly handsome rogue who viewed women, all women, as objects of his pleasure. Was Mama a little in love with him too? She would not completely admit to it. "I was," she said, "at one time quite warm." How warm, I wondered. Warm enough to creep between the sheets with him? It was a thought that tantalized and intrigued me! In my mind's eye I began to see the exquisite possibilities of a long-ago love affair between my mother and your father.

Listen! Fear is my spur. Fear of poverty and insignificance made me marry Charles. But the fear of lack of love, the awful, unimaginable fear of *lovelessness*, led me to greater sins.

It was impossible to tell you the plain, unadorned truth. So I hinted at deeper reasons. I told the lie I had in mind since my mother's death. I told you that your father, Thomas Winslow, sired me as well. I erected the barrier of consanguinity between us.

You see how perfect it was. A complete resolution of my passion and my fear. We were all—Buzz, myself, you—to be half related. We were all petrified in love, like the three figures in the lava of Pompeii, stretching out their hands to touch fingertips together.

I told you, Claus, and for the moment I believed it myself. Then I caressed you good-bye and went on to my other life.

I read and reread the words. With that one monstrous, romantic lie, she had held me in thrall even more than she knew. She had shriveled my capacity to love.

The last entry was dated today, April 15, 1934.

What more to tell you? Only that the *Astoria* sails tomorrow. You *could* be there with me. Will you be there, I wonder? What more to say? You hesitate. You forget even the loving children that we were. You don't believe that we can realize our dreams. But a man's reach (and a woman's too, but Browning never mentioned that) should exceed his grasp. Or what's a heaven for?

I felt no anger, although I knew I *should* feel anger. Perhaps that will come. Perhaps that will be part of my voyage back.

I closed the pages of the journal and walked out to the hot-water stove in the stableyard. Njomo stood by with a silent, puzzled look as I opened the front of Catherine's iron stove and, one by one, threw in the leatherbound volumes.

TWENTY-NINE

The track led up between red rocks taller than either of us, until suddenly I could see a fringe of trees above me. Beyond the treetops a waterfall leaped off the mountainside and plunged somewhere out of sight among the trees.

Dust rose from under our feet. Each step upward dislodged stones that rattled and bounced down toward the road. She smiled at me a few times and once stretched out a hand to haul me up a particularly steep slope. Strange birds were chattering in the trees on the top of the crest. The sun struck us with a sullen fury.

And then we passed between two tall rocks, the gateway to a green, cool oasis beneath towering acacia trees. A smaller waterfall fell to spurt and trickle across flat rocks that formed the lip of the deep pool.

"God, it's hot," she said. She ran forward into the bushes.

I came forward more slowly, calling to her. "Did you and Buzz swim here together?"

"I did. Buzz didn't swim," Pamela called back.

Through the latticework of leaves I could watch the light playing on her brown body as she took off her shirt and slacks.

I lit a cigarette. "Why did you bring me here?" I asked her.

She dived from behind the bush, flashed brown across the water, and slipped below the surface. The water rippled over her naked figure as she drifted slowly across the bottom of the pool. Then with a powerful kick she drove upward and her head broke the surface. "I don't know why I brought you here," she said, pushing her dark hair from her face. A single stroke brought her to the edge of the pool. "I don't have explanations for all I do."

I sat down on the rock. Reversing the cigarette I was smoking, I put the cork tip in her mouth.

"Mm," she said. "Du Maurier."

She stood shoulder-high in the pool; her arms up, her elbows resting on the flat rock, the deep cleavage of her breasts visible beneath the sparkling level of the water.

"What do you want?" I said. "Out of life, I mean."

"You," she said, smiling.

I crushed the cigarette on the rock.

"And you?" she asked me. "What do *you* want?"

I reached out and touched her shoulder. "Do you think," I said, "that we can persuade your father to give up his dream of Southend?"

She frowned. "Give up Southend?"

"And come and live with us at Ngong."

She pressed the palms of her hands on the rock and lifted herself from the water. She knelt there a moment, her bright teeth against her tanned, shaded face. I knew she was more beautiful than Diana—even if it had taken me half a lifetime to see it.